Sorry Not Sorry

SOPHIE RANALD

bookouture

Published by Bookouture in 2019

An imprint of StoryFire Ltd.

Carmelite House
50 Victoria Embankment
London EC4Y 0DZ

www.bookouture.com

ISBN: 978-1-78681-752-5
eBook ISBN: 978-1-78681-751-8

In loving memory of j, one of the good guys

Chapter One

When I got in from work, Maddy and Henry were still there – just. Their hired van was parked in the street outside the house, and they were standing in the hallway surrounded by their stuff. I wondered whether they'd decided not to wait for me but then changed their minds – the same way I'd almost gone for a drink after work but decided to come home instead, to say goodbye.

'Oh, you're here, Charlotte!' Maddy said, with a cheerfulness that sounded a bit forced.

'Yes!' I said, with equally forced cheerfulness. 'I mean, Briony and Alice were going to go to Quag's for a cocktail, but I didn't… I couldn't…'

I stopped. I tried to meet Maddy's eyes, but somehow I couldn't do that, either. There she was, my best friend, her face as familiar as my own, standing in our familiar hallway wearing the 7 For All Mankind jeans we found in TK Maxx six years ago, which I'd watched go from new to worn to distressed, and fished out of the washing machine more times than I could remember. There were her green eyes behind the cat's-eye glasses, her dark, cropped hair, the dimple on her left cheek that was almost always there, because she was almost always smiling.

Not now, though.

Henry cleared his throat. 'We left the keys on the hook in the hallway,' he said.

'We were going to drop them off at Wankerson's,' Maddy said, smiling as she used our joke name for the letting agent. 'But we ran out of time, and they'll be closed now.'

'It's no problem,' I said. 'I'll do it tomorrow.'

'And we've done all the stuff with the bills,' Henry said. 'Council tax, water, Npower, broadband – and we've signed up for three months of mail forwarding. But just let us know if there's anything we missed.'

'Odeta's coming to clean the place on Monday,' Maddy said. 'Remember, she's going back to Romania for two weeks after that, but the agency said they'll send someone else. I told them you'll be in touch about the direct debit.'

'Ollie at Wankerson's called to say the landlord's arranged for someone to come round tomorrow and do some stuff in the garden,' Henry said. 'Cut back that tree, hopefully. But he might not turn up. You know what they're like.'

Maddy said, 'Our new fridge freezer isn't coming until next week, so we've left some stuff – ready meals, and that chilli I cooked the other night. It's all yours. You're so busy, Charlotte, I know you don't have time to cook.'

'And it's not like we're moving to Siberia,' Henry said. 'We'll only be in Bromley. It's only, like, an hour and a half from here on the train.'

An hour and a half on three separate trains and a bus, I thought. It might as well be flipping Siberia.

When Maddy had told me six months before, with amazed delight, that an inheritance from Henry's grandmother was going to enable them to buy a place of their own and finally put an end to the precarious, expensive annoyance of renting in London, I'd imagined an elegant flat in one of the nearby developments, all industrial chic with a view of the canal. Or maybe a Victorian cottage that they could lovingly restore, with original fireplaces and polished floorboards.

Instead, they'd opted for a three-bedroom semi with a big garden in *actual* suburbia. I knew what it meant: it wasn't just the physical distance; it meant that Maddy and Henry were moving on to a totally new phase of their lives. One that would involve being close to good local schools, spending the weekends gardening, and dinner parties with Henry's sister, who apparently lived nearby. It meant they weren't just buying a house, they were growing up with a massive, rocket-powered whoosh and leaving me far behind, still paying rent each month, getting the same Tube to work each day, and going to bed alone each night. Except I'd be doing it all without my best mate there to share it.

I realised I'd been staring down at my shoes – taupe kitten heels that had looked comfortable in the shop but were viciously pointed and had been killing my feet all afternoon – and forced myself to look up again, at their concerned, guilty faces.

Then I burst out laughing. It was just as well, otherwise at least one of us would have started to cry.

'You guys!' I said. 'I'm twenty-seven, you know. I can do adulting. I've been doing it for lots of years. I know how to pay the gas bill and let the cleaner in and harass the estate agent. I hold down a responsible job. I haven't even passed out on a night bus for, like, ages. I'll be fine.'

Maddy laughed too, and said, 'God, I'm sorry, Charlotte. Of course you'll be okay. It's just… weird, you know. Moving. After all this time. I'll bloody miss you.'

'I'll miss you, too. But, like you said, you're only moving to south London.'

'Are you sure you don't want to come round tonight?' Maddy said. 'We can order pizza, and you can help us build our Billy bookcase.'

For a moment, I was tempted. Then I told myself not to be ridiculous, and said, 'No way! Don't be daft. It's your first night in your new home. You need to be alone together to kiss the walls and shag in the kitchen and stuff. And assemble your own bloody Ikea bookcase.'

'Are you sure, Charlotte?' Henry asked. 'You'd be totally welcome. We can shag in the kitchen any time.'

But I could see, however carefully he concealed it, that he was relieved. Of course he was. Since he and Maddy first got together, when Maddy and I advertised for a new housemate and he moved in, and after a couple of months vacated his own room to share with Maddy, I'd been there too. Not all the time, obviously – I work long hours, and I'd been on holiday with other friends, nights out with my colleagues and stuff (dates, though? Not so much). But still, for the whole two years of their relationship, I'd been a third person in the household. However well we got on – and we did get on fabulously – I knew it couldn't always have been easy for them. For Henry, especially.

Now, they'd have space to be on their own together at last. And in five months, thanks to a swoon-makingly romantic proposal in the restaurant at the top of the Shard (don't worry, I wasn't actually there that night, but Maddy told me about it in minute detail afterwards, several times), they were getting married. They didn't need me hanging around like a needy, squeaky third wheel.

So I declined their Domino's-and-flatpack invitation again, more firmly this time, and helped them carry the last of their things to the waiting van.

'You won't be here on your own for long, anyway,' Maddy said, looking a bit teary again. 'The new girl's moving in on Sunday.'

'Yes.' It seemed like a very long time ago that we'd posted the ad for the room online, and even then I'd only skimmed through emails from people wanting to move in, partly because there'd been so many of them but mostly because I was in denial about this day ever actually happening. 'What's her name again? Pansy?'

'Something like that,' Henry said. 'I can't quite remember.'

'But Henry really liked her,' Maddy said. 'He thinks you'll get on great. It's a shame we couldn't be here to meet her, though.'

'Yeah, I'm really sorry about you having to do the showing-around thing at the last minute,' I said to Henry. 'But we'd arranged all the viewings and then there was that major Brexit thing when Theresa May invoked Article 50, or triggered it or whatever she did, and I got home at four in the morning because Colin made everyone stay in the office in case the markets went mental.'

'Oh, don't worry about it! Anyway, I was doing an after-hours shift at the surgery,' Maddy said. 'But yeah, she sounds really nice.

And she might be able to get you amazing discount clothes from The Outnet.'

'Not The Outnet,' Henry said. 'The other one. She's a buyer there, or something.'

'BrandAlley?' Maddy said.

Henry shook his head.

'Luxeforless?' I said.

'Think that's the budgie,' said Henry. 'Anyway, Tansy – that's her name, not Pansy, my bad – said she'll turn up on Sunday. I told her she'll have to pick up the keys from Ollie tomorrow, so if you could drop them round, Charlotte, if it's not too much hassle…'

I said it was no hassle at all. It wasn't like I had an action-packed weekend ahead of me, after all. Since when did I ever?

'Although I might not be here when she arrives,' I said, 'because we've got brunch, remember, Maddy? Third Sunday of the month, like always?'

It was Maddy's turn to look down at her shoes. They were battered Converse that had been white, once upon a time, and I bet they weren't hurting her feet one bit.

'Yeah, I don't think I'm going to make it this month,' she said sheepishly. 'It's just – you know. We'll have so much to do in the new place. The guy said he'd start tiling the bathroom this weekend, and if I leave Henry to sort it out we'll end up with a brick pattern instead of herringbone. So, yeah. Sorry to be flaky. I was going to post on the WhatsApp group, I just haven't had a chance. But the others will be there – Molly, Chloë… And you'll get to hear all about how William's sister's wedding went last weekend.'

'That's right.' I brightened briefly. 'And Molly wore her cerise satin slip dress and pants of steel. How could I forget?'

It was true – Molly had kept us entertained for the past few brunches with tales of her sister-in-law-to-be's bridezilla antics, while saying, 'God, I really need to go on a drastic diet if I'm going to fit into that stupid dress and look so stunning William will propose to me on the spot,' then stuffing her face with bottomless steamed buns and Bloody Marys along with the rest of us. But I knew that Maddy was reminding me of it to distract me from feeling sad that she wouldn't be there, and wondering how many times in the future she would also not be there because she and Henry were doing couply, weddingy things that were more important. Fortunately for her, Henry was on back-up distraction duty.

'And then in a week or so, Adam's moving into my old room,' he said.

'Right. Adam.' I'd been kind of distracted about it all, I realised – in denial, most probably. I'd been quite happy to let Maddy draft the ad on SpareRoom ('Are you sane, solvent, clean and reasonably sensible? Two double rooms available in gorgeous, spacious house in Hackney. New bathroom. Cleaner weekly. Courtyard garden. Modern kitchen. Vacant owing to the moving-in-with-boyfriend thing. You'll be sharing with my mate Charlotte, who's always up for a laugh but often works long hours, so professionals preferred. M or F, late 20s to early 30s. Inbox Madeleine or Henry…'), and for them to vet the candidates. And when Henry had said that his cousin (or second cousin, or something) was coming back from a couple of years working abroad and would need somewhere to live, I'd said, 'Great! That sounds great!' and dashed off to work, leaving a slice of bread in the toaster that went black and set off the smoke alarm.

'He's been in, what, Dubai, was it?' I said.

'Iran. His mate Amir has a start-up there, not Uber but like Uber. But it's launched now, so Adam's coming home. He's hoping to find freelance work writing apps, but for now I guess he's at a bit of a loose end. I haven't seen him for years but from what I remember he fills the sane, sensible, et cetera, brief, so you won't have to worry.'

He looked around, picked up his cricket bat and pads from the floor and slung them into the van.

'Right,' he said. 'Looks like we're good to go. Maddy?'

'Good to go,' Maddy said. Then she said, 'I'll just have a final check upstairs. Coming, Charlotte?'

I followed her back into our house – or rather, the house that used to be ours, which I'd now be sharing with two total strangers. It looked the same, mostly. The kitchen was only missing Henry's space-age espresso machine – I'd have to invest in a replacement – and the fancy food mixer Maddy had bought to make cakes in, which I'd definitely have no need of. The living room was much the same as always, only a weird mix of tidy and messy – the rug had been hoovered, but there was dust on the bookshelf where Maddy's recipe book collection of Ottolenghi, Mary Berry, Deliciously Ella and all the rest had accumulated. The floor had been swept, but there were scuff marks on the walls where Henry had wheeled his bicycle in and out, over and over.

It would be the same in the bathroom, I knew: my stuff all still tidily there in its place; a ring on the counter-top where Henry had kept his wet-shaving kit; a faint smell of Maddy's peony body lotion in the cabinet. And the bedrooms – the one where they'd slept, and the other, where all Henry's clobber had been allowed to accumulate, because although the house had three bedrooms, there was only one bathroom and we couldn't be arsed to get a fourth housemate.

'I think we're done,' Maddy said.

I swallowed the lump in my throat and said, 'All done. Listen, have an amazing first night in your new home. I'll miss you guys, but you know how made up I am for you, don't you?'

'I know.'

And then the two of us kind of launched ourselves into each other's arms and had the most massive hug outside the closed, silent doors to their empty rooms.

I didn't go back downstairs with Maddy. I went and lay on my bed and looked at Tinder for a bit, swiping left and left again until it got too depressing to carry on. I went downstairs and made a gin and tonic and drank it while I considered baking a cod fillet wrapped in foil with herbs in it, like Jamie Oliver does on the telly. But I thought, 'Sod it,' and put some frozen chips in the oven and ate them standing at the kitchen counter, looking out as the summer sky slowly darkened from intense blue to slate grey, because it felt too weird to sit down.

Then I walked to the corner shop and bought a tub of Ben & Jerry's – I didn't even clock what flavour – and ate that in bed, continuing to stare blankly at my phone.

I'd been single for three years. Three years since I'd realised that although Liam and I still lived together, sharing our flat in Newcastle and kind of vaguely drifting towards marriage and kids,

I wanted something more. He was a nice guy. He'd be a good husband and a great dad. But I'd found myself looking at his head next to me on the pillow every morning and spending the few minutes before I had to get up and put the kettle on thinking, *Shit. Is this all there is?*

I might have kept my head buried firmly in the sand on that one, and let things carry on until we no longer just didn't love but barely even liked each other, but then two things had happened quite quickly, in the space of about a month. Mum, who'd been single herself for years and years, pretty much since Dad buggered off when I was little, announced that she was moving to Spain. Jim, the bloke she'd started seeing the year before, was a locksmith who'd made such a success of his business that he was able to retire to Alicante, where his daughter lived with her husband and two kids. And Mum was going with him, apparently without so much as a backward glance at me. And then I was offered the job of my dreams in London, and that had given me the spur I needed to make big changes.

Which was all very well, only it seemed like for those whole three years nothing else had actually changed. My life had fallen into a different kind of routine, but it was still a routine: work, nights out with colleagues, work, drinks in the pub with Maddy and later with Maddy and Henry, work, monthly brunches with Maddy's friends – who'd accepted me into their group without really becoming my own friends – work…

Until now. Now, with Maddy and Henry gone, I realised how empty not just the house, but my whole life felt. Maddy and Henry had each other. I didn't have anyone. Once again, that question loomed in my mind. *Shit. Is this all there is?* And more to the point, I hadn't had so much as a sniff of a shag for over a year.

I scraped the last dregs of Caramel Chew Chew out of the bottom of the tub with my finger and licked it. It left a sticky smear on my phone's screen when I typed into Google, 'How to find love, sex and happiness.'

One thing was for sure: I wasn't the only person searching for this stuff. The internet was full of advice on how to write a Tinder profile that would get my ideal bloke swiping right so fast he practically dislocated his finger; how to harness the energy of the Universe to make my dreams come true; how to get from zero to 'Ooooh' in the sack through tantric lovemaking. There was even a local spiritual healer who promised to cast a spell that would make me irresistible to the man of my dreams, for a small fee. Although I was impressed by his SEO skills – the site came up at the top of the second page of my search – I decided to pass on that one.

But right below that was a page I did click on. The title caught my eye straight away: 'Sorry Not Sorry (a bad girl's guide to love and sex)'.

The site was simply designed: there was an image of a woman, taken from the back, wearing a swishy red coat and walking over a bridge – Brooklyn Bridge in New York, I guessed it was, because the Manhattan skyline filled the background. I'd always wanted to go to New York, but it had never happened. And if I carried on the way I was, it never would.

There wasn't much text on the page. It just said, 'Hi and welcome to *Sorry Not Sorry*, a series of podcasts I've recorded to help single girls – and guys – navigate the choppy waters of dating. I call this a bad girl's guide to love and sex, even though I have to admit to being a bit more vanilla than I'd like to be, myself. But I want to try and channel that side of me – to tap into my daring, out-there, fun side. And since you clicked on this site, I guess you do, too! But I'm a talker, not a writer, so why not have a listen?'

Okay, Bad Girl, I thought, *show me what you've got.* I scrolled down the page, glancing at the dates on the audio links. They'd all been recorded a while back – the most recent was almost five years old. But dating couldn't have changed that much in half a decade – even the dating app Bumble had been around almost that long, I told myself. There were loads of links: how to write a killer online profile, dating safety tips and reviews of lingerie and sex toys ('I've tried these so you don't have to. But you might just want to!' she wrote). I was feeling about as saucy as my empty ice cream tub, so sexy knickers and vibrators felt a bit advanced for the moment. But one category caught my eye: 'Take these challenges and set your dating life on fire!'

Even though I didn't need to, because I was alone in the house, I plugged in my headphones before I pressed play.

Hey girlfriend! Welcome back to Sorry Not Sorry *– the bad girl's guide to love and sex. If this is your first time listening, a huge hello to you and a massive hug to go with it.*

If you're a regular listener, you can tune out for this next bit. Switch your hairdryer on, send a WhatsApp, blend your smoothie, whatever – I'll see you back in a couple of minutes while I give the newbies a bit of background.

A year or so ago, I decided to document my journey in this series of podcasts. Listeners who've been around for a while will have heard me tell about some of my dating adventures – and misadventures; believe me, there were plenty of those. They'll have been right here with me when I went on that disastrous date with BO Boy – remember him? I sure do. Once smelled, never forgotten. They'll know what I'm on about when I mention Psycho Man, who – and I am not kidding you – lived in his late mom's house with all her stuff still right there like her wedding photo in a frame on the wall and even clumps of dead hair in the brush on her dressing table. Not to mention, he expected me to do it in. Her. Actual. Bed. Spoiler: I didn't. Call the cops, that is. And I didn't bone him, either.

But listen to me – I'm going way off track! I was meant to be telling you what this new series of podcasts is all about.

I've noticed something recently, in my dating life as well as in my personal life. I've realised that I've kind of got myself into a bit of a rut. So I'll be setting myself a series of challenges that I hope will inject some adventure back into dating, make it seem less goal-oriented and less of a chore. And, hopefully, make me more fun and more dateable at the same time. What's not to like about that?

Because, you see, this whole dating journey isn't just about Mr Right. It's about you – and me, obviously – discovering ourselves. It's about enjoying adventures, pushing boundaries, learning more about ourselves. Hell, having amazing orgasms! I want a piece of that. Do you?

You said yes, right? Then why not join me in taking these challenges!

So let's get started. The first challenge I've set myself is a simple one, although it seems like climbing Mount Everest right now…

Chapter Two

I guess I fell asleep before the podcast finished, because when I woke up the next morning I still had a headphone in one ear. The speaker wires were tangled around my neck and the empty ice cream carton was next to me on the pillow. My mouth tasted sour and I felt hot, sweaty and quite honestly a bit gross. Sunlight was streaming into my bedroom through the open curtains – that must have been what woke me.

Then I heard a man's voice, directly under my window. 'Oliver? Yeah, mate, it's Tim Gladstone here. I'm at number 65 but I don't think there's anyone in.'

Shit. It must have been a knock on the door that had woken me. The tree guy, who Henry had told me to expect. I pulled on a pair of jeans and hurried downstairs in my bare feet.

I opened the door.

'Sorry, sorry,' I said. 'I was…'

'Having a lie-in,' the man on the doorstep said, smiling. *Fuck.* Opening the door to a stranger with yesterday's make-up still on, my hair unbrushed and morning breath, would have been bad enough if the stranger didn't look like he'd stepped straight out of a Google image search for 'hot tradesmen'. He had bright green eyes and floppy, shiny brown hair. There were deep dimples in his cheeks, not quite concealed by a layer of stubble. His high-vis jacket was unzipped, showing what looked like an impressive chest and a full set of ripped abs under a white T-shirt.

'I'm here from Tim's Trees,' he said, and I realised I'd been standing there like a numpty, staring at him. Fortunately, I hadn't taken my bra off the night before, so although I was highly dishevelled and had quite obviously just woken up, at least my boobs weren't flopping all over the place under my vest top.

'Tim's Trees,' I parroted.

'I'm here to take a look at the branch that's overhanging your neighbour's roof,' he said.

'Overhanging branch,' I said. 'Right. Got you. Of course. Er… it's in the garden.'

The dimples in his cheeks got deeper, and although his lips didn't move, I realised he was suppressing a smile. Or more likely a hoot of laughter at my stupidity.

'Right,' he said. 'I'll just get my gear from the van.'

'Great,' I replied. 'I'll leave the back door open for you. I'll be down in just a few minutes.'

I legged it upstairs to the bathroom and locked myself in. I turned the shower on full and sat on the edge of the bath, my face in my hands. Surely things couldn't have got so bad over the past few years that I couldn't even talk to a good-looking man without stammering and blushing like a twat? Not to mention with yesterday's ice cream smeared around my mouth. But, I told myself, I talked to good-looking men all the time. Only that was at work, when we were all there for a reason, and weren't expected to like one another. *But this bloke, this Tim, is working, Charlotte*, I reminded myself. *Now get in the shower, put some clothes on, and go down and flirt with him.* Flirt with him? Where the hell had that idea come from? Then I remembered. The *Sorry Not Sorry* podcast.

Her first challenge, which I must have heard just before I drifted off to sleep: flirt with a stranger. Flirt? What was that again? I literally couldn't remember the last time I flirted with anyone. Oh, wait – it must have been the summer before last, when I was at the Creamfields festival with Henry and Maddy. We were queuing for ramen noodles when the guy in front of us started chatting to me. I chatted back, our eyes met and then, just as I was thinking, *Hold on, is he flirting with me?* his girlfriend appeared and chucked a full pint of Pimm's over his head. Not exactly Romeo and Juliet, was it?

You don't have to, I told myself. *Go on. Fall at the first fence. Or you can woman up and do it. It's not like you're ever going to see him again.*

So I had a shower and put on a pair of shorts and a different, clean vest top, and looked at myself critically in the mirror. At brunch a few months back, we'd got talking about politics – well, kind of. To be perfectly honest, we were discussing whether it was more likely that Melania Trump or Victoria Beckham would ever be seen to crack a smile. And then Maddy had said, 'You know, Trump's daughter Ivanka's the total spit of you, Charlotte.'

I pointed out that, while Ivanka and I both had straight blonde hair and were somewhat puddingy about the face, she was six foot tall and I was five foot five, and we probably both weighed the same. So if you squashed Ivanka down as if you were tamping coffee, and put the result into cheaper clothes and a Geordie accent, you might get someone who slightly resembled me, only not really. Especially as my father was about as far from being a billionaire as you can get. And now, whenever I looked in the mirror, I wondered whether other people looked at me and thought, *My God, she's like a shorter, chubbier Ivanka Trump only with less good teeth!* And you can imagine what that did for my self-esteem.

I followed the whine of what I guessed must be a chainsaw downstairs and out into the blazing sunshine. The paving stones were littered with leaves and twigs, and several smaller branches, but at first I couldn't see Tim, although I could see Freezer, the neighbour's white cat, watching from the safety of an upstairs window, looking majorly pissed off. Then the noise stopped and I heard his voice say, 'I'm up here!'

I don't know how I'd imagined tree surgeons worked. Ladders, I guess. But he was actually in the tree, right up high, perched astride one of the branches, safety goggles obscuring his face but not making him look any less fit.

'I'm almost done,' he shouted down. 'Then I'll clear this mess up and be on my way.'

I said, 'Can I offer you a cup of tea, or something? Something cold? It's hot today.'

God, you sound like an actress in a bad porno, Charlotte, I thought, cringing. But he didn't seem to mind.

'That sounds great,' he said, switching on his chainsaw again and getting back to work. I stood for a moment and watched him. There was something about him – about a man doing a skilled, physical, dangerous job – that was undeniably sexy. The way his body stayed firm and still, anchored on the branch by the strength of his thighs.

The way his face had gone all sort of stern with concentration. The way he seemed entirely unfazed by being several metres above the ground with a bit of kit that could have had his arm off in seconds if he wasn't careful. Of course, it helped that he was young and hot. I'm pretty sure I wouldn't have felt the same about a middle-aged, beer-bellied tree surgeon, if they even existed. Perhaps they didn't. Perhaps they all fell to their death or lopped off a limb or lost their head for heights and retired.

Reluctantly, I stopped watching him and went inside. There were some cans of Diet Coke in the fridge, and a few bottles of beer Henry had left. Presumably Tim wouldn't want one of those as he was working and driving (and wielding a deadly chainsaw) but I'd offer anyway. And I put the kettle on for good measure. My hands were shaking a bit, I noticed, which was ridiculous. I remembered the words of the narrator of the *Sorry Not Sorry* podcast – the Bad Girl, as I found myself thinking of her.

Now don't be nervous! You don't have to sleep with him, you know! Just a bit of fun, a bit of flirting. Just catch his eye, say something witty, laugh when he does. Maybe even a bit of physical contact, the brush of an arm, that kinda stuff.

How hard could it be? I knew the answer: it was going to be really bloody hard. When it came to flirting, I was as rusty as Paul Gascoigne making a comeback to football.

I waited while Tim lugged all his gear back to his van and tidied up. Then he came into the kitchen, and said, 'All done. Your neighbours won't need to worry about their roof tiles now.'

'What can I get you to drink?' I asked, gesturing vaguely towards the kettle and the fridge.

He'd taken off his working jacket and my suspicions about his body were confirmed. His arms were so muscly they stretched the sleeves of his white T-shirt, which was now stained from the sap of the tree and damp with sweat where it clung to his torso. There was more serious muscle action going on under his jeans. Very, very, very hot.

'Just a glass of water would be great, if you don't mind,' he said, and I realised I'd been staring at him again.

I filled a pint glass from the tap and added some ice cubes, wishing I could rub one over my burning cheeks. Or over his taut abs, where it would instantly melt on contact with his skin and run in a lickable rivulet down towards his— *Charlotte! What are you even thinking?*

'So, what you were doing up there, is it very dangerous?' I asked.

'It's like anything, really. It's dangerous if you don't know what you're doing.'

He stepped over and took the glass from my hand. This close, I could smell him: his deodorant, or shower gel or whatever, and the smell of the tree clinging to his hands, and himself – that musty, sexy, masculine scent. I thought, *This is dangerous. I don't know what I'm doing.*

'What is it you do for a living?' he asked.

'I work in finance,' I said. 'I'm an admin assistant for a hedge fund in Mayfair. Not as exciting as what you do.'

'It's not always exciting. Only sometimes.'

He looked down at me, and I looked back at him. We held each other's gaze for a long moment, and something changed, right then. I knew he knew what I was feeling, and I knew he felt just the same. The quiet, sunny kitchen was suddenly as charged with sex as if it had been the dance floor of a club or the honeymoon suite of a flash hotel.

I'd caught his eye all right (plump Ivanka lookalike or not), but I couldn't think of a single thing to say, witty or otherwise.

He took a long drink of water, then handed the glass back to me, taking one step closer, his eyes still on my face.

'Your other half isn't home, then?' he asked.

I'd only listened to one episode of *Sorry Not Sorry*, and not even the whole of that, because I'd fallen asleep. But I was pretty sure I knew what the podcast's narrator would have done in my position.

She would've channelled her inner bad girl and said, 'As it happens, I'm single,' while glancing at him through her eyelashes and flicking her hair.

And then she'd have taken one step forward herself, the only step there was room to take. She'd have reached out a hand and touched his arm, where his bicep bulged out from his sleeve, and discovered that his skin was as hot and smooth as it looked, the muscle beneath as hard and strong. She'd have smiled and tilted her face up to his, and waited for his kiss, his touch, and whatever happened after that. Or maybe she'd really give it some and go in for a snog herself.

But me... I did none of those things. I bottled it. I heard my voice blurting out, 'Actually, I'm expecting him home any minute.'

And he said, 'I'd best be on my way, then.'

I waited until I could no longer hear the engine of his van, and then I collapsed on the sofa, fizzing with excitement. I hadn't touched him. I hadn't even properly flirted. But I'd done *something*

– a part of me that I'd forgotten was even there was wide awake again. I felt more alive than I had for months.

Oh my God, Charlotte, you almost shagged the tree surgeon!

I didn't tell Molly and Chloë about my almost-adventure at brunch the next day. If Maddy had been there, I might have said something – even spun the whole thing out into a bit of a story, bigging up the hotness of Tim and downplaying my own wimpy response – but she wasn't, so I didn't.

Instead we talked about the chances of Molly's boyfriend William ever asking her to marry him (remote, I thought; they'd been together for years and as far as I could tell William was far too content having Molly cooking his dinner every night and doing all his ironing to have any need to change anything at all), about Chloë's seemingly perfect new bloke Gareth (who she'd met online a few months after having her heart broken by Sam, spiralling into a decline and losing so much weight she hadn't even had to suck her cheeks in when she took selfies for her Tinder profile), and about how I was going to get through the next week at work without going insane and attacking Piers (who wasn't even my boss, but still treated me like his skivvy) with a stapler.

It was only when I got off the Tube much later, tipsy on margaritas, that I realised I had forgotten all about my new housemate moving in. Poor girl, I thought, turning up to find the place deserted. Still, at least she'd have had a chance to have a nice private poke around and take her time deciding which of the two available bedrooms to move her things into. I quickened my pace, hurrying round the corner into our road and only pausing briefly to scratch Freezer, who was perched on the wall outside the next-door house, presumably waiting for his humans to come home, under his bristly white chin. It was seven o'clock – there was still time for the two of us to pop to the pub and get to know each other.

But when I unlocked the front door and called out, 'Hello?' there was no response. I called again, then I went upstairs and had a look around. Both bedrooms were still empty, and had that forlorn look unoccupied rooms do: even though Henry hadn't slept in his for many months, it had still felt used when he'd lived here, with his clothes in the wardrobe and his skis propped up in the corner.

Oh well. Tansy was bound to turn up soon, and then the place would feel properly lived-in again, and I wouldn't be rattling around on my own any more. But, for now, I felt a bad case of the Sunday-night blues creeping up on me. My eyes felt heavy from the brunch cocktails and I had the beginnings of a hangover. Dispirited, I stuck a load of washing on, then stared into the fridge for a bit, but couldn't think of anything I wanted to eat. In the end, I made a pot of tea and took a packet of Hobnobs up to my room, got into bed and watched *Jamestown* on my tablet.

I must have fallen asleep, because the next thing I knew I was being jerked awake for the second time that weekend by the pounding of the door knocker and the corresponding hammering of my heart. I looked at my watch – it was half past eleven.

What the fuck? Who moves into a house at almost midnight on a Sunday? Or what if it wasn't Tansy at all, but someone else? Luke and Hannah, who lived next door, had woken us up once when they'd been to the pub and forgotten their keys, and needed to climb over our fence to break into their house from the back. Or what if it was the police? What if something had happened to Maddy or Henry? Thoughts racing through my head – each more dreadful and unlikely than the last – I pulled on some clothes and ran downstairs.

There, standing on the doorstep with a bulging backpack on her shoulders, a massive holdall on the path next to her, and a huge bunch of pink roses in her hands, was a Victoria's Secret Angel. No word of a lie – she was so stunning that all I could do was stand and stare at her. She was way taller than me, and had long honey-blonde hair that managed to be both tousled and silky. Her eyes were violet, framed by long, feathery black lashes, and she was incredibly slim but incredibly curvy, too. Her mouth was a perfect rosebud pout until she smiled, revealing even, pearly white teeth.

'You must be Charlotte,' she said, in a slightly husky voice that matched her ridiculously sexy appearance. 'I'm so sorry to turn up so late. The day – things just got out of hand and I didn't realise the estate agent would be shut, so I didn't get to pick up my key and I didn't have your number. I'd have waited until tomorrow but I had nowhere else to go.'

I realised I'd been blocking the door – perhaps she thought I wasn't going to let her in. Mortified, I moved aside and muttered something about her coming in. She tripped over the rug and only just managed to right herself, dropping her flowers, and I realised she was totally shitfaced.

For a second I was absolutely furious with Henry. What had he been thinking? We wanted a housemate who, while not necessarily a teetotal hermit, was at least moderately sensible, and he'd landed me with this flaky pisshead. Then I looked at her again, and I could see how it must have gone.

Henry would have tried his best to ask this girl questions about herself, her work and social life, but there was no way, faced with her off-the-scale hotness, he would have been able to take in any of the answers. She could have told him she was a crack dealer, or on the run from the Feds, or had been evicted from her previous accommodation after burning it to the ground for the lolz – anything at all, really, and he would still have decided she was the ideal housemate. Not that Henry was some kind of lecherous creep, or anything – he was properly smitten with Maddy – but still. Faced with Tansy, any straight man would have lost the power of rational thought.

Tansy dumped her backpack on the floor and rooted around in it, then produced a bottle of champagne, which she handed to me along with the slightly battered roses.

'These are for you,' she said. 'Honestly, I'm just so sorry about all this.'

I wondered how on earth, if her day had been as chaotic as she'd said, she had still managed to find an open florist that sold seriously gorgeous bouquets and an open wine merchant that sold Perrier-Jouët Belle Epoque, but I didn't ask. I thanked her and said, 'Shall I show you round?'

'Please don't worry. I can see I got you out of bed, and I'm totally knackered myself. If it's okay with you I'll just hit the sack.'

I said that was absolutely fine with me, and she followed me upstairs, looked around and then turned and went into the room that had been Maddy's.

'I'll leave you to get settled in,' I said. 'The bathroom's just there, and my room's next to it. The one next to yours is empty too, but there's someone moving in this week, so then we'll be a full house again.'

'Great!' Tansy said, smiling her devastating smile and then yawning. Even her tonsils looked beautiful. However annoying the way she'd arrived had been, I had a feeling I was going to find it impossible not to like her.

I went downstairs and turned off the lights, then I remembered the beautiful bouquet of roses. If I didn't get them in some water they'd be dead by morning. I rummaged in the kitchen cupboards and found the jug we sometimes used for Pimm's, filled it with water and ripped the cellophane off the flowers. There were so many of them I could only just manage to squeeze them in. I was about to chuck the packaging in the recycling when I noticed a white card attached to it, with swirly florist's writing on it.

You were amazing last night, as always. Travis.

Chapter Three

Standing on a packed Tube train on a boiling Monday morning, my face pressed into the armpit of the man next to me (*BO Boy, is that you?*), I was finding it hard to love anything: not the chirpy narrator of *Sorry Not Sorry*, not the world at large, and certainly not my boring self or my tedious routines.

After Tansy's arrival I'd lain awake for what felt like hours, listening to the muted thumps and crashes as she tried to be quiet sorting out her stuff but, like any pissed person, failing totally, doing a lot of noisy tiptoeing and whispering, 'Oh shit,' every so often. Once she'd finished, I'd stayed awake for a bit longer, hoping she wasn't going to vom everywhere. But she didn't; the house was silent and only a faint smell of flowers, which might have come from the roses she'd brought with her or from Tansy herself, let me know she was there at all.

And now, scratchy-eyed and narky, I was in no shape to face a full-on week at work. I edged off the train and out of the station, wondering as I did almost every morning what possessed hedge fund owners to base their offices in Mayfair, where you had to fight through crowds of tourists who'd apparently never used a train before, rather than in the City, where dead-eyed, robotic commuters shuffled swiftly through the tunnels as if powered by some kind of remote control.

But as soon as I stepped through the doors into the fish-tank-lined lobby of the building where I worked, I felt my spirits lift. It sounds a bit tragic, I know, but I loved my job. Obviously there were times when I bitched and moaned about it, but mostly, the sense of excitement and potential I felt the first time I saw the building, when I'd come for my interview, had stayed with me.

I remembered sitting opposite Margot, the Head of Operations, in a squashy cappuccino-coloured leather chair, the shiny blond expanse of the meeting room table between us, and thought, *I want this*. I'd looked at her gorgeous rust-coloured wool dress, severe but feminine, and imagined one day owning a garment like it, and one day achieving her air of assured authority. I imagined interviewing someone like me, and her not having the slightest idea that I'd grown up in a council house and been on free school meals. I'd been apprehensive and overawed, but at the same time filled with a sense that this was where I belonged – or at least where I wanted to belong.

I remembered Margot saying, 'Don't think this job will be all glamour, Charlotte. It's not. It's a junior position. You'll get to sit in on client meetings and prepare presentations, and you'll assist Piers, our Head of Sales, with marketing when he needs it. But also, if there's no one else available to make coffee for a meeting, you do it. If the sales team are crunching numbers for a presentation at two in the morning and you're doing the PowerPoint slides, you stay until they're done. If someone needs their dry-cleaning collected… You get the picture.'

I got the picture. And, to my amazement, I got the job, along with a salary that seemed dizzyingly high until I realised just how hard I was going to have to work to earn it.

As soon as I stepped out of the lift and into the Colton Capital office that Monday morning, I could hear Colin shouting. I had hardly anything to do with Colin day to day, thank God, but he was still my boss – everyone's boss, because he owned the firm – and it wasn't a bit unusual for him to shout. But him getting going so bright and early pretty much set the tone for the week, and not in a good way.

On my way to my desk, I glanced surreptitiously through the glass wall of the fishbowl-like meeting room where Colin's bollockings usually took place. (Unless someone was actually going to be sacked, in which case they were invited into one of the private meeting rooms and joined by the Head of HR and the Head of Legal, then escorted out of the building by security, and had to send someone later on to take away their belongings in a cardboard box.)

So I knew that whatever had enraged my boss that morning, it was unlikely to be terminal. I couldn't make out many of his words, just the occasional 'stupid, incompetent fucker' and 'trying to fuck over this entire firm' – standard stuff for Colin's rants. What did surprise me, though, was the identity of the victim.

Colin was pacing up and down, as he generally did while delivering a proper roasting, practically bouncing on the balls of his feet, his short, stocky body puffed up with rage and his jowls wobbling so he looked a bit like a furious frog: almost comical, unless you were on the receiving end.

The man listening to his harangue, in contrast, was standing still, his back to the glass wall, preserving some dignity by not allowing the rest of the office to see his face. But I'd recognise that back view anywhere. No one else was so tall, or had such lean, broad shoulders clad in such flawless Italian tailoring, nor such immaculately styled, glossy dark hair.

Renzo had been headhunted a few months back from a rival fund, and until today had been the blue-eyed boy of Colton Capital. He'd been given a portfolio of five hundred million pounds to manage – a serious wedge for a new joiner – and had been consistently and often spectacularly up. I sometimes allowed myself to dream wistfully about the size of the bonus that would be coming his way, and wonder what I'd do with it if it were mine. I could put down a deposit on a flat – actually, never mind that, I could buy a flat outright, and still have change left over for enough shoes to last me for years, a luxury holiday, even a car if I wanted one. I could take my nan to the Bahamas for a holiday, although to be honest she'd probably prefer Blackpool.

Other times, I allowed myself to dream for just a few moments about Renzo himself, wondering what those broad, hard shoulders would look like without the austere workwear covering them, whether his hair would be as silky to touch as it looked, and whether his performance in bed would be as aggressive and as expert as it was at work.

Whenever I found my mind straying along those lines, I brought it firmly back where it belonged. I knew where that road led: I'd seen it happen to Larissa, who'd made the mistake of sleeping with one of the other portfolio managers. He'd never spoken to her again afterwards, but his colleagues had. In fact, they'd all had bets going on who'd get to shag her next, and in the end it got so intolerable that she left. So I knew that nothing good at all would come of a crush on Renzo, or indeed on any of the other fiercely ambitious, gym-honed, suited men who strutted their stuff at Colton Capital, wearing their masculinity and their success as brashly and competitively as they wore their thousand-pound leather shoes. The men I worked with were strictly off-limits for me.

But the price Renzo and the rest of them paid for their huge income was high. Not just the brutal hours and the certainty that, sooner or later, it would be their turn to get called into the fishbowl and ranted at, but the pressure: the awareness that, every day, they were effectively gambling millions of pounds and that sooner or later they'd lose. No matter how robust the data provided by the research analysts and the quants was, no matter how confident they were that they knew the markets they were buying into inside out, it was still not that different from betting the entire contents of your bank account on a fifty-to-one outsider in the Grand National because it's got adorable floppy ears and you feel sorry for it. I knew it, and they knew it, too – hence the banter and the swagger, the relentlessly macho culture that sometimes made me feel as if I was paddling through pure testosterone when I walked to my desk.

I put my bag down and turned on my computer. I was dying for a coffee, but walking to the kitchen would mean passing the fishbowl again. Instead, I decided to apply myself to the presentation I was putting together for Piers, which I was due to deliver that evening. Looking at how much there was left to do, I braced myself for lunch at my desk and a late evening.

As I opened my PowerPoint file, I saw the glass door swing open and Renzo and Colin emerge. Colin's face was blotchy and sweaty, and I could see a bulging vein in his forehead. I always worried that he would go too far during one of his bollocking sessions and simply drop dead. Renzo, in contrast, was deadpan – for all the emotion he showed, he and Colin might as well have been discussing the weather or the cricket or something. I tried to look tactfully away as he passed my desk, but he caught my eye and gave me the merest ghost of a wink, and I couldn't help blushing.

I worked until lunchtime, polishing my pie charts and toning down the worst excesses of Piers's OTT language. Just as I was considering whether to do a global search and replace every use of 'whilst' for 'while', I became conscious of someone hovering over my desk.

I looked up. Not someone, but two people: Briony, one of Colin's three executive assistants, and Xander, another newish joiner, whose role in the business I didn't really understand.

'Hey,' I said. 'What's up?'

'Actually, I wanted to ask you for a favour,' Briony said.

'Oh,' Xander said. 'So did I. But I can see how busy you are, so…'

I looked at my screen, then at the two of them, imagining my lunch break and my chance of going to the gym on my way home melting away.

'Go on,' I said. 'Who got here first?'

'You did,' Briony said to Xander.

'No, no,' he said. 'After you. I insist.'

'Okay,' Briony said. 'Thanks. Charlotte, it's just that Svetlana rang, she's in a massive state about Lucinda's birthday party and asked me if I can meet her to talk about it. The others are really busy – Craig had to find a venue for that drinks thing at the last minute, Alice is organising the trip to Silverstone—'

'What do you need me to do?' I interrupted.

'Only the Ocado order,' Briony said. 'I'd put it off until tomorrow but we're almost out of smoked salmon and you know what they're like...'

I did. If the staff fridge wasn't kept bursting with high-quality protein, there'd be a mutiny. It would be almost as bad as running out of coffee (or running out of the single-estate El Salvadorian roast that was currently in favour and having to resort to Nescafé like normal people). I also knew that doing the Ocado order would take most of the afternoon and test my patience to its limit, but there was no getting out of it. At least I didn't have to deal with Colin's five-year-old daughter's birthday party and the off-the-scale expectations of his wife.

To be fair to Svetlana, she's done seriously well for herself. The official story was classic rags-to-riches. Well, not rags exactly, because Svetlana was apparently working in the menswear department at Harrods, and one day about ten years ago, Colin took some clients out for lunch at Galvin at Windows, and during the course of the meal – the first course, actually; the story isn't short on detail – Colin spilled gazpacho down his Dolce & Gabbana tie (see, I told you, detail). Not wanting to lose face at his next appointment, he popped into the nearest shop to buy a replacement, saw Svetlana, and fell in love at first sight.

The story was actually quite plausible, partly because everyone who'd ever been to lunch with Colin knew that he couldn't finish a plate of food without looking like he'd been in a fight with it, and partly because Svetlana was a knockout by anyone's standards. She was about eight foot tall – or at least that's how it felt to me – with razor-sharp cheekbones, wings of black hair, a figure that she put a huge amount of work into achieving and Harley Street surgeons put even more into maintaining, and a husky, Russian-accented voice that I imagine men interpreted not so much as, 'Come to bed,' but, 'Get on that bed and pass me the spanking paddle – now.'

And so the truth – the alleged truth, anyway, which everyone claimed was just a rumour while pretending to believe the tie thing – was that Colin had met Svetlana through a high-class escort agency: one which had certain specialisms. The detail got a bit hazy at that point, and to be honest I never asked for the whole (alleged) truth. The man was my boss, and the last thing I wanted to do was imagine him trussed up like a Christmas turkey and being… Anyway, I sometimes wondered whether that cringe-making image might be helpful to his employees when the door of the fishbowl closed and Colin started to shout.

Svetlana's past career aside, she retained – or just naturally had – the ability to terrify everyone who dealt with her, coupled with almost magnetic charm. I knew this because shortly after I joined the fund, when Briony was off on maternity leave, I got volunteered to work with Colin's other executive assistants helping Svetlana organise his surprise fiftieth birthday party. It sounds mad, I know, but that's how it worked. The fund belonged to Colin, but Svetlana, and by extension their four children (and the three Colin has from his previous marriage, and the two from the one before that), expected and got full access to its staff. Of course, though we all knew and accepted this, the birthday party had to be planned without Colin knowing about it, so the EAs and I had to deal with it all in addition to our normal workload.

It was brutal. It made the triggering of Article 50 – when Britain's deadline for leaving the European Union was set and no one knew how the fuck the markets were going to respond, and I was at work until dawn organising blow-up mattresses for people to sleep on and endless deliveries of sashimi from Nobu – look like taking the afternoon off and going for a pedicure.

So I said to Briony, 'Of course, no problem, leave it with me. Let me know if you need a hand with the party.' We exchanged sympathetic glances and she hurried off.

Then I turned to Xander. 'And what can I do for you?'

Like I said, Xander's role in the fund wasn't entirely clear. He was an economist who worked for the World Bank until Colin lured him away with the promise of more exciting challenges and even more exciting cash in return for his expertise in emerging markets. He'd worked all over the world – in South America, the Asian sub-continent, the Middle East, and most recently Washington, DC. (I knew all this because Piers had chucked his CV at me a few weeks back and said, 'Here, write this up for the website, would you, darling.')

A couple of days after his CV landed on my desk, Xander himself appeared at Colton Capital, and since then he'd been floating about with his laptop – sitting with the analysts one day, with the quants the next, with the traders after that – and leaving chaos wherever he went. If the fire alarm went off, you can be sure it's Xander who's burned his toast in the kitchen (he avoids the high-quality protein, being a vegetarian). I did offer, when Xander first told me this, to organise a regular Paxton & Whitfield order of expensive, smelly cheese, but he said it was absolutely fine, he liked getting out and exploring in his lunch break, because he'd never lived in London before. I gave him a look that was like, 'WTF, you think you're going to go out at lunchtime?' but he just smiled and headed off to make himself a cup of tea, colliding with Pavel's desk on the way, almost knocking over a can of Red Bull and not even noticing Pavel's death stare.

'It's just my pass, again,' Xander said apologetically. 'I think I must have left it on the Tube. I'm sure I had it with me when I left the flat this morning. I stopped off at Pret for a croissant; I suppose I might have left it there. Fortunately Renzo got here at the same time as me this morning, otherwise I'd have been hanging around outside the door looking like a lemon.'

I made a mental note to mention to Margot, my line manager, that when we moved to our new offices on the two floors above, which were currently being refurbished at vast expense, we could maybe replace the card system with passcode access. Except even then, I suspected, Xander – in spite of having a brain the size of a planet – would forget the code and it would need resetting every couple of days so as not to compromise security. Maybe I should suggest biometrics instead – even Xander couldn't lose his own fingerprints.

'Okay, I'll give you a new one,' I said. 'This is – what – your fourth in two months? Strong work.'

'I'm sorry, Charlotte.'

I smiled. 'It's no problem. But I'll have to extract a fee.'

Xander raised an eyebrow. He had nice eyes behind his glasses, I noticed. I hadn't really paid much attention to his looks before. In his scruffy tweed jacket and jeans, he kind of got overshadowed by all the other men in the firm, rocking their sharp suits and hundred-pound haircuts.

I lowered my voice. 'What was that about with Renzo and Colin, earlier?'

It was another thing I'd noticed about Xander. Although he hadn't been with Colton Capital long, he seemed to have his finger on the pulse of everything. People told him stuff. Just the other day I'd found him and Briony deep in conversation in the kitchen about Briony's one-year-old daughter's habit of waking up at three in the morning, and how knackered Briony was as a result. I walked in just as Briony was saying, 'I just wish she'd leave my boobs alone and let me get some sleep.' And Briony never, ever said anything about being a mum at work, because she worried that it was career-limiting.

So I thought it was likely that whatever blunder Renzo had made, Xander would have the low-down.

He said, 'Oh, yeah, he took a client to Gaslight.'

It was my turn to raise an eyebrow – or try to, I'm not sure I actually managed it. 'And?' I said.

It's not like I approved, but entertaining clients in strip joints – or 'Gentlemen's Clubs', as they were referred to on their websites when I went on to book VIP rooms for Piers (although I didn't get what's so gentlemanly about paying some surgically enhanced stripper to shove her tits in your face) was standard operating procedure at Colbert Capital.

'Change of policy,' Xander said. 'Apparently, the portfolio manager who left a while back – Larissa, I think her name was – is suing for sex discrimination. So they've all been told to clean up their acts. And I guess Renzo didn't get the memo.'

That, I thought, explained Renzo's wink as he passed my desk. It had meant, 'Look what a naughty boy I am, breaking the rules by looking at writhing naked women on expenses. And he can't even sack me because I'm so shit-hot at my job.' Although, of course, it didn't even begin to explain how Colin could square his own relationship with Svetlana with this new squeaky-clean image.

'Right,' I said. 'Interesting. I'll bear that in mind.'

He paused for a second and then said, 'And quite right too, if you ask me. Most workplaces wouldn't consider that kind of thing any more. I mean, like, the nineteen eighties called, they want their client entertainment back. But I guess that's not a popular view around here.'

I considered shrugging diplomatically and keeping my mouth shut, but I couldn't. 'It is with me.'

I handed Xander his new plastic access card, and then I sent off an email to all staff saying that the deadline for additions to the Ocado order was four o'clock, and braced myself for the requests for Febreze, langoustines, shaving gel and Grey Goose vodka to start flooding into my inbox.

Chapter Four

Hello again you gorgeous things, and welcome back. Today, I'm going to be inviting you to take part in the second of our challenges – and it's a doozy! I don't mind admitting it – I'm kind of nervous about it. But excited, too. Because this is all about being daring, embracing my wild side and fricking living a little – or, I hope, living a lot.

Let me explain. Back when I was a teenager, there was a saying: good girls go to heaven; bad girls go everywhere. And that's what this series is all about. Not being a bad girl in the sense of doing bad things, or – worse – being a bad friend, but in the sense of going places. Spreading your wings. Learning not to say no. (Well, obviously, there are situations in which saying no is absolutely fine – when it's the right thing to do – but we'll talk more about that later.)

So today I'm going to be challenging myself by trying something new. Are you up for joining me?

I pushed myself up in bed and adjusted the pillows behind me, wishing I'd thought to make a cup of tea before hitting play on this latest podcast. But now I'd started, I wanted to know what was going to happen: what the Bad Girl had in store for herself and – I took a deep breath – for me.

I listened to her explain how she'd decided she needed to broaden her horizons and meet new people.

Like my friend Ashley, who randomly decided a year or so back to go to a swingers' night, and now she's, like, totally into the scene. I could do that! Haha – who am I kidding? I so could not do that. But I can push my boundaries in other ways.

So the Bad Girl decided to start out relatively slow. She'd try new activities, join clubs (although maybe not swingers' ones) or even just go somewhere in her city where she'd never ventured before. And even if this didn't lead to love at first sight, it could lead to her becoming a more exciting version of herself – and having a bunch of great stories to tell her mates.

It all sounded fairly predictable, objectively speaking. But I couldn't help admiring the Bad Girl, and wanting to keep listening to her story. There was something about her determination, her feistiness, that appealed to me. She was like me in some ways: she had a job she loved and worked hard at, although she wasn't specific about what it was. She lived in a cool, hip part of town. She spent a big chunk of her salary on clothes, and then worried she was never going to go anywhere where she could wear them.

But, unlike me, she was making changes to her life. She was pushing herself beyond the familiar, facing the prospect of failure and rejection and not being daunted by it.

She was like me, only brave.

And maybe, if I did as she said, some of that courage would rub off on me, if I accepted her dare. So I opened Facebook and did a search for groups and events near me. There were loads, unsurprisingly – our corner of East London is as community-minded as they come. But not very many of them looked like they held enormous potential for finding excitement, hot dates, or even someone to share an awkward fumble with after too many wines down the Prince George.

There was a Saturday singing session for parents and toddlers at the local church hall, which would have been great if I was in the market for meeting a lonely single dad with a caring nature and sad eyes, only I wasn't. There was a furniture restoration workshop, which sounded interesting, except I didn't have any furniture to restore. There was a taxidermy course starting, but even the Bad Girl wasn't going to persuade me to attempt that.

I was about to give up when I remembered the podcast's firm instruction: 'Come on now, girl! I know what you're going to do! You're going to browse the web for a bit and then you're going to go, "Nah, sorry, none of that shit is for me. I'll try again next week." No. You. Won't. You'll get right out there and do it, because I say so and because I'm going to be doing it too and anything I can do, you can do better, right?'

Right. I promised myself that the next event I found, however random, would be the one. I swiped down so that my screen scrolled so swiftly it blurred, and as soon as it came to a stop I tapped.

Fuck. It was a running club.

'Hackney Huffers,' the page description read. 'We're not your everyday running group or time trial. We're local, we're small, we're friendly AF and we welcome runners of all ages and abilities. No need to register – just turn up with your trainers on and a sense of adventure.'

They started at nine o'clock and it was just gone eight. I couldn't even use being too late as an excuse not to go, especially as they were just down the road. Reluctantly, I pushed the duvet aside and rummaged through my wardrobe for a sports bra.

'Bad Girl, whatever your name is, if this goes tits up I am holding you solely responsible,' I said aloud.

*

Two hours later, I staggered into the kitchen. I hadn't seen Tansy all week, not since she'd moved in, which isn't as weird as it sounds – typically, I was out of the house before half seven in the morning, and that week I'd worked even later than usual on a couple of evenings, been round to Maddy and Henry's new place for a takeaway, and actually made it to a Pilates class for once. I presumed Tansy was busy, too: honing her incredible figure in the gym; seeing Travis, whoever he might be; and no doubt working in her enviably glamorous-sounding job in fashion.

Occasionally I heard music playing quietly behind her closed bedroom door at night. The smell of Maddy's toiletries in the bathroom had been replaced with a different, muskier scent. One evening I'd come home to find the washing machine full of damp, clean clothes. Another morning, there'd been a couple of huge packages in the hallway with an address in Cornwall on the labels, which I guessed Tansy was planning to take to the post office on her way to work. There was no sign of her ever using the kitchen, not even to make a cup of tea – but then, there was no sign of me doing that, either. And I knew, at least, that she hadn't moved out and wasn't lying dead in her room like the poor woman in that *Dreams of a Life* documentary I'd seen when I was at uni.

But now it was Saturday, and she was there in the kitchen, eating toast. In my head, I realised, I'd built her up into some mysterious, fragrant goddess who I wasn't worthy to share a home (and certainly not a tub of chocolate mini-rolls) with. But she looked completely normal – if ridiculously pretty – in her white denim shorts and faux suede T-shirt. When she saw me, she dropped her breakfast and it landed Marmite-side down on the floor.

'Jesus Christ, Charlotte, what happened to you?' she gasped. 'Are you okay? Do I need to call the police?'

I managed a laugh. 'Maybe. But only to report the Hackney fucking Huffers for breaching the Trade Descriptions Act.'

'The what?'

'I've been "broadening my horizons",' I said, doing air quotes. 'Trying new things. So today I went to a running club. I know, I should have known better and I'm ridiculously unfit and it's all my fault. But they said they were relaxed and friendly. They said they welcomed runners of all abilities. What they didn't say was that they were doing a special training session today for the Tough Mudder.'

'The what?'

'Nope, me neither,' I said. 'I googled it on the way home. It's this insane thing that mad, obsessed fitness masochists do that involves crawling through ponds and climbing over combat nets and ridiculous, pointless, painful stuff like that.'

'It sounds kind of fun.'

'No,' I said. 'It does not. Trust me. This wasn't even the actual race and it was insane. I mean, look at me.'

Tansy looked, and I saw her stifle a giggle. To fair, I was quite the sight. I was literally caked in mud from the neck down, and there were splashes of it on my face, too – I could feel it drying there like a dodgy pore-tightening treatment. My vest top was ripped in about a dozen places from crawling under barbed wire. My leggings were ripped too, and I'd taken all the skin off both knees.

'But did you meet anyone nice at least?' she asked.

'No! Of course I didn't. There were more men there than women, to be fair. But they were all these terrifying ripped types who think it's fun to bench-press their own body weight and go fell-running and – well, do shit like this. And they were all so damn cheerful about it. You should have seen them at the start, bouncing up and down on their toes and making jokes about how much it was going to hurt. Bloody healthy bastards. And the women were worse. All glowy and cheerful, even at the end when they were covered in mud and sweat.

'And,' I went on, 'to add insult to injury, there were actually showers there, and a really nice-looking café that did fried breakfasts, but I didn't read that bit on the Facebook page so I didn't have a change of clothes with me and even if I'd wanted to flirt with some Terminator type over coffee afterwards I wouldn't have been able to because I stink of goat poo.'

'Well, I didn't want to mention it, but to be perfectly honest you are a bit whiffy. I didn't know there were goats in London.'

'Nor did I,' I replied grimly. 'But it turns out there are these things called city farms, where people take their kids for fresh air and a glimpse of the natural world, and this was one of them. And there were goats.'

Tansy's face twitched again.

'And I was right at the back all the time,' I went on. 'So there was no one to help me over the stupid obstacles – or under them – until the people in front caught up with me, and they were all so hardcore and fast that I didn't want to let them help when they offered so I said I was fine. I wasn't, obviously. I almost cried when I got to the end of the first lap and realised I was meant to go round again.'

'I totally would have cried,' Tansy said. 'I can't believe you didn't just stop. Why didn't you? I would have. I'd have sat down and cried and then one of the ripped hot men would have stopped and asked me what was wrong, and then…'

'Then,' I said, 'even if one had stopped, and I wouldn't guarantee it – okay, maybe they would, for you – he'd have said, "Come on! A winner never quits, a quitter never wins." Or maybe, "One day, this is going to be your warm-up."'

'"When you're face down in the mud, keep reaching for the stars,"' Tansy suggested.

'"Anything worth having doesn't come easy."'

'Exactly! Bastards.'

'I hate them all. Every last fit, toned, motivated one of them.'

'Tell you what,' Tansy said. 'Why don't you jump in the shower, I'll stick your gear in the washing machine – I was about to put a load of my stuff on anyway – and we can head out and have a massive brunch, with bacon and crumpets and prosecco.'

'Now that's a great call,' I said. 'Maddy said the coffee shop up the road does amazing brunch and they've just got a booze licence. But don't worry about doing my washing – this stuff is trashed. And the leggings give me the worst camel toe. I'd forgotten why I haven't done any proper exercise for so long, and now I know.'

So I showered and dressed and Tansy and I walked up the road to The Daily Grind, except it was closed for a function and absolutely heaving with teenage girls – evidently a celeb called Gemma Grey was doing a book signing. So we got the Tube into town instead and had matcha green tea sours and dumplings and all the fizz, and it was so much fun I didn't particularly care that no one tried to pull us.

If Tansy's arrival in the house had been somewhat dramatic (okay, dramatic by my standards; I lead a quiet life), Adam's couldn't have been more different. One day the door to Henry's old room stood open and the space beyond it was empty. The next, I came home from work to find the door closed and Adam presumably in residence. That was it. There was no other sign of him. Just that closed door.

It stayed that way for several days. Occasionally I'd be woken in the middle of the night by the sounds of him moving around the house – a tap running in the kitchen, footsteps on the wooden floor, the toilet flushing or the microwave pinging.

'It's like having a fricking ghost in the house,' I complained to Maddy and Henry over drinks at their local pub. 'Not even a fun poltergeist that rearranges your belongings and stuff. Just a kind of sullen haunting one.'

'A boring ghost,' Henry replied. 'That sounds like the cousin Adam I remember.'

'I don't think I've ever even met him,' Maddy said.

'Yeah, you have, he came to James's wedding, remember?'

Maddy said she couldn't remember a thing about Henry's brother's wedding, given that it had been months ago and she'd been so nervous about meeting all his family that she'd drunk a bottle and a half of prosecco and had to go to bed soon after the dancing started, before the bride had even thrown her bouquet.

'Not that it mattered, because you asked me to marry you the week after anyway,' she finished, and the two of them exchanged one of the long, intense looks that made me feel kind of awkward and kind of jealous, but also really happy for them.

'You danced with him,' Henry reminded her. 'Right before you fell in the fishpond. You can't not remember.'

'Oh God, don't. Not the bloody fishpond. Dying.'

Henry said he was trying to remind her about Adam, not about the fishpond, and they bickered amiably for a few minutes.

Then Maddy said, 'Oh hold on, I do remember him! Really tall, and kind of hot in a geeky way. Dark hair, glasses, and a beard? Can't manage to string a sentence together without blushing and tripping over his words?'

'That's him.'

I said, 'Right, so if I find some dark beardy dude in the kitchen one morning, at least I'll know not to call the police. But seriously, he never comes out of his room. And Tansy spends almost every night shut in her room too, FaceTiming her family, apparently. The Addams family, more like, given she does it at two in the morning. It's like living in a morgue. I really miss you guys.'

'We miss you too,' Maddy soothed me, and she and I had a bit of a hug while Henry went to get another round.

She meant it, I knew – in a way. But I also knew that it was different for her. She'd moved on, she was planning a wedding and having a new kitchen fitted, and who knew, maybe in a few months she'd be telling me she was having a baby. And even if something made all that not happen – if Henry jilted her at the altar, say, and she moved back into her old room, not that I would ever wish anything that awful on my best mate, obviously – things would never go back to how they were.

I allowed myself a brief moment of nostalgia, remembering how Maddy and I would sit in the kitchen together on Saturday afternoons, drinking tea and painting our nails and gossiping, while Henry went to the pub to watch the football. How we'd declared Tuesday nights white wine and takeaway night, and sat together stuffing our faces with chicken tikka masala and naan from the Queen of Kashmir and putting the world to rights. How we always knew when the other would want to chat, or want to be left alone.

But then I dragged my mind back to the present, and asked how the wedding plans were coming along.

'It's going to be really chilled,' Henry said. 'Marquee in my parents' garden, ceremony at the church down the road, only about a hundred and fifty guests. It'll be the week before Christmas so everyone will be partied out.'

'Basically we don't want a load of stress,' Maddy said. 'Although we do need to get the invitations out this week, and…' she lowered her voice and spoke softly in my ear. Tactfully, Henry got up and went to the loo. 'There's this dress designer in Brighton. I saw one of her frocks in a wedding magazine – not that I've been buying loads of them, don't look at me like that – and her work is stunning. Like, fantasy fairy-tale stuff, all lace and tulle and pearls, and just, aaaah.'

'That sounds amazing,' I said. 'Are you going to buy one, then?'

Maddy laughed. 'If only it was as simple as that! She's got a waiting list months long. But I've been stalking her on Instagram, and apparently one of her brides has cancelled, and she's got a free appointment tomorrow and when I called she said she might just be able to get a dress made for me in time. I haven't told Henry but I've taken the day off work and I'm going to drive down and see her. You'll come, won't you?'

I looked at her eager face and remembered the memory stick Piers had chucked on my desk earlier that afternoon, saying casually, 'This is the presentation I'm doing to SkyBridge in New York. Take a look, would you? See if you can zhuzh it up a bit? I don't need it until lunchtime tomorrow.'

Coming from Piers, the suggestion that I might be able to improve on work he'd done was a massive vote of confidence. Normally, I'd have stayed in the office and done a few hours' work on it that evening, but I hadn't wanted to let Maddy and Henry down. Instead, I'd planned to be at my desk at seven the next day.

'Maddy, I'd love to, you know I would, but…'

'Go on! Chuck a sickie, just for once. It'll be fun.'

I shook my head. 'I can't. Piers has given me this thing to look at, and it's urgent, and…'

She rolled her eyes. 'Everything's urgent with that posh bastard. He's just taking you for a mug.'

'Yeah, maybe he is, but it's my job to be taken advantage of by him. I'm sorry, babe, I can't do it. Can't you reschedule with this whatsername?'

'With Conchita Villamoura? Like I said, she's booked up months in advance. It's no biggie. I'll see if Bianca can go instead.'

But I knew Maddy well enough to know that, whatever she said, and whether or not she had a great time shopping for dresses with Henry's sister, it was a biggie. She was hurt and annoyed and I felt dreadful about letting her down, even though I knew there was absolutely nothing I could have done about it.

After that, although we had another round and shared a plate of poutine (which Maddy said was the trendiest thing in the world right now but to me just tasted like chips and gravy, although not as good as the ones from the chippie on the corner where I grew up), I was aware that it would take me over an hour to get home and I'd have to be up at half past five, and couldn't stop myself looking at my watch and yawning.

So I made my excuses and went home, and coming out of the bathroom on my way to bed, I literally bumped into Adam.

At least, I presumed the dark-haired, bearded stranger on our landing must be Adam. Either that or Tansy had brought a bloke home – the mysterious Travis, maybe, although there'd been no trace of him since the bouquet of roses had withered, died and eventually been thrown in the bin by Odeta – or our house had been broken into by a burglar who carried a laptop with him when he went to use the facilities.

'Hi,' I said. 'I'm Charlotte.'

He and Henry were only first cousins so there was no reason why they'd look very alike, and they didn't. Adam had Henry's lanky height and a similar way of stooping his shoulders, as if he was worried he'd bump his head on something, but the resemblance ended there: he had none of Henry's easy confidence. He blinked, blushed and shied away from me.

'You're Adam, right? Nice to meet you at last. I've just got back from seeing Maddy and Henry. They said hi,' I said, even though they hadn't.

'Oh. Er, hi back, I guess.'

I wasn't sure whether he meant the greeting to be for me, or to be somehow subliminally passed back to my friend and her fiancé. And anyway, I was too knackered to stand around trying to make conversation with this monosyllabic stranger.

'I'm off to bed,' I said. 'Early start.'

And I watched as Adam turned around, went back into his room and closed the door behind him.

Chapter Five

I slept horribly that night, and the next. Added to my worry about work and guilt that I was abandoning Maddy over her wedding planning, I was still getting used to the unfamiliar sounds Tansy and Adam made in the house. They weren't noisy, just different. Tansy sometimes played music late at night, not nearly loudly enough for me to want to knock on her door and ask her to turn it down, but loudly enough that I could hear a faint whisper of sound through the wall. Sometimes I could hear her talking, too – far later than I'd ever ring any of my friends for a chat, which was weird. The walls of the house were too thick for me to make out any actual words, but the rise and fall of her voice jerked me out of almost-sleep and interrupted my dreams. I'm sure Adam could hear her too, and I could hear the scraping rumble of what must be the wheels of an office chair rolling across the wooden floor and occasionally the heavy tread of his feet as he moved around the room. For a slim man, he could certainly fucking stomp, I thought, pulling a pillow over my head and willing myself to sleep.

It must have worked, because I woke up on Saturday from a horrible dream about being on my way to Maddy and Henry's wedding, except for some reason I was trying to get to south-east

London on the train and the other train and the bus, and then I realised the train I was on was one to Brighton and I needed to find Conchita Villamoura's shop and pick up Maddy's wedding dress, and it was getting later and later and Maddy wouldn't have anything to wear and she'd never forgive me. And, of course, once I was awake enough to realise that it had only been a dream, I couldn't get back to sleep.

Scratchy-eyed and miserable, I made my way downstairs and put the kettle on. It was ridiculously early for a Saturday – not even seven o'clock – and neither of my housemates were up yet. Not surprising, I thought sourly, given the fact that they'd both apparently been awake half the night.

The weekend stretched uninvitingly ahead of me. I could go to the gym or do a Pilates class, but although I knew I'd feel better afterwards, I felt too rubbish to make myself go. And I definitely wasn't going to go back to the Hackney bloody Huffers. I could go into the office and make a start on another presentation Piers had asked me to look at, but the thought of staring at a screen for hours made me want to scream. I could get the bus to Westfield and wander round the shops, but I'd bought a much reduced, but still hugely expensive, pair of shoes online the previous day and my credit card couldn't take more punishment.

So I slumped on the sofa with my tea and surfed through the channels on the telly and the internet on my phone, and mindlessly ate my way through four slices of toast and peanut butter instead. And – newsflash – it made me feel even worse.

I was yanked out of my fug by the crash of the door knocker. For a moment I considered not answering – I knew that no one would call round without arranging to first, and I couldn't face turning away some poor Jehovah's Witness or man selling cleaning products to get back on the straight and narrow after being let out of prison (even though I'm pretty sure people who do that are actually casing the joint before breaking in and nicking everything).

Then I remembered my beautiful shoes, realised it was almost ten o'clock and the post was due, and ran to the door, opening it just as the postie was filling in his 'Sorry we missed you' card. A minute later, feeling considerably more cheerful, I was ripping open the cardboard packaging with the help of a bread knife.

Inside the plain brown cardboard was a glossy white box. I slowed down, wanting to savour the moment when I lifted off its lid and inhaled the fragrance of new leather for the first time. But inside, under a cloud of tissue paper, instead of my reduced Rag & Bone boots, was a set of La Perla lingerie that must have cost twice as much.

It was black lace: a feather-light bra that wouldn't have a hope in hell of containing my thirty-two F chest and a pair of minuscule knickers that I was fairly sure I wouldn't be able to get past my knees. Which was a huge shame, because if Amazon was going to send me the wrong stuff, they could hardly have chosen nicer wrong stuff than this. Not that I had any occasion to wear smalls like this.

I'd like to say I couldn't remember the last time anyone had seen me in my underwear, but I could – all too clearly. It was also the last time I'd swiped right on Tinder – a bloke called Nick had liked me, said hello, and not sent me a dick pic, which made him pretty much a keeper from the off. We chatted online for a couple of weeks, then arranged to meet for a drink. You know how these things go – as the frequency of our messages ramped up and the evening of our date got closer, I started to get massively overinvested, and by the time we met I'd practically named our babies.

So when I realised, about five seconds after meeting Nick, that there was no chemistry whatsoever between us, I wasn't going to let that stop me. Maybe it would be one of those slow-burn things, I told myself, drinking my gin and tonic far too quickly and ordering another. He was a nice guy, I insisted in my head. He had a good job, he was funny. He said he wanted to settle down.

He was the Clarks shoes of men. And even though, by the end of the night, I was still feeling none of the feels, I went home with him anyway. God, it was awful. He was a wet, sloppy kisser. He tweaked my nipples with his fingers like he was trying to find Five Live on his car radio. It was one of those shags you think is never going to end.

It hadn't quite put me off sex for life, but it hadn't exactly left me keen to try again with someone else. So I'd hardly been in the market for lingerie that was so clearly made to be put on, shagged in, and then taken off again before being tenderly hand-washed and probably rinsed in unicorn tears or something. Reluctantly I set aside my fleeting dream of somehow transforming into a size eight sex goddess, and folded the bra and pants back into the tissue paper. They'd have to go back and be sent to whoever had ordered them. Then I noticed the delivery note sticking out from between the layers of tissue. That was definitely our address, but my name wasn't on it; there was no name on the label at all.

'Shit,' I muttered. 'Why didn't I check?'

I considered shoving everything back into the box, returning it to the sender and denying all knowledge, but then I remembered that I'd signed for the parcel, and also that I was, after all, an adult and this was an innocent mistake. And then I heard Tansy's door opening and closing and her feet on the stairs, and felt myself come over all cringy with embarrassment again.

'Morning, Charlotte,' she said cheerfully, strolling into the kitchen in a strappy vest top and hot pink boy-short knickers. 'Did I hear the postman?'

It was just as well I'd answered the door, I thought – if she had, the poor man would probably have dropped dead of a stroke on the spot.

'Yeah, you did,' I said. 'I'm really sorry – I was expecting something from Amazon and I opened this by mistake. Is it yours?'

I handed her the box and she rummaged excitedly through the tissue paper.

'Oh,' she said. 'This came, did it? Nice.'

She seemed surprised, and also somewhat casual about her purchase, which seemed odd to me. If I'd splurged hundreds of pounds on underwear, I'd be overwhelmed with a mixture of excitement, guilt and buyer's remorse. But maybe it was different for Tansy – from what I'd seen of her clothes drying on the airer, she owned loads of designer stuff, although I'd assumed it was mostly freebies and samples from her work as a fashion buyer. A junior fashion buyer, though, which surely would mean that something like this was a rare purchase. But it was none of my business – if my housemate wanted to blow the equivalent of half her monthly rent on pants, let her knock herself out. *But if she's buying sexy kecks, she can't be single. So where's her boyfriend? She's never even mentioned Travis. Is she or isn't she?* I wondered, then I pushed that idea to the back of my mind, too – after all, weren't women's magazines always telling us we should dress for ourselves and not for men? Didn't someone even write a book about buying things that sparked joy? Or was that just about getting rid of things that didn't?

'Very nice,' I said. 'Sorry about – you know.'

'Don't give it another thought,' Tansy replied. 'Um… Charlotte, I hope you don't mind me asking, but are you okay? You look kind of tired.'

She put the box back on the counter and turned tactfully to fill the kettle.

'I'm fine. I just haven't been sleeping very well.'

To my surprise, Tansy blushed absolutely scarlet, like I'd have expected her to when she realised I'd seen her fuck-me lingerie.

'I wasn't keeping you awake, was I?' she said. 'I mean, I was talking until late on FaceTime. My mum and my sister both work shifts, and that's often the only time we're all online together, but I didn't realise…'

'I hardly heard a thing,' I assured her. 'It's just that work's a bit stressful and Maddy wanted me to go and look at wedding dresses with her and I couldn't, and now I feel bad. It's nothing, really.'

'If your friend's getting married, you've got a whole load of that to look forward to. It sends everyone a bit mental, I think. I remember when my sister got married. We thought at one stage we were going to have to call the men in white coats. Perdita used to ring me at five in the morning because she'd woken up and had some out-there idea like turning the curtains in the venue back to front because she didn't like the colour. She was pregnant at the time, too, which I guess made her extra bonkers. Mega stress.'

'I guess,' I said. 'But Maddy has always been really down to earth. And I'm worried I've hurt her feelings.'

'It'll blow over,' Tansy said. 'Trust me. Give it a few days and ring her for a chat. If she doesn't ring you first, which she probably will. How do you guys know each other, anyway?'

I explained how we'd been next-door neighbours in Cramlington, up in the North East, when we were little, best friends all the way through school, and stayed in touch throughout uni, even though I'd gone to Manchester and Maddy to Glasgow, and how when I'd been offered a job in London, I'd got straight on WhatsApp and asked Maddy if she needed a housemate, and our friendship had picked up as if it had never been interrupted.

'That's so lovely,' Tansy sighed. 'Once her wedding is over she'll totally go back to normal, you watch.'

I wasn't convinced, but I was encouraged. I asked Tansy what her plans were for the day, and she looked out at the brilliant sunshine and said she was going to put on a bikini and go and lie in a park somewhere, and did I want to join her?

I looked at her slim golden limbs and thought of the contrast with my own milk-bottle-white legs. I started to say no, then told myself not to be so ridiculous.

'I'll go and get changed,' I said.

When I was halfway up the stairs, I bumped into Adam coming out of his bedroom, and I watched him head downstairs, clock Tansy in her nightwear, turn absolutely scarlet and shoot into reverse, before disappearing back into his room and slamming the door. Poor bloke, I thought – living with Tansy was going to be a mixture of nightmare and dream come true for him.

Tansy and I hung out in the park for most of that day, working our tans along with crowds of others also taking advantage of the gorgeous summer Saturday, reading a stash of magazines we'd picked up at the newsagent, and occasionally chatting idly about matters of great importance like whether David Tennant or Matt Smith had been better in *Doctor Who*, and whether Maltesers Buttons were the best or the wrongest chocolates ever.

Once it got too cold to lie outside any more, we made our way home via the supermarket to pick up a posh ready meal and a bottle of wine.

Tansy did a detour through the aisles, filling her basket with random things like tins of beans, boxes of biscuits and packets of sanitary towels, and I wondered why she had picked this particular moment to do her weekly shop. But then, on the way out, she dumped the whole lot in the food bank donations box, and I felt terribly guilty because I'd walked past it so many times and never put anything in.

Back at the house, we had dinner together and just as I was about to suggest heading out to the pub, Tansy yawned and said she was going to go upstairs and FaceTime her sister, then go to bed.

Resigned to the prospect of a night in on my own, I powered up my laptop and opened the epic spreadsheet I was composing for Margot ahead of our office move the following year. We were only moving two floors up in the same building, but given the amount of work and planning it was taking, you'd think we were invading Syria. Architects had been hired almost a year before to refit the new space, complete with three kitchens (each of which would have to be stocked when the weekly Ocado order arrived), a palatial gym which was apparently going to be staffed by an on-site personal trainer, and five meeting rooms.

To make the whole thing even more fiendishly complicated, the move itself was going to have to happen when the stock markets were closed, so the traders wouldn't lose even a minute of online time and thus money. And the task of arranging it all had fallen to Margot, who'd delegated it to me. I gazed mindlessly at the columns and rows for a bit, daunted as I always was by the scale of the task, then sighed, poured another glass of wine, composed a text to Maddy, deleted it and sighed again.

I was about to give up and go to bed myself, when there was a knock at the door. It was almost nine o'clock, so definitely not the postie this time, or a Jehovah's Witness, but possibly a reformed convict selling dusters, or a determined nocturnal chugger wanting me to sign up for a direct debit to support Save the Children.

I closed my laptop and hurried to the door.

'We're so sorry to bother you so late.' It was Hannah and Luke from next door, owners (or parents, depending on how you see these things) of Freezer the cat.

'I hope we're not disturbing you,' Luke said.

I muttered that they weren't, at all, which was true, and asked if they wanted to come in.

'No, thanks,' Hannah said. 'It's just – we're knocking on all the doors around the neighbourhood to ask if anyone's seen our cat.'

'Freezer,' Luke said. 'He's white, with one green eye and one blue eye.'

'I've seen him, he's gorgeous. He comes into our garden sometimes, and then legs it over the fence when you call him home for dinner. But he hasn't been around for a while,' I said.

'We haven't seen him since Friday morning,' Hannah said. 'He's only been allowed out recently, so we're worried he might have got lost.'

'He's not even a year old,' Luke carried on. 'So only a kitten really.'

'We've been calling and calling him,' said Hannah. 'He isn't deaf – people think all white cats are, but he's not.'

'Normally he comes running when he hears the Dreamies packet rustling,' said Luke.

I shook my head. 'I'm so sorry. God, you must be so worried. Have you tried local Facebook pages?'

'We've posted on social media,' Hannah said, 'and put signs up along the road, and in Luke's coffee shop.'

'The Daily Grind,' Luke explained. 'I don't think I've seen you in there?'

Of course, I walked past the coffee shop every day on my way to work, and I remembered now that I'd seen Luke in there almost every morning, through the window. But, because when Tansy and I had tried to go there for brunch it had been closed, and in the mornings I was always in a mad rush and had access to unlimited high-quality coffee at work anyway, I'd never been in. Maddy and Henry had been regulars, though.

I explained this, and took one of their leaflets (which seemed pointless as I already knew what Freezer looked like, but refusing would have seemed as if I didn't care).

'I'll ask my housemates,' I promised, 'and keep an eye out for him myself. I'm sure he'll come back. He's probably got stuck in someone's shed or something.'

We said goodnight and I watched them walk off down the road in the twilight, holding hands and clutching their little stack of printed flyers. Poor them, I thought, and poor Freezer, wherever he was. They looked so sad, but at the same time so united, a team of two on a mission to find their little lost cat. I felt tears sting my eyes – but blinked them away and went back to my spreadsheet until the words and numbers started to swim in front of my eyes.

Then I had a bath, idly flicking through Tinder while a protein treatment soaked into my hair and a glycolic acid mask hopefully sloughed dead skin cells off my face.

Chapter Six

Hey you! Welcome back to Sorry Not Sorry, *the bad girl's guide to love and sex. Today's podcast is all about going back to basics. I know, I know, everyone knows online dating is where it's at… except when it isn't! Some of the happiest couples I know met offline, many of them through friends. After all, your buddies know you better than anyone else, so when a girlfriend tells you she wants you to meet someone, listen to her! It might not be love at first sight, but he could still be Mr Right for Now. Know what I'm saying? I mean, I've had some pretty amazing times with guys who I've known I don't have a long-term future with. Guys who have become good mates. Guys who've turned into regular booty calls. Guys who I've hooked up with and had hot sex with in spite of knowing they'd never be the father of my children. So that's my challenge for today. I'm going to call three of my besties and ask them to introduce me to a single friend. There! That's not so hard, is it?*

'It's been totally frantic, to be honest,' Maddy said. 'Who knew renovating a house while also planning a wedding would be kind of stressful? Not us, clearly!'

'You don't look stressed,' I said. 'You look amazing, and so does the house.'

It was true. Maddy had lost weight – but then doesn't everyone, when they've got a wedding dress to fit into? Although her dress-hunting trip to Brighton hadn't resulted in The One (dress, obviously). When I called to ask how it had gone, and apologised again for not being able to come, she'd brushed me off and said it didn't matter, sounding so down that I'd almost bottled the challenge of asking her if she and Henry could set me up with one of their single friends. But I went through with it, and she responded, sounding suddenly much more like herself, saying she'd arrange a dinner party in their new kitchen. Although the idea of meeting Henry's cricketing crony hadn't exactly filled me with excitement, I'd replied saying that I'd love to come, and asking what I should bring. Which felt weird in itself, because in the past when Maddy had hosted dinner parties in our shared kitchen I hadn't needed to ask anything. I just hung around while she bossed me about telling me what to chop and wash up and sending me on emergency missions to the corner shop to buy stuff she'd forgotten.

The house, which when I'd last seen it had been a sea of cardboard boxes, with the flatpacked carcass of the kitchen in bits all around the walls, now looked like a home. A proper home. The glass doors were open to the garden, letting in the warm evening air, and I could see pots of roses and herbs planted on the freshly laid flagstones. There were fairy lights draped over the mantelpiece, forests of candles everywhere, and an actual tablecloth covering the Ikea kitchen table around which we were sitting.

Or rather, where Henry, Henry's sister Bianca and her husband, who I'd been introduced to but whose name I had completely forgotten, and I were sitting. Maddy was standing at the cooker stirring something, and hovering behind her was Magnus, my 'date' for the evening.

I don't want to sound ungrateful, because after all setting up single friends with each other is never easy, but he hadn't exactly had me at hello. Not least because his 'hello' had been accompanied by a kiss that had missed my cheek and left me with a clammy ear, and then as if that wasn't bad enough, he'd gone and repeated the process on the other side and I'd had to wait until he wasn't looking to wipe my ears on my jumper. He was fair-haired and pink-faced and somehow sort of squashy-looking, in spite of a bushy beard that was clearly intended to be edgy but made him look a bit like one of the Seven Dwarfs. Possibly Sneezy, given the colour of his nose. His voice was all posh and public school and he talked just a tiny bit too loudly and a tiny bit too much, and was currently dissing Maddy's rice. Yes, her rice.

'Of course, arborio is a perfectly acceptable choice for a risotto,' he said. 'But I find that carnaroli gives a superior, creamier result. It's what they always use at Locanda Locatelli. Last time I was there for lunch I had a risotto with lobster and summer truffle that was positively ethereal.'

'Well, this one's got chicken and peas in it, and I'm working on ethereal,' Maddy said, stirring determinedly.

'Organic, I hope,' Magnus said. 'One simply can't make decent stock out of an intensively reared bird. And a risotto stands or falls on the quality of the stock – it's more important even than the rice itself, I feel. Anna Del Conte says in her book that…'

I tuned him out and turned to Henry, asking him how work was going. It was weird – it wasn't a question I would ever have asked him when we were living in the same house, because I'd just know, depending on whether he came home in a grump or came home late or took calls on his mobile long into the evening. But now, I had to ask, same as I'd had to ask Maddy how the wedding plans were going, rather than her slamming the front door, flopping down on the sofa and staring to whinge about how there wasn't a single florist in the whole of London that didn't charge an absolute fortune and her mother-in-law-to-be was determined to invite everyone in Surrey.

By the time Henry had finished telling me about the latest developments in the world of graphic design and opened another bottle of white wine ('I do feel Gavi is rather overrated,' Magnus said), Maddy had plonked the dish of risotto and a bowl of salad on the table and was passing round grated parmesan cheese. She was hardly eating anything herself, I noticed, but was knocking back the overrated wine at speed. I took a huge gulp from my own glass – drinking through it seemed like the only way to survive an evening of Magnus's company.

'This is delicious, Maddy,' Bianca praised, taking a tiny forkful of risotto. 'You're such a fantastic cook.'

'Henry's a lucky lad, aren't you?' Magnus said, looking rather too hard at Maddy's cleavage. 'What's on the menu for the big day then? What delights can we look forward to? I was at a wedding at Pembroke Park last weekend and, I must say, the food was disappointing for a venue of that calibre. The beef was overcooked and the salmon mousse was underseasoned.'

'Disgraceful,' I said, catching Maddy's eye across the table and hoping I would make her laugh, but she didn't; she gave me a tense little frown.

'So we're thinking of doing a street food vibe,' she said. 'You know, like carts or stalls with different themes from all over the world. Sliders and enchiladas and fresh oysters and noodles and stuff.'

'That sounds amazing!' I said.

'A brave idea,' Magnus chipped in. 'Little chance any of it would be at all authentic, of course. When I was last in Chongqing I ate *mala* at several – well, I suppose a layman would call them street food stalls, but the locals regard them as restaurants. Remarkable stuff. There's such a contrast between the real thing and the ersatz versions that are attempted here. One was made with duck intestines – the intensity of flavour was something quite special.'

'I can imagine,' I said, rolling my eyes ever so slightly at Maddy, who frowned at me again.

There seemed no way forward but to drink more wine, so I did, and when my glass was empty I filled it up and drank that, too.

After the risotto, there was tiramisu, which gave Magnus the chance to mansplain the difference between authentic Italian mascarpone cheese and the inferior stuff which Maddy had bought from the supermarket and used in her version, and give us all a lecture about the superiority of freshly ground coffee beans over Nespresso pods.

Just as I was beginning to hope that it was nearly time to go – or nearly time for everyone else to go, so that I could have a proper gossip with Maddy and Henry about, well, anything really – Magnus said that he'd brought something really rather special as a gift for

Maddy, and far be it from him to disrupt the menu planning, but he did rather feel that no meal was complete without a morsel of cheese. And he produced a huge chunk of pecorino and a jar of honey that he said was flavoured with black truffles, and tasted like the smell I'd noticed coming from Adam's bedroom. We all ate some, and I stifled a yawn and wished again that everyone would stop eating and drinking and talking about the cuisine of various exotic places I'd never been to (and, at this rate, would probably never make it to), and go home to bed.

At last, Bianca said she and Michael (of course!) really must be off because they were taking their daughter to a circus skills workshop in the morning.

'Charlotte, you're going to Hackney, aren't you?' Magnus asked. 'My flat's in Old Street, so not that far. Shall we share an Uber home?'

I could have kicked Henry for telling him where I lived, because I certainly hadn't. And I wasn't about to share a taxi home with him.

'I was planning on getting the night bus, actually. I love the night bus! Especially on a Friday night, all the way from Bromley to Dalston. It's great, all human life is there! Best place to people-watch! So I'll give Maddy a hand with the clearing up before I head off. Unless you'd care to join me?'

I'd read him right. He looked horrified, whipped out his phone, and Ubered the fuck out of there. Bianca and Michael followed shortly afterwards in a whirlwind of air kisses, but not before I overheard a whispered exchange between Bianca and Maddy in the hallway, as I was stacking the dishwasher.

'So, it's three o'clock tomorrow afternoon, right?' Bianca said. 'Sorry Conchita didn't work out, but you'll love Studio Monty, I just know you will.'

'Yes,' Maddy said. 'But why don't we meet earlier, at two, and we can have a sneaky cocktail before we head to his studio? I can't try on wedding dresses stone cold sober, after all.'

And I heard them both doing a not-quite-silent 'Squeeee!' of excitement, and then Henry clocked me standing there with a tea-towel in my hand, no doubt looking a bit stricken, and said, 'Come on, Charlotte, we can't have you slaving away. Sit down and I'll put the kettle on and you can tell me all about how your new page three girl housemate is getting on.'

I sat down. Actually I didn't think I could have stood for much longer even if he hadn't made the offer – my legs were suddenly feeling a bit weird and my head a bit spinny. And sitting there on my own like a loser, with the 'Squeeee!' ringing in my ears, I was feeling shocked and hurt, as if I'd been punched in the stomach.

After all, I was Maddy's chief bridesmaid. Wasn't I? But then I realised that she'd never actually asked; I'd just sort of assumed. But surely with that task would come loads of others – arranging her hen do, helping her choose between tasteful pink roses and tasteful embossed curly writing on her invitations, and – obviously – going 'Squeeee!' with her at the prospect of choosing a dress. She hadn't asked me to do any of those things. She'd obviously asked Bianca to do at least one, because when she'd asked me, I'd let her down. And, I realised, the wedding was just four months away. I was used to organising work functions at ridiculously short notice, but people took much, much longer with weddings generally, didn't they?

So by the time Maddy came back into the living room and Henry had handed me a mug of tea, I'd built up a head of steam wondering what the hell was going on.

I said, 'Why were you…'

At exactly the same time, Maddy demanded, 'Why were you…'

And Henry muttered something about putting the recycling out, and sidled away.

We both paused, but Maddy was the first to resume.

'Why were you so foul to Magnus?'

'What? He's a wanker, Maddy. A pompous twat who looks like a Percy Pig. Why did you even think I'd be interested in him?'

'He's not a wanker! He's lovely. He's kind and generous and he's even offered to go to France with Henry and me to choose our wedding wine. It'll save us a fortune. He was so excited about meeting you and you just sat there not talking to him and gurning whenever he said anything. What were you thinking?'

'Come on, Maddy!' I lowered my voice, 'I know he's a mate of Henry's, but seriously? Really?'

'Fine. Be picky. Look where it's got you so far. Exactly one whole shag since you moved to London. Well, since that's working out for you so well, carry on. Good luck with it.'

I wanted to ask her to understand, to explain that it was exactly because sex with Nick had been so awful that I didn't want to risk another disastrous night with a man I didn't fancy, and that going out with Magnus just because he was there and it would please her and Henry would be wasting his time as well as mine.

But I had more important matters to address with the woman I'd thought was my best friend.

My voice went a bit quavery when I asked, 'Maddy, are you going wedding dress shopping with Bianca tomorrow?'

I saw a tide of pink start to creep up from her collarbones, but it stopped before it reached her face.

'Yep,' she said. 'Bianca's married. She's been through it all. She knows how shit works. I trust her taste, and I know she's going to have time to help me with stuff. You're too busy, Charlotte. And honestly, you're not that interested. I needed to make a decision, and I have. You're my...' there was a tiny pause, where a very important word would have fitted, 'friend, and you always will be, but I've asked Bianca to be my chief bridesmaid. I'm sorry.'

There wasn't much to say after that. I thanked them for the lovely evening and got a solitary, extortionate Uber home (surge pricing saw me coming), spending the first half of the journey trying not to cry and the second half trying not to let the driver hear me crying.

Chapter Seven

'Just type this up, would you, darling, when you have a sec?' Piers said, chucking a USB stick on my desk. 'It's not urgent, I only need it for mid-morning tomorrow.'

I looked up from my screen, where the office move spreadsheet had been doing its numbing work on my brain. In between, I'd been flicking over to Maddy's wedding planning Pinterest page, which seemed to have been taken over by images of Audrey Hepburn in *My Fair Lady*. It appeared that she'd decided on a theme; she just hadn't said anything to me about it.

'What is it?' I asked.

'I had breakfast with a chap from Nicaragua at the Chiltern earlier,' Piers said. 'Frightfully interesting. He had lots to say about real estate, agribusiness and even fintech. I thought it could make a decent article for the website. He'll need sign-off, of course, and we're falling behind on the content schedule, so if you wouldn't mind…'

He made a little tapping gesture with his fingertips in mid-air, then turned and strolled away.

I rolled my eyes. 'A minute' was more likely to mean about four hours of trying to decipher Piers and the man from Nicaragua's words over the roar of conversation and clink of cutlery while I transcribed their meeting, and then I'd need to try and make sense of it all and cut it down into a thousand-word blog post. And then, of course, both Piers and his breakfast companion would want to make innumerable changes to make themselves sound more important and remove anything even slightly controversial, even though they'd been perfectly happy to say it at the time.

And I'd been planning to sneak off on time for once, because I was meeting Tansy for a drink.

'Let's go to the Ritz,' she'd said. 'Go on, Charlotte, I've always wanted to go to the Ritz for a cocktail and I bet the talent there will be fantastic.'

So you are single then, I'd concluded. Poor Travis must have been told to sling his hook, roses or no roses.

I sent her a text. *Really sorry, going to be stuck at work for a bit. Not sure what time I'll finish. Still on for cocktails and sheik-pulling but it will have to be later. Let me know if you'd rather reschedule for another night.* I added an eye-roll emoji and one of a martini glass, then I plugged in the USB stick, put headphones in my ears and started typing.

As I'd feared, it was hard going. The background noise was a problem, as was Ernesto Gonzalez's heavily accented English and Piers's regular interruptions as he pressed more coffee 'or perhaps a Bloody Mary, my dear chap – the sun's almost over the yard arm' on his guest. I thought I'd probably best leave that little gem out of my transcript.

I was five thousand words in and could feel tension wrapping itself around my neck and shoulders, when I became conscious of a bit of a commotion coming from the kitchen.

'Where the fuck is Briony, anyway?' Renzo was asking. 'Skived off home already?'

'It's only six o'clock,' Pavel said. 'Does Colin pay her to work fucking part time, or what?'

'Well, someone's going to have to sort it out.' Renzo's tone clearly implied that it wasn't going to be him.

'Ask Charlotte,' Pavel said.

I saved my document and pushed back my chair. Best to be proactive and go and ask what the crisis was and come up with a solution before Pavel came over and shouted at me. Even better to find out and implement the solution before he reached my desk, so when he started shouting at me I could tell him coolly that it was already sorted.

I saw Xander approaching with a glass of water and called him over.

'What's going on over there?' I asked.

'We're out of coffee, apparently,' he said.

'Oh for God's sake, is that all? You'd think that one of those grown men would be capable of walking twenty yards down the road to Sainsbury's and buying some. But no, apparently not.'

Xander said, 'To be fair, it is coffee we're talking about here. I know I've not been around that long, but it does seem to play a kind of central role in this place.'

'True enough. Right, I'd better stave off World War Three and a meltdown in the markets, then.'

I stood up, slinging my bag over my shoulder.

'I can go, if you like?' Xander offered. 'You looked like you were pretty busy.'

I explained about Piers's last-minute request and said, 'To be honest, I could do with a break.'

'Nicaragua?' Xander asked. 'I know a bit about the Nicaraguan economy. I wrote a paper on it a couple of years back. If you email me what you've got, and the audio file, I can write up Piers's article for you. No point you transcribing loads of irrelevant chatter.'

'Oh my God, would you? That would be amazing. I'm meant to be meeting my friend later and I thought I was going to have to blow her out, but now I can get away at a reasonable time and – anyway, thanks.'

'Don't mention it. But remember, you owe me. No telling me off next time I lock myself out of the building.'

'Deal,' I said, clicking send on my email and legging it to the shops. Xander, I reflected, might be the most hapless individual ever to walk through the doors of Colton Capital, but he was kind, which was more than could be said for a lot of my colleagues. There was no reason for him to have offered to help with what was – even by the standards of my job description – a mundane and thankless task, but he had. I wondered why: there had to be more to it than preemptive gratitude for a new access card. Maybe he was planning to write some searingly brilliant economic analysis and claim the credit from Piers. Well, if so, good luck to him, I thought.

When I got out of the lift ten minutes later, mission accomplished, it was clear that a different kind of crisis had erupted in the office.

Tansy was standing in reception. She was wearing a simple little white dress, loose and unstructured, but short enough to show the full tanned, toned glory of her legs. Her hair was hanging loose down her back and she was wearing high-heeled, open-toed silver shoe boots that matched her silver nail polish. The heels made her almost as tall as Renzo, but not quite. I could tell, because they were standing right next to each other, both with their phones in their hands.

Pavel was stalking away towards his desk with the air of a cat that has been hissed at by another cat and beaten a strategic retreat before it could eat any of the tuna.

The air was positively vibrating with testosterone.

'Charlotte!' Tansy said. 'I got your text, and I thought I might as well come and wait here for you, then we can go on whenever you're ready. I hope that's okay.'

I handed Renzo the pack of coffee. He smiled his breathtaking smile and thanked me – to my amazement – then said to Tansy, 'I'll call you,' before turning and striding away to his desk.

Tansy winked at me and did a very subtle fist-pump, saying, 'Boom.'

I left her waiting in reception while I answered a couple of urgent emails, then switched off and spent a few minutes topping up my make-up in the ladies', wishing that I'd worn something a bit less drab and corporate than my grey Reiss shift dress. Next to Tansy I'd be even more invisible than usual.

But, I thought resignedly as I swished bronzer onto my face, trying to create the illusion of cheekbones, there were few if any outfits in the known universe that would make anyone look at me when Tansy was there also. Look at Pavel and Renzo – both of them had worked with me for months and barely given me a second glance, and within about five seconds of setting eyes on Tansy they'd been practically challenging each other to a duel to settle which one of them would get to ask her out.

I added a defiant slick of red lipstick and combed my hair. That would have to do.

'You look great, Charlotte,' Tansy said. 'I love your shoes. Shall we go?'

We walked down the road and into the fragrant gloom of the Ritz, and found a table in the bar.

'Oh my God,' Tansy breathed. 'This is so cool. They've got a pianist. And a caviar menu. I suppose you come here all the time?'

'I wish! At twenty quid a cocktail it's not exactly my local.'

I saw her clock the prices on the menu and flinch. But she said, 'Well, this is my shout. Since you've accidentally done me a massive favour! I'll have a Perfect Gentleman, please.'

'An Iron Lady,' I said to the hovering waiter.

Tansy spent a few minutes enthusing about the awesomeness of our offices and asking me how hedge funds worked, and I did my best to explain without going into loads of boring and unnecessary detail about alternative investments, institutional portfolios and active versus passive strategies. But she didn't seem at all bored – she listened eagerly and asked intelligent questions. It would have been flattering, except I knew that she was embarking on a crash course in preparation for a very important test.

Her self-control was impressive. It was only after we'd ordered our second cocktail and received our second bowl of olives that she said, 'So. Tell me more about him.'

'Renzo?' *Of course Renzo, Charlotte. Duh.*

'Mmm hmm,' Tansy said.

'Well, he's thirty-two. From Rome originally. Degrees from Cambridge and MIT. Worked at Deutsche Bank for a few years and then…'

But she didn't want to know about the man's CV, obviously. She wasn't interviewing him for a job – if anything, she was preparing to apply for one. I racked my brains for details I knew about Renzo that couldn't be found on his LinkedIn profile (which I was sure Tansy would start looking up as soon as I got up to go for a wee).

I took a sip of my cocktail. 'He's a Capricorn. Birthday's the fifteenth of January. He follows Formula One and supports Lazio football club – not Roma, that's important. He's got a huge family, I think – he's forever asking the EAs to go and buy birthday and christening presents for his nieces and nephews.'

'Awww, that's so lovely,' Tansy said, and I resisted the temptation to point out that it would have been even lovelier if he made the effort to buy them himself.

'His favourite restaurants are The Square and Sketch. He lives in a flat in Marylebone, just off Harley Street. I've got the address somewhere if you want to do some hardcore stalking.'

Tansy giggled. 'No, that's okay. Well, maybe another time. He hasn't got a girlfriend, has he?'

'Nope, no girlfriend. He's been single since he joined the firm earlier this year, as far as I know.'

'Ever been married?' Tansy asked.

'No. But, look, if I'm being honest, when I first met him I stalked him a bit myself. You know how it is. He's dated Tabitha Whitely – the model, you know – some girl off *Made in Chelsea* whose name I can't remember, and Minty Hastings-Herbert, who *Hello!* magazine says went out with Hugh Grosvenor at one stage. So he's highly selective – you're in good company. But it looks like he goes through women at a rate of knots.'

'I like a challenge. Come on, let's have another drink.'

We ordered, and talked about other things for a bit, but I could tell that Tansy was itching to get back to the subject of Renzo.

Eventually she snapped. 'He's not going to call, anyway, I don't know why I'm even bothered.'

'I'd be very surprised if he didn't.'

'Why?' she asked, suddenly looking all excited and hopeful.

'Well, for one thing, look at you. You make her off *Made in Chelsea* and Minty Whatshername look like right munters. I know, I googled them. And for another thing, Renzo doesn't mess about. All the guys at work are the same: they make snap decisions and they act on them. He'll call.'

'Well, in that case I'd better make a booking to get my roots done and have a spray tan in a couple of weeks.'

'Why only in a couple of weeks?'

'I don't want him to think I'm too available, do I? I'm playing the long game here.'

I thought admiringly that Renzo might just have met his match in Tansy. But I said, 'Well, don't go falling in love with him, whatever you do. I'd hate you to get hurt.'

And looking at her lovely, eager face and remembering how kind she'd been when I was worried about Maddy, how she'd spent the day with me when she knew I was lonely and how she'd casually dropped thirty quid's worth of stuff in the food bank box, as though it was something she did every time she went grocery shopping, I realised it was true.

*

The next week must have been really hard for Tansy. The effort of will it must have taken for her not to ask me every day whether Renzo had been in the office, whether he'd been out the night before, whether he'd gone out for lunch and who with, whether he'd asked me anything about her, must have been immense, but she managed it.

I know what you're thinking. *What? She's known him five minutes! Is the woman some kind of bunny boiler?* But if there's one point in relationships at which even the most sane, normal person manifests bunny-boilery tendencies, in my experience, it's not when they end, or when you suspect infidelity – it's right at the beginning, when hope, uncertainty and insecurity are running their highest.

I'd love to be one of those women who, when they meet a man they fancy and give him their number, take the view that if he calls, he calls. If he doesn't, it was never meant to be, they say, sending their mates text messages using the manicure emoji before moving on with their lives without a backward glance. But I'm not, and I guess Tansy wasn't, either.

Although Tansy somehow managed to resist quizzing me about Renzo on a daily basis, there were other signs that she was preparing for the moment when he eventually called. Instead of her usual crisps and cups of tea, packs of salmon fillets and bags of kale appeared in the kitchen. Big parcels of clothes kept arriving from Topshop and Asos, and then being left in the hallway, repacked and slightly smaller, for Tansy to take to the post office and return, alongside her mysterious parcels with a Truro postcode on them. The bathroom revealed that she'd laid in enough acid toners and rosehip oil to start a shop.

But she didn't say anything. I was home late most nights, because work had kicked off big time, and I think that must have been some comfort to her – if I was pulling eleven-hour days, she must have guessed that Renzo was putting in even longer hours, as indeed he was.

It was more than a week after Tansy's and my drink at the Ritz when I left the office just after nine o'clock, noticing that it was already dark outside and realising that, depressingly, summer seemed to be almost over before it had properly begun. I pressed the down button to call the lift, and as the doors opened, Renzo hurried over and stepped in after me.

He looked as gorgeous as ever, but shattered, too. He needed a haircut and his stubble was not so much designer as not-had-time-to-shave. His suit was a bit crumpled and although his hazel eyes were as Bambi-lashed as ever, there were dark shadows under them.

'Heading out?' he asked me.

'God, no. Home to bed. You?'

'Meeting some mates for drinks at 5 Hertford Street.'

Part of me was impressed by his stamina – he'd be at his desk at seven the next morning, having spent an hour in the gym first. No wonder he looked knackered. Then I thought, if he's got the energy to go out on the lash with his cronies, why hasn't the rat called Tansy?

'Well, hope you have a fun—' I began, but he interrupted me.

'Charlotte, your friend who was here the other day...'

'Yes, Tansy.'

'Have you known her long?'

'Couple of months. She moved into our house in July.'

'She's not a vegetarian, is she?'

'Nope, fully committed carnivore,' I said. 'See you tomorrow.'

And then I legged it home to tell Tansy that he'd asked, and that this must, must mean he was going to call.

I found her in the living room, slumped in front of the telly with a glass of pink wine, tapping idly at her phone. She was still in her gym kit (although it was cool leopard-print leggings and a baggy cutaway grey top through which I could see the neon-yellow crisscross straps of her sports bra, and would have made a perfectly respectable outfit without the need to suffer through CrossFit or whatever the hell she'd been doing), and she looked tired, too.

'Renzo was asking about you,' I said, faux casually.

'Was he now?' she said, glancing sharply up at me and then returning to her phone.

'He asked if you're a vegetarian. As in, he's not just going to ask you out, he's going to ask you out, out. For. Dinner. Or maybe lunch. But anyway, a proper date.'

'Well,' Tansy said. 'I guess I'd better put this on silent, then.'

She pressed a couple of buttons on her phone, stood up, stretched, said goodnight and strolled off upstairs. But she wasn't fooling me – I heard the sound of her trainers doing some kind of victory dance on the landing outside her room.

I went into the kitchen and checked the contents of the fridge without enthusiasm. There was a block of cheddar that hadn't been wrapped properly and was all dry and cracked round the edges, a carton of milk past its best-before date, a crumpled pack of butter with just a scraping left, half a bottle of wine and a tub of tomato pasta sauce I'd bought the night before and been too tired to eat.

Spaghetti for one it was then, I decided, sloshing some of Tansy's rosé into a glass and making a mental note to buy her another bottle.

Adam, I reflected, had left as little sign of his presence in the fridge as he had in the rest of the house. In the cupboard next to my pasta were a few sachets of instant noodles, a big box of tea bags and several tins of tuna, neatly stacked on top of one another. Well, Adam was a big boy – if he gave himself scurvy it wasn't my problem.

My life, I reflected as I ate my solitary supper, was narrowing down to a pinprick. I went to work, I came home, I slept. I had no realistic prospect of meeting anyone, unless I got my swiping finger limbered up and put some serious effort in on Tinder. I'd go so far as to sit through another dinner with Magnus, especially if it meant seeing Maddy. But she and I had only exchanged a smattering of text messages since I last saw her.

I imagined Tansy, when eventually she gave in and answered the call that Renzo was totally going to make, getting dressed to meet him at 5 Hertford Street or some other exclusive venue that made the bar at the Ritz look as low-key as your local Wetherspoons. I knew how she'd feel, the butterflies fluttering like bastards inside her so she was practically airborne with nervous excitement. I remembered the glorious, almost sick-making thrill of connection you get when you meet someone's eyes and just know: *He fancies me. I fancy him. This is going to happen.*

I knew it was mathematically unlikely that it would never happen for me. But at the same time, I couldn't see how it possibly ever would.

Chapter Eight

Hey girlfriend! How are you doing? Welcome back to Sorry Not Sorry. *I hope you're having a great day, and even if you're not… go on, give me a smile and get ready for today's challenge!*

I'm not going to lie. It's a tough one. When I'm chatting to my single friends, we all say the same thing: 'I just never meet any guys!' But when we interrogate that a little, it always turns out not to be true. We do meet men! There's the hottie on the bike next to me in my spin class. The fella who services my car. The stranger who sat on the other side of the boardroom table in a work meeting yesterday. See? I've got to admit it – they're everywhere! So, for today's challenge, I'm going to get one of those guys' numbers. And then – you saw this coming, didn't you? – I'm going to pick up my phone and I'm going to call him.

'Charlotte?'

I looked up from my chicken and avocado salad. It was Monday, and a particularly frantic Monday at that. Leaving the office for lunch was out of the question, so I'd helped myself to the low-carb cornucopia in the kitchen instead of going out and buying the cheese and pickle sandwich I was craving. I'd decided to grab ten minutes to listen to another podcast before cracking on with personalising a bunch of emails to clients, which Piers said had to be done manually, because each one needed to begin, 'I hope this finds you well <name>,' and I couldn't figure out a way to make Outlook automate it.

Then I saw who it was standing over my desk, looking impatient, because I'd been so engrossed in my lunch, the podcast and the mindless task of copying and pasting names into emails, I hadn't noticed him there. It was Colin.

Colin never talked to me, ever. And thank God for that. Not being talked to meant not being shouted at. I was still too junior to warrant his attention, and I hoped that by the time I did, it would be for all the right reasons. Instead, he'd caught me listening to a podcast with a mouth full of half-chewed salad.

'Sorry,' I gulped, tugging the headphones out of my ears. 'What can I do for you?'

'Meeting this afternoon,' he said. 'Architect who's designing the new office. I can't do it, Margot can't do it. He's coming in at three. Just take a look at the drawings, will you, ask whatever questions, get the visuals off him and send them on to us with your notes, okay?'

'Yes, of course. No problem, Colin,' I said. And to my relief he turned and stomped away back to his office.

Once he'd gone, I felt the beginnings of panic. What did I know about architecture, or the layout of the new office? All I'd done so far was try and plan the logistics of the move. What if the designs were all wrong, and the toilets ended up opening off the boardroom and the kitchen off Colin's office, or something equally ridiculous?

What if the designer had had a rush of blood to the head and was going to propose painting everything sunshine yellow or baby pink and I wouldn't have the courage to tell him it was a bad idea, and wouldn't even know whether it was in the first place?

I looked around for Margot, but her desk was empty – presumably she was unable to attend the meeting because she'd been dragged into another, more important one.

At least, I supposed, her and Colin's willingness to blow this architect out at short notice must mean that whatever we were going to be discussing wasn't that important – maybe just some sort of routine catch-up about the progress of the work, I thought hopefully.

I glanced at my watch. I had an hour and fifteen minutes – enough time to make some headway into Piers's emails before whatever his name was showed up. I returned to my spreadsheet and my salad, but I left the headphones off this time.

After a few minutes, though, I was interrupted by an email pinging into my own inbox. It was from Margot, an invite to the meeting.

Thanks for helping out here, Charlotte, she'd written. *Sorry to dump you in it but my nanny's gone off sick and there was literally no one to pick the twins up from school. We briefed Myles thoroughly last time so it should be pretty routine – just let him go through the latest iteration of the drawings and forward the digital files to Colin and me. Here's their website for background. PS – he's hot. You can thank me later.*

She'd pasted in a link to Taylor + Associates. The plus sign was a bit naff, I thought, but maybe architects liked that kind of thing. I clicked and found myself on a shiny homepage with images of space-age office buildings and enormous apartments scrolling across the screen, but I didn't look at those – I clicked through to the About Us page.

When Myles Taylor founded Taylor + Associates in 2010, he was already regarded as one of the rising stars of British architecture. Since then the practice has… It went on to list a load of (I presumed) highly prestigious projects and a clutch of awards, but I skimmed past these to the Meet the Team section. And when I saw the picture of Myles Taylor, I heard myself give a sharp intake of breath. Maybe this meeting wouldn't be so bad after all.

To my shame, I spent the next hour googling interviews with the man I was about to meet, giving him a good old stalk on LinkedIn, and gawping at images of him wearing a hard hat and gazing up at buildings, poring over what I presumed were CAD drawings in a glass-walled office overlooking Chelsea Harbour, and – most enticingly of all – looking utterly edible in dinner jackets at awards ceremonies.

So, when Briony dialled my desk phone to let me know that the man himself was waiting for me in reception, I was flustered and totally unprepared. I ducked into the ladies', tidied my hair, topped up my lipstick and even emptied a ton of perfume over myself. Then I thought, what if he hated scent on women or was asthmatic or something, and tried unsuccessfully to wash it off. And then I told myself to stop being unprofessional and ridiculous, and go and attend my meeting like a grown-up.

In the flesh, Myles Taylor was even more gorgeous than his photographs. I wouldn't have thought such a thing were possible, but oh my God, it literally was. He was tall and lean, his long limbs and broad shoulders shown off to perfect advantage in a charcoal grey suit, which he wore with an open-necked black shirt and no tie.

Startlingly, his hair was grey, too, which it hadn't been in the photos I had seen. Surely the stress of running an acclaimed architectural practice, while obviously significant, wouldn't be enough to make someone's hair go white practically overnight, the way women's did in melodramas? Then I looked again and realised it was dyed – no one could possibly have hair that perfect, glossy shade of pewter naturally.

He's gay, I thought. He's totally, obviously gay. That's why there was no mention of any wife in any of the interviews I'd read, and no glamorous women in frocks clinging to his arm in any of the awards ceremony pictures.

Then he smiled at me, gave me a cool, appraising stare, shook my hand, and said, 'Charlotte.'

Oh my good God. Okay, so very not gay. Definitely not. Don't ask me how I knew – my gaydar's not all that – but I knew for sure. It was like (and I know exactly how cheesy this sounds) a little jolt of electricity went through my entire body when he took my hand, and carried on zapping me when he held it for ever so slightly longer than was normal. His palm was warm and dry, his fingers were strong, his nails were manicured – and all I could think of was how his hands would look cupping my breasts. It was bizarre – like my body had woken up after a long nap and had come charging into my head going, 'Hello! Let's have some fun!' I pushed my totally inappropriate thoughts to the back of my mind and said, 'Meeting room one, right, Briony? Could you organise coffees and some water, please?'

To my amazement, my voice sounded completely normal, even though as I led the way down the corridor it felt as if my legs had been replaced with wet spaghetti.

'Here we are,' I announced, and Myles Taylor actually pulled out a chair for me and waited for me to sit down. Literally, he did. I don't think any man's ever done that for me before – in fact, I only knew what I was supposed to do because I'd seen it in movies, and also because my knees really weren't doing such a great job of holding up my body.

He sat down too, not opposite me but at right angles to me, at the head of the table, and took a sleek silver MacBook out of his bag. The bag must be new, I thought – I could smell the rich, heady scent of leather. Or maybe that was some sort of cologne he was wearing.

'Colin sends his apologies,' I mumbled. 'He's been called into an urgent meeting with the regulator.' Which might or might not have been true – I didn't have access to the secrets of Colin's diary – but it sounded good. And made me come across as more composed than the alternative, which was, 'This boardroom table is more than big enough to fuck on, don't you think?'

What's got into you, Charlotte? I thought, shocked by my rampant imagination. *Him!* I internally answered myself. *I want* him *to get into me!*

'That's not a problem,' Myles said, and smiled at me again. 'Not a problem at all. This is just a routine update on the project, to set your mind at ease and confirm that everything is going according to plan.'

He powered up his laptop and angled it slightly towards me. I leaned over so our shoulders were almost touching. *Don't ask to use the projector*, I prayed, and he didn't.

'As you know, we're entering phase two of the project now,' Myles explained. 'The internal construction work is complete, and the design team are moving in now to finalise the fit-out of the space. The brief was comprehensive, but there are just a few questions.'

'Of course I'll try to help,' I said. 'But this isn't really my area, so I may have to escalate and get back to you once I've met with Colin and Margot.'

We spent the next half-hour discussing interlocking hexagonal pods, shifted floor plates and the amalgamation of crystalline forms. Or rather, Myles discussed them and I thought about how much I wanted to touch him: to stroke the back of his hand as it moved over the trackpad; to let my knee brush against his under the table; to slide my hand up his thigh, which was enticingly muscular under the sombre grey fabric of his suit.

Eventually, it was over. I managed not to spill my coffee, not to entangle my high heels in the wheels of my chair when I stood up, and – crucially – not to say, 'You are the sexiest man I have ever seen,' before showing him out.

Instead I said, 'Here's my card if you need to contact me for anything.'

'And here's mine,' he replied and smiled again, looking down into my face for what felt like hours.

I said goodbye to him at the lift, and then I went straight to the shredder room. I looked at his card and thought about feeding it into the machine we used to destroy confidential documents, and watching it come out the other end in ribbons as fine as the spaghetti he'd reduced my legs to. And then I remembered the Bad Girl's latest challenge: *Pick up your phone and call him.* I'd do it, I resolved, even though I hadn't actually needed to follow through with the bit about asking him for his number, because he'd given it to me himself. I'd definitely do it. I'd take on the challenge. I'd pick up my phone and I'd call him. Maybe.

'He's not going to call, is he?'

It was three nights later and Tansy and I were, unusually, both home by seven o'clock. I was draped over the sofa, legs hanging over the arm, watching an old episode of *Love Island*. Tansy was leaning over the ironing board, making her way through a pile of clothes – mine as well as hers, because when I'd come home and seen what she was doing, she'd said, 'Need anything ironed? I'm doing my stuff, so bring it on. I like ironing. Weird, right?'

She hadn't needed to offer twice. But actually, neither of us was particularly engaged in what we were doing, because we kept breaking off to stare at our obstinately unresponsive phones. Tansy had been waiting for Renzo to call for more than two weeks now; I'd only been wistfully imagining that Myles might do, sparing me the embarrassment of having to call him, for a few days. But, at exactly the same time, we both decided enough was enough. 'Fuck this, why don't we go to the pub?' I asked.

'Or to The Daily Grind,' Tansy agreed enthusiastically, folding the ironing board away even though my stuff was finished and hers wasn't. 'They've started opening late on Thursdays and Fridays, and they've got a food cart outside doing wood-fired pizza. They put a flyer through the door. Special offer – three for two for local residents.'

I felt a brief pang of guilt as I remembered the last flyer Luke and Hannah had handed out to their neighbours, about their missing cat. I hadn't seen Freezer at all since then. I hoped he was okay, and wished I'd done more to help them find him, although quite what I could have done, I didn't know.

'Deal,' I said. 'Let's go and eat pizza and drink cocktails and leave our phones at home.'

'And let's ask Adam if he wants to come along,' Tansy suggested. 'Poor bloke spends all his time alone in his room. It can't be good for him.'

'Good point. He'll get rickets or something, sitting there staring at a screen all day. I'll put this stuff away and get him.'

I took my still-warm shirts upstairs, hung them in my wardrobe, and knocked on Adam's door. He opened it a crack and peered out at me. He was wearing a grey T-shirt with unidentifiable stains on it, his feet were bare and his hair unbrushed. There was a strange smell in the room, that smell that single blokes' rooms tend to have, which somehow vanishes as soon as they get a girlfriend. I've never worked out what it's composed of: dirty socks and wanking, presumably. Possibly not unconnected.

Anyway, Adam's room smelled like that, with an undertone of something else that I couldn't quite identify. I wrinkled my nose and stepped back from the gap, making a mental note to check with Odeta, our cleaning lady, and ask whether she ever managed to get in there and freshen the place up. If she didn't, I'd have to have a word with Adam and tell him to clean up his act before we got a mouse infestation and a bollocking from the letting agent.

'Tansy and I are popping out for a drink and some food. Fancy coming along?' I asked.

Adam looked down at his feet, then longingly back into his room.

'Um…'

Fine, I thought. *I can deal with social awkwardness – if I've learned nothing else working at Colton Capital, it's that.* Some of the quants literally hadn't spoken a complete sentence in years, and communicated purely through spreadsheets, emojis and grunts.

'We're leaving in five,' I said, with what I hoped was a bright and breezy smile. 'Come along if you want. If you're not too busy.'

Back downstairs, Tansy met me with enquiringly raised eyebrows.

'No idea,' I mouthed. 'He's so weird.'

Tansy nodded definitively.

We loitered around for a few minutes, then I said, 'Right. Let's head off. But first…'

I gave a last, lingering look at my phone, like a mother saying goodbye to her first-born child on their first day of school. A problem child, mind – one that'd been uncooperative for days, and one you'd been tempted to chuck in the bath and destroy once and for all. Okay, maybe not so much like an adoring mother, then.

I put the wretched, silent thing down on the kitchen counter, and Tansy put hers next to it with a little sigh.

'Fuck the lot of them,' she said.

'Too right.'

Laughing, we headed out into the night. It was still warm, the sky a washed-out blue behind fading gold clouds, and it suddenly felt liberating to be doing this nice, normal thing with a new friend. I felt almost excited to be heading out for a drink and a pizza on a Thursday night, like it was some kind of big adventure. *How has my life come to this?* I thought. *Maddy and I used to do this stuff all the time.* But I was too excited at the prospect of this tame evening out to let missing my best friend ruin my night.

We'd almost reached the end of our road and could see the retro neon sign of The Daily Grind gleaming invitingly up ahead, when I heard the sound of pounding feet behind us. I spun around, tightly clutching my handbag. Even though our bit of East London has long lost the edgy roughness Maddy told me it used to have and is getting more gentrified all the time, as our rising monthly rent proves, it still has its dodgy moments.

But it wasn't a mugger sprinting up the road towards us; it was Adam. He'd had a shower, or at least stood under running water for long enough to get wet. His hair was slicked damply back from his face, he smelled of some sort of citrusy shower gel, and he'd changed out of the grimy T-shirt into a white linen shirt and put on clean jeans. He looked… not exactly fanciable, but a whole lot less like a dysfunctional neckbeard than he had ten minutes earlier.

'Sorry,' he panted. 'I had some stuff to do. Thanks for asking me.'

I said it was no problem, and Tansy said it was great that he could join us, and we pushed open the heavy glass door of The Daily Grind.

The place was packed. I don't know how good Luke was at making coffee, but clearly when it came to running a business the man had what it takes. The battered wooden tables were all full, crowded with beer bottles, wine glasses and pizza boxes. The jukebox was playing The Lumineers, but it was barely audible over the hum of conversation and laughter. The industrial-style filament bulbs lit up a horde of London hipsters, all seemingly having all the fun.

It was a world away from the places I booked for lunches, drinks and dinners for Piers, Renzo and the others at work. There wasn't a starched tablecloth or a wine waiter in sight – nor, for that matter, a lingerie-clad eastern European pole dancer. I wondered whether Tansy was aware of the contrast between her local bar and the venue Renzo might choose for a date with her, and whether she was as happy about coming here as I was. But I had no chance to ask, even if I'd known how to, because she'd sprung right into organising mode.

'Right,' she said. 'We need a strategy. That table there are just finishing up. Adam, you go and hover, and as soon as they get up, nab it. I'll order our food – there are only three kinds of pizza so I'll get one of each. Charlotte, you're on drinks. Mine's a large chardonnay.'

Galvanised by her managerial skills, Adam shot off towards the back of the room. I just managed to grab his sleeve and say, 'Drink?'

'Oh. Beer. Whatever,' he said, giving me what I thought might have been the beginning of an actual smile before he disappeared into the crowd.

I made my way to the bar. To my surprise, Luke was taking orders himself, rather than delegating to cheap, hourly-paid staff as I would have expected.

I caught his eye and he grinned and made a gesture that meant, 'One second.' It was less than a minute before he was smiling and asking what he could get me.

'Two large chardonnays and a beer – craft, I guess. What's good?'

'The Hungry Locust is great if you like a classic IPA,' he said. 'Or there's the Woofer if stout is your thing.'

'It's not for me, so I don't really know. Maybe something kind of… lagerish?'

'Then I'd go for the Kissing Cousins. Everyone likes that. Kind of hoppy, but still light.' He turned to pour our drinks. 'Great to see you here, Charlotte.'

I smiled, pleased and surprised to be remembered. 'Did you find your cat?'

'You know,' he said, leaning over the bar counter, 'it's the weirdest thing. No one responded to the leaflets or posted on the Facebook page, or used the #FindFreezer hashtag. Our friend Gemma's got this YouTube channel that's gone totally huge, and she even posted about it on social media, but there was nothing at all. Apart from a few stalker types sending pics of other white cats to Gemma, but she's used to that. Not cats, obviously – she can't stand cats – but other stuff. Then a few days after we called round yours, Freezer turned up again.'

'Oh wow. You must have been so relieved.'

'We were. And he didn't look thin or traumatised or anything. We took him to the vet – Hannah insisted, even though he seemed okay – and he'd actually put on weight while he was missing. But then a couple of days later he disappeared again. We haven't seen him since.'

His cheerful face fell a bit. I became conscious of the thirsty crowd behind me and said I was sure Freezer would turn up, knowing that it was of little help to Luke. Then I thanked him and turned away, carefully balancing our drinks as I navigated a path through the crowd.

Tansy and Adam seemed to be getting on remarkably well. She was listening intently to what he was saying – some anecdote, I thought, about his travels in the Middle East. Not for the first time, I regretted how little of the world I'd seen, having lived in Newcastle, been to uni in Manchester, returned home, then moved to London, with a few budget Ryanair flights abroad thrown in in between.

At the table next to them, I noticed a pretty girl with violet hair talking enthusiastically into her phone, which she was holding high up above her head. As I watched, she turned her phone around and filmed the pizzas on her table and the cocktails she and her boyfriend were drinking. I wondered if she was the vlogger friend Luke had mentioned, giving The Daily Grind some free publicity.

As I approached the table, Tansy broke into laughter – the climax of the story, I supposed – then a voice called, 'Tansy? One Quattro, one Neapolitana, one Special!' and she jumped up to collect our order while I put the drinks down.

Adam looked at me and I looked at him, and his face reverted to what I imagined was its default expression: a sort of closed-in sullenness. I tried to ask him about his day, about his work in Iraq (except I got it wrong, and it turned out to have been Iran where he'd worked, coding for a ride-hailing app start-up; that would have been impossible in Iraq, he told me, with something that was almost but not quite a sneer). But, until Tansy came back with our food, he was monosyllabic and basically downright rude, and when she sat back down, he talked only to her and not to me at all, until Tansy kindly started a conversation with me about whether flatform trainers were still going to be a thing going into winter, which by default shut Adam out.

And then, when we got home, Tansy had a missed call from Renzo. There was nothing from Myles – not that I had expected there to be. I'm not a believer in Fate or Destiny or any of that nonsense, but still I had a deep instinctive sense that the *Sorry Not Sorry* podcast was influencing my life somehow. Myles wasn't going to call me, because I had to call him.

I picked up my phone.

Chapter Nine

Sooo… welcome back to Sorry Not Sorry *and to our next challenge! Did you woman up and make that call after our last one? I did and let me tell you, I was nervous as hell! But I did it. I asked the hot boy from my spin class for his number, and I called him. I did it! I felt so great afterwards, all empowered and shit. Like I could take on the world! And we've been exchanging texts for the past week or so, and as soon as we can find a free slot in our calendars we'll meet up.*

But that brings me to my next challenge. I reckon it's time to up the ante ever so slightly in those text messages. Know what I mean? No, I'm not talking full-on sexting. Sending intimate images of yourself to someone you don't know well and don't trust completely is a bad idea, and you don't need me to tell you that. But just, like, get a little frisky, right there on WhatsApp. Go on – you can do it!

After keeping Tansy hanging for more than two weeks, when it came to actually arranging a date with her, Renzo didn't mess about. That Saturday night, I watched – not without envy – as she paraded in and out of my bedroom in one stunning outfit after another.

'I think this is a bit too try-hard,' she said, spinning around in a ruched black cocktail dress. 'It's Dolce & Gabbana; it was a sample. I love it but I think it's a bit much, even for Nobu, don't you?'

Regretfully, I told her it probably was.

'What the hell do people wear there, anyway?' she demanded. 'You've been, right?'

'Only once. We had our Christmas do there last year, so everyone dressed up, obviously, which isn't much help. But I walk past every evening on my way home from work, and honestly, people seem to wear all sorts. The WAGs go full Kardashian with their tits out and their fake tans on. But lots of other people wear jeans and trainers.'

'Hmmm.' Tansy pulled the dress off and headed back to her room in her bra and pants. I hoped for Adam's sake he wasn't going to choose that moment to emerge from his lair.

A few minutes later, she was back. 'Any good? It's the grunge look.'

She was wearing ripped jeans and a cropped white T-shirt, and underneath, showing through the rips and above the waistline of the jeans (only they were so low-rise it was more like a bikini-line), black fishnet tights.

'That's seriously sexy,' I said. 'But no. Too fashion-forward. He won't get it. He'll spend the whole evening wondering if you know your hosiery is showing.'

'Damn it. I suppose you're right. Back to the drawing board.'

This time, she dropped the jeans on my bedroom floor and the tights outside Adam's door. If he spots those, he'll have a coronary on the spot, I thought, deciding I'd wait to tidy up until Tansy had made her final outfit selection and left.

'Okay, how about this?'

'This' was a jumpsuit, pale grey, sleeveless and high-necked, with wide legs that should have concealed the perfect shape of Tansy's own legs, but actually accentuated them.

'That's good,' I said. 'I'm liking it. Demure.'

'Or not so demure,' she said, turning round. The whole back was open, showing off her toned, golden shoulders and everything beyond, all the way down to where her knickers would have been if she was still wearing any, which I was pretty sure she wasn't.

'My God,' I said. 'It's amazing. You've nailed it. But you'll get arrested going on the Tube in that.'

'I'll put a jacket on,' she said. 'And get an Uber. Fuck, it's seven already and I still need to tong my hair and do my make-up.'

I perched on her bed and made soothing noises while she applied primer, foundation, three different contouring powders, blusher, at least six shades of eyeshadow and two of lipstick, and finished looking like she was wearing hardly any make-up at all, having spent the day sunbathing on the beach.

'Blimey,' I said. 'Skills. You're going to have to give me a crash course before I go on my date with Myles.'

'Which will be never,' Tansy said. 'If you carry on telling the poor man you're busy every time he asks you out.'

'I know! But it's not my fault. The podcast said to pick up my phone and call him. I was shitting myself, but I did it. It was sooo awkward. I was like, "I really enjoyed meeting you and wondered if you'd like to have a coffee sometime, outside of work." And he said, "Charlotte, I'm flattered." Which totally sounded like I was going to get mugged off.'

'But you weren't.'

'No, I wasn't. He said, "I enjoyed meeting you too, a lot." But then he had to go. I thought that was it, but then he called back the next day and we had a bit more of a chat, and we've been texting each other ever since.'

'So when are you seeing him then?'

'This is the problem! The next bloody episode of the podcast was all about playing hard to get. I have no idea why I keep listening to the stupid thing – she annoys me a bit and she contradicts herself constantly – but somehow I can't stop. So whenever he's asked to meet me, I've said I'm busy.'

'Treat 'em mean, keep 'em keen,' Tansy said.

'Exactly. She says you should play it cool, at least at first. So by agreeing straight away to go out with Renzo, you're totally breaking all the rules.'

Tansy rolled her eyes. 'I know, I know. What could I do, though? I waited ages for him to call, and then he was like, "I've booked a table at Nobu," and I just heard myself going, "OMG really?" and then it was too late to play it cool. You'd have to be superhuman to turn down dinner with Renzo at Nobu anyway, and I'm just not.'

'Well, if he dumps you after one date…'

'I'll have eaten the black cod in miso. My life will be complete. He won't dump me after one date though, will he?'

With Renzo, I thought, anything was possible. Then I took another look at her in her jumpsuit, and said, 'He won't.'

'If I survive tonight, I'll do your make-up for you when you stop treating Myles mean,' she said. 'Right, shoes. Heels, obviously. Red or silver?'

I considered for a moment. 'Silver. Keep it neutral.'

She slipped on a pair of pewter mules with heels so high her hair almost brushed the door frame as she swished out. Then she turned around and hugged me, almost asphyxiating me in a cloud of Elnett and Jo Malone.

'Thanks, Charlotte.'

I knew that what she meant was nothing to do with the fashion advice I'd given, because she would have come to just the same conclusions on her own.

'Have fun,' I said. 'You look stunning.'

Tansy hurried downstairs to her waiting cab and what she hoped would be the last first date she ever went on. I was excited for her – of course I was – but I felt oddly apprehensive, too. She'd invested so much in the idea of Renzo – not just in all those workouts in the gym, dinners made up entirely of kale, acid toners for her face and argan oil masks for her hair, but in hope and anguish and sleepless nights. I hoped the date wouldn't disappoint her. I hoped Renzo was taking it as seriously as she was. He was so successful, so good-looking, he literally could have anyone he wanted, I thought, leaning back on Tansy's pillows. But then, so could she.

And so, from what little I had seen of him, could Myles. If Tansy was on a not-quite-equal playing field, I was batting way out of my league. I stood up and gathered Tansy's discarded clothes from the hallway and my bedroom floor and draped them on her bed. If she was going to sleep with him tonight – and because I knew he was a bit of a player, I hoped for her sake she wouldn't – they'd go to his Marylebone shag pad, not come back here. Wouldn't they? The idea of walking into the bathroom in the morning to find Renzo in his boxer shorts brushing his teeth was too cringe even to contemplate.

Instead, I took out my phone and read Myles's latest message.

I'm in the office, just looking at those drawings for your boss. But I keep thinking, what would Charlotte like? Stop distracting me from my work!

I'd been too busy when I received it to reply with anything much more than a few emojis and 'x's, but knowing that he was thinking of me had left me feeling glowy and excited all day. Now though, if I was going to go through with the challenge, I had to up the ante, as the podcast had instructed.

My thumbs hovered over the keyboard. I felt a tight knot of embarrassment in my stomach. What was I going to say to him? I was so out of practice, so unused to thinking of myself as someone who was desirable, or someone who even had desires. Christ, the last time I flirted was with the bloody tree surgeon and that was barely a flirt! This challenge was *hard*.

I'm lying in bed now, I typed. It was Tansy's bed, and I was on it, not in it, but I figured a bit of creative licence was allowed. *And I'm thinking, what would Myles like?*

Then I dropped my phone like it had just bitten me, put my arms over my face, and waited.

I didn't have to wait long. Just two minutes later, he replied. *Myles would like to know what you're wearing.*

Shit. I was wearing ripped jeans that were meant to be baggy but had got a bit tight over the past few months, and a jumper with a hole in the elbow and a stubborn stain on the front where I'd dropped ketchup down it.

I'm wearing a cream jumper and a white bra and pants. Jumper is soft and fluffy. Underwear is lacy.

All that was perfectly true, I assured myself, even if the picture it painted wasn't.

I wish I could see you. But imagining looking at you is doing the trick right now…

A shiver ran down my spine as I tapped out my reply. *I'm imagining you looking at me. Maybe you wouldn't just look? I wouldn't just look. I'd have to…*

And we were off. We spent the next half-hour texting back and forth, until my phone's screen was practically steaming up and I was more turned on than I could remember being. Ever.

When at last he said he had to go (which involved us texting back and forth several times, *Good night then. You still there? Yes. Good night.* Pause. *I'm still here. Me too. Good night. Thinking of you.* Kisses. More kisses), I tugged myself back to reality and realised I was still in Tansy's room, which felt all kinds of wrong. I got up, stubbing my toe painfully on a bulky holdall just sticking out from beneath her bed. Surely she hadn't had this much stuff when she moved in? What was she keeping under there anyway, dead bodies? I went to the bathroom and spent the next hour conditioning, exfoliating, depilating and polishing myself to within an inch of my life. I slapped a thick layer of cream over my face that promised to leave me looking as radiant as if I'd had eight hours' sleep, and went to bed, hoping to up the ante by getting eleven.

As I lay in bed, I was still buzzing from my earlier sizzling exchange with Myles. The next time he texted me – and now I was confident that he would – I was going to make a plan to meet him. Not for some stupid, awkward coffee, but for a proper date in the evening. And I was going to look as good for it as he'd imagined me looking while we texted. The Bad Girl would be proud!

But first, I had to get through the next day's Sunday brunch. I had my suspicions it was going to be a less jolly affair than usual…

'I'll have the almond granola, please, with extra blueberries,' Bianca said. 'And do you do coconut yoghurt? I'm dairy intolerant. And a skinny soy chai latte. And my daughter will have… Tell the lady, Charis.'

'Poached eggs and avocado,' Charis piped up. 'But only if the eggs are free range. And a blueberry and banana smoothie, but make it with oat milk, I've gone lactose-free.'

You're six, I thought, *isn't that starting a bit young on the food fads?* And then I felt a bit bad for judging a child.

'Of course they're free range, sweetie,' Bianca said. Then she fixed our waitress with a steely gaze and said, 'Aren't they?'

The waitress smiled a smile that looked only slightly forced. 'All the food here at Gilbert and Gwen's is responsibly, sustainably and locally sourced,' she said, which was of course rather different from confirming that the eggs were free range – they could have been responsibly, sustainably and locally sourced by sending the work experience girl round the corner to Nisa. But it seemed to be good enough for Charis.

'I'd like an egg white omelette with a green salad on the side,' Maddy said. 'No dressing on the salad, please. And another bullet-proof coffee, and please could you bring another couple of jugs of water with fresh lemon slices?'

'What, no margaritas?' I asked, only half joking.

'Margaritas?' Bianca curled her lip like I'd suggested ordering a pitcher of cold sick. 'Aren't those terribly noughties? Or are they having a moment again? I wouldn't know, I never touch spirits. So bad for the complexion.'

Put firmly back in my place, I looked at the menu without enthusiasm. I wanted a sausage sandwich even more than I wanted a margarita, but neither was on offer at what I guessed was Bianca's choice of brunch venue. The food was heavily biased towards chia seed muffins, organic oatmeal and tofu scramble, and the most interesting drink on the menu was fermented kombucha tea. I tried that once at work, when Briony put it on the Ocado order, and quite frankly I'd rather drink my own sweat.

'I'll have the avocado on toast, please,' I said meekly.

'They'll serve it on little gem lettuce leaves if you prefer, Charlotte,' Bianca told me. 'Bridesmaids' dress-fitting right after this, remember? Bread is so bloating.'

'Really?' I said, wishing I'd thought to have pre-brunch breakfast. 'That sounds really, um, crunchy. I'll try it. And a black Americano.'

Chloë ordered a pumpkin and walnut muffin and Molly went for scrambled eggs, hold the toast, and a carrot juice.

Our food came and we ate it – or rather, most of us did. Maddy picked unenthusiastically at her omelette and sipped water in between discussing wedding couture with Bianca.

'So we went for the third fitting for my dress on Wednesday, and it's still not quite right,' she said. 'They're having to take it in again, and that means redoing loads of the beading, and now the lace doesn't match up properly at the back.'

'They're really great at Studio Monty,' Bianca said, 'but even the best couturiers need a few goes to get it spot on. And, of course, your wedding diet is working its magic. You should expect your shape to change a bit more between now and the big day.'

I said, 'You're looking amazing, Maddy, honestly. You really don't need to lose any more. Get some chips down you, woman!'

Privately, I thought that Maddy had already lost more than enough weight, wedding or no wedding. She'd always been slim, but now she looked almost gaunt – there were deep hollows under her cheekbones and her forearms looked so delicate they were almost frail.

'I actually dreamed about chips last night,' Maddy sighed, 'and my God, how guilty did I feel when I woke up? They were proper beef dripping chips too, like we used to get at the Almighty Cod back home, remember, Charlotte?'

'With mushy peas and a portion of scraps,' I said. 'We used to sneak out of school at lunch on Thursdays, when they gave us that grim watery beef stew, and stuff our faces with chips and go back stinking of vinegar.'

We laughed, and for just a second all the closeness between us was back.

Then Bianca said, 'How you didn't end up the size of a house, I will never know,' and gave me a look that quite clearly said that she knew exactly how I'd ended up – by her standards, which clearly meant anything over a size eight – the size of a house.

'Honestly, Charlotte,' Maddy said, 'it's a wedding thing. The camera packs on pounds and I do want to look my best in the photos. Once I've got that ring on my finger I'll be back to stuffing my face, I promise. You'll be the same when you get married.'

Molly looked a bit pained, the way she always did when she was reminded of the prospect of friend after friend getting married, and William still not popping the question.

'If Charlotte ever does get married, of course,' Bianca said. 'If she ever stops being so fussy, and actually dates someone.'

She rolled her eyes and looked around the table, hoping for a round of giggles. But no one laughed, especially not me. Her comment stung, not just because it was so casually bitchy, but because it meant she and Maddy must have been discussing my love life, most likely telling each other that I should have begged Magnus to go out with me, because I wasn't going to get anyone better.

'Actually, I've met someone,' I couldn't stop myself replying. 'We're going on a date in the next couple of weeks. We'd have gone already but I've been too busy. He's an architect, and he's gorgeous.'

Chloë squealed with excitement.

Molly said, 'Oh my God, best news ever! We need to know all about him. How did you meet him?'

I was about to embark on a long description of Myles, starting with his perfectly cut pewter hair and working my way down via his chiselled jawline, broad shoulders and muscular arse all the way to his Italian shoes, when Bianca said that we should get the bill or we'd be late for our dress-trying-on session, and the wind was well and truly taken out of my sails.

We paid for our meal – admittedly considerably less than was usual, thanks to the meagre portions and severe lack of booze – and followed Maddy and Bianca on the route to the bridal emporium, which was familiar to them, but not to me.

I hurried to catch them up, suddenly struck by fresh guilt about how little attention I had been paying to the preparations for my best friend's wedding. I worried that she might be feeling that since Tansy had come on the scene, I had moved on to a new phase of my life just as easily as she had. But before I could talk to Maddy, I had to wait for Bianca and Charis to finish nattering on, which didn't look like happening any time soon.

'Elephant's Breath,' Charis was saying, as we walked along a street lined with what had presumably been warehouses of one kind and another and were now divided up into luxury apartments. 'Mizzle. Stiffkey. Dimpse.'

'And how about that one there, sweetie?' Bianca said.

Charis paused, her head on one side. 'Railings. No, Black Blue.'

Bianca laughed. 'Black Blue is right, I think. Clever girl.'

I nudged Maddy and gave her a look that said, *WTF?*

'Charis knows all the Farrow & Ball paint colours,' she said. 'It's a game they play, spotting them on people's front doors, isn't it, Bianca?'

Bianca nodded. 'Charis has such an eye for design. Not just interiors – which she gets from me, of course – but her fashion sense is amazing too. As we're about to find out. Here we are – Studio Monty.'

We all stopped in front of what looked like a charity shop. Not how they are now, obviously, now they've got professional window-dressers to arrange someone's Reiss coat from two seasons ago on a mannequin alongside someone else's slightly worn L.K.Bennett boots and dress the whole lot up with a Primark scarf so it all looks like an expensive boutique, but how they used to be when I was growing up. The window was cluttered with old sewing machines and taxidermy, and in the middle of it was a life-size wooden puppet draped in old net curtains.

'How cool is it?' Maddy breathed. 'Every time I come here I stop and just go, "Aaaah."'

Bianca pushed open the door and immediately a fifty-something man with a beard and heavy black-framed glasses came bustling to meet us, closely followed by a wheezing black pug.

'Sweeties!' he said. 'Madeleine and Bianca, my favourite girls. And you must be the other bridesmaids.'

He bestowed kisses on us all, then ushered us through to the back of the shop, which widened into a huge, glass-roofed, cobble-floored space flooded with light and lined on all sides with garment rails holding a host of dresses swathed in protective white bags.

'Now, whose fitting shall we do first?' Monty (I presumed) said.

'Mine,' Charis said. 'Last time, my dress looked like a sack. I hope those darts you put in worked.'

Monty looked taken aback, and then managed an ingratiating smile. 'I hope so too. Come on then, little flower girl.'

'My name's Charis,' she said sulkily, but she followed him into the fitting room, Bianca hovering closely behind.

Chloë, Molly and I perched on a reclaimed wooden church pew and waited. Charis emerged a few minutes later in a flounced, black and white striped frock. It seemed an odd choice to me, but I had to admit she looked adorable.

'She doesn't know who Audrey Hepburn even is,' Monty cooed. 'But she's totally rocking the look.'

'I do know, too,' Charis said, pouting. 'I've seen *My Fair Lady* five times and I know the words to all the songs.'

She started carolling the lyrics to 'Wouldn't it be Loverly', twirling round the room until she cannoned into a table holding a vintage typewriter and some wax flowers under a glass dome and almost sent the whole lot flying.

But I wasn't really watching. I was thinking, *Oh my God, does this mean we're all going to be got up like something out of* My Fair Lady? I should have seen it coming, but somehow I hadn't. Had I really not been paying attention? I felt guilty all over again. A few minutes later, we were all standing in front of the mirror in matching fishtail sheaths, banded with more black and white stripes. Curvy Molly and slender Chloë could just about carry it off. I, on the other hand, just looked like a quarterback in drag.

My heart sinking right down to the soles of my feet, I tried to make a joke of it. 'Looks like the Newcastle United team put their shirts on sideways by mistake.'

Bianca looked us up and down. 'You might want to lay off the carbs just a bit, Charlotte.'

'Maybe you could give Charlotte some of that skinny tea you drink, Mummy,' added Charis.

Chapter Ten

Hi again, and welcome back to Sorry Not Sorry! *Today I'm going to be talking about a subject that's very close to all our hearts: the first date! You know, I've been on a lot of dates in my time. A lot. And some of them have been baaaad. You know when Sansa meets Ramsay Bolton in* Game of Thrones? *Okay, maybe not quite that bad. But I've kissed a few frogs, I can tell you. Or not kissed them, actually, because eeewww!*

But anyway, right now, I'm about to get ready to go on a date with a new fella (he's the one from the spin class and he's got the sexiest butt I've ever seen). And I want to feel sexy too, so I'm wearing some absolutely stunning new lingerie. No frills or lace here, ladies: just sheer black mesh and lots of straps that give it an almost bondage vibe. Even if he doesn't get to see it – and he may well not, because you never know how a first date is going to pan out – I'll know it's there, and that will make me feel smoking hot.

So here's your challenge for today. Have a rummage in your underwear drawer, find the sexiest things you own, and wear them, just for you.

I wondered enviously what else the Bad Girl had done to get herself looking her best for her first date with the man with the sexy bum. She'd have had her nails done, and probably had every imaginable bit of herself waxed, and maybe treated herself to – what do they call it in New York – a blow-out.

Maybe she'd have spent the day reading and rereading the text she'd composed taking the plunge and actually asking him out, and his response. I did, anyway. I spent almost as long looking at it afterwards as it had taken me to write in the first place. I wanted to sound casual, but not no-care; keen, but not desperate. Sexy, but not like I was just arranging a hook-up.

In the end, I'd gone for, *All these texts are making me want to see you again! Drink after work on Wednesday maybe?*

Then, pathetically, I'd shut my phone in a drawer like it might run away, and gone and had a bath. When I'd finished, Myles had replied. *A drink sounds delicious – almost as delicious as you.*

He thinks I'm delicious! I read those nine words over and over, thrilled, delighted and sick with nervous excitement. Maybe the Bad Girl had read and reread her text messages, too, in between the manicurist and the hair salon.

What she wouldn't have done was spend the hour before she needed to leave – and the half-hour after she really, really needed to have left – moving furniture.

It was Piers's doing, of course. I was sitting at my desk wondering how long would be too long to spend in the ladies' doing my make-up, when he wandered over and said, ever so casually, 'Got a moment, Charlotte?'

'Of course,' I replied, knowing there was trouble in my future and already mentally composing the text I'd send to Myles telling him I was going to be late. But I didn't realise just how bad it would be.

'So, the briefing tomorrow morning,' Piers said. 'A few of the media people can't make it. I know you set up the room for seventy-five, but we've only had forty confirm. So we're going to do it boardroom-style, not theatre-style. Change things around, would you, and let the caterers know?'

'No problem,' I responded, thinking, *Fuck you, Piers, you entitled Old Etonian twat. It is a massive problem and you know it.*

That morning, with the help of Greg, Colin's second PA, and Maurice, who looked after the post and picked up dry-cleaning and generally helped out, amazingly without ever stopping smiling, I'd moved seventy-five chairs into rows, moved the table to the back of the room, set up the projection system and made sure everything was as it should be.

Now, because Piers didn't want to be shown up by a load of empty seats, I'd have to shift thirty-five chairs out again, somehow move the massive boardroom table back into the centre of the room and arrange all the chairs around it again. And I'd have to do it alone, in half an hour, in high heels, and without ending up a sweaty mess.

The prospect made me want to cry, and only the knowledge that if I did I'd be a red-eyed, blotchy-faced sweaty mess stopped me.

I called the caterers to halve our order, apologising profusely and knowing that they'd be cursing me as much as I'd cursed Piers and as silently. Then, feeling like whoever the bloke was in the Greek legend who had to clean ten years' worth of horse shit out of a stable for some reason that I've forgotten (possibly because Piers couldn't be bothered to do it himself), I got started.

It was even worse than I'd thought. The chairs were too heavy to stack, and had to be dragged out of the room one at a time, but eventually I moved them all. The table, though, was another matter. The damn thing was huge. I tried to lift one end and my arms almost fell off. I tried to push it, but it wouldn't budge. It was impossible.

I looked at the chaos of the room in despair, and thought about walking out and never coming back. But that would mean no job, no reference to help me get another, and no way of paying the rent. I looked at my watch. It was half past six and I was meant to be meeting Myles at seven. Panic gave me renewed strength, and I gave the table an almighty heave and managed to move it about a foot before my hands slipped and one of my nails snapped clean off against its smooth walnut edge.

'Fuck!' I shouted. 'You fucking bastard of a fucking thing.' I put my throbbing finger in my mouth and sank down onto the carpet, tears beginning to sting my eyes.

'What the hell are you doing, Charlotte?' said a voice. 'Are you okay?'

I looked up. Xander was standing in the doorway, his jacket on and a laptop bag slung over his shoulder, evidently on his way home.

'Does it look like I'm okay, or does it look like Piers confused me with a removals man and made me shift a ton of furniture for his stupid press conference?'

'He made you…' Xander's eyes widened behind his glasses. 'Jesus. Has the man never heard of health and safety? You could have put your back out and sued the company for a fortune.'

'Can I sue for a broken nail?' I said, standing up and trying very hard not to cry. 'Come on, give me a hand please, since you're here. I'm running late.'

'Don't be ridiculous.' Xander turned and left the room.

I didn't feel like crying any more – I felt absolutely furious. What was he like, flouncing off without even bothering to help? Bloody jobsworth, thinking that because he had a first in economics he was too special to move some furniture.

'Fucking snowflake,' I muttered, grabbing the table again and giving it another heave.

Then I heard Xander's voice behind me again. 'Charlotte, stop.'

He was standing in the doorway, and behind him were Pavel, impassive as always, and Piers, looking distinctly shame-faced.

'As I explained to these guys,' Xander said, 'I'm all for equality in the workplace, but expecting one woman to do a job like this on her own is pushing it a bit. Right?'

'Er, I hadn't quite thought of it that way,' Piers mumbled.

Pavel didn't say anything. He just took his blazer off and hung it on the coat rack, the muscles in his neck and shoulders bulging in a manner I usually found slightly menacing but now looked perfect for the task in hand. Xander took his jacket off too, and dropped it on the floor.

'Right,' he said. 'Let's get this sorted. Charlotte, there's no need for you to wait. You said you were running late.'

'Ah, yes, off you trot, darling,' Piers said. 'And don't worry about setting anything up in the morning, I'm sure we'll have it all under control.'

For a second, I considered breaking into a flood of apologies for my weak and feeble double-X-chromosomed body and offering to stay and help. But Xander must have noticed my indecision, because he shook his head ever so slightly and winked, and I realised, impressed with his tact, that he knew Piers wouldn't want another witness to what he'd see as humiliation.

'Okay, then,' I said, making do with a flood of silent thanks to him for rescuing me. 'I'll be off. See you in the morning.'

I grabbed my bag and dashed for the lift. There was no time to sort my face – no time to do anything, really. I was just going to have to leg it to the bar where we'd arranged to meet, and Myles was just going to have to take me as he found me.

Then I remembered the Bad Girl's words: *You might be keen. You might be so keen you're tripping over your own feet! But take a breath. Remember, this isn't the first first date you've been on, and it might not be the last. Have fun, be yourself, and see where the night takes you. That's what I'll be doing – or trying to. Wish me luck!*

So instead of sprinting to meet Myles, I sent him a text saying that I was running a few minutes late. Then I went to Fenwick's and got a lovely girl at the Chantecaille counter to do me a full face of make-up in return for selling me a bottle of expensive foundation I didn't need. Then I bought a pink and red Deco-print silk blouse to replace the grey one I'd worn to work and sweated in and put it on in the fitting room. I doused myself with Roja scent on the way out and strolled into the street, confident that I might be almost half an hour late but at least I looked fabulous and smelled of five-hundred-pound perfume. And, thanks to the podcast, I was wearing the foxiest underwear I owned: a dark red satin bra and thong printed with black roses.

*

Owing to Piers's intervention in my plans, I hadn't had a chance to find the bar on Google Street View, study the menu so I could make a swift and nonchalant decision, or spend ages analysing what Myles's choice of venue said about him and, more importantly, about what he thought of me. An upmarket place would have been a clear statement of intent – see Renzo's choice of Nobu for his first date with Tansy – or it might have simply meant that the only places he knew were upmarket (again, see Renzo…). Something generic, especially if it was part of a chain, would mean he hadn't given it much thought at all. A hotel bar could mean that he was hoping to put thoughts of a shag upstairs in a four-poster bed into my mind – entirely unnecessarily, because those thoughts were there already, and had been since he first shook my hand and I'd felt that jolt of electricity between us.

But I was totally unprepared for his actual choice. *The Latimer*, he'd texted me, with a link to a map. It could have been anything, but I was completely surprised by what it was: a pub. An ordinary pub on a quiet street off Grosvenor Square. A pretty, chichi one, admittedly, with hanging baskets of geraniums outside and a crowd that seemed to be made up more of fashion types than estate agents, but still a pub. My heart sank. He couldn't be even slightly keen. Not that it mattered, because I was so late he would probably have the hump and leave after one drink, and I'd ripped the tags off my new top so I wouldn't even be able to cut my losses and return it.

But he hadn't left. He was still there, at a table for two in the corner, an almost empty glass in front of him, staring at his phone.

'Hello,' I said.

If I'd been worried about lack of keenness, I wasn't any more. His face broke into a delighted grin and he stood up and kissed me on both cheeks. He'd snuck past the Fenwick's scent counter on his way here, too, I thought. Or more likely he had a whole cupboard of expensive, sexy-smelling cologne to choose from.

'I'd almost given up,' he said. 'I thought you'd changed your mind.'

'I'm really sorry,' I said. 'It's just so busy at work at the moment. Anything can happen. I did get held up for a few minutes, but it's only… Oh God, is that really the time? Poor you.'

He laughed. 'You're worth waiting for. What can I get you to drink?'

So much for scrutinising the cocktail list in advance and selecting something delicious yet classy, that didn't come with an umbrella in it to poke me in the eye or a stick of celery to drip down my top. Not that this place served cocktails in the first place, I realised.

'Just a glass of wine, please,' I said. 'White. Er… Viognier, if they have it.'

Get you and your sophisticated ways, Charlotte, I told myself. *Maybe next time pick a wine with a name you can actually pronounce.* But Myles didn't seem to have noticed. He just smiled and made his way to the bar, and I sat down on the other side of the little wooden table, wishing I was facing the room so I could at least people-watch while I waited, instead of staring blankly at the wall. I longed to get my phone out of my bag and scroll through Instagram, or get out my hand mirror and check that my make-up was still as perfect as it had been five minutes before, but I knew that the first would be rude and the second tragic.

'So,' Myles said a moment later, putting our drinks down on the table. 'How's the world of high finance?'

'Gold futures are up. The yen is down, but we're short on that and long on the Mexican peso, so that's all right. Cryptocurrencies are still rising, but there's so much volatility there at the moment. Many analysts are predicting another hard fork in the bitcoin blockchain and anticipating a surge in Ripple.'

He blinked, and I knew exactly what he was thinking, because it was what I'd spent roughly my first six months at Colton Capital thinking: *This person just said some words. Yes, they were definitely words, and almost certainly words in English. I just don't have a clue what any of them mean.*

He said, 'That sounds fascinating.'

I laughed. 'Nice try. I pretend I understand that stuff, but mostly I don't. And anyway, the highlights of my day today were ordering bite-size eggs Benedict for forty people, and moving furniture.'

'That's a relief,' Myles said. 'The first time I met your boss, I asked him about market performance, just to break the ice, and ten minutes later he still hadn't shut up and I hadn't understood a word. After that, I learned not to ask.'

'But your job's just the same, surely? Don't people ask you about it and you start talking about something you think is interesting, like, I don't know, flying buttresses or whatever, and then you realise you lost them right at word one?'

'Flying buttresses are only in churches,' he said, 'but I take your point. Maybe talking shop should be restricted to people who work in the same shop you do.'

'I used to work in a shop,' I said. 'Tesco. I was a checkout girl at weekends all the way through uni.'

Then I blushed. That wasn't something I particularly wanted him to know about me: the image I was trying to cultivate was of someone who'd moved effortlessly into a world of houses in Mayfair and thousand-pound bottles of champagne, and didn't find any of it strange in the slightest. Which was totally not the case. The first time Piers asked me to go with him to lunch with a new client ('He likes a bit of blonde totty, darling,' he'd said), I'd spent several hours watching YouTube videos about how to hold a knife and fork the right way.

Myles said, 'I know the feeling. I grew up in a council flat in Bermondsey, and here I am designing houses for people who already have six, and offices where enough money gets traded every day to wipe out the debt of a small country. But it's okay. I'm not insecure.'

We met each other's eyes and we both laughed, and I felt a strange sensation inside me – sinking, or was it soaring? Like being in a lift travelling very fast to the top floor, when your body hasn't quite caught up with its acceleration. Fuck. I didn't just fancy this man rotten. I actually *liked* him.

'Nor me,' I said. 'Not insecure in the slightest. About anything.'

'I was going to take you out for dinner, but there's something I'd like to show you, first. Can I get you another drink or shall we go?'

I remembered the Bad Girl's sensible advice: *Meet in a public place, stay in a public place until you're sure you're safe. Tell a friend where you're going. Know what your red lines are.*

Shut up, woman, I told her in my head. *I don't care about that. There's no time. And anyway, if this man's dangerous, it's the kind of dangerous I want.*

'Go on then,' I said. 'Show me.'

Myles stood up, and I took a moment to admire the length of his legs in his suit trousers, and imagine what he'd look like without them on. Once again, I was disconcerted by the effect he had on me. To use a technical term, he gave me the raging fanny gallops. Then I stood up too, while my legs would still let me.

'It's just round the corner,' Myles said, holding open the door and waiting while I walked through ahead of him. The interior of the pub had been gloomy, and I was taken by surprise by the bright sunlight outside. I followed him down the street, through a leafy square full of tourists and office workers sitting on the grass with picnics, and into a quiet road lined with stucco-fronted houses. One of them was surrounded by hoardings advertising the Considerate Contractors scheme, and branded with the Taylor + Associates logo.

'It's still a building site, officially,' Myles said. 'But don't worry, you won't need high-vis or steel-toed boots. Come on.'

He took out a bunch of keys and unlocked a door emblazoned with a sign saying that authorised personnel only were permitted to enter, pushed it open, then tapped a few numbers onto a keypad to silence the beeping of an alarm.

'Wait,' I said. 'Where are we? Are we breaking in?'

Myles said, 'Does it look like we're breaking in? With my key and my access code? The security system even knows my face, look.'

Behind the hoarding was a normal-looking front door, painted a deep, inky blue. I wondered whether Bianca's daughter would be able to name the colour. Myles paused in front of it, looking into a tiny, barely visible lens. There was a beep and a click, and he pulled the door open.

'It's five inches of solid steel,' he said. 'My client's kind of hot on security, with good reason.'

I said, 'There's no letter box. It looks totally ordinary, apart from that.'

'Exactly.'

'But how does he get his post?'

'I don't think Oleg Shchepotin is all that interested in pizza takeaway flyers,' Myles said. 'Or council tax bills, come to that. But he pays them, obviously, through his family office. He likes to look legit.'

He gestured for me to step inside. Part of me thought, *Stop, Charlotte. This is too weird.* But a far bigger part was fascinated, avid to see inside and to be alone with Myles.

The air inside the house was cool, chilled by air conditioning against the summer evening. The floor was marble – at least what I could see of it was; it was mostly covered by an enormous Oriental rug.

'Oleg who?' I asked.

'Shchepotin. My client. He's a Ukrainian billionaire. Made his money in property, and by taking bribes, and – allegedly – by hacking into Western banks' systems and extorting money. But that's all in the past now, and Oleg has turned over a new leaf and is moving to London to lead a quiet, respectable life with his wife and kids.'

'Really?'

'Probably not,' Myles admitted. 'But why should I care, so long as he pays me on time? And he does. This project has been worth north of eight million to the business so far.'

'Wow,' I said. 'If I'd known, I'd have studied cyber crime at uni. Not sure they offered it as a course though. I can't think why.'

Myles chuckled. 'Want to do the grand tour? We're almost done here; the interior decorators should be finishing next week. But we're project managing, so we've got full access to the site until it's time to hand over the keys.'

'This feels kind of wrong,' I said. 'It's like trespassing.'

But, in spite of myself, I found I'd walked into the hallway and was gazing up at the huge, branched staircase ahead of me. The stairs were marble, too, and there was gold everywhere: on the bannisters, on the legs of the vast table that dominated the room and held a vase of what looked like hundreds of pink peonies, and on two giant paintings of the Virgin Mary that stared balefully at each other from opposite walls.

'Oleg – or rather, Mrs Shchepotin – takes a "more is more" approach to interior design,' Myles said. 'I'll show you the basement first. It took three months to dig it out, and three times as long to persuade the neighbours to let us. The earth-moving equipment they used is still buried under there – there's no way of getting a JCB out in a project this size, so they just write them off. Come on.'

He reached out his hand and I took it, grateful for its warmth. He led me through a door and down another marble staircase.

'The servants' wing's through there,' Myles said. 'They've got two nannies, a full-time butler and housekeeper, and Mrs Shchepotin's PA will live here, too – at least when they're not travelling. Then the whole circus goes with them.'

'What's down here?' I asked, as he led me to the top of yet another staircase.

'Oleg's pride and joy.'

A familiar smell and a blast of much warmer, damp air hit me as he pushed open the glass door at the bottom. A swimming pool, its water unnaturally blue, filled almost all of the basement. On one side was a bar (marble, of course) with white and gold leather-covered seats lined up in front of it and hundreds of bottles arranged behind it.

'You've supplied all this stuff?' I said in amazement.

'Everything,' Myles said. 'Every last ice cube, every last towel. Let's have a drink. Don't worry, I'll replace it. I value my kneecaps far too much to nick Oleg's booze.'

He opened a fridge concealed in an expanse of white marble and took out a bottle of Pol Roger champagne.

'When in the oligarch's house…' I said, starting to giggle in spite of my fear that what we were doing was very, very wrong.

'Exactly.' Myles eased out the cork and carefully filled two flutes. 'Cheers.'

We clinked glasses – extremely gently in my case, so as not to risk chipping the crystal – and I sipped the wine.

'You know what I'd like to do right now?' Myles asked.

'Test the swimming pool?' I joked.

'Definitely. But first, I'd like to kiss you.'

Before I could object, he reached out and brushed my hair back with his fingertips. I felt the cold from the champagne bottle and then the warmth of his skin on my face. His lips brushed mine, and then the kiss became deeper, more intense, and I felt my eyes closing and heard my breath coming in little gasps. I fumbled my glass onto the bar top, knowing that if I tried to keep hold of it I'd drop it for sure.

I hadn't kissed anyone for a long time – so long, I'd almost forgotten how it felt. But I did know that, as kisses went, this was up there with the best. His cheek against mine felt slightly rough with stubble but his lips were soft and gentle, exploring mine slowly at first, and then more urgently. His shoulders were strong and hard underneath my hands. After all those months, I was being kissed by a man and kissing him back, and I never wanted it to end.

Chapter Eleven

'So did you shag him?' Tansy asked.

It was the night after my date with Myles, and the two of us had decamped to The Daily Grind. It was the first chance we'd had to catch up since Tansy's date with Renzo as well – she'd been absent for most of the weekend following it, arriving home after I'd gone to bed on Sunday evening, and then the usual mixture of her gym habit and my working hours had meant our exchanges had been limited to brief 'hello's as we passed on the way to the bathroom in the morning and text messages arranging to meet up this evening, because we were itching to tell each other what had happened properly.

'Wait,' I said. 'We need wine. Be right back.'

I went to the bar, hoping that Luke would be there so I could ask him if there had been any more sightings of Freezer, but he was down the other end, deep in conversation with another customer. So I ordered a bottle of red and a bowl of olives from the barmaid and returned to Tansy.

'I'm proud to tell you that I did not shag Myles,' I told her. 'But my God, it was tempting.'

I sipped my wine and allowed myself to remember for the mil-lionth time the intoxicating sensation of Myles's lips against mine, how his hands had moved gently and insistently over my neck and shoulders before his mouth travelled down my throat, his breath hot on my skin. I remembered how his back had felt through the fabric of his shirt, hard and warm, and how I hadn't been able to stop myself pulling the shirt out from his trousers and sliding my palms over his muscular shoulders, then round to the front, caressing the firm warmth of his chest.

I hadn't shagged him, but we had come pretty damn close. Close to the point where he'd unzipped my skirt and slid it down over my hips, letting it fall to the floor, then unbuttoned my top and dropped that as well. I'd stood in front of him in my sexy bra and pants (thank you, Bad Girl!) and my high heels, and I heard him gasp with longing.

'My God, Charlotte,' he said.

The look in his eyes was mesmerising. To see this gorgeous man, who I desired so much I could hardly think straight, looking at me with the longing that I knew was mirrored in my own face, gave me a thrilling sense of power. I'm no sex goddess, but in that moment I felt like the Wonder Woman of snogging. I didn't think about the half a stone I wanted to lose, or care that my lipstick was smudged: seeing myself through his eyes, I felt beautiful and desirable. It was even more intoxicating than the champagne.

So I stepped back into his arms and kissed him again, unbuttoning his shirt and sliding it off to join my own clothes in what was becoming a disorderly heap. His body was as perfect as I had hoped: smooth, muscular, tanned. I could feel the hard heat of his cock pressing against my hip, and I ran my hand down over his abdomen to touch it, feeling his body jerk as he pressed himself against my hand.

'It was pretty close, if I'm honest,' I said to Tansy. 'We had most of our clothes off, and that swimming pool was right there, and the bottle of champagne and everything. Although I've never had sex in a swimming pool. Have you?'

'Yep. It's massively overrated. The water washes away all the lubrication and the chlorine gave me a raging case of thrush. So I guess you dodged a bullet there.'

I laughed. 'I guess I did. Although there were loads of lounger things we could have used – proper luxury ones with cushions on them, not those flimsy plastic jobs. And of course the whole rest of the house, which I didn't get to see. Imagine if I'd shagged in a Ukrainian oligarch's bedroom – I swear I'd be so terrified of him finding out, I'd never get a good night's sleep again.'

'But you didn't,' Tansy said. 'Why not?'

'I just thought – you know, in *Sorry Not Sorry*, she says you should ignore anyone who says a man won't respect you if you have sex on your first date. She says if you do, and then he ghosts you, he wasn't worth it in the first place… But I… I guess I wanted to keep the anticipation building.'

'Even though you were stood there in your undies practically gagging for it?'

'Even then.' I took a big gulp of wine, remembering how I'd interrupted Myles's kiss to do the same, only out of a crystal flute instead of a repurposed jam jar. I'd dipped a finger in the cold, fizzy liquid and run it over Myles's chest, making him shiver.

'We need to stop,' I'd said.

'Why?' he asked. 'Don't make me stop.'

I said, 'I'm afraid I am going to make you.'

If, subconsciously, I'd set Myles a test, he passed it with flying colours. He put his shirt back on, although to my delight he didn't do the buttons up. I reached for my top, too, but he said, 'At least let me look at you,' and I felt a renewed surge of power, like in the novel I read recently where girls got this freaky ability to zap men with a touch.

So I said, 'I suppose you can look.'

He looked, and he touched too. We sat on one of the padded loungers and finished the champagne, and in between sips we kissed each other and stroked each other and he told me what he wanted to do to me until I was so turned on it was all I could do not to lie back and let him. It was light years away from Nick's awkward fumbling and sloppy kisses. But I didn't let him – I kept the boundaries I'd arbitrarily set, and he respected them.

And when the bottle was finished, we left the house, removing all evidence of our presence and restoring the fortress-like security behind us, and he took me to a restaurant round the corner he knew and we ate lobster rolls and chips and drank negronis and talked. I told him about my first job, working as a cashier in a high-street bank in Newcastle. I told him how I'd realised, almost literally overnight, that Liam and I weren't going to be together forever, and how it had felt to leave him and that familiar world to move to London on my own, and how I hoped that if I carried on saving up I might be able to buy a flat in a couple of years. He told me about starting his own business, and what a leap into the unknown that had been, too. Once again I felt that sense of real connection with him. My heart lurched as I realised I was on a date with a man I really liked, who I hoped really liked me.

'So when are you seeing him again?' Tansy asked.

'I'm not sure. We've been chatting, but he's flying to Portugal tomorrow for a week with work, so we can't see each other until he gets back. So you'll have to wait a bit for your full report on date number two. Now come on – you and Renzo. Spill.'

'Oh my God.' Tansy smiled, looking all misty-eyed, as I supposed I must have been. 'He is so hot. And so nice. He really made me laugh.'

'Really?' I asked, amazed. In the months I'd worked with Renzo, a sense of humour hadn't exactly struck me as outstanding among his many attributes.

'Sure,' she said. 'He told me all about his family in Italy – he's got five sisters – he's the baby of the family and they kind of bullied him, but also spoiled him rotten – and all his little nieces and nephews. There are loads of them, and he's so cute when he talks about them. You can tell he really loves kids. And he told me about the cycling club he's joined, and how all the other blokes are way fitter than him, but because he's so competitive he makes himself go on these mad long rides at weekends and ends up so knackered he can't even climb a flight of stairs.'

I'd heard Renzo mention his cycling hobby in the office, but the version he presented to us had been quite different, and probably less accurate.

'And the food was amazing,' Tansy said. 'He ordered loads and loads, because he said he wanted me to try everything, and of course we couldn't finish it, and he made them pack it all up for us to take away. But we didn't eat it, because I gave it to a homeless guy we passed on the way to the Tube.'

'You got the *Tube*?' Renzo never got the Tube. He drove in his fancy car or he got taxis or, if he was going to a meeting nearby, he power-walked at dizzying speed.

'Sure,' Tansy said. 'To his apartment, which is totally amazing. And we made coffee – his coffee machine is insane, it's got, like, twenty different programmes and he didn't mind me playing with it for ages – and we watched an episode of *Billions* and he got all annoyed when they got things wrong about what hedge funds are really like, and he laughed when I took the piss out of him for being annoyed. And then I said I should probably go home, and he ordered an Uber for me.'

'You didn't shag him?' I asked disbelievingly.

'Nope. You're not the only one who can play that game, you know.'

'Blimey,' I said. 'I literally can't believe this. When are you seeing him again?'

'Oh, I already have. Next morning, Sunday, when you were out. I'd just woken up and I was wondering whether I should text him, or try and play it cool, when he called.'

'And?'

'And I was still half asleep, so when he asked me if I had plans that day I didn't have the chance to make something up, and I said I didn't. He said, "I'll pick you up in half an hour." And he did. He drove us out into the countryside, to West Sussex. It was so pretty, all the little villages and the trees just starting to change colour. And we had lunch in a pub and then we went for a walk, and he told me the names of loads of plants and birds, and then he drove me home. In his Lamborghini. Oh my God, how cool is that car? Have you seen it?'

I said I'd not only seen it, but arranged to have it valeted, paid Renzo's parking tickets, and booked a driver to collect it from Heathrow when he'd been late for a flight to New York and couldn't be bothered to use the long-term parking.

'I keep forgetting how well you know him,' Tansy said enviously, and I thought that if she was having longing thoughts about doing Renzo's life laundry for him, she must be really far gone.

'I guess I didn't know him anything like as well as I thought I did,' I said. 'Are you sure you're dating Renzo and not his mild-mannered identical twin brother?'

'He doesn't have a brother,' she said patiently. 'Only all those sisters, remember?'

'I was joking. And what next? When are you seeing him again? Have you kissed properly, at least?'

'We did on Tuesday,' Tansy confirmed, and I said that to make time for three dates in less than a week was giving it some, and Renzo must actually be truly keen.

'I took him bowling,' she went on. 'It was hilarious. I haven't done it for years but I used to go with my little sister, and I haven't lost the old skills, because I thrashed him. He's not a sore loser at all. And then we had burgers and chips and he kissed me goodnight outside the Tube station. And it was amazing.'

'Wow,' I said, literally at a loss for words. Renzo bowling. More importantly, Renzo being beaten at bowling and not chucking a strop about it? We were living in strange times.

'And this weekend he's taking me to Paris,' she said. 'He said he'd book the Eurostar and the hotel and everything. And he asked if I wanted separate rooms, but obviously I was like, "Duh, no."'

'Wow,' I said again. 'Tansy, this sounds so amazing. I'm so pleased for you.' And I was, apart from the feeling that I'd stepped into a parallel universe.

But the excited smile had slipped off Tansy's face. She tipped the last of the wine into our glasses and said, 'Charlotte, if I tell you something, will you hate me?'

'Of course I won't. Unless you tell me you've murdered someone, or something. And even then I don't think I'd literally hate you.'

'The thing is, I need to marry a rich guy. I know how it sounds, but hear me out. When I was growing up, we were properly poor. Well, not at first. My parents had a house in Reading that they sold to move down to Cornwall. Mum was a set designer, working in the West End, before I was born, but she couldn't go back to doing that because the hours are so antisocial and anyway she'd always wanted to paint. So she was going to do that and Dad was going to be a cabinet-maker, like, making proper, bespoke pieces of furniture, instead of being a joiner on building sites, which he hated. They bought this little cottage and we were all going to live the dream there by the seaside. It was going to be like the Famous Five, Mum said.'

'It sounds lovely,' I said, contrasting the cute little cottage by the sea with the one-bedroomed flat where I'd grown up.

'Yeah, it was. It was properly lovely. But then I realised they hadn't moved just so they could be by the sea. Dad always liked a flutter, but he'd been gambling more and more before we moved. I guess Mum thought – maybe they both thought – that a change of scene would stop him. But it didn't. It got worse and worse over the next few years. Horses, dogs, poker machines – whatever. It got really bad.'

She lifted a hand to her mouth and started biting a cuticle, almost savagely.

'Go on.'

'Dad borrowed money against the house. He didn't tell Mum. She didn't find out until all the equity they'd had in it was gone. And by then there were other, massive debts too, and they couldn't pay those and pay the mortgage. And Dad wasn't working because he was so busy chasing that one big win that never fucking happened. Mum couldn't sell her paintings for enough money to get by – seems she wasn't the only one who'd wanted to be an artist by the seaside; the market was totally saturated, as they say. And round about then the house got repossessed. I was thirteen and Perdita was eleven.'

'Oh, babe. That must have been—'

'It was. It was shit. Mum got a job in a supermarket worked her arse off, double shifts, but Dad would tell her some sob story and take her wages too and lose those. Sometimes she didn't eat so that my sister and I could. It was that bad. I'm not clever or anything really – I just managed to scrape into uni and I've got a decent eye for fashion and I work bloody hard, but my job doesn't pay that well and I'll never be management material. So I'll never earn shedloads on my own. But I just want to feel secure. I want my kids never, ever to go through what I went through.'

'Of course not.' I couldn't imagine what it must have been like for Tansy, having had what she thought was a stable home and then losing it. Okay, I kind of could, because my life had changed equally tumultuously, only in a different way, when Mum met Jim.

'I want to be able to help Mum,' Tansy went on. 'Like Dad was meant to and never did. I send her money when I can, but you know how it is. I'm skint every month by pay day with the rent and the bills and stuff, and no matter how much money I give her it never feels like enough, because it all gets sucked away so fast. I send her parcels of clothes from work, and I tell her they're for her and Perdita to wear but we all know they're for her to sell, just to get by. So I've made up my mind I'll marry someone rich. And then I'll never have to worry again, and nor will Mum.'

Loads of possible replies spun through my head. I could tell her that money wasn't everything. I could tell her that my mum had been a single parent when I was growing up and brassic skint, too, and I'd chosen to make my own way in the world. I could tell her that however much money you had it was never actually going to be enough, there'd always be someone who had more, and anyway it couldn't buy happiness. I could tell her that in Renzo, she'd found another man with a bit of a gambling habit, albeit one of a different kind and one at which he generally won. Then I remembered how she bought groceries for the food bank every time she went shopping, as if it was a kind of insurance policy, in case things ever got that bad for her family. I imagined what it must be like to be evicted from your home when you're a teenager and everything is changing so fast and terrifyingly, anyway. And I knew I was in no position to judge or preach. So I said, 'Well, it looks like you're on the right track there.'

Tansy stopped looking anxious, and the happy, dreamy smile came over her face again. 'Yes, but you know what? I never ever imagined that I might meet someone who wasn't just rich, but actually nice, too.'

*

As it turned out, I needn't have worried about Myles forgetting about me during his week away. The next day, a huge bunch of roses arrived for me at the office with a note that said:

I can't stop thinking about you, Charlotte.
When you see these, maybe you will think of me too. M.

Which, of course, I did. I felt my face turn as pink as the flowers, and Xander, who was passing my desk on his way to a meeting, stopped and said, 'Secret admirer? It's not your birthday until next year, is it?'

I was surprised he knew, but of course everyone's birthday was listed on the intranet, there for all to see in a spreadsheet I kept updated. 'An admirer, I guess. Kind of.'

'One whose PA has slightly unoriginal taste in flowers.'

'Ouch,' I said, immediately wondering if Myles had actually got his assistant to place the order and think of the wording on the note, the way Colin did whenever he sent Svetlana flowers. Greg, Alice and Briony basically know whenever Colin's had a shag, which would be awkward if they weren't privy to every single other detail of his life as well.

'So who's the lucky bloke?' Xander asked. There was a slight edge to his voice that wasn't there normally, but I was too elated to give it much thought.

For a moment I was torn between the urge to talk about Myles and a sense that, given we'd met through work and our contract was worth a sizeable whack to his firm, it was probably best to be discreet. Besides, what if there was some clause, buried deep in the HR manual, about not shagging suppliers? Discretion won.

'Just someone I met online.'

Xander paused, looking like he might be about to say something, but then he glanced at his watch.

'Nice work,' he said, and strolled away.

I waited until lunchtime before texting Myles to say thank you, and almost immediately received a reply. *I've just come out of a meeting with my client. Her name is Carmen. I kept calling her Charlotte. If we get sacked I'm blaming you.*

It would teach you an important lesson about keeping your mind on the job, I texted back.

Impossible, he replied. *My mind is on you. And I wish it wasn't just my mind. I can't stop thinking about your body. I want to…*

And he went on to tell me in graphic detail that would have made even the Bad Girl blush, until my own concentration was shot to pieces and I typed 'US presidential erection' instead of 'election' in the report I was compiling for Piers, noticing just before I sent it to him. The idea of Trump's todger was sufficiently off-putting to drive all thoughts of sex from my mind, and I determinedly shut my phone in my drawer for the afternoon and didn't reply to Myles until I was in bed that night and could give his filthy texts my full attention. And so I did, marvelling at how much easier it had got with practice, how the replies I sent him came not from the imagined voice of the Bad Girl in my head, but from someone uninhibited and real and seriously fucking sexy, who was actually me and must have been there all along. At last I fell asleep and dreamed that I was back in the Mayfair mansion with him, only this time I didn't tell him to stop, and just as he was preparing to thrust his gloriously hard cock inside me, Oleg Shchepotin turned up with two security guards, and then… You get the picture.

So of course I had to describe the dream to Myles in great detail the next day, and he added some embellishments of his own to the fantasy, and I ended up having what was probably the least productive day I'd had since joining the firm.

The next day, a parcel arrived on my desk. I never got online shopping delivered at work – I don't know why, since almost everyone else did; it just seemed like it would be taking the piss somehow. So, intrigued, I ripped open the brown cardboard with the fork I'd used to eat my lunch.

Inside was a plain linen bag, and inside that was the softest gold belt, curled up like a slender snake. It was simple and unadorned except for the buckle, which was a small heart made of steel. I looked at it for a second, stroking the leather, which felt almost like velvet between my fingers, then tucked it away in my bag to admire later, relishing knowing and not knowing who it was from.

Just as I was focusing on work again, my phone lit up with a message.

Do you like it?

God, technology, I thought. There was no way to play it cool when Myles had been notified by text – and probably email too – that his present had been delivered and signed for.

It's beautiful. I love it. Thank you.
I'm imagining you wearing it, and nothing else. I can't wait to see you. I wanted you to know I think about you all the time.
Me too.

I wondered whether he meant he thought about my body, about us finally doing in real life all the things we'd described doing to each other by text, or whether he meant something else, something deeper. I couldn't help it, but whenever I saw his name appear on my phone's screen, I felt more than the delicious pinpricks of arousal his words gave me. I felt surges of emotion: excitement, happiness, longing and sick disappointment if I got back from a meeting and there was no reply to a message I'd sent.

It wasn't just my inner bad girl Myles was bringing to the surface, but something deep in my heart that I'd forgotten how to feel. And it was scary. It was too soon. So the next day I pleaded pressure of work and left his texts unanswered for as long as I could bear to. This wasn't as hard as it sounds, because I kept getting distracted by texts from Tansy agonising over what to pack for her weekend in Paris. It was downright weird seeing Renzo strutting around the office, looking even more glossy and assured than usual, and knowing that he'd be spending that night in bed with my housemate. It was just as well I had met Myles, I thought, otherwise I'd be feeling seriously envious; as it was, I just felt excited for both of them, especially when Renzo asked me to book a table for two at La Truffière.

Then, for just a moment, his air of unshakeable confidence wavered. 'Do you think she'll like it, Charlotte?' he asked.

I tapped the name into Google, spent a few moments admiring photos of the intimate, low-beamed, candle-lit rooms and salivating over the menu, and said, 'She'll love it.' Then a slight sense of mischief overcame me and I added, 'She's quite the foodie, you know. She might have been there already,' even though I knew from what Tansy had said about the precarious state of her finances that there was about as much chance of that as of her having flown into space on Virgin Galactic.

'Shit,' Renzo said. 'Seriously? Should I book somewhere else?'

I laughed. 'Nah. You'll be fine.'

He looked briefly furious, then laughed too and walked away. Even weirder than picturing him shagging Tansy, I thought, was the realisation that Renzo was actually human. There might be more to him than his flash car, designer suits and dazzling good looks – underneath all that, perhaps he had insecurities and dreams and a sense of humour, and was just highly skilled at keeping them hidden.

I remembered what Tansy had said about meeting a rich man who was also a nice person, and for the first time I thought that she might actually have struck gold. I texted her to tell her I'd booked a restaurant for their dinner, but no matter how much she pleaded, I refused to tell her where. I wanted it to be Renzo's surprise.

Chapter Twelve

Helloooo and welcome back!

So you might be wondering how it went with Butt Boy. We had an okay time. He's hot, and he's kind of funny. But I'm just not sure he's right for me. And it's tough, because part of me is thinking, 'But he likes you! He asked for a second date! Just because he's not perfect, doesn't mean you shouldn't give him a chance! It's better than being single, right?'

But that's got me thinking. Is it better to be going out with someone you're not sure about than to be single? Is it better to be with someone who makes you unhappy than to be alone?

And you know what? It's not. So this isn't just a challenge for today: it's one for my whole dating life going forward. If something's not working for me, I'm going to be honest about it. I'm not going to pretend to myself that being single is worse than dating someone who's not right for me. And most important of all, I'm not going to kid myself that he's going to change.

'Right!' Bianca said, tapping a teaspoon against her coffee mug. 'Can I have everyone's attention please? Charis, please could you use headphones, my sweetie, or Mummy will have to take the iPad away. Molly, would you mind just moving the fresh fruit platter to one side while I fetch my laptop? Great.'

There was a brief pause in the proceedings while Charis threw a strop over not being allowed to share the latest masterpiece from the creators of *Horrible Histories* with the assembled bridesmaids, I topped up everyone's coffee, Chloë went to the loo and Molly took a call from William. Eventually we all quietened down and were sitting in a more or less orderly fashion around the table in Bianca's kitchen, which was done up like a Provençal farmhouse with bunches of herbs hanging from the distressed wooden beams, vintage furniture and rush matting on the quarry-tiled floor. I remembered Maddy telling me that Bianca was an interior decorator; presumably her own home was a showcase for her skills.

This was a serious occasion, after all. It was only three months until Maddy and Henry's wedding, and there was, as Bianca had stressed, a lot of work ahead for her five bridesmaids. Four, I supposed, if you didn't count Charis, who couldn't realistically be expected to contribute more than looking cute in photographs.

The problem was, it felt too serious. It should have been fun: we should have been giggling together, squealing with excitement, eager to be part of Maddy's special day. But I'd barely spoken to the bride-to-be since our dress-fitting; the texts I'd sent her had been read but only one had been replied to, and that with a brief, *OK*, when I'd asked her how things were going. She hadn't asked me how things were going with Myles, or about work, or anything else at all.

It hurt like hell, and I couldn't think of a way to make it right, apart from be the best bridesmaid I could.

'So, ladies, I hope you all received the agenda I sent round on the Slack group?'

Typically, Bianca had made us all get set up on a communications platform that was clearly designed for work and sent chirpy motivational messages every time you opened it.

'Excellent. I've also circulated calendar invites for the key dates we have coming up, just to make sure that there are no avoidable diary clashes. If you're rushed into hospital with appendicitis, I might just let you off, but otherwise I'd really appreciate one hundred per cent attendance. After all, Charis will be available for all of them and I can assure you her social calendar is far busier than any of ours!'

'I've got my singing class on Tuesday and my Mandarin lesson on Wednesday and pony club on Thursday and ballet on Friday,' Charis informed us. 'And Calliope's birthday party next Saturday, but I don't want to go to that. Parties are boring and you have to share.'

Bianca gave a tinkly little laugh. 'You're good at sharing, though, aren't you my sweetie? Almost as good as you are at Mandarin. So, anyway, ladies, please double-check that you have clear availability for all these: final dress-fitting, hair and make-up trial, bridal shower, the stag do for those of us whose partners are involved in that—' as she knew perfectly well, her other half was the only one who was— 'rehearsal and rehearsal dinner, the wedding itself. And of course the hen! But more on that later.

'Please let's all remember that this is a proper wedding we're organising here, and we all need to focus!'

'Right,' I said. 'Not like those improper weddings you hear about.'

I thought my little joke would lighten the mood, but no one laughed. Bianca gave me a frosty look and carried on.

'First of all, I just wanted to have a quick word about accessories. As you know, the bride and groom are kindly footing the bill for all of our gorgeous bridesmaids' gowns. So I do hope you'll all attend the final fitting. If you don't, and your zip won't do up, I won't be held responsible!'

'Eating too many carbs makes people fat and then their clothes don't hang right,' Charis said. Although she didn't look up from her screen, it still felt as if her comment was aimed at me. Instead of telling her daughter that looks weren't important and it was what you were like on the inside that mattered, Bianca just laughed again. I suppose someone had once told her what a charming laugh she had – light and feminine – so she wheeled it out at every opportunity. To me, it was beginning to sound like nails on a blackboard.

'But, yes, accessories. The feathered skull caps have been designed by Monty and are being made by the same milliner who's doing the mothers of the bride and groom's hats, so there's no need to worry about what you'll be wearing in your hair. Otherwise, I've put together a little Pinterest board with some guidelines as to what is and isn't acceptable. It's shared with you all so you can check up on it at any time, but I'll just run through the key points.'

She swivelled her laptop around so we could all get a good look at her Pinterest. I was surprised she hadn't set up a projector especially for this high-level bridesmaids' summit, to which we'd all been sent an official invitation the previous week, when she'd Slacked us for the first time. There'd been a flurry of protests from Molly, who was meant to be watching William play five-a-side football;

Chloë, who'd been planning to put up shelves in her bathroom;
and yours truly, who'd had a call from Myles saying he was back
in London, and could I meet up. But Bianca had laid it on thick
about how important it was to Maddy that everything on her big
day was absolutely perfect and how she, Bianca, was shouldering
by far the greatest burden of all the planning, and basically guilted
us all into giving up a Saturday morning to wedding planning.

Surreptitiously, I checked my phone. There was a text from
Myles. *How's it going, beautiful? Any chance you'll be free this afternoon?
I've got plans later but could meet at three. I've missed you.* And a long
row of kisses.

I dithered over a reply, longing to see him as much as he said
he longed to see me, but at the same time not wanting to give the
impression that I could fit into the small window he'd proposed,
and settled for saying I'd see how it went.

I'll be at Oleg's, he texted. *There's some stuff that needs doing there.
Just turn up – you know where to find me.*

I allowed myself a few seconds of delicious anticipation, then
forced my attention back to Bianca.

'No jewellery except wedding and engagement rings,' she was
saying. 'Sheer nude tights only, shoes to be black courts with a heel
of exactly four inches – apart from Charis, of course, who will be in
white tights and adorable little ballet flats. All tattoos to be covered,
please – if you need assistance with this, Daniel, who is doing our
make-up, is happy to help, but he'll need to allow extra time, so please
let me know in advance so I can put it on the schedule for the day itself.'

'He's going to do my make-up, too, isn't he, Mummy?' Charis
said.

'Now, sweetie, remember we talked about this?'

'You said I'm not allowed make-up for the wedding because I'm too young, but I said I don't want to look washed out in the photos, and you said you'd think about it.' Charis's bottom lip was trembling.

'Sweetie, you know Daddy doesn't approve of—' Charis let out a wail, and Bianca said, 'Well, maybe just a little bit of lip gloss and some clear mascara. Now, moving on to the bridal shower, I'd like to ask you all to prepare an ice-breaker activity for the group. Remember, there will be thirty ladies attending from all age groups, from Charis's cousin Poppy, who's only two, all the way up to Maddy's granny, who was eighty last year. So please keep them clean, but fun.

'And speaking of fun! Girls, we have a hen to arrange! I know it's ridiculously short notice, given it will be taking place just five weeks from today. But to be perfectly honest, very little planning had been done before Maddy asked me to take over as her chief bridesmaid.'

She shot me what I can only describe as a glare. Stung, I forced myself to smile sweetly instead of glaring back.

I said, 'Actually, when I discussed it with Maddy ages ago, when she and Henry first got engaged, she said she didn't want a hen do. She said they're tacky and unnecessary, and being a wedding guest involves so much time and expense anyway, it's unfair to ask people to—'

'Oh, Charlotte,' Bianca said pityingly. 'When you've been a bridesmaid as often as I have – and been a bride, of course – you'll know that everyone starts off saying that. But then they get into the swing of it and realise they want all the things! And rightly so! So, venues. We've looked at various options but I thought I'd throw it open to the group and see if anyone has any inspiration.'

'How about Butlin's?' Chloë suggested. 'It's cheesy, I know, but it's actually really good fun, and they do spa treatments now and everything, and if Maddy is worried about costs…'

A look at Bianca's face stopped her in her tracks.

'Butlin's?' Bianca repeated in a tone of incredulous disgust, as if Chloë had suggested that we all roll ourselves in fox poo and parade naked down Oxford Street. 'I. Don't. Think. So. We're not a gaggle of slappers from Newcastle. Sorry, Charlotte, I know that's where you're from. I meant… Maddy will want something more upmarket, that's all.'

Maddy is from Newcastle, too, I thought, biting my tongue.

'I thought about a country house hotel,' Bianca went on. 'But all the decent ones seem to be booked up already, which I suppose is unsurprising. We're on the waiting list at Calcot Manor but I don't hold out much hope. And it's high season – half-term, you know – so it would be a bit pricy for those of us on limited budgets.'

'We could stay in London,' Molly said, and I knew she was thinking that that would mean her not having to be away from William overnight. I sometimes wondered if she believed that by being in his field of vision at all times, she'd be sure not to miss the moment when he decided out of the blue to propose to her. 'An activity in the morning, spa treatment in the afternoon, cocktails then dinner somewhere, then head out clubbing.'

'Yes, that would be convenient, I know,' Bianca said. 'But it seems a little… unimaginative, I suppose. After all, we all live here, and we go out here all the time. I wanted Maddy to have something different, a bit special.'

My phone's screen lit up again and I glanced down at it. Myles, this time. He'd sent a photo of a double bed – one of the beds in Oleg Shchepotin's house, I presumed, since it was covered in an enormous faux fur (or possibly, given what little I knew of Oleg, real fur) throw, and had a huge oil painting of a naked woman eating a peach hanging behind it. Damn it. The sooner I could get bloody Bianca to make a decision, the sooner I could get out of here and see him.

'How about Portugal?' I asked. 'Someone I know has just spent a week in Lisbon with work and he – they – said it's amazing. Cheap, beautiful, fantastic food, and the flight's not too long.'

'Now there's a thought,' Bianca said. 'Charlotte, would you mind awfully doing a bit of research on that one? Maybe cost up five different hotels or Airbnb apartments, compare flight prices from a few airlines, that sort of thing? And circulate a spreadsheet with options? In the next couple of days, please, because we really do need to make reservations.'

It was fair enough, I supposed. Back when… back when things had been different between me and Maddy, I'd assumed I'd be doing loads of this sort of thing for her wedding. And I wouldn't have minded a bit. In fact, I was actually looking forward to it. I did, however, mind being ordered to do it by Bianca.

But I forced myself to smile. After all, she'd done a lot of hard work herself, with her Slack channel and her fresh fruit platter.

'Sure,' I agreed through gritted teeth.

'You could ask your… friend… for recommendations,' Bianca said.

Before I could stop myself, I said, 'Yes, I suppose I could. He's working on a major project out there so he goes every couple of weeks. He'll be able to give me loads of tips. It's Myles, actually, my new boyfriend. I was going to let Maddy know that I'd be bringing a plus-one to the wedding after all.'

One date was hardly boyfriend territory, let alone plus-one territory, I knew, but I couldn't help feeling that I was backed into a corner and a bit of exaggeration for effect was necessary. And effective it certainly was – Bianca's mouth hung open in affronted astonishment.

'Really?'

'Really,' I said. 'Actually, Bianca, you may have heard of him, in your line of work. Myles Taylor, from Taylor + Associates. With a plus. I'm off to meet him in Mayfair now and I'm running a bit late, so I'll love and leave you all. Thanks for the coffee!'

I grabbed my bag and swished out, literally skipping with pleasure as soon as the front door closed behind me.

This time, I didn't say no. I couldn't have even if I'd wanted to and, believe me, I didn't want to. I rushed from Bianca's house to the station, hastily applying some make-up on the Tube. I considered doing an emergency dash to Selfridges to buy some nicer underwear, or at least a new top, but seeing Myles suddenly seemed even more important than the way Myles saw me. And anyway, I was wearing the supple leather belt he'd sent me, threaded through the loops of my black denim skirt. And from the moment he opened the Shchepotin fortress, still shrouded in its blue hoarding, and took me in his arms, I knew it was going to be all right.

It was. It was actually quite a lot better than all right, thanks partly to all the texts we'd sent each other describing what we liked, what we wanted, how we'd touch each other. (Thanks for that, Bad Girl!) I'd been simmering with desire for him for more than a week, and it took just a few deft touches for me to reach boiling point.

In fact – and I'm slightly ashamed to admit this – we didn't even get inside the house. Myles closed the outer door, waited for the alarm to beep, then took me in his arms like I was the most precious thing in the world, but with a kind of urgency too, which was almost – but not quite – rough. The smell of him, the feel of his denim shirt under my fingers, even his stubble grazing my face, all seemed too erotic to bear. I kissed him, hard, and guided his hand under my skirt so he could feel through my knickers how much I wanted him.

He didn't wait. He pushed the fabric aside and touched me, and I gasped, 'Don't stop,' and he made me come right there, pushed up against Oleg's front door, like the kind of brazenly sexual woman I'd never dreamed I could be.

'That's a good start,' he said, smiling, once I'd finished juddering and bucking against his hand.

'Not too bad,' I gasped, thinking, *How? How, exactly, have I become this person?*

'I suppose we should go inside,' he said, and we did.

Even Myles, I guess, didn't have the audacity to fuck in Oleg and Mrs Oleg's master bedroom. Instead, we found a downstairs room that I suppose was intended for a nanny, and grabbed a towel to put on top of the mattress, and we did it there, and then we did it again on one of the loungers by the swimming pool, and then we took our clothes off and tried again in the pool itself. Tansy was right – it didn't work particularly well, but I didn't care and neither did he.

'You're full of surprises, Charlotte,' Myles said, once we'd dried off and were perched on the white leather bar stools, somewhat dressed again but mostly not, drinking another bottle of borrowed Pol Roger bubbly.

'I am? What, did you find a bunch of coloured handkerchiefs up there, or a white rabbit?'

He laughed. 'Maybe next time. And maybe a different kind of rabbit. Do women even use those any more or are they a bit 2005?'

'I couldn't possibly comment.' I couldn't, actually, but I didn't want him to know that, and I wasn't about to tell him about the newest challenge from the Bad Girl, and the order I'd placed online the previous day. 'Maybe I like my sex toys old school, like my men.'

'I'm only thirty-five,' he protested, and I laughed and said again that he was, indeed, ancient.

'Silver fox,' I said, running my fingers through his silky pewter hair. 'What do you mean, anyway, about me being surprising?'

'You seemed so proper, when I first met you,' he said. 'All straight-laced in your suit. Sexy as hell, but kind of intimidating, too. And yet, under it all, you're properly filthy.'

'You know what they say?' I said, quoting the podcast. 'Good girls go to heaven, bad girls go everywhere – including heaven.'

'It looks like they do,' he said, pushing me back, kneeling between my legs and slowly, tenderly, flicking his tongue against my clit and easing his fingers in and out of me until I found myself where I thought it wouldn't be possible for me to go again until I'd had a good long rest.

Afterwards, I couldn't move or open my eyes for a few minutes. I just let myself flop back against the bar in a haze of bliss, the part of me that had been dormant for so long and been savagely reawakened now drowsy again. And it felt amazing. Why had I left it so long?

When I opened my eyes, Myles was fully dressed again, tucking the empty bottle into his bag and carefully drying the crystal glasses.

'Getting rid of the evidence,' I said. 'You've been picking up on Oleg's master criminal skills.'

'I learn from ze experts,' he said in a cod Russian accent. Then he added absently, 'The hoarding comes down next week, and then Oleg's staff will be moving in. Our work here is done, I think.'

'Well, you can stay over at mine, although it's nothing like as luxurious as this. I can't promise a swimming pool or the pelts of endangered species on the bed.'

'Poor, Charlotte, very poor,' he said, chucking my skirt over to me. 'Come on, get dressed, I have to go now.'

I felt a stab of disappointment. He must have seen it in my face, because he stepped over to me, suddenly serious again, and wrapped his arms round me.

'Hey,' he said. 'Just because Oleg's project is finished, it doesn't mean you and me are. We're just beginning.'

'We are?'

'I hope so. Don't you?'

I nodded, suddenly feeling overwhelmed with a rush of emotion I couldn't let myself express.

'What are you doing tonight, anyway?' I asked, forcing myself to sound casual. 'Anything nice?'

I imagined another swanky awards dinner, or perhaps an evening in the pub with friends, and realised how little I knew about his life.

'Not really,' he said. 'I'm having dinner with my ex.'

The haze of post-coital bliss that had enveloped me vanished like it had been whipped away by a gust of wind. I shivered and put my shirt on.

'Ex-girlfriend?'

He sighed. 'Ex-wife.'

'Oh,' I said, my voice sounding small and tentative. 'I didn't know you were divorced.'

Don't be an idiot, I told myself. *He's in his mid-thirties, what did you expect? That he'd been single all these years, just waiting for you to come along?*

'Separated, actually,' he said. 'Look, Charlotte, I know it's not ideal. My situation at the moment – it's complicated. If I could have timed things better, I would have. But it is what it is. My marriage is over – everything that's left is just detail. I didn't expect – I didn't even want – to meet someone else so soon. But now I have, and I don't want to throw away what you and I have because of a stupid mistake I made three years ago.'

Three years. Less than ten per cent of his life. But still, he'd loved someone enough to think that he might spend all of the rest of it with her. They'd have a whole shared history, a home they'd built together, pet names for each other and in-jokes no one else got. An ex-girlfriend – someone he'd been with for a few months and was meeting up with as a friend – would have set my insecurities on red alert; a wife, even a soon-to-be-ex-wife, was something else altogether.

'I didn't know,' I said again.

He sat down next to me and took my hand. 'I'd have told you, Charlotte, of course I would. I should have done already. I'm sorry. I was worried about how you'd react, that you'd end things between us. And these things... there's just never a good time, is there?'

As timing went, right after we'd shagged for the first time (well, the third, I suppose, strictly speaking) was pretty diabolical.

'No, I guess not,' I said, hating how feeble I sounded.

'Look. I wasn't looking for another relationship. Far from it. The last few months have been so tough, it's almost broken me. I thought I'd be on my own for a bit, focus on work, take some time to get over it. But then I met you.'

I looked up from our clasped hands and met his eyes. His face was very still and serious.

'I don't know if I can do this,' I said. 'I mean, you're still married.'

'Only technically,' he said. 'In every way that counts, it's been over for months. Years even.'

A horrible thought struck me. 'Do you still live together?'

He sighed. 'Yes. Yes, we do. Separate bedrooms, separate lives, but in the same house, at least for the time being. It's bloody hard, to be honest. But it won't be for long. Once we get a court date, get all the formalities sorted out, we can put the house on the market and then I can finally move on properly. Practically, I mean. Emotionally, I reckon I moved on in the boardroom at Colton Capital a few weeks ago.'

He reached out a hand and gently caressed my cheek, and I felt a surge of emotion – desire, regret, anger – that was almost too strong to bear. I forced myself to stay calm. Everything he was saying made me feel safe and desired, as I knew he intended it to. But it wasn't feelings I needed; it was facts.

Dry-mouthed, I asked, 'Do you have children?'

'No,' he said. 'No kids, thank God. I mean, this would all be even harder if we did. For them, for her, for me… and for you. That was part of the problem. I wanted kids, I really want to be a dad. And I thought she did too. But she kept putting it off, because she wasn't ready and work had to take precedence, and all that stuff. Nothing unreasonable. But then I realised that "later" actually meant "never".'

'So that's why you're splitting up?'

'*Have* split up,' he said. 'The house – seriously, Charlotte, it's just a detail. We haven't shared a bedroom since Christmas. I'd have rented a place of my own, but I didn't realise how long the process would drag on. And I didn't think it mattered, particularly. I'm away with work a lot so we barely see each other. It didn't matter, until I met you.'

'But now you have met me.'

'I have,' he smiled. 'And I'm so bloody glad I did. You're quite something, you know. You're special, Charlotte. Not just because you're beautiful and fucking you is off the scale, but because you're so together, so focused. I love that you don't need me. It makes me realise how much I need you.'

Love. He hadn't said he loved me. He'd said he loved an aspect of me: one I wasn't even sure I recognised. But the word was still there, hanging in the air like a promise.

I said, 'I'm going to have to think about this.'

'Of course. I don't want to rush you. I don't want to put any pressure on you at all. But I really think you and I could have something special. I never expected to feel like this again – not for a long time anyway. But I do, and here we are.'

'Here we are,' I echoed. 'But now you have to go and meet your wife.'

He sighed and glanced at his watch. 'I do have to go. I don't want to be late, it would just stir up more bad feeling between us. We're going to go through a load of paperwork from the lawyer tonight. Full financial disclosure, they call it. I've never hidden anything from her, and she's not dependent on me financially, but it's still got to be done, and it will be even less fun if we start off having a row.'

I wondered why their going through lawyers' paperwork couldn't happen during the day, over a coffee, instead of over dinner on a Saturday night, but I didn't say anything. It was none of my business, and anyway, he'd been away. They probably hadn't had time, what with her full-on career that meant she couldn't give him the children he longed for.

'Okay,' I said, letting go of his hand and standing up. 'I don't want to make you late.'

'I hate saying goodbye to you, Charlotte,' he said. 'Especially now, when I can see you're upset. But please think about it. Please give us a chance.'

And then he kissed me and I got on the Tube with a Saturday night at home alone to look forward to.

Chapter Thirteen

For the second time, I typed Myles's name into Google. Before, I'd done so out of idle curiosity, wanting to be at least semi-prepared for a meeting at which I'd be representing my boss, and then disappeared down a rabbit hole of speculation and fascination. Now, it was a whole other matter.

Standing on the baking Central line train, the smell of his body still clinging to me, I typed Myles's name into my phone. I could see my hand shaking as I added a word afterwards: wife.

The train pulled out into the tunnel and my phone's connection dropped before the results could load. Then, when they did, I found a load of random results. There were lots of people called Myles Taylor, it turned out, and lots of them had wives. And there were people called Myles something else married to women whose surname was Taylor. And then the connection dropped again. But at Tottenham Court Road there was a delay and I refined my search, adding quote marks and the word 'architect'. Then I knew her name.

Feeling sick, I typed it in and clicked the images tab. There were none of them together, at least not on the first page. But there she was. Even on the tiny thumbnails, her personality seemed to radiate off the page. A small woman, extravagantly curvy but toned and slim, who made up for her lack of height with killer heels and piled-up hair. A woman who clearly spent a lot of time on her make-up and had a penchant for ultra-feminine, retro fashion. A woman whose job apparently involved attending loads of events with people I didn't recognise, but who seemed to be celebrities of a sort. A woman with a smile so warm and dazzling it was impossible to imagine not liking her, but also with a distinct air of taking no prisoners.

'Stop right now, Charlotte. That way madness lies.' I hadn't realised I was speaking out loud, although at least under my breath, but I noticed the Sikh man standing next to me edge away a bit, shepherding his children down the carriage with him. *Madness indeed, Charlotte. Next thing you know you'll be joining her two hundred thousand followers on Instagram or turning up at her Soho office and demanding to know just how over her marriage is.*

As the train pulled into Liverpool Street and I automatically gathered my stuff together to change onto the Overground that would take me home, I resolutely closed the window on my phone. Whatever decision I made about my relationship with Myles, I wasn't going to make it on the basis of stalking his wife online.

Although it was almost eight o'clock and beginning to get dark, the evening was still warm. People were spilling out of The Daily Grind and the Prince George onto the pavement, smoking and vaping and drinking and talking. A few months ago, Maddy, Henry and I might have been there too. I could have told Maddy what Myles had told me earlier, and she would have told me what to do. Or, at least, she would have told me what to think in order to make the right decision for myself. I wanted so much to talk to her, ask her what I should do, listen to her wise advice and act on it. I knew that whatever she told me, she'd include a hug and say something to make me laugh. But she wasn't there, and if I called or texted her I wasn't sure she would even answer. She and Henry were in Bromley, no doubt hosting a dinner party or discussing the seating plan for their wedding reception. Or maybe just flopping on the sofa arguing about what to watch on Netflix and whether to order pizza or curry from Uber Eats, the way we all used to do on Saturday nights. And I was going home alone, to a house with no Maddy and no Henry, only Adam's unsettling presence. Because Tansy, of course, was in Paris. Lucky Tansy, having a glamorous and romantic weekend away with a man who was not only hot and rich but also apparently mad keen on her. And, crucially, single. Renzo might have his issues as a boyfriend, as I'd warned Tansy, but an undisclosed wife wasn't one of them, I knew for sure: Colton Capital's background checks were nothing if not rigorous.

I let myself into the house and walked straight through to the garden. It was a beautiful evening – it was getting dark earlier and earlier each night, but the sky was a clear, perfect turquoise still and the moon was just rising – and if I was going to spend it alone, I might as well sit outside and drink, maybe indulging in a bit of online shopping while I was about it. The garden had suffered since Henry's departure; there were weeds flourishing in the flower beds, which were choked with fallen leaves, and the ivy was encroaching seriously from Luke and Hannah's next door. I looked dispiritedly around, wondering whether I could be bothered to do anything about it, deciding I couldn't, and turning to go back indoors.

A flash of white caught my eye and I spun around – but there was nothing there. Had I glimpsed Freezer's tail disappearing over the fence? I hoped so, but I wasn't sure, and anyway I had more pressing matters to consider, and I needed a drink while I considered them.

To my surprise, Adam was in the kitchen. I hadn't seen him downstairs more than a handful of times; his coding, or whatever obscure work he did, he did in his bedroom, and any laundry or cooking happened while Tansy and I were at work. It had been several days – maybe even a week – since I'd seen him at all. It was a bit like living with a ghost, if ghosts used shedloads of Lynx and ate lots of tinned tuna.

He was sitting at the table, drinking tea and reading something on his tablet, and looked pretty normal, although as pale and hollow-eyed as he'd been every time I saw him. He was wearing tracksuit bottoms and a faded T-shirt that looked like it had been a freebie at some gaming conference, and his long, thin feet were bare and, I couldn't help noticing, a bit grubby. Although to be fair to him, the kitchen floor was none too clean either. Now that Maddy wasn't around, gently pointing out to Odeta what needed doing in between asking her about her family in Romania, all of whom she'd seemed to know by name, Odeta was letting her standards slip. If I was ever going to invite Myles round to spend the night, I'd have to have a word with her or, more likely, do some cleaning myself. *Damn it, Maddy, I miss you.*

'Hi,' I said to Adam. 'How's it going? It's such a nice evening, I was going to have a drink in the garden.'

'Hello,' he muttered back.

I opened the fridge and saw only an almost-empty bottle of sauvignon blanc, which wouldn't cut it at all, the way I was feeling.

Then I remembered the bottles of tequila and triple sec Maddy had left in the cabinet under the telly.

'You never know when you'll need an emergency margarita, chick,' she'd said.

Well, I needed one right now. And there were even some limes, only slightly withered, that Tansy must have left in the fruit bowl.

'Fancy a cocktail?' I said to Adam.

'I'll pass,' he said.

'Suit yourself.' I squeezed and stirred and salted, and when my cocktail was ready I sipped. It tasted pretty damn good. Fishing my phone out of my bag, I headed towards the garden.

Then Adam said, 'How does it feel, knowing that you're doing something so evil?'

I froze, my mind whirling. He didn't know about Myles. He couldn't. And anyway, Myles wasn't married – at least not very. Not married, married. But Adam didn't even know who he was, or where I'd been.

'What are you talking about?' I asked, trying to sound cool and unflustered, but actually sounding guilty and a bit panicky.

'Your job, obviously. Working in the industry that caused the crash and the recession. Making money off people's misery. You know how many people are homeless right now, in this country, because of people like you? You know how many kids are living below the poverty line?'

For Adam, it was quite the speech, and the shock of not only what he said, but hearing him say anything much at all to me, left me dumbstruck for a second.

Then I said, 'You know I'm just an office assistant, right? I type letters and make coffee and order sandwiches. Or I would order sandwiches if anyone ate them, which they don't, so I order sashimi. I'm not some financial mastermind.'

'An office assistant,' he said mockingly. 'Yeah, right. How much would you earn in the public sector, doing that? If they even had people to order their lunch and make their coffee and type their fucking letters, which they don't, because cuts. Not enough to live here, that's for fucking sure.'

I couldn't have been more surprised if he'd chucked his mug of tea at me. Silent, surly Adam suddenly coming out of his shell to have a go at me for – of all things – my job. It was bizarre. It could only have been more bizarre if he'd come out of his shell to join me in a drink and chat pleasantly about who was going to win *Strictly Come Dancing*.

'You live here, too,' I pointed out. 'And your cousin Henry only doesn't any more because his grandfather passed away and left him enough money to buy a house. Which is hardly honestly earned income, is it?'

'Don't bring my family into it,' Adam said.

'What? I'm not bringing your family into anything. You started this. For God's sake, I get home, all I want to do is have a quiet evening, I offer you a drink and you start having a massive go at me for nothing at all. What's wrong with you?'

'What's wrong with questioning the mechanisms that keep wealth in the hands of one per cent of the population?' Adam demanded. 'What's wrong with objecting to a system that lets the rich derive profit from war and famine? What's wrong with having a problem with offshore shell companies that let people avoid paying millions of pounds in taxes that could make a real difference to the most disadvantaged people on the planet? You might want to ask yourself those questions, instead of asking what's wrong with *me*. I'm perfectly all right.'

'Okay, since we're talking about disadvantaged people,' I said, 'maybe you'd like to tell me how much Colton Capital donated to charity in the past year? You don't know? Well, I do. Four hundred thousand pounds. Maybe you'd like to know about the foundation Colin set up to help disadvantaged youths in deprived areas go on to further education, and how many of them he's helped. I'll tell you. Seventy-four. Two of them went to Cambridge last year. How's that for keeping wealth and power in the hands of the elite? Maybe you'd like to hear about the micro-lending scheme we invested in, and how many women in rural Pakistan it's lifted out of poverty. But no, you don't want to hear about those things, because they don't suit your silly dewy-eyed keyboard warrior agenda. Now I'm going to sit outside and enjoy my drink. It's been nice talking to you.'

Adam stood up. For a second I wondered whether now was the moment when he was going to twat the dregs of his PG Tips at me, and what I'd do if he did. But he didn't. He rinsed the mug in the sink and put it in the dishwasher, and I bit back a comment about how wasteful water consumption in the western world was contributing to global scarcity, not least because I wasn't sure whether it was, or how.

'Whatever,' he said and stomped upstairs, leaving me standing open-mouthed, wondering what the hell had just happened.

It was as if an element of the house that I'd got used to being mildly annoying in a particular way – the rug Maddy bought last year for the hallway, for instance, which tripped us up every time we came and went for months until we learned to step carefully onto it rather than dragging our feet and letting it have its wicked way with us – had suddenly risen up and revealed itself to have an agenda we couldn't have imagined.

Adam didn't like me – he'd made that pretty clear by avoiding me and then, when me being there was the price he had to pay for going out for beer and pizza with Tansy, by being openly rude to me. Being disliked by someone I shared a house with wasn't ideal, obviously, but given how little our paths crossed, I could deal with it. I'd mentally prepared myself for the awkwardness of living with strangers when Maddy and Henry had moved out, and it had been an unexpected bonus that Tansy had turned into a friend. Although, I thought sadly, now that she and Renzo were an item she'd be around less often, leaving me and Adam orbiting each other in silence like hostile planets.

Then a horrible thought struck me. Adam was Henry's cousin. In her preamble to today's bridesmaids' conference (had it really been just this morning? It felt like about a hundred years ago), Bianca had said something about how we were all going to be divided up among the tables, each with one of the groom's ushers as our opposite number.

'It might mean that you won't be at the same table as your partner,' she'd said, and I remember noticing Molly wince. 'But luckily, some of us don't have partners.'

Yeah, cheers for that. Nice of you to rub my face in my single status. Again. And, if I knew Bianca, she'd take charge of the table plan and make sure that I was seated with Adam, especially if she got so much as a whiff of the news that he and I didn't get on.

But I wasn't technically single – was I? I'd met Myles. I'd told Bianca I'd met him. He'd told me he had feelings for me, even though he hadn't asked me to be his girlfriend, not as such. But then, he was almost ten years older than me. He would probably think that was childish and unnecessary, now that we were sleeping together. Surely that made us exclusive? Exclusive, that was, apart from the minor detail of him having a wife. Not a wife, I reminded myself. A soon-to-be-ex-wife. Just as soon as all the details were ironed out.

I wasn't a bad person. I wasn't a home-wrecker who went around shagging married blokes just because I could. I hadn't even known. *And if you had known, Charlotte? If he'd told you in the beginning what he told you today, what would you have done?*

I didn't know, at first. And then I thought about it some more, about how it felt when Myles kissed me, touched me, fucked me. I heard in my head the words he'd said to me, the sadness he felt about his loveless, empty marriage, the future he saw us sharing together. *You're special, Charlotte*, he'd said. The memory of him made me shiver with happiness. I could make him as happy as he made me.

And it wasn't like we were living in the Dark Ages, or the 1950s or some other time in the distant past when having relationships with divorced people was shameful or even sinful. In fact, I remembered reading just the other day that even the Catholic Church was softening its stance on the issue – and when the Catholic Church softens a stance on something, you know public opinion on it must have changed forever ago. Chloë's boyfriend, the wonderful Gareth, had been married before and had a little boy, who stayed with him every other weekend. Margot at work was married to her second husband. Colin was on marriage number three, for heaven's sake. No one thought anything of it.

Except he's not divorced, is he, Charlotte? niggled the annoying voice in my head, which I was beginning to suspect might belong to my conscience. *He isn't even properly separated. The. Man. Lives. With. His. Wife.*

I remembered the instant, reflexive guilt I'd felt when Adam had said, 'How does it feel, knowing that you're doing something so evil?' I hadn't known, that was the whole point, that was why Adam's accusation had felt so unfair, even though it had turned out to be about something quite different. Which reminded me, I'd have to ask Xander, who was work's resident expert on ethical investment, just how evil Colton Capital really was in the grand scheme of things. He'd know. And anyway, surely, if the firm was that bad, on a moral scale of angelic to reprehensible, someone ethical wouldn't be working there in the first place.

But this wasn't about work. Deep down, I was pretty sure that Adam was wrong, and anyway I didn't much care what he thought of me. But I cared what I thought, what my friends would think, even what the Bad Girl would think. Was this the sort of thing she'd meant when she said, 'Know what your red lines are'? I strongly suspected it was. Even if what I was doing wasn't evil, it wasn't right either.

Myles said he was going to leave his wife. He said he'd already checked out of the marriage in every way except the fact of a house needing to be sold and assets divided up. But the point was, those things hadn't happened yet, and until they had, I realised, I simply couldn't carry on.

I wandered back into the kitchen in a bit of a daze, tipped the remaining margarita out of the cocktail shaker into my glass, made another and nicked a tube of Tansy's Pringles from the cupboard. It was going to be a good long while, I guessed, until anyone saw me naked again, so I might as well trough the lot, and to hell with my bridesmaid's dress.

Then I went and sat outside again, and started to compose a long text to Myles. I explained about how Adam had inadvertently made me realise that sleeping with Myles went against all my principles. I told him that however happy I was when we were together, that happiness would be tainted by the knowledge that he wasn't properly mine, and that I was doing something I was ashamed of. I told him that if what we had together was worth anything at all, it would still be there in six months, or after however long it took for him to extract himself from his marriage.

And then I read over it all again, thought what an overwrought, navel-gazy load of bollocks it was, and deleted it all. Instead, I texted him just two simple sentences.

I don't date married men, sorry. It was fun.

Then I finished my drink and the crisps, mindlessly, not really tasting either of them. I felt like crying but somehow I couldn't get around to it, even though I knew a good old howl would probably make me feel better. I thought about texting Tansy or Chloë and begging for reassurance that I'd done the right thing, but I knew perfectly well that I'd be hoping they'd reply saying, 'Don't be a crazy woman! Text him back right now and tell him you've changed your mind!' and what they'd actually say would be, 'What a sleaze, not telling you until after you'd shagged him! Run for the hills and don't look back!'

It was after midnight when I finally realised I was too cold to sit outside any longer. I went upstairs and had a hot shower, washing the memory of Myles's body off me for good and not caring if the sound of the running water woke Adam. But when I went to bed I could see from the crack of light under his door that he was still awake.

I slept horribly, disturbed not only by imaginary texts from Myles begging me to change my mind, but by skittering, scratching sounds that seemed to be coming from the landing. Great. Not only was I single once again and apparently doomed to remain so, but my reclusive weirdo housemate who hated me had been eating in his bedroom and now we had mice.

Chapter Fourteen

Hi there and welcome back to Sorry Not Sorry! *I've got a challenge for you today that I promise you're going to love, because it's one that's gonna bring out your inner bad girl. But when I tell you what it is, I don't want you to freak out. You're not going to freak out? Good. Because times have changed, and nowadays you don't have to go into some sketchy shop on Times Square full of creepy old men in raincoats to buy these things. You can order them discreetly online, and they don't just feel great, they look great too. You see where we're going with this? You're ready for the challenge? I knew it!*

'Oh my God, it was so totally amazing,' Tansy said. 'He'd booked us a suite, seriously, with a dining table and everything, and this enormous marble bathroom with Diptyque toiletries – full-size ones, and they replaced them every day so I brought loads home, take whatever you want – and fluffy bathrobes, and fresh flowers and a fruit platter and champagne on ice and everything. It was so fabulous, but as soon as we walked in I just looked at the bed and that was all I could think about, and I started to feel really nervous.'

'I can imagine,' I said. 'So carry on – did you jump on him then and there?'

'No! I kind of wanted to, obviously, but, like I said, I was so nervous. We unpacked our stuff and it was so awkward, we were really formal with each other, just sort of dancing around the room trying not to get in each other's way, even though we'd had such a laugh on the Eurostar on the way. And I was really embarrassed when I put my stuff in the bathroom because his is all from Aesop and mine's, like, Superdrug own brand.'

I laughed. 'Shamed by your toiletries. I bet he didn't even notice. And then?'

Tansy chucked a handful of spinach leaves into the stir-fry she'd offered to make for us both, having said that she'd eaten so much over the weekend she'd been craving green vegetables all day. She'd spent quite a bit of time telling me all about the confit duck, oysters with mignonette sauce (she had to explain to me what that was), and crêpes with Nutella, and my stomach literally started rumbling listening to her. What with that, and the fact I'd spent most of the previous day in bed making further inroads into her stash of Pringles and Penguin biscuits, I was all too glad of a healthy dinner myself.

'Then he asked if I wanted to go out and explore or have a drink or something, or if I was tired and wanted to lie down for a bit, and he actually blushed, and I realised he was just as nervous as me.'

'Renzo, nervous? I knew he liked you but this is serious stuff.'

'I know!' She turned away from the cooker and did a sort of delighted squirm. 'He really was. Bless him, it was so sweet. So I said what I really wanted was to have a shower, because even though we'd been in first class and got a taxi from the station, you know how manky travelling makes you feel.'

I said I did know, although travel for me had always tended to be packed into a Ryanair cabin with groups of lairy stags, and it was hard to imagine the luxury of first class on the Eurostar.

'He said, "Shall I meet you downstairs in the bar?" because obviously he thought I'd be embarrassed about getting undressed in front of him. Although honestly, Charlotte, that suite was so huge we could have lived in it for a week and not seen each other naked if we hadn't wanted to, and anyway there were two bathrooms. Seriously! So I said it was fine, and he said in that case he'd shower too, and we did, but not together, obviously.'

There was nothing obvious about it, but I didn't say so. I plonked a couple of bowls on the table and found some chopsticks left over from a long-ago takeaway, and put the chopping board and knives Tansy had used in the dishwasher while she added various finishing touches to our dinner, which smelled way better than anything so healthy had any right to.

'And it was so funny, Charlotte. We came out of the shower – the showers – at exactly the same time. He wasn't wearing the hotel bathrobe and nor was I; we were both just wrapped in towels. And we just looked at each other and smiled, and I knew there was no point in waiting, really, it was going to happen right then.'

'And it did?' I picked up my chopsticks. I wasn't feeling hungry any more; there was a sudden hollowness inside me that I knew food wouldn't fill. It was envy, I realised, because if there wasn't going to be a happy ending to Tansy's story I would know by now, and she didn't yet know the unhappy ending mine had.

'Mhmm,' she said, tackling her food with enthusiastic expertise. 'Ah, it was lovely. He's lovely. I won't go into details because you have to work with the bloke and you don't need to be thinking about his penis when you meet over the photocopier, or whatever. But I can confirm it's right up there with the best. Like, not just the size, but the—'

'Tansy!' I covered my ears with my hands.

'Sorry, sorry,' she said, and then she mouthed, 'Not sorry.'

'Anyway,' I said firmly, 'if you've quite finished mooning over Renzo's tackle, what did you do the rest of the weekend?'

She inhaled some more food and beamed. 'All the things! We went out for dinner that night to this amazing restaurant, and I was so glad we'd got the sex out of the way, because otherwise I wouldn't have been able to eat a thing. But we were both starving, and we had four courses and champagne and this amazing red wine he chose, from Château Pétrus or something. And then the next day we just walked and walked, and he didn't mind when I made him go into all the high-end fashion boutiques so I could stroke things and make some notes about trends for next season. It's so weird, you know, Charlotte, I meet the marketing people from the top houses at shows and they're perfectly nice and everything, but I could tell going into those shops that they knew Renzo could spend money there but I couldn't.'

Her face had kind of clouded over.

I said, 'Don't give it another thought. They're notorious in those shops for being vile to people unless you've practically got an Amex Platinum card surgically attached to you. Go on about your weekend.'

'He paid for everything,' Tansy said. 'He wouldn't even let me buy a coffee, even though I kept offering. So I could afford to buy gifts for Mum and Perdita and my niece and nephew – I'll show you later what I got, they'll love them. And he bought me this gorgeous scarf, look.'

She produced a tissue-wrapped parcel and carefully opened it, holding up a square of silk, patterned like a Fabergé egg, only slightly abstract and scribbly, in pink, mint green and gold.

'It cost five hundred euros,' she said. 'Imagine! For a scarf. But all the French women wear scarves all the time. They're so stylish, Charlotte, you won't believe. They've all got perfect messy hair and they rock a bold lip, and they have perfect skin and look like they've spent hours in front of the mirror even when they're wearing jeans and trainers. And they're so thin! I suppose it's because they all smoke.'

'Lung cancer: a small price to pay for being a size six,' I said.

Tansy laughed. 'Don't worry, I'm not about to start on the fags. I did spend about an hour in front of the mirror watching scarf-tying videos on YouTube, though. And Renzo didn't even mind. He watched and made suggestions and told me when I'd got it right. He's so lovely. And he speaks fluent French, did you know? As well as Italian, obviously, and a bit of Russian.'

'They're all like that at work. Pavel speaks seven languages, all of them narkily.'

But Tansy didn't want to talk about polyglots in the finance industry.

'And then on Saturday night we went out again, to this amazing little place on the Left Bank – it was really casual, not posh at all, but oh my God, the food! We had oysters and steak and the most perfect lemon tart, and then we walked some more – all along the river in the moonlight, it was amazing. There's this bridge where people used to put padlocks to represent commitment, and we stopped there, and he kissed me, and I thought maybe if we'd had a padlock… But it's too soon, isn't it?'

'Yes, probably,' I said. 'But it sounds like you had such an amazing time! Who knew Renzo was so…'

So what, I wondered. So generous? That didn't surprise me. I knew how much he earned, and I knew a weekend in Paris, even with all the stops pulled out and a five-hundred-euro scarf thrown in, was roughly equivalent to going to Westfield and buying a pair of jeans at New Look and a sandwich at Pret for me. So romantic? Why wouldn't he be, taking a beautiful girl away for a weekend when he was planning to sleep with her for the first time? I remembered Tansy's words before, about how his kindness had surprised her, and that surprised me too. She was describing a side of my colleague I'd never seen – a tenderness, a patience, a willingness to do small things that pleased her. But then, why would he show that side of his personality at work, in an environment where winning was everything, and risk-taking and ruthlessness were what got you there? For all I knew, he was a total pussycat with all his girlfriends. He was Italian, after all, and I knew all the clichés about Latin lovers.

'Do you think he really likes me, Charlotte? I'm so worried that I wasn't cool enough. Maybe I should have played hard to get, but I just couldn't, you know? Seeing him there in the bedroom, wrapped in a towel. I was just, like, phwoar.'

If I saw Renzo wrapped in a towel, straight out of the shower, in a glamorous Paris hotel, I'd have been, like, phwoar too. But I didn't say so to Tansy – the last thing she needed was to think I fancied her new boyfriend, when I spent every day with him at work.

Instead I said, 'It really, really sounds as if he likes you. I'm so excited for you. When are you seeing him again?'

'Well, he asked me to go back to his on Sunday night, but I said no. I wanted to, but then I thought we'd both have to be up early for work the next day and it would be all rushed and stressful, and I wanted to keep the magic going a bit.'

'Quite right too,' I said. 'There's no harm in taking things slow at first. Not being too eager.'

'Oh, bollocks to that! I don't want to play games with him. I really like him and I don't care if he knows it.'

'I'm fairly sure he knows it already,' I said. 'And I bet he feels the same way. Just, you know, be careful.'

'I'm on the Pill!' she protested. 'And we used condoms, obviously.'

'That's not what I meant,' I said, but I knew she knew that.

'Anyway. Enough about me! I almost forgot, you saw Myles again at the weekend, too. How did that go?'

Reluctantly, gloomily, I told her.

'Oh Charlotte,' she said. 'Oh no! I can't believe it. What a bastard!'

'You don't think he was telling the truth, then? About his marriage being basically over?'

Tansy chewed briefly at a fingernail, then stopped, looked at her hand and got out a nail file. 'Maybe. Maybe he was. But he should have told you earlier. It's just not fair, is it? Not giving you a piece of information like that, which is kind of central to whether you decide to have a relationship with a guy.'

'But let's say it is true,' I said. 'And I've told him to get lost. What if I've thrown away my only chance with him?'

Tansy shook her head. 'You'll find out. You've done the right thing. I'm so sorry.'

And I had to be content with that. She wasn't going to give me permission to fling myself into a relationship with him regardless, I realised – no one was.

I saw less of Tansy over the next couple of weeks. When she wasn't at work or at the gym, she was with Renzo or asleep. Her long night-time chats with her mum and sister seemed to have stopped almost completely, so I assumed their shifts must have changed to day ones, and she didn't play music in her room at night any more, either.

But then, I was working crazy hours too – we all were, including Renzo, although I did notice that he was managing to leave the office by nine most nights, presumably to take Tansy for dinner at posh restaurants and then have ecstatic sex with her in his fabulous flat while I went home and got into bed alone.

Not that I was jealous, or anything.

Glumly, propped up on my pillows, I looked at the plain black box on my bedside table. When it had arrived, I'd almost forgotten what it was, because when I'd ordered it I'd felt so different. All daring and sexy, ready to discover new things about myself and my body like the Bad Girl said I should. Now I just felt lonely and forlorn, wishing I could go back to Oleg's basement and the delight I'd experienced there.

Well… maybe I could. But it would have to be alone, in my head.

I opened the box and inspected the object inside. It was innocent enough to look at – pretty, even. A gently curved silver wand, shaped a bit like a candle flame, although quite a lot bigger. If I left it on my dressing table or plugged into a USB port on my laptop to charge, and Adam or Odeta saw it, they probably wouldn't even know what it was.

Okay, they *so* would. Who was I kidding?

I lifted it out and pressed one of the buttons. There was a faint buzzing sound, and a gentle but powerful thrum made my hand tingle.

Cor. Feeling ridiculously self-conscious, I turned out the light and slid the vibrator under the duvet.

I'd think of Myles, remember the last time we were together, and even though I'd never see him again, I could at least relive some of the pleasure he'd given me. I closed my eyes and parted my legs and let the magic happen. And OMFG, it really did. I went from 'oh' to 'oooh' to 'yasss!' in just a few minutes.

And then it all went wrong. Seriously, horribly wrong. Just as my pleasure peaked, the face I was imagining in my mind changed. Instead of it being Myles kneeling between my legs, exploring me with his expert fingers and tongue, my imagination pulled a bizarre switcheroo. As I was about to orgasm, my lover stopped being him and became… Xander. Work Xander. Xander with a smile on his face and an impressive erection that he plunged inside me just as I came.

I was left limp with pleasure and burning with embarrassment. I didn't even fancy the man. And I had to see him in the office every bloody day. How the hell was I going to meet his eyes without him guessing the utterly filthy thoughts I'd accidentally had about him? And, even worse, what if I bumped into him in the lift or somewhere and started having them again?

Chapter Fifteen

Hello and welcome back to Sorry Not Sorry. *I'm recording this podcast with my hair in rollers and a sheet mask on my face and let me tell you, it's just as well you can hear me but not see me, because you'd run screaming for the hills! Girlfriend, tonight I am going out, out! One of my besties is turning the big three-O and a group of us are hitting the town. I. Can. Not. Wait. I'm going to talk in a little while about friends, and how important they are, especially when you're dating and it feels like it's taking over your life to the exclusion of everything else.*

But first, my challenge to you tonight: hit the town, let your hair down and have some fun! Drink, dance, laugh until your sides ache – reconnect with your friends and your carefree, single self. And if you end up making out with some stranger on the dance floor – well, I won't tell anyone!

Maddy's hen weekend got off to an inauspicious start – and then got worse. As I sat alone in a cab on my way to Gatwick to meet the others and catch our flight to Lisbon, I remembered again how much I'd been looking forward to this – even more than the actual wedding, to be brutally honest, because weddings aren't a whole lot of fun when you're single. But that was before I'd spent hours, when I should have been working, hunting for apartments that would meet Bianca's standards – and be as lovely as I wanted our base for Maddy's special girls' weekend to be, of course – researching local bars and restaurants using websites that were mostly in Portuguese so I couldn't make head or tail of them, and trying and failing to organise the local equivalent of an Ocado delivery. So now that the weekend was here, I realised I was dreading it. It felt as if, in our group of five, we were divided into Team Bianca and Team Charlotte and, increasingly, like the only person on Team Charlotte was me. To make matters worse, Bianca had decreed that this was to be a tat-free event: no cock deely boppers, no penis straws, no L plates, no fairy wings, no tiaras, not even any T-shirts with 'Maddy's Hens' screen-printed on them in glitter – none of the fun, naff stuff I'd imagined us all wearing, giggling about, Instagramming and no doubt cringing over in years to come.

Still, I reminded myself, if that was what Maddy wanted, that was what Maddy must have. It was her weekend, and I resolved to be as cheerful as I could and not be the cause of any rows, because if it all went wrong because of me, I'd never forgive myself.

The taxi pulled up with plenty of time to spare, and I got my bag from the boot. There were no new messages in the Slack group so I decided I might as well go and check in, and find the others once I'd been through security.

Then, just as I was turning towards the glass doors of the airport, a huge, pink stretch limo with tinted windows pulled up. I waited, trying not to look as if I were staring, but looking forward to seeing its deely-boppered, tiara-wearing, matching-T-shirted occupants spill out, no doubt already half pissed, nailing their hen weekend tat-fest.

But when the pink doors opened, out climbed Molly, Chloë, Bianca and Maddy.

To be fair, they did look totally mortified when they saw me.

'Hello,' Maddy muttered.

'Isn't the limo cool?' Molly said. 'You really should have come.'

'We thought maybe you couldn't pay your share of it,' said Chloë, which was a bit much given that she was the one who was always complaining about being skint.

'I guess Charlotte preferred to make her own way here,' Bianca said, with a sweet smile that looked to me like pure poison. 'Seeing as how she thinks limos are a bit… tacky, was it?'

I opened my mouth to protest, but then forced myself to stop, not wanting to get Maddy's weekend off to a bad start.

'You know how it goes. I'm trying to save for a deposit on a flat and sometimes you just have to cut back. Anyway, at least we're all here now. Hope you enjoyed the ride.'

In awkward silence, we all trooped into the airport and dropped off our bags, then made our way straight to our boarding gate. There was no talk about finding somewhere to have a drink, I noticed. There wasn't much talk at all, in fact. I thought I heard Maddy say something, and then I heard Bianca laugh.

'Look at that queue,' I said. 'I can never understand why people stand and wait when they've got seats booked and they know perfectly well all the priority boarding people and wheelchair users and so on will get on before them anyway. Let's sit and wait for them to call our row.'

But the other four didn't sit and wait. Maddy and Bianca carried on past me, heading for the front of the queue.

Chloë grabbed my arm and said, 'Come on, Charlotte! We're all in business class.'

Molly saw the expression on my face, and said, 'We got upgraded, remember? Because Bianca's hubby's got loads of air miles. She organised it.'

'Did you not get the message about that?' Chloë asked.

'No, I guess I didn't. My ticket is definitely economy, so I'll see you in Lisbon then, I suppose.' Tears stung my eyes as I joined the back of the queue.

Presumably in business class the free champagne would be flowing like water, and I resolved to make sure it did the same in cattle class. When the stewardess came round with the drinks trolley, I said, 'I'd like some fizz, please. As much as they'll let you give me.'

I watched as the poor woman thought about it, glanced at the rows and rows of customers waiting impatiently to be served, and decided that not only was I a respectable type and unlikely to get pissed and rowdy on a three-hour flight, but she couldn't be bothered entering into an argument about it. She handed over three miniature bottles of sparkling wine, and I spent the rest of the journey steadily making my way through them.

So, when we landed in Lisbon and saw the blue skies and radiant sunshine through a mellowing haze of alcohol, we were all prepared to set aside hostilities – whatever their cause – for the time being. We shared a taxi to the apartment I'd found after hours of research on Airbnb, which Bianca had eventually approved and allowed me to book, and to my relief it was gorgeous, with stone floors and high ceilings and views of the castle through the haze of purple bougainvillea that surrounded the windows, and three luxurious bedrooms with en suite bathrooms.

'Well done, Charlotte,' Bianca said. 'I can see all your experience in booking international travel for bankers has paid off.'

I decided to ignore the fact that she was clearly being as patronising as fuck, and said thanks.

'There should be a load of cava, or espumante, or whatever it's called, in the fridge,' I said, 'and I asked them to get some ham and olives, and bread and coffee and stuff, in for us too. So we won't starve.'

For the first time in what felt like ages, Maddy met my eyes and gave me a proper, genuine smile that filled me with happiness and relief.

'Thanks, babe. Honestly, thanks, all of you. It's so amazing to be here, I can't believe you've organised all this for me.'

'Never mind that,' Molly said. 'It's your hen do. We have a sacred duty to go out and party.'

So we did. We all showered and changed and did our make-up together around the kitchen table, just like Maddy and I had done when we were teenagers getting ready to go out on the razz in the Bigg Market, and headed out into the warm night, and those of us wearing heels immediately regretted it when we discovered that every street in the entire city was not only insanely steep but cobbled, too. But after a few drinks we didn't care too much about that, and we managed to stagger round a few bars without anyone faceplanting, and then we had a delicious dinner in a restaurant I'd found, and then we went on to a club – at least, four of us did; Bianca said she had a migraine and got a cab back to the apartment.

As soon as she'd left, what little tension there had been in the group did, too. I ordered a round of margaritas, and we drank them and then ordered another. Maddy laughed the raucous laugh I used to hear so often, and started to slip back into the Geordie accent I thought she'd shed long ago. Molly stopped checking her phone to see if William had texted her. We all got up and danced around our handbags, throwing shapes and shrieking with laughter.

'Hey, Charlotte!' Chloë shouted over the music. 'See that man over there? The hot one in the leopard-print shirt? He so fancies you. If you didn't have a boyfriend…'

I looked across the room and clocked leopard-man. He was leaning against the bar, holding a beer, and seemed to be looking at the room in general. But when he saw me notice him, he met my eyes and smiled.

'See?' Chloë said. 'Go on, go and talk to him – double-dare you! What happens in Lisbon stays in Lisbon!'

I wasn't quite brave enough to leave my friends, but I couldn't help glancing over to him again. This time, he smiled and raised his glass to me, before draining it and putting it back on the bar. I smiled back and then, just to see what would happen, made a little 'come over' gesture.

Amazingly, he did. He slipped through the crowd and joined us, and suddenly there weren't four of us dancing together, but my three friends and then him and me, in the same group but somehow separate. I felt my body's rhythm change, not cheesily sending up the dance moves any more, but moving confidently, my eyes fixed on his face while my muscles seemed to know exactly what to do.

The track merged smoothly into another, a trancey techno one I didn't know, and I wondered if the others were going to sit down. But they didn't. I kept dancing, kept meeting the eyes of the tall, smiling stranger. The press of people around us grew thicker and we moved nearer together, so my hips brushed his as I swayed them in time to the music. He reached out a hand and touched my waist, pulling me even closer.

I let myself be pulled, and when his face lowered towards mine and I knew he was going to kiss me, I let that happen, too. For the whole of the next two songs, our bodies and our mouths were locked together as we snogged like we'd invented snogging.

It was brilliant. I didn't care that I didn't know his name and would never see him again. I was just there in the moment: thrilled to have become someone who caught a man's eye in a club, danced with him and kissed him, right there, not caring who saw us. It felt daring and almost dangerous – but safe, too, because my mates were there and wouldn't let things go too far and would make sure nothing dodgy happened to me.

And maybe it was because I'd had so much to drink, but it felt like the Bad Girl was there too, looking out for me and cheering me on as I completed her challenge.

And when, after a bit, I felt a tap on my shoulder and Maddy said, 'Chick, sorry to interrupt you, but Molly's not feeling great,' I gave him one final kiss, smiled and turned away, back to my friends.

We frog-marched Molly to the toilet and held her hair while she threw up, and afterwards she said she felt way better, and she loved us all, and we bought more espumante, which Chloë tried to order in Portuguese before discovering that the barman spoke perfect English. The man in the leopard-print shirt had gone, but I didn't care.

It was almost two o'clock in the morning when we reeled drunkenly and happily back to the apartment, which I discovered was wired for sound, so we found a playlist of retro nineties music and danced like loons and drank more fizz, and after a bit Molly said she was fading and went to bed, and Chloë passed out on the sofa, and then it was just Maddy and me left.

'Happy hen weekend,' I said, topping up our glasses for what I knew should be the last time that night, but was fairly sure wouldn't be. 'Are you having fun?'

'The most fun. Being here with all of you, my best mates, in this amazing place, getting married in six weeks… I'm just, awww.'

She spread out her arms and leaned back on the sofa, looking as happy as I'd ever seen her, just like the old Maddy, her eyes all bleary behind her stylish specs with her dark fringe flopping over her face.

'Are things okay with you, Maddy? With us?' I asked. I knew I shouldn't do anything to rock the boat, but the booze had loosened my tongue and I just couldn't hold it in any longer. 'I know it's all so stressful and stuff, but I've been worried you're mad at me. For some reason. Or something.'

'Charlotte, I'm not sure I can talk about this right now.'

She'd sat up again, although a bit wonkily, and wrapped her arms around herself.

I said, 'It's okay. Whenever. I don't want to fuck up your hen do. It's just, I'm worried I've done something to hurt you, and…'

Then the door to the bedroom Maddy was sharing with Bianca opened and Bianca emerged, looking smudged with sleep and also furious.

'I don't want to break the mood,' she interrupted, 'But remember we've got our first activity booked for ten a.m. and our bride needs her sleep! And that music is, like, really loud; we do need to consider our neighbours! Shall we call it a night?'

I looked at Maddy and she looked at me, but the moment was over.

'Is that really the time?' I asked no one in particular. 'Night, then.'

And Maddy said goodnight too, and we poured ourselves big glasses of water and she went off to the room she was sharing with Bianca and I went to the room I had to myself, and went to sleep when the world eventually stopped spinning.

I could tell the second I woke up the next morning that the mood had changed overnight. This wasn't down to any leap of intuition on my part, but rather the fact that what had woken me up was Bianca and Chloë having a massive row in the kitchen.

'Why the rush?' Chloë was saying. 'Weren't we just going to spend the morning chilling out and having breakfast and stuff, then go to the spa thing this afternoon? I've got such a foul hangover, I need some Berocca and tea and then maybe to go back to bed for a bit.'

'We said we were going to book a pole dancing class,' Bianca hissed. 'That's what we agreed. It was on the Slack group. And it was your job to do it.'

Great, I thought. A pole dancing class. Just what I needed with a hangover. Surely even the Bad Girl would draw the line at that?

'Well, I didn't,' Chloë said sullenly. 'Sorry, okay? I guess I forgot. Or maybe I think pole dancing is a terrible idea.'

You're not the only one, I thought, reluctantly levering myself out of bed. I pulled on some clothes and cautiously left the safety of my bedroom.

'Well, look what the cat dragged in,' Bianca said snidely. 'I hope you slept well, after keeping the rest of us up all night.'

'Good morning.' I smiled cheerfully, remembering my promise to be all sweetness and light. 'Coffee, just what I need. Where's Maddy?'

'She went for a run,' Molly said. 'I was going to go too but I haven't got any trainers and anyway I had to throw up again. I feel better now though.'

'We were just discussing breakfast,' Chloë lied. 'I was going to head out and get some pastries.'

I said I'd keep her company, and we left the apartment for the sunlit street.

As soon as the door closed behind us, Chloë blurted out, 'Honestly, fucking pole dancing. What is she like? As if anyone wants to do that. She basically ordered me to book it, for ten o'clock in the morning no less, when anyone would have known we'd all be feeling terrible.'

I said tactfully that it wasn't the sort of activity I would have chosen, myself.

'Well, exactly,' Chloë said. 'And Maddy has zero co-ordination and would probably end up falling on her head. So I did us all a favour, except for Bianca, who does pole dancing classes at that ridiculously posh gym she's a member of, and wanted to show the rest of us up with her stripper moves.'

We wandered into a bakery and stocked up with a load of croissants, wholemeal bread for Maddy and Bianca and a dozen custard tarts because Chloë said if she didn't get some sugar in her she'd probably faint.

'Chloë, do you know what's going on?' I asked. 'I mean, with Maddy and Bianca? I don't really mind about the limo and the flight upgrades, though I thought it wasn't really like you guys. But I could have afforded my share, you know I could. And I didn't say I thought it was tacky. It just seems really weird, leaving me out of things. What did Bianca say to you?'

Chloë took a tart out of the box and bit off a corner of it. 'Look, Charlotte, I feel really bad about this, to be honest. The thing is, Bianca said that you'd said that finding the apartment had taken loads of your time and you didn't want to be involved in the organisation any more. She said that your nose was really out of joint because you weren't going to be chief bridesmaid, and you and Maddy had fallen out over it, and everyone knew that Maddy didn't want you to come on her hen weekend but if you were uninvited it would just cause even more bad feeling.'

I suddenly felt as sick as Chloë looked. 'Is that true? About Maddy, I mean?'

'I don't know. She hasn't said anything to me, honest. But it's been obvious that the two of you haven't been seeing each other as much as you did, so when Bianca said there'd been some big row, I believed her. But now I just don't know. When Maddy and Henry moved and they basically became neighbours and started seeing loads of each other, I thought Bianca was good fun. She's got this amazing life, you know, with her business and her perfect child and her banker husband and everything. But I think actually she's a bit of a bitch.'

Chloë might be a qualified solicitor but, bless her, she's never been the sharpest knife in the drawer.

'Cheers for that revelation, Sherlock,' I said, and she laughed. 'But it's not Bianca's hen weekend, or Bianca's wedding.'

'It might as well be,' Chloë said, 'the way she's, like, taken over the whole thing.'

I looked up at the dazzling sky, feeling the beginnings of tears and wishing I'd brought my sunglasses. I knew groups of women were meant to be prone to bitchiness and infighting, but it had honestly never been the case with our friends, up until now. And now, at what should have been a happy and exciting time that we could all enjoy together, everything seemed to be breaking down into a horrible mess.

'Look, this isn't about us,' I said. 'I just want to make everything okay for Maddy. I wish I knew what was going on with her, but I don't. I tried to talk to her about it last night but then Bianca came barging in. I hope she's just gone a bit off the rails with the wedding planning stuff and things will go back to normal soon.'

'She hasn't, though,' Chloë said. 'She's not being a bridezilla at all. She's really relaxed about it. It's Bianca who's being mental.'

I said she might have a point.

'The thing is,' Chloë carried on, 'I don't think Bianca's actually got very many friends. She sees some of the mums at Charis's school obviously, but that's more about the kids. And she has these flash dinner parties but I think that's mostly for her hubby Michael's friends and their wives. I think she's fallen out with loads of people and that's why she's latched onto Maddy.'

I wondered if I'd underestimated Chloë. Her analysis of the situation sounded spot on to me, but even if she'd nailed the inner workings of Bianca's psychology, that was no help to us now.

'Look,' I said. 'There's really nothing we can do about this right now. It's all so pathetic and bitchy and silly and boring, but we're stuck with it. We've got to go back in there, eat our breakfast, neck some paracetamol, and put up with whatever plans Bianca's made. Even if it does involve winding ourselves round poles in our knickers.'

'I shagged a Polish guy once,' Chloë said. 'I quite enjoyed winding myself round him in my knickers.'

So the two of us were giggling like idiots when we returned to the apartment.

'You took your time,' Bianca huffed. 'I hope you've brought some fruit, or granola, or something. Some of us are watching our figures.'

'I don't give a fuck about my figure right now,' Maddy said. 'I'm starving. That run nearly killed me.'

'You got croissants!' Molly said. 'Angels! And there's jam in the cupboard, I saw last night. I was thinking we could make some kind of jam-based cocktail, which in hindsight would have been a really terrible idea.'

'Gin and jam,' I said. 'The guy from Disrepute who just won mixologist of the year doesn't have to worry about the competition just yet.'

We all laughed, except Bianca, who had a face on her like she'd just taken a sip of a gin and jam cocktail.

I said, 'We got some wholemeal bread, though, if you're not in the market for carbs and lard.'

'Wholemeal bread is just as…' Bianca said. 'Oh, never mind. I'll just have a coffee.'

'Don't be daft, Bianca,' I soothed. 'Chloë and I went past an organic shop on our way back from the patisserie. They had loads of amazing-looking fruit outside, and I bet they'll have goji berries and cold-pressed juices and every hipster food known to man there. This is Lisbon – it's practically a suburb of Shoreditch. I'll pop out again, just tell me what you want. It'll take five minutes.'

Bianca looked startled, then she smiled. 'Are you sure, Charlotte? That's really sweet of you. Just some fresh berries, if they have any, and some nuts, only not roasted, salted or smoked, obviously, and some coconut yoghurt if they have it. And maybe a chai latte? But don't put yourself out.'

'It's no bother,' I said. And I sprinted down the stone staircase, full of the righteous glow of someone who's turned the other cheek. If we could only keep up this level of charm offensive, I thought, the weekend might yet be salvageable.

The organic shop, which I'd barely glimpsed when we passed it the first time, because Chloë and I had been so deep in conversation, turned out to be quite the happening place. Gorgeous people in yoga gear were browsing its aisles, sipping water from eco-friendly aluminium bottles. There was a pop-up stall selling freshly ground nut butters and a poster advertising mindfulness workshops (I don't want to give the impression that I'd suddenly acquired a working knowledge of Portuguese, but the fact that it said, '*Grupo semanal de Mindfulness*' was a pretty clear giveaway) and aisles packed with every wholefood known to man.

I browsed happily for a few minutes, enjoying my flirtation into a world which, while of course I'd known about, I'd never considered particularly relevant to me as a lazy, non-spiritual consumer of meat, cheese and fried egg butties. I allowed myself a little daydream in which I became a yoga-practising, mindful vegan, and moved to this beautiful city, where I'd find an equally beautiful, ripped, dark-haired boyfriend, because of course my new healthy lifestyle and serene outlook would have rendered me slender and swishy-haired with a pelvic floor that would drive a man wild.

Then I remembered that my existing pelvic floor had driven Myles mad without the need for core strengthening of any kind. God, I fancied him. I missed him. I wanted…

But now wasn't the time for idle fantasy, I told myself – I'd embarked on this errand to cement a fragile truce between Bianca and my friends. *Focus, Charlotte*, I told myself. In a sort of hippy Supermarket Sweep, I filled a basket with almonds, goji berries, hemp milk and something called spirulina powder, and then I queued up and bought a coconut chai latte. And then, feeling as zen and virtuous as if I'd just completed a six-hour yogathon in aid of endangered marine plankton, I hurried back to the apartment.

It was the strangest thing. When I left, the atmosphere had been congenial, if a bit tense. The bonds we'd reformed the previous night had seemed to be holding, and, if anything, Bianca had appeared to be on the outside again, rather than dividing us from within.

But the moment I opened the door, I could tell that something had changed. Everyone was standing around, dressed and made up, impatient to leave. There was a hum of chatter and a burst of laughter, but the moment I stepped into the kitchen, everyone fell silent.

'Here you go.' I put the brown paper carrier bag down on the table. 'The latte should still be hot.'

Maddy said, 'Actually, we really need to make a move now.'

'The pole dancing studio managed to fit us in after all.' Molly looked down at the floor.

'We've got an Uber on the way,' Chloë added, not meeting my eyes either.

'Oh. I haven't showered, though. Do I have time?' I asked.

Maddy said, 'No, sorry. You don't.'

I looked around at them. No one was smiling, except Bianca. She looked straight at me, and she smiled as gleefully as a child on Christmas morning.

Chapter Sixteen

Hi and welcome to this week's podcast. Over the past seven days, I've been going through a bit of a low time. I know I've talked a lot about how much fun dating is – and it is fun – but you know what? There are some really dark moments too. There are times when I wake up alone, or – even worse – wake up next to someone, and think to myself, 'What the hell am I doing here?' Times when I think I might as well give up on the whole dumb shebang and be alone forever.

So the challenge I have set for myself today is kind of simple, but also really hard. Don't give up on love. If you're feeling a bit sad and alone as you listen to this, give your head a wobble, woman! That's what I'm telling myself to do. I will find love – or it will find me!

I don't want to create the impression that I'm some kind of push-over. Honestly, I'm not. But I'll admit that I did, for just a second, consider meekly going along, unshowered and unbreakfasted, to the pole dancing class and sweating espumante all over the poor instructor, and spending the rest of the day looking like some scruffy minger my friends had brought along with them out of pity.

I considered it, but then I unconsidered it straight away. 'Look, I'm sorry, but I can't go anywhere like this. I need fifteen minutes to get myself ready. If you really need to leave now, that's okay. Let me know where to catch up with you later.'

'Fine,' Bianca said. 'We'll see you later then. Someone text Charlotte and let her know the plan.'

'Bye, Charlotte,' Chloë said.

'See you later.' Molly kind-of waved, without smiling.

Maddy didn't say anything. I watched as they all trooped out, and as soon as the door closed behind them, I flopped down on the sofa, suddenly exhausted.

What the fuck was the point of all this? So Bianca wanted a new group of friends. Fine. Our group had never been cliquey or exclusive – after all, I'd been accepted myself, without question, because I was Maddy's friend, new to London. The same could have been the case with Bianca, if she wanted to join in. And if she wasn't a total bitch, obviously.

And why was she picking on me? Okay, I was Maddy's best friend – if 'oldest' meant 'best'. But it's not like we had some rigid friend hierarchy going on, with me at the top and Bianca at the bottom. Maddy had loads of other mates – women from work she went to lunch with, women from her spin class she went for coffee with, even a couple of guys whose pug she'd had to put to sleep, and she'd been so lovely about it when they overstayed their appointment for half an hour because they couldn't stop crying, and now she and Henry got invited round to their anniversary party every year. I didn't care about any of them – I wasn't jealous. Because I wasn't twelve years old.

I picked up my phone and checked for texts, but there was only one – a message from Tansy asking how my weekend was going. I tapped out a short reply: *Fucking DIRE. Will tell you all when I'm back.* Thinking about going home made me realise that, actually, there was nothing stopping me doing just that. I could pack my stuff, get a taxi to the airport, take the hit of a few hundred quid for a new ticket (which, while annoying, would be a fair price to pay for being out of this nightmare) and be back in London before teatime.

But I ruled that idea out almost immediately. Whether it was loyalty, stubbornness or a belief that somehow the situation could be fixed, I don't know, but I forced myself to get up, shower and dress. I hadn't had any breakfast, but looking at the scattered remains of the croissants and custard tarts just made me feel sick. Not to mention the bloody goji berries I'd just spaffed fifteen euros on for her royal highness.

There was still no text from anyone. I checked Slack too, just in case, but there was no message there, either. So I was going to have to text them, cap in hand, like the no-mates I was beginning to realise I was.

But who to text? Not Bianca, obviously. Not Molly or Chloë, who both seemed quite willing to take part in Operation Ostracise Charlotte. It would have to be Maddy. I remembered how the previous night, just for a bit, it had felt like we were friends again, like nothing had changed. Surely we could get back to that?

Hey, I tapped. *I'm ready now. Let me know where to meet you and I'll jump in a cab.* Then I added a few random emojis: a bottle of fizz, a smiley face and the dancing lady, for want of a pole dancer.

I didn't expect Maddy not to reply at all, but I was pretty sure she would take her time about it. That was okay with me, I thought – it wasn't like the pole dancing class had been right at the top of my bucket list anyway. But, to my surprise, my phone buzzed almost straight away.

I glanced at the reply. *An offer I can't refuse! Unfortunately I'm in Lisbon with work again. God, I miss you.*

What the actual… I picked up my phone and then almost dropped the stupid, treacherous bit of kit in horror.

I'd texted Myles. Fuck, I'd gone and sent him a message, after keeping so strictly to my vow of silence all these weeks (and deleting the only text he'd sent me without even reading it) because his name was right below Maddy's on my contact list and looked similar enough to my distracted eye. And maybe there'd been some kind of Freudian slip at work as well, who knew. But he'd replied. And he was here. Right here, in this city, presumably working on his museum project. And he missed me. Was this some kind of sign?

I knew the right thing to do, of course. I should delete his text and block his number, right away. No explanation, no apology, nothing. And I was about to do it, when another text flashed up. *Just so you know, I'm leaving her. I'm moving out as soon as I get back to London. I told you in my last WhatsApp message, but you didn't read it.*

And that was it. My resolve snapped.

Fuck, I'm so sorry – that text was meant for my friend. Random – I'm in Lisbon too, on the hen weekend from hell.

Can you escape the hellish hens and meet me for a drink?

No, said my brain. *Yes,* went my thumbs on the keypad.

Come to my hotel? He named a place I remembered investigating when I was looking for places for Maddy's hens to stay, and spent far too long lusting after before ruling it out as being off-the-scale spendy. And, I remembered, it was just a few minutes' walk from our apartment.

Give me an hour, I texted. If Maddy messaged me, I promised myself, I wouldn't go. I really, really wouldn't. But my heart was pounding with excitement and my stomach felt hollow with longing and, I realised, lack of food. But there was no way I could eat anything now.

Instead, I flew into action. I straightened my hair, which I'd left to dry into a crinkly, frizzy mess after my shower. I smoothed tinted moisturiser on over the normal moisturiser I'd slapped on earlier. I peeled off the ordinary bra and pants I'd put on for pole dancing and got into the lacy black set I'd brought to wear that night, on the off-chance that I might pull a handsome man. I changed my shorts and vest top for a floaty maxi dress. I put on earrings, lipstick and perfume. I didn't stop to ask myself what the hell I was doing.

I checked my phone one final time, telling myself that if there was a message from Maddy or any of the others, I'd change right back again and head off and join them. But there wasn't. So I picked up my bag and walked the few minutes to Myles's hotel, although it actually took me almost half an hour because I was so nervous I went the wrong way at first and the cobbles were a nightmare in my high heels.

It was just as fabulous as it had looked online. It had a huge, flagstone-floored atrium with a glass roof, Oriental rugs and potted plants everywhere, and glamorous people sitting drinking sherry.

A glossy-haired doorman welcomed me and showed me the way to the bar.

And there, even more glamorous than any of the other guests, was Myles. He was sitting at a small table by the window, overlooking the castle and the sea beyond it. There was a bottle of the same Pol Roger we'd drunk at Oleg's house waiting in an ice bucket. *He remembered!* I thrilled. He was wearing jeans and a white linen shirt, and his hair was damp from the shower. When he hugged me, he smelled of limes and soap and hunky man.

'I'm so glad you came,' he murmured, his breath warm in my hair. 'I'm so glad you're here.'

I wasn't sure about either of those things, but I said, 'It's good to see you.'

And it was. It was so good that I quite literally couldn't take my eyes off him. I watched as he poured champagne into two glasses, then clinked his against mine.

'So, tell me about the hen from hell,' he said. 'What happened? Rival bridesmaids wanting to shag the male stripper? Someone was sick in someone else's Louboutins? Clutch bags at dawn?'

I laughed. 'Something like that.' And then I found myself pouring out the whole sorry story to him, trying to make light of it at first, but not succeeding as a lump appeared in my throat and got bigger and bigger until my voice started to sound all croaky and my nose started to run.

'Sorry.' I dug in my bag for a tissue. 'It's pathetic. And you didn't ask me here to hear me moan about my so-called friends.'

'It's not pathetic at all,' he said. 'It sounds really hurtful. You've every right to be upset.'

I turned my face away, feeling like an idiot and pretending to admire the view while I dabbed ineffectually at my eyes and nose.

'I'm so sorry,' I said again. 'It's just so mean and petty, and I don't even know what I've done wrong.'

He reached over and took my hand. 'Group dynamics are strange. And at a time like this, emotions running high, everyone expecting to have the best time ever – people can act in uncharacteristic ways. It's like those meltdowns that happen at family Christmases, right? Auntie Susan goes a bit cray on the Baileys and tells Auntie Debbie what she thinks of her new settee, and Debbie says Susan's never cooked a decent turkey in her life, and Susan says Debbie's children are all spoiled little scrotes who have learned their manners from their mum, and then their other halves pile in and punches are thrown and the neighbours call the peelers, and everyone goes off swearing they'll never speak to one another again. And then the next year they come back and do it all again. Or was that just my family?'

I laughed again, properly this time. 'No, mine got kind of like that too. Well, they did the last time I went home for Christmas.' I thought about explaining that since Jim had come on the scene, Mum's home wasn't my home any more and she didn't even really feel like my mum, because she was so wrapped up in what she clearly thought of as her new family. But I didn't. I just said, 'Maddy and Henry and I stayed home last year with some of our mates. We were her urban family, she said. I guess we won't be doing that this year.'

A wave of hurt at the unfairness of it all washed over me again, and this time I couldn't stop myself – I started to cry properly, gulping sobs and great splashy tears that washed all my make-up off onto the inadequate tissue.

'Charlotte,' Myles said. 'Come on, let's get out of here.'

He put his arm around me and helped me to my feet, saying something to one of the hovering waiters as we left the bar and got into the lift.

'I'm up in one of the towers,' he said. 'The view's stunning. You'll see it when you've finished crying, it'll still be there.'

The lift doors swooshed open and he guided me along a corridor with more flagstones, oriental rugs and potted plants, and up a stone spiral staircase.

'Just a second.' He produced a plastic card from his pocket and clicked the door open. 'Come in. The bathroom's just in here.'

'Thanks,' I muttered, and shut myself in, surveying the blotchy, swollen wreckage of my face. I splashed cold water on my eyes, but it didn't help much, and blew my nose as quietly as I could, which wasn't nearly quietly enough. There was no point trying to repair my make-up, I decided – I was liable to start crying again at any second, especially if he carried on being so kind.

When I emerged, he was sitting on a chaise longue by the window. The bottle of fizz was on a table, presumably brought up by a waiter, and the glasses had been refilled.

'Now,' he said. 'Come and admire the view, talk to me, have a drink, and cry some more if you want.'

I did all of those things, although not in that order, and after about an hour I'd finished crying and we'd finished the bottle, too.

I checked my phone again for messages, but there was nothing.

I said, 'I don't know what to do. I mean, I don't even know where they are. I can't go back to the apartment and be sitting there on my own when they get back from wherever they've been.'

The idea of that humiliation made me feel like crying some more, but I couldn't. I was done.

'No,' he replied. 'I can see why you don't want to do that. Do you want to try calling one of them again? You could do it from my phone, or the landline here, if you think they won't answer your number.'

I looked at my messages again. Maddy had read the one I sent earlier, in a panic after seeing that I'd sent it to Myles by mistake: she'd read it more than two hours ago. 'No. If she's not talking to me, she won't talk whichever number I call her from.'

Myles nodded and said nothing.

'I suppose I could just go back to London,' I said. 'There'll be a flight this evening.'

'Or,' Myles said, 'we can go back there and fetch your things and you can stay here with me. I can't promise that I'll dance round your handbag with you to "All the Single Ladies", but I'll buy you dinner. And sleep on the floor, if you'd rather.'

'Because of your wife?'

'Charlotte,' he told me gently. 'It's over. Me and her.'

I said, 'Okay. I mean, yes, please.'

And so that's what we did. We walked together back to the apartment, Myles holding my hand. I paused at the door and listened, but I couldn't hear anything.

'It's all right,' he said. 'You've got this.'

But there was no one there. The remains of breakfast were still on the kitchen counter, so they hadn't been back. Which meant they could turn up any minute.

I packed my bag in record time, and left a handwritten note, weighted down by the coffee pot, saying:

I can't stay for the rest of the weekend. I hope we'll talk soon and make things right. Have fun, C.

And then Myles and I walked out together into the afternoon sunshine, and I felt as if an enormous weight had been lifted from me – although that might just have been him insisting on carrying my suitcase.

The rest of the weekend felt like honeymoons must feel. Back at Myles's hotel, in his room, I kind of collapsed into his arms, weak with gratitude, and he held me tight, and the next thing I knew we were kissing each other, pulling off our clothes and falling onto his bed, avid with longing for each other. It was as good as the last time – better, actually, because along with the raw desire I felt for him, there was even more tenderness, a sense of security that hadn't been there before, and new knowledge of what felt good for me. I felt not just wanted, but cherished, too. And I felt something more, too – a kind of swelling emotion in my chest that could only be released by telling him how I felt. But I didn't – it was too soon.

Afterwards, we lay next to each other, holding hands while the sweat dried on our skin and the sunset flooded the room with amber light. I must have fallen asleep for a bit, because when I opened my eyes again it was dark, I could hear the shower running and I was hungrier than I'd ever been in my life.

Myles came out of the bathroom a moment later, naked, damp and fragrant, and if I hadn't been absolutely starving I would have wanted him all over again.

'Your turn,' he said. 'Then we'll go out. Unless you'd rather get them to bring something up here?'

For a moment, I was torn between longing to go out with him – to be his proper girlfriend at last – and the prospect of somehow bumping into my friends, or former friends.

'Don't worry,' he said. 'There's a place near the museum where I'm working. It's a quiet part of town – no tourists go there yet.'

He was right: the restaurant was a small room down a quiet street, with candles and paper cloths on the tables, and the waiter knew Myles's name and brought us bread and olives, which I devoured. Then we ate garlicky mussels and roast pork and tomato salad dripping with olive oil, drank a bottle of red wine, and chatted about things totally unrelated to my friends or Myles's marriage. When I wasn't stuffing my face with food, I was smiling, or laughing, or being kissed.

Satiated, we walked back through the warm darkness, admiring the moon shining off the sea and stopping to admire the view and each other, and snog some more. So by the time we climbed the stairway to his room – our room – I was alight with lust for him again, in spite of being as full as a python and absolutely knackered from all the food and emotion.

I was woken the next morning by the smell of fresh coffee and Myles's fingers gently caressing me, and although I couldn't have imagined wanting him again so soon, so urgently, I found that I did, and the coffee was cold by the time we drank it.

We spent the morning wandering aimlessly through the cobbled streets, and Myles showed me the former hospital that was being developed into a museum, designed by his firm. Like the Mayfair mansion, it was surrounded by hoardings and ribbed with scaffolding, but this time we didn't go in.

'I'll bring you here when it's finished,' he said. 'For the grand opening,' and I felt a thrill of pleasure at the idea that he expected us to still be together when this wasn't a building site any more – that he saw a future for us together.

We stood, holding hands in the sunshine, looking at what we could see of the old stone walls of the building and the glass box sticking out of its side.

'When we get back to London, will we... I mean, what are your plans?' I asked.

He sighed. 'I'm here for another week. But I've got the keys to a flat in Shoreditch. I haven't moved in properly yet, but I will when I get back. So the next time I see you, it will probably be there.'

I said, 'I should get ready for my flight home.'

And all at once, the honeymoon melted away and the reality of my situation came thudding back, a solid weight in my stomach that made me feel sick. *I'll make sure I get to the airport late*, I decided. *I'll cut it as fine as I possibly can. And if I see them, I'll say I couldn't get a flight yesterday and I stayed in a hotel. What's the worst that can happen?*

But they didn't see me. I was the last to board and got allocated a seat right at the back, and there was no sign of Maddy's remaining hens at the airport or on the flight. So I sat down and fastened my seatbelt and opened the copy of *Architectural Digest* I'd bought to remind me of Myles, but before I'd got through the first ten pages I'd conked out. I slept deeply all the way back to London and, as far as I can remember, didn't dream of anything at all.

Chapter Seventeen

Hello and welcome back to Sorry Not Sorry. *You guessed it – it's challenge time again! And this is a fun one for you all. One thing you don't know about me (well, I guess there are a few things, given that I keep these podcasts anonymous) is that I am the unluckiest person in the entire world, ever. Like, I never win stuff. When I play poker, I get the rubbish cards. The last time I matched any numbers on the lotto was, like, two years ago and I won three dollars. I don't let it bug me, because I know I'm blessed in so many other ways. But this week I won an actual prize, through a sweepstake thing at work! I can't believe it! I won dinner for two at Le Bernardin, which in case you didn't know is one of the hottest restaurants in Manhattan right now. I am so excited! And I get to ask someone to go with me to this amazing place. So that's your challenge today. Think of somewhere you've always wanted to go, but you've put it off because you're single and stuff like that's for couples, and go! Go with a girlfriend, or with your mom, or even on your own if you're super-brave. Treat yourself – you deserve it.*

'Charlotte, you're free later this morning, aren't you?' Margot said. She was as immaculate ever, today wearing a scarlet trouser suit, her dark hair bundled up on top of her head. But, instead of gliding around the office like she normally did, as if her stiletto heels were those things with wheels underneath that kids wear, which allow them to strike a pose and suddenly go shooting off (usually across a crowded shopping mall, and then they collide violently with your ankles and their parents glare at you as if it was all your fault), today she was actually, visibly rushing.

'Sure,' I said. 'What's up?'

'Problem with the servers,' she said. 'Pavel's working on it. But I'm meant to be going to Sexy Fish at eleven thirty for the menu tasting for our Christmas do and there's no way I can leave the office today. Can you go? The chef's preparing everything: there's six canapés and five other courses, plus the vegetarian options, plus four desserts. And the wine.'

Normally, the idea of being able to skive out of the office and spend a couple of hours stuffing myself with Michelin-starred food and fine wine would have appealed to me a great deal. And I had the podcast's challenge to complete: treat yourself. And if it was Colton Capital treating me, that was even better – even if I wasn't properly completing the Bad Girl's challenge, because it wasn't my choice of treat. And even if she, the smug, jammy cow, was getting to do it with someone she liked, not on her own like a saddo. Then I thought, *Maybe I don't have to do it on my own, either?* Of course, I was conscious of the approaching day when I would have to fit into my humbug-striped bridesmaid's dress, and even more conscious that Myles would be back in less than a week. In anticipation, I'd even ordered a black basque from Mimi Holliday, and it was currently just a tiny bit too tight, giving the effect of an overstuffed sausage rather than the sexy siren look I was aiming for.

'Sure, I'll go,' I said. 'But, wow, that's a lot of food.'

'Take someone with you,' Margot said, as if she'd read my mind, and looked rather wildly around as if she expected a contestant from *Man v. Food* to materialise next to the trading desk. No one did, of course, but Xander happened to be passing.

'Hey,' I heard myself say. 'You don't eat meat, do you? Want to come along and sample the veggie tasting menu at Sexy Fish?' Margot hurried off, leaving him looking puzzled and me blushing furiously, remembering again the graphic sex fantasy I'd had about him by mistake.

'What's this about?'

'Christmas menu tasting,' I said. 'I need a volunteer to come and help me eat all the food. It's just up the road.'

'I can think of worse ways to spend a Monday,' Xander said.

I looked at the forty unread emails in my inbox, at least half of them from Piers, and all of those bearing red 'urgent' tags, and decided that I could, too.

'They're expecting us at half eleven.'

'Just as well I didn't have breakfast,' Xander said.

For the next two hours, I tried my hardest to focus on work. But it wasn't easy, because there was a sense of mild commotion in the office. Some of my emails sent without a problem, but others bounced back. The level of noise and number of obscenities from the trading floor were higher than usual. Renzo was pacing up and down like an angry tiger, talking rapidly into his phone and not so much tapping as bashing at a tablet in his other hand. Pavel and Colin were locked in the fishbowl and I could see Colin's face turning redder and shinier as the morning wore on, while Pavel hunched over his laptop, a dark diamond of sweat spreading across his back.

And, of course, I had to try and stop myself checking my phone every five minutes for messages from Myles. I failed, but there weren't any.

So, all in all, it was a relief when Xander strolled over to my desk and said, 'Shall we go?'

I stood up and put on my coat and watched as he pulled on a rather stylish tweed number over his jumper, a shabby grey cable-knit that was either the height of Scandi style or had come from the Oxfam shop. I still didn't quite understand how Xander got away with so blatantly breaking the office's dress code. Nowhere was it actually written down that dark suits – grey, pin-striped or, at a push, navy blue, and the more expensive the better – were obligatory for men, but nonetheless that was what everyone wore, except Xander.

'How was your weekend?' he asked, pressing the button to summon the lift. 'You went to Lisbon, right?'

I was about to ask him how he knew, then remembered his uncanny ability to know everything that went on in the office, just by listening to people. Hopefully he couldn't read minds, too, I thought, otherwise his ears – and probably other bits too – would be on fire knowing what I'd accidentally imagined him doing to me. Well, I wasn't about to spill out the sorry tale of Maddy and Bianca, and the happier one of Myles, only to have the entire office know about it. Although, I realised, Xander didn't pass on the intel he seemed to gather so effortlessly. He knew things about people, but mostly he kept them to himself. Unless I was badgering him for gossip.

'The weather was lovely,' I said neutrally. 'Not like here.'

The sky was a depressing slate grey and gusts of wind lashed drizzle against our faces. It seemed as if winter had arrived with a vengeance while I'd been away, robbing London of its colour as it stripped the last of the leaves from the trees, sending everyone digging through their wardrobes for black, charcoal and camel clothes. Even though it was still November, the Christmas lights had been switched on in Regent Street.

Inside the restaurant, though, there was brilliant colour everywhere. A huge tank of tropical fish filled one wall. The bar and seats were scarlet. More fish – or models of fish – were suspended from the ceiling.

'How fabulous is this?' I breathed.

'A bit like walking into a box of Quality Street,' Xander said dismissively, but he was smiling.

Before I could tell him off for being sarcastic, a beautiful girl in a black dress welcomed us and showed us to our table, and seconds later the maître d', the head chef, the chief mixologist and the sommelier all came over and introduced themselves.

'Please do let me know if you need anything at all,' offered the maître d'.

'Ms Clark asked us to suggest a selection of wines,' said the sommelier, 'but if you would like to try anything else from the list, we'd be delighted to bring you a glass.'

'Here is one of our signature cocktails for you to try,' offered the mixologist, reverently placing two glasses on the table in front of us.

'Your amuse-bouche will be with you very shortly,' said the head chef.

'Wow,' I whispered to Xander. 'This is what it must feel like to be… I don't know, a celebrity, or something.'

'Not a celebrity,' Xander said. 'Just dropping twenty grand on lunch for forty people. Forty people who entertain clients with lavish budgets, and don't think about how much they spend when they go out with their friends or their girlfriend or whatever. Money might not buy happiness, but it certainly makes people suck up to you.'

I remembered what Tansy had said about the assistants in the Paris boutiques, how completely differently they'd behaved towards her when she'd been with Renzo to when she'd been alone, and realised he had a point. But before I could think it through, two plates appeared in front of us, laden with what I knew was food but looked more like tiny works of art, or maybe jewellery.

The chef explained what they were, which was so complicated I forgot almost straight away. I ate mine anyway, and took a gulp of my cocktail, which was apparently gin flavoured with wasabi, pepper, beetroot and other things I couldn't remember.

'That good?' Xander asked.

'It's lovely,' I said. 'But I have to admit I'm more of a margarita girl usually.'

He deconstructed his canapé, showing impressive chopstick skills, and ate it too.

'You must be used to all this,' he said, 'aren't you? You've been with the firm long enough.'

'Yes. But this is only my second Christmas party. Last year's was amazing, but I was so worried about using the wrong fork I hardly ate anything, and just got shitfaced. It was okay though, because everyone else was shitfaced too. I don't get to take clients out for posh lunches or anything like that. Not yet, anyway.'

'Is that what you want?' Xander asked. 'Piers's job? Margot's job? Or Colin's, even?'

Two glasses of champagne had appeared in front of us, and another pair of plates was presented.

'Sea bass with yuzu and miso, madam,' said the waiter. 'And for you, sir, burrata with kimchi and basil.'

I ate my fish while I considered Xander's question.

'God, no, not Colin's,' I said. 'Or Renzo's. I know my limits. But I can organise stuff, and I can be nice to people. So, in theory, I could do what Piers or Margot do, and earn the kind of money they do, too.'

'You're ambitious,' he said. 'I thought I was, too. That's why I accepted this job. And don't get me wrong, I'm looking forward to the Christmas do and the bonus. But I think it's going to be my last one.'

We were presented with more wine and more food. I drank and ate, although I was starting to feel distinctly less hungry. Even though Xander hadn't been around that long, it was weird to imagine the office without his aimless, jeans-clad figure in it, fitting in at once everywhere and nowhere, a bit like how he'd appeared without warning in my sexy fantasy. But I pushed that thought out of my mind before a tell-tale blush could flood over my face.

'Why?' I asked. 'Where will you go?'

'I wanted to see what this world was like, I suppose. To experience the forces – this is going to sound totally wanky, bear with me – that shape the places where I used to work. Take tantalum, for example.'

'I'd prefer not to, thanks. I hate spiders.'

'What?'

'Isn't that a kind of spider? Those massive hairy ones?'

Xander laughed. 'I think you're thinking of tarantulas. I saw one in my kitchen once, when I was living in Bogotá, and they are fucking terrifying.'

'So what's tantalum, then?'

'It's a metal,' he said. 'They use it in mobile phones and laptops and stuff. It's got similar chemical properties to platinum, but that's massively in demand as a precious metal, too, for jewellery. So suddenly, everyone wants tantalum, and the price on the markets is going crazy.'

'And funds are finding ways to trade in it,' I said, on surer ground now. 'And making money for our clients.'

'Of course,' he said. 'But when you look at it from the other end – from the point of view of the countries that produce it – it's a bit different. Suddenly you've got a commodity boom that can make some people incredibly rich.'

'And that's good,' I said. 'Countries that have been wrecked by war and… I don't know, colonialism, and stuff, are sitting on these massive asset pools that can turn their economies around.'

'Except when they don't,' he said. 'Thank you, that looks amazing. Could we have some water, as well, please?' he said to the waiter, before turning to me. 'Except when they turn up in countries like the Congo, which is already massively politically unstable, and suddenly you've got a massive shitstorm blowing up. Sorry. I need to shut the fuck up and let you enjoy your lunch.'

'I am enjoying my lunch,' I said, determinedly eating some tuna sashimi. 'But you're reminding me of my housemate, who gave me the most massive telling-off the other day for the same thing. And I was like, for fuck's sake, I'm just doing a job.'

'And so am I,' Xander said. 'Look, I'm benefiting from this too. Loads of people are. But I keep asking myself, what happens next, in fifty years or— shit.'

For the first time since we'd sat down, he was looking at his phone. Mine was still in my handbag; I'd been so interested in chatting to him it was almost like the world around our table had ceased to exist. Now, though, I could see he was on WhatsApp, and messages were flashing up every couple of seconds.

'What is it?'

'The server thing. It's not just a regular IT glitch, it's a full-on attack. Pavel's going mental, apparently. We should probably get back.'

'But what can we do?' I asked.

'Probably nothing. But I want to see what happens next.'

I felt a huge rush of adrenaline, and realised that I did, too. So we thanked the staff profusely, said we were sorry that we couldn't finish all the wonderful things they had prepared for us but we were sure everything would be perfect for the party, and hurried back to the office to face the meltdown.

We went from being pleasantly mellow, enjoying the excellent food and drink – which tasted even better for being free and consumed during working hours – to an atmosphere of total shock and chaos.

Not knowing what to do, I joined a little group that included Colin's three PAs, who were literally wringing their hands.

'What's going on?' I asked.

'It's a DDoS attack, apparently,' Greg said. 'Or maybe just a DoS attack, Pavel said.'

'I don't know what the difference is,' said Briony.

'They've shut down all our computers,' explained Alice. 'And I was busy doing the guest list for Colin's mother-in-law's birthday party. Svetlana's going to fucking freak out if it's late.'

'Is a DDoS attack like what happened to the NHS back in summer?' I asked. 'Loads of people couldn't get into A&E and appointments got cancelled and stuff?'

'And there was that guy who worked out what the hackers were doing and stopped it,' Greg said. 'I remember that.'

'And then didn't he get arrested in America? I wonder what happened to him,' I thought out loud.

Xander appeared to be doing his usual thing of drifting around the office, having a word here and a word there, until I knew he'd know as much about what was going on as anyone else in the office, even though we'd missed the initial drama.

We watched as Pavel burst out of the fishbowl office, shouting into his phone. 'They've used the UDP on our TCP/IP protocol stack to flood the ports,' he was saying.

We all looked blankly at each other. As I'd told Tansy, Pavel speaks seven languages – and he could have been using any of them for all the sense it made to me.

'So reboot the fucking server,' I heard Colin shout. 'You're the fucking CTO, I pay you to keep our systems fucking running, you…'

He launched into a torrent of abuse that was off the scale, even for him.

Greg, Briony and Alice looked frozen with fear.

'Surely if rebooting the server was going to help, Pavel would've done it by now?' I asked.

'He needs to find the kill switch, apparently,' Xander said, joining our group. 'The server is being bombarded with traffic that it can't handle, so it's fallen over and we can't process any transactions, which means no one can trade. Which is bad, obviously, but it's worse that fraudulent trades could be being carried out in the background on our account, or funds could just be being moved out.'

'What's a kill switch?' I said. Trust Xander to know exactly what was going on within a few minutes of walking into the office.

'I haven't got a clue,' he admitted. 'Renzo reckons there must have been a piece of code sent to someone's email, and they opened it, and… well, it all went pear-shaped.'

We looked at each other. I could tell from Greg, Alice and Briony's faces that they were all thinking the same thing I was: if it was me who did that, I'm toast. *Surely I didn't, though*, I thought. I wasn't stupid. I knew about phishing scams and even spear-phishing, even if I wasn't sure what the difference is. I knew not to click on links in emails purporting to be from Nigerian princes offering me a share of a vast fortune in return for my bank details.

'Alice, stop coffee-housing and get in here!' bellowed Colin, and Alice turned white and went.

'Is he going to sack her?' I asked Xander.

'Shouldn't think so,' he said. 'Unless she's a closet hacker, which I doubt.'

'He must be going to sack someone, the mood he's in.'

'Well, you and I weren't even here at the time, so I guess we're safe.' He grinned. 'Who knew stuffing ourselves with cocktails and canapés would turn out to be the perfect alibi? So we can just keep our heads down and watch the drama unfold.'

We watched Colin gesticulating furiously and Alice nodding mutely.

Pavel was back at his desk, still talking on his phone, only now he'd switched to Russian, which I didn't understand but could at least recognise. Renzo was standing by the traders' desks, watching the figures scrolling on the television screens overhead. He looked outwardly relaxed, but his hands were clenching and unclenching by his sides.

The door to the fishbowl opened and Alice hurried out, wide-eyed and alarmed.

'Do it right now!' Colin shouted after her.

'Are you okay?' I asked.

'Just,' she said. 'I'm to go back to Colin's house and carry on doing the party stuff there, with Svetlana. Apparently she's not happy.'

She did a sort of hunching thing with her shoulders that I think may have been the first time I've ever seen anyone literally shudder, grabbed her bag and rushed to the lift, without even putting on her coat.

Once again, I was filled with awe at the fact that, even with his entire business potentially imploding and billions of pounds at stake, Colin was still concerned about how his wife would react if her mother's social life was disrupted.

'And he wants a coffee,' Alice said, over her shoulder. 'Greg, will you… And he wants you in there now, Briony.'

'I'm on it,' Greg said, dashing towards the kitchen as if the hounds of hell – or even Svetlana herself – were at his heels.

Briony, perhaps because she'd been with Colton Capital for longer and knew Colin and his ways better, was able to maintain her composure during her little chat with our boss. I watched her nodding reassuringly, and the flood of colour receded from Colin's face as she did so. A few minutes later she joined us again, trembling only slightly.

'They've called in a cyber security expert, Colin says,' she said. 'When she arrives, Greg, will you find Pavel and make sure they've got everything they need?'

She glanced at her shorthand notebook and brandished her pen, reminding me a bit of the scene in *Game of Thrones* where Arya Stark holds Needle for the first time. She took a deep breath and returned to the fishbowl, where she remained at Colin's side for the rest of the day.

For the rest of us, although the sense of high drama remained, there wasn't much to do. We'd been told not to use our mobile phones in case security was further compromised, so we all hung about, at once tense and bored.

The cyber security expert arrived, turning out to be a pretty young woman with long dark hair, wearing skinny jeans and carrying an even skinnier laptop. She joined the group in the fishbowl, and the door remained closed for the rest of the afternoon.

In the meantime, some of the traders started a poker game, using different coloured Post-it notes for chips. I found out afterwards that Xander ended the afternoon four and a half thousand pounds up and Piers took a bath.

*

It was after nine when I left the office. The servers had been restored, I'd answered forty of the two hundred emails clamouring for attention in my inbox, and I'd even managed to put in a rather pared-down version of the Ocado order for delivery the next day. Several people, including Pavel, Colin, Margot and Renzo, looked like they were settling in for an all-nighter, but I was too knackered to join them. I'd get in early, I promised myself, and try and make some headway in my mountain of missed work.

The rain that had been falling in thin, needle-like gusts when I'd walked to the restaurant earlier with Xander – hard to believe it was only a few hours ago – had properly got into its stride now, and was coming down in determined, icy sheets, accompanied by gusts of wind. Huddling down into my coat, I made a dash for the Tube station.

It was still raining when I got out at Hackney, and the usual crowds of hardy smokers who gathered outside The Daily Grind and the Prince George were sheltering under umbrellas, looking like they were in two minds about whether their nicotine fix was worth the discomfort and hassle.

Inside The Daily Grind, I could see Luke behind the bar and Hannah at a table drinking red wine with the same impossibly gorgeous couple I'd seen at the table next to ours when Tansy,

Adam and I had our awkward pizza dinner. Hannah waved when she saw me passing, and I considered popping in to ask if Freezer was still AWOL. But I was too wet and too knackered, so I just tapped my watch and rolled my eyes regretfully, hurrying down the road towards home.

The lights in Adam's window upstairs and the front room downstairs were on, which I guessed meant both he and Tansy were home. I wondered if I could expect another lecture from Adam about the evils of capitalism, and wished I had Xander's knowledge so that I could refute what he said. I wondered whether Renzo had filled Tansy in on the day's drama, or whether he'd been too busy. I wondered whether they'd had plans to meet up that evening and he'd let her down, and whether the first shadow of disillusionment would be setting in for Tansy.

Mostly, though, I was thinking about a hot, bubbly bath and texting Myles from bed to explain why I hadn't been in touch, and see if he was able to meet up later in the week at his new flat. The prospect made me all shivery with pleasurable anticipation, so I forgot the rain and the wind for a moment and I also almost didn't notice the man standing outside our front door.

He was wearing a waterproof jacket of some sort – an anorak or a parka, only without any fur trim, and jeans, which were soaked with rain from the knees down. He was shortish and thinnish and had pockmarked skin and a weak chin. He was holding a huge bunch of red roses, wilting by the second.

I took him in with a quick glance, and the instinct that everyone – every woman, at least – develops over time kicked in without the need for rational thought. This wasn't a Hermes or DPD driver delivering an order late. There was no van, for a start, but also, the man himself looked all wrong. There was no lanyard round his neck, no tablet or scanning device in his hand. He didn't have the air of purposeful haste delivery drivers did, the manner of someone who was going to knock on our door, give us ninety seconds tops to open it, and then dump the flowers in our recycling bin and perhaps leave a card saying they were in a safe place before departing at speed for the next stop on his rounds.

This was someone who'd been hanging around outside our house in the rain for some time, or walking up and down the street looking for our house, which was odd in itself because the number on the door was large and easy to spot against the red paint, and the street wasn't one of those where the numbers didn't line up or make sense; it was all logical, from number 1 on the left and number 2 on the right all the way to number 65, where we lived, and beyond.

So, as I say, my spider senses tingled, but they didn't register danger, just oddness. Something not right.

I paused and took my phone out of my bag as well as my keys, almost dropping my umbrella in the process.

'Can I help you?' I asked.

'I'm looking for Saskia.'

So he knew the person he was looking for, because he'd known I wasn't her. Otherwise his question would have been, 'Are you Saskia Whatever-her-last-name was?' Or he would have knocked on the door and said to whoever answered – which would have been Tansy, because I'd never known Adam to leave his room to open the door in all the months we'd lived together – 'Delivery for

Saskia Whatever,' and Tansy would have said, 'Sorry, you've got the wrong house. There's no Saskia living here.' That meant he hadn't knocked. And he wasn't a delivery driver – there was no question of it. His voice was almost posh, not public school like Piers's, but certainly without the East London or Eastern European accents the drivers who delivered our parcels usually had.

'There's no Saskia living here,' I replied, after my lengthy internal analysis. 'You've got the wrong house.'

He looked at me for what felt like quite a long time. I waited for him to say sorry and go away, so I could let myself in, which I wasn't keen to do with him standing right there watching. I didn't feel tired any more – I was alert, not scared exactly, but anxious enough to feel my heartbeat.

Then he thrust the roses at me and said, 'When you see her, give her these. Tell her Travis brought them.' Instinctively, I reached out to take them, but the shock at hearing that name made me hesitate for a fraction of a second, and I didn't grab hold of them properly. The cellophane wrapping was slippery with rain and so was my phone, and I fumbled to keep my umbrella up and ended up dropping the lot.

He didn't stop to help. By the time I'd gathered everything up from the pavement, he was already halfway back up the road, walking fast towards the station.

Struggling not to drop everything again, my hands wet and clumsy with cold, I eventually managed to get my key in the door.

Tansy was standing right there, in the hallway next to the radiator where we keep our keys and the post, which always ends up being a litter of pizza leaflets and 'For the attention of the homeowner' letters that we knew were from estate agents so didn't pass on to the landlord, but which felt too official to throw away. She was holding her phone too, and she looked wide-eyed and alarmed. I watched as she glanced over my shoulder at the empty street beyond, then seemed to relax.

'God, Charlotte, you're soaked! You poor thing,' she said. 'Such vile weather. But look at your beautiful flowers! Who are they from?'

'I could do with a cup of tea. How about you?' I replied.

'Actually, I was just…'

I waited. Then she said, 'Oh, go on then.'

We walked through to the kitchen and I dumped everything on the table, took off my wet coat, slung it over the back of a chair and switched on the kettle.

'These are for someone called Saskia,' I said.

Tansy gave a little gasp, but her face only registered mild curiosity. 'Is that someone who lived here before?'

'Maddy and I lived here for three years before she moved out with Henry. I can't remember the names of the girls who lived here before, but I'm fairly sure if one of them had been called Saskia, it would have rung a bell.'

'It's an unusual name,' Tansy mumbled.

She turned to get mugs and tea bags from the cupboard. Her hands were trembling, I noticed, and then there was a clatter as she dropped a mug onto the floor.

'Shit,' she said, with a laugh as shaky as her hands. 'Thank God for that indestructible Ikea quality.'

'The man who brought the flowers said they were from Travis. That's an unusual name, too,' I continued.

'Sure is,' Tansy said. 'My dad used to read these old detective stories about a guy called Travis McGee, who lived on a boat in Florida. I thought it was quite a cool name then.'

'But you don't any more?'

Tansy said, 'Charlotte, it's late. I think I'll take my tea and head up to bed.'

I looked at her. Her face was composed but her eyes were still wide, darting around as if she wanted to run away but wasn't sure where was safe.

'Tansy, come on,' I pressed. 'When you moved in here you gave me a bunch of flowers just like this. You must have forgotten to take the card off. They were from Travis. I know you know who he is. If you're frightened, just tell me. We can figure something out.'

'I'm not frightened. Not of him, anyway.'

I waited, and then, as if she had lost the will to stand up any more, she flopped down into one of the hard chairs, wrapped her hands around her mug of tea as if they were very cold, and told me the truth.

༚

Chapter Eighteen

Hello, you gorgeous things, and welcome back to Sorry Not Sorry *and the latest in the series of challenges we're taking on together. Ready? Today, I'm talking about connecting to – or finding, if you haven't already – your inner sex goddess. Now don't tell me you don't have one! You do. I do, every woman does. It's the bit of you that puts a wiggle in your walk when you go down the street, the bit that drives your partner wild in bed, the bit that makes you smile when you look at yourself in the mirror.*

And keeping that side of yourself alive and zinging might seem impossible when you're single, or you're stressed out at work, or you think you're not looking your best, but it's really not. It can be as simple as taking some me-time with an erotic novel, or going out without any panties on, or wearing a pair of killer heels to the office. So today, I'm going to think about what makes me feel sexy, and I'm going to do it. With me?

I stood in front of the orange door in the stark, concrete-floored lobby, my stomach feeling as if the lift that had dropped me here hadn't stopped and let me out, but had instead descended at speed

back to the ground floor where the polite, blank-faced concierge
had taken my name, then shot back up again, then down.

Connect to your inner sex goddess, the Bad Girl had instructed
– and here I was, wearing my new basque, about to do just that.
I was tinglingly aware of every part of my body: my lips parted,
freshly slicked with red lipstick; my nipples hard from the cold and
excitement; my thighs pressing together under my skirt, and the
space between them. My palms were damp and I could smell my
perfume coming in waves off my hot skin.

Part of me wished I could get a grip; part of me hoped that, if
Myles and I were still seeing each other in a year's time, or two, or
ten, I'd still feel this hopeless, melting desire, somewhere between
pleasure and pain, at the prospect of being with him.

I raised my hand to knock on the door, but it opened before I
could, and there he was, tall and lean in a denim shirt that matched
his eyes.

'Hello,' I said.

He didn't say anything for a moment. He put his arms around
me and hugged me tight and kissed me hard, then pulled me inside
and closed the door behind us. I heard a heavy thunk as it closed,
and there was a muffled click as the lock engaged.

'It's a bit like Fort Knox here,' he said, brushing his lips over
mine again. 'I'm glad you made it through the cordon. Did you
find it okay?'

'Eventually. Google Maps sent me the wrong way at first. And
the guy downstairs takes no prisoners – or maybe he does, he looks
like he might have worked for the Gestapo in a previous life.'

'But you're here.' He kissed me again.

'Come on, aren't you going to show me around?' I handed him the bottle of champagne I'd brought. 'Happy housewarming. Sorry it's not the posh stuff, I think the off-licence down the road had sold out of Pol Roger.'

'Thank you,' he said. 'That's sweet of you. You didn't have to. It's only temporary, after all.'

'Is it?' The unease that had vanished when his arms closed around me returned in a rush. He hadn't said anything about temporary. He'd only said that he'd moved into a flat near Old Street, now that he'd left the house he and his wife shared. But, I supposed, it was far too quick for that to have been sold, so perhaps he was just renting here until he could find somewhere that would be properly his.

But he said, 'My mate Chris is an estate agent. He's marketing this place. The owners have gone their separate ways but they're not short of cash and they're in no hurry to sell. So I'm basically squatting here – with their permission, obviously – until the sale goes through. Could be three months, could be a year. Now, let's open your fizz. There's a balcony out the back with a great view of the canal and a hot tub – we'll have to try that out sometime. But I didn't have time to get it hot, and it's arctic out, so that's going to have to wait for another night.'

I followed him across the polished concrete floor. I could see why his estate agent friend wasn't sure how long the flat would take to sell: it was huge, but had an unfinished look about it. There were lighter patches on the walls where paintings must have hung, and wires dangling where a television screen had been removed. Apart from a huge red suede sofa, there wasn't any furniture at all.

I wanted to ask him how he was feeling about living in this empty, forlorn-feeling place. How he had broken the news that he was leaving to his wife, and what she had said. How long it would take before things were finalised between them and I could put the last shadows of guilt I felt about our relationship behind me, and look forward to our future. How soon I could give myself permission to put a name to the feelings I was developing for him.

But I didn't. I watched his strong hands untwist the wire from the champagne bottle and ease out the cork, as expertly as they brought me from tight containment to open readiness, and I asked, 'Why don't you show me the bedroom?'

He laughed. 'It's worse than this, I'm afraid. The owners are two young lads and they didn't keep the tidiest house. There's just bare mattresses and dust bunnies in there now, and the sleeping bag I used last night. Don't worry, Chris is going to get decorators in and they'll work their magic, and then it'll make Shoreditch House look shabby. But until then, it's the sofa for us.'

We sat down and put our drinks on the floor. He kissed me again in the way that was beginning to become familiar, although my body's reaction to his touch was no less intense.

'You're beautiful, Charlotte,' he said. 'I love how you look dressed like that.'

'Like what? It's just a suit.'

'Exactly. All stark and severe, and yet, underneath…'

My stomach did another slow-motion somersault and I felt a tight thread of excitement run from my collarbone, where his thumb lazily circled, down to my breasts and then lower. I loved the way my body looked with his hand on it: the pallor and softness of my skin, which looked flabby when I looked in the mirror, was transformed into creamy lushness when I imagined how it felt to him.

He undid the three buttons of my jacket, then, slowly and surely, all those of my blouse. Underneath was the black lace basque I'd bought to wear for him.

'My God,' he said. 'Stand up.'

I did as he said. I stood in front of him, sipped my drink, and watched his face as he slid the jacket and top off my shoulders onto the floor, then unzipped my skirt and eased it down over my hips. I wasn't wearing any pants (in the interest of full disclosure, I'd worn them all day, just whipped them off in the lift and put them in my handbag; I wasn't *that* much of a bad girl after all. And the word 'panties' was cringy AF, so I'd had to get over that hurdle), only hold-up stockings and high heels.

Once more, I felt the electric thrill of excitement his desire gave me. My inner sex goddess was doing her thing, sending what felt like bolts of lightning through me. I totally got what the podcast had meant: I felt so powerful, but at the same time I knew I was helpless to change the way my body and my heart responded to him. Then he put his hands on my waist and pulled me towards him, his lips brushing the inside of my thighs and moving upwards to the wetness waiting for him, and all my thoughts dissolved into a hot pool of pleasure.

Afterwards, we lay together on the sofa, but it was hard to find a comfortable position. The suede was slippery and although the room was warm, I felt awkward being naked with him in this huge, empty space. I got up and started to put my clothes back on.

'What are you doing that for?' Myles asked lazily.

'What if your mate shows up with people wanting to view the flat?'

'They'll ask if you come integrated. Anyway, he won't. We agreed. He'll give me half a day's notice. I said if I was a proper tenant it would be twenty-four hours, no messing, and I could say no if I wanted to, so he's getting a good deal.'

'Squatters' rights,' I said. 'You could form an anarchists' collective, like those guys who got chucked out of that place in Mayfair. Except you'd have to move into Oleg's place for it to have the desired impact.'

'ANAL,' Myles said. 'No need to look alarmed. That's what they're called. The Autonomous Nation of Anarchist Libertarians – a slightly tortured acronym. Shall we order some food?'

I said I was starving, and while he opened the Deliveroo app on his phone, I went to the bathroom. It was as sad-looking and empty as the rest of the house. There was a tube of toothpaste, Myles's toothbrush and razor on a shelf next to the basin, a bottle of shower gel in the shower and a single, slightly threadbare towel. I glanced into the bedrooms. One was empty apart from a bare king-size bed; the other had, as Myles had said, a sleeping bag chucked over the mattress, a clean, ironed shirt on a wire hanger on the back of the door and an overnight bag with a few items of clothing spilling out of it.

I imagined cuddling up with him there, lighting candles, waking up in the morning with light flooding through the bare window and having sex again. The idea should have felt romantic, although admittedly in a slightly studenty way. But it didn't; it just felt uncomfortable and even a bit squalid. And, in my lace underwear and work suit, I felt like I didn't belong there at all.

Quickly, so he wouldn't think I was snooping, I hurried back to Myles. He was looking intently at his phone.

'Ramen's on its way,' he said, tipping the rest of the wine into the paper cups we'd used.

But when the food came, there was no plastic cutlery or even chopsticks with it, and none in any of the kitchen drawers.

He looked at the plastic containers of hot noodles, chicken and vegetables, swimming in delicious-smelling broth, and so did I. There was no way we could eat this stuff without ending up looking like we'd been in a fight with it.

'Fuck,' Myles laughed. 'I'm so sorry, Charlotte. Epic love-nest fail.'

I tried to laugh too, but suddenly this wasn't feeling like fun, and not much like love either. It was late; I needed to shower and sleep and be in the office by seven. I was hungry and I could feel the beginning of a headache.

'I'll take you out,' he suggested. 'There are loads of places around here that are open late. It's only ten o'clock.'

But I just wasn't feeling it. 'Next time. When you're more settled in. Then I can even stay over. But now I should go home.'

I might have imagined it, but I could have sworn that, for just a second, he looked relieved.

'Or you can come to mine,' I said. 'I can't promise gourmet cooking but at least I can offer knives and forks to eat it with.'

'Charlotte, you should know by now that it's not your cooking I'm interested in,' he said, pulling me close and kissing me.

I kissed him back, but when his hands moved round to the buttons of my jacket again, I moved them gently away. 'I really must go.'

I put my coat on and he promised he'd call me the next day, and I left and walked round the corner to the bus stop, deep in thought. I looked up to the window three floors above me that I thought was the room where Myles was sleeping, but there was no light showing at all.

Our house was in darkness too. Tansy and – unusually – Adam were both out. And there was no stranger – no Travis – loitering in the street. I knew, because I checked, looking both ways up and down the street, before I opened the front door. I glanced up at the neighbours' upstairs window, too, just in case I'd see Freezer's little white face peering down as I sometimes had, but there were only the closed shutters.

I didn't feel hungry any more. I switched on all the lights downstairs, and checked that there was no one there. Then I went up to my room and changed into pyjamas and a dressing gown. Both Adam's and Tansy's doors were closed, but I knocked quietly, then opened each in turn, flicking the light switch on, glancing around, then shutting off the light and closing the door. I knew Travis wasn't there – no one was – but I had to check, just in case.

Adam's room still smelled musty but, apart from two empty cereal bowls on the floor and a pint glass with some water in by his desk, it was very neat. Evidently the passive-aggressive reminder I'd sent to our house WhatsApp group about tidiness had had some effect on him, at least. His computer was on, blue lights flashing intermittently from it, but both screens were off. His laptop lay closed on the bed.

Tansy's room was just the same as always. The make-up scattered on her chest of drawers, the smell of her perfume, the wardrobe ajar with clothes on hangers bulging out. The bags stuffed underneath the bed. I knew what was in them now that Tansy had opened up to me, but I wasn't going to look.

I checked the locks downstairs one more time, and then I went to bed.

'Yes, darling,' Colin said into his phone, brushing past me as he left the boardroom. 'I was in a meeting. Yes, of course Alice will help. I'll tell her to call you. Or would you prefer her to just pop round? I'll let her know. Alice!' he yelled across the office.

The rest of the meeting attendees followed him out more slowly. Greg, clutching a Dictaphone; Renzo, already on his mobile; a man and a woman I didn't recognise, presumably clients; and Xander.

While Greg showed the clients to the lift – unnecessarily, as it was right there – I hurried in to tidy up the detritus of coffee cups, milk jug and sugar bowl (unused) and platter of bacon rolls (untouched).

Xander followed me back into the room. He'd abandoned his usual jeans and jumper in favour of slightly smarter jeans, a white shirt and a jacket, I noticed, presumably in honour of the client meeting.

I started stacking things onto a tray, and he stacked, too.

'You don't have to do that,' I said.

'It's no problem,' he replied, picking up three cups in one hand so they rattled together and a chip of white porcelain pinged off the edge of one, then fumbling them and dropping them all. A dark rivulet of espresso dregs spread across the table.

'For God's sake,' I snapped. 'Really, please don't. I can manage. This is my job. Go and do yours.'

'And you can do your job far more efficiently without my ham-fisted attempts at help. Sorry, Charlotte.'

'That's okay,' I muttered, immediately feeling guilty for having bitten his head off when he was only trying to be nice. I turned towards the door, but he was way ahead of me – he'd already hurried out and was reappearing with a roll of paper towels.

'Charlotte,' he said, handing them to me, 'is everything all right?'

'What do you mean?' I blotted up the spilled coffee, stepped back and assessed the damage. There wasn't any – no need for spray cleaner, even.

'You look tired. And you don't usually shout at me when I make your life difficult.'

I looked up at him, the burden of the questions I hadn't been able to ask anyone heavy on my mind. I'd promised Tansy I'd look into some things for her, to help put her mind at rest, but so far I simply hadn't any idea how to begin.

Adam, I knew, understood the internet as if it was the house he'd grown up in. He was an app developer, after all – but an app developer who wasn't talking to me. I'd suggested to Tansy that she ask him herself, but she'd blanched and said, 'No fucking way. Cringe-tastic.'

Renzo, who was pretty tech savvy, wasn't even a candidate, for obvious reasons.

Pavel had been closeted in meetings for the past two days with the cyber security firm we'd brought in, so was a non-starter even if I hadn't been too terrified to say much more to him than 'Good morning,' and 'Would you like two cases of Red Bull on the order, same as usual?'

That left Xander. Even if he didn't know the answer, I trusted him to keep whatever I said in confidence. And, right now, the idea of unburdening myself to someone who'd listen and try to understand even if they couldn't help was hugely appealing. 'Can I ask you a question? I don't expect you to know the answer.'

'Of course,' he said. 'Although I probably don't.'

'How could you find someone's address, if you didn't know their name, but only what they looked like? I'm asking for a friend.'

Xander looked at me steadily for a second. Then he said, 'It's nearly lunchtime. Shall we go out?'

I thought about my overflowing to-do list and the hair-trigger on which Piers's temper seemed to be operating right now. Then I imagined trying to talk to Xander here, with so many people able to overhear, one of them Renzo. And I remembered Tansy's face, white and frightened, and heard her saying, 'Don't tell him, Charlotte. Please, please don't tell him.'

'Sure. Let's do that. Thanks.'

Ten minutes later, Xander had guided me to a street food market where he said he often came for lunch, and we were perched on a bench under heat lamps, surrounded by twinkling Christmas lights, eating flatbreads stuffed with grilled cheese and vegetables and drinking hot chocolate. I genuinely hadn't realised how hungry I was until the first bite of food, but now I was tearing through my lunch as if I hadn't eaten for days.

'What's with the early Christmas thing?' I said. 'It's only November. Doesn't this really piss you off?'

'On the scale of things that piss me off, from one to ten,' Xander said, 'this rates a two, at best. Come on, what about people who get to the front of the queue in Pret and *then* start thinking about what they want to order? What about the way Pavel crushes his Red Bull cans after he's finished drinking them, like he's Chuck Norris or something? What about Boris Johnson?'

'Okay,' I said. 'Fair point. At least early Christmas isn't trying to single-handedly ruin the country and put tens of thousands of people out of work.'

'Still though,' he said. 'A two is a two. Mild, but still annoying. But tell me about your friend.'

I finished my halloumi wrap, wiped my greasy fingers on a paper napkin and sipped my hot chocolate. I wasn't sure where to begin, or how much to say. Enough for him to help Tansy – if he could – but not enough to give away her secret.

'So, my friend is really worried, because someone turned up at her house who isn't supposed to know who she is, or where she lives.'

'Right,' Xander said. 'But they know what she looks like? They've met in person? Or just like through a social media account or something?'

'Something like that,' I said. 'Not in person. She has Twitter and Snapchat accounts, but they're not in her real name, and they're not linked to the accounts that are, if you see what I mean.'

'Could she have posted a picture of herself from the main account onto one of the anonymous ones?' he said. 'If she did, a reverse Google image search could find her real profile pretty quickly.'

'She says not. She says she was really careful. And anyway, he – they – don't know her real name, only where she lives.'

Xander asked, 'Could there have been anything in any of the pictures that gave away her location? Like, a selfie by the Tube station, or in a local pub or something?'

I shook my head. 'They were all taken in her home, in her bedroom. And they weren't pictures, although some of them were. Mostly they were videos.'

'Could this person have seen her typing a password, or something like that, in one of the videos?'

'She says she was really careful. And anyway, if he'd done that he would have known her name and email address and stuff too, surely? Not just where she lives.'

'And he's never sent things to her?' Xander had abandoned the neutral pronoun, I noticed. There was no point pretending that the person trying to find my friend wasn't a man. 'Money to a PayPal account? Or Verse or Venmo?'

'Yes, he has. Quite a lot of money. But it was a while ago – like, a couple of months. She hasn't been in touch with him since then, and she thinks all the transactions were secure.'

'How about gifts? Like, through an Amazon wishlist or something like that?'

I nodded miserably, remembering the parcel I'd opened by mistake months before, with our address on it but no name, containing the beautiful lingerie set that had cost hundreds of pounds. 'That too. But again, all anonymous.'

'Not necessarily,' he said. 'I wonder whether, if the item was dispatched through a third-party seller – so not by Amazon itself

– the seller might include the address on the dispatch confirmation it sent to Amazon, and that could somehow show up on the
customer's account. It's vanishingly unlikely, though. Amazon are
super-careful about data. They have to be.'

I drank some more of my hot chocolate, then stopped. I was
feeling a bit sick.

'Charlotte, this is really a friend you're talking about here, isn't
it? Not you?'

I thought about how everyone told Xander things, and I
wondered whether he told people things in turn. I could say that
it was me I was describing, not Tansy, to make sure that if he said
anything to Renzo about our conversation, it would be me who he
said it about, not Renzo's girlfriend. But I couldn't do that. I was
as sure as I could be that Xander wouldn't spread gossip about me,
but I couldn't gamble my career on it. I had lots of friends. I could
be talking about any one of them.

'It's not me. It's a friend. Honest.'

'She's doing webcam work, isn't she?'

I tried to keep my face expressionless, but nothing could have
concealed the hot rush of colour that flooded my face.

'Yes. How did you know?'

'You told me,' he said. 'There wasn't anything else that fitted with
what you said. Videos, Snapchat and Twitter accounts, everything
done from her bedroom at home, some man sending her money
and gifts and then turning all stalkery when she wasn't doing what
he wanted any more.'

Helplessly I said, 'I didn't know it was even a thing. I mean, I
kind of did, but not a thing that anyone I know would get into.'

'When I was working in Colombia I had a colleague whose daughter did it,' Xander said. 'She was one of the ladies who cleaned our office, working on a low wage, struggling to make ends meet. She had six daughters, and the eldest had a job in a call centre, she told her mother, to help put the younger ones through school. Except she was working for a webcam studio. It's a huge business there. When Maria found out what she was really doing, she went mental and chucked Valeria out of the house. After that, she didn't just do webcams any more. And she was murdered by a punter six months later. Maria was broken by it.'

'That's so awful. Poor Valeria.'

Poor Valeria, and poor Tansy, too. She hadn't crossed the line into actual porn, and certainly not actual prostitution – she'd reminded me of that, over and over, in between making me promise that I would never tell Renzo. I remembered the soft music I'd heard coming from her bedroom through the wall, and how I'd thought she was chatting to her mum and sister in Cornwall, and what she'd really been doing there, alone, was being watched by strangers online.

'But why did you do it, Tansy?' I'd asked. 'I mean, did you enjoy it?'

'For the money,' she said. 'Why else? I told you about my dad having a gambling problem, remember? Earlier this year, it got really bad. Mum was struggling to pay the bills. Her credit cards were all maxed out and the rent was two months in arrears and the landlord was getting nasty. And I was skint, too, after Christmas. At first I thought it would be easy money, but I got that idea out of my head after a few weeks. It was kind of fun at first, when you're sitting there in your nightie chatting to people and they're telling you you're so hot, you're so witty, and they're paying you money for it. And I wasn't even doing anything, literally just sitting in my room in some lingerie, that's it.'

'But that's not what it's about, really, is it?' I asked. 'I mean, it's just not, right?'

She gave a hard, unamused laugh. 'Nope. I guess if guys wanted to have a nice chat to a woman in a nightie they'd do that with their wives in bed, right? They might tell you that's what they want, at first, and then they start wanting more, you know?'

I hadn't known, but I'd nodded anyway. I watched Tansy's face and I could see her deciding whether – and how much – to tell me. I suppose she must have wanted to talk to someone about it for a long time, because once she started, it was like she couldn't stop.

'There's public chat, which is quite casual and innocent, lots of banter and stuff, and when everyone watching your room has paid in enough money, you take your kit off. It's like a sliding scale, but a hundred quid in total gets you naked. And then some of them disappear off to watch someone else, and if you're lucky someone asks you for a private.'

'Right,' I said.

'I figured out pretty quickly that the way to make it work is to get regulars, guys who come into your room a couple of times a week and get to know you.'

'Like Travis?'

'Yeah. I mean, I had other regulars too, but he was my main one. The day I moved in here, that's what I'd been doing, why I was late and pissed. I ended up having to get drunk to go through with it. I was online all afternoon, talking to him. That's the weird thing about Travis. He didn't want any of the other stuff, just to talk. But he used to keep me there for hours and hours sometimes, asking me questions about myself, and I'd have to lie and make stuff up because I was scared if I let too much out he'd find out who I really am. I was caning the wine that day to get me through it. He sent me the flowers and the champagne I gave you, through a wishlist so he wouldn't have my address. Not that I wanted the stupid things – what use were they to me? They wouldn't help Mum. But I was so careful, Charlotte, I really was. You can't let people know your real name, or where you live. It's not safe. And now he does.'

'Are you scared of him?' I asked, although the question was pretty pointless, really. Looking at her huddled, trembling body, it was obvious that she was terrified.

'Not of him, exactly,' she said. 'I mean, I spent hours talking to the guy online, so I got to know him, in a weird kind of way. He never wanted me to do any weird shit. But I fucked up, that day when I moved in here. I ended up telling him about Mum and why I was doing what I was doing. I shouldn't have. I wish I hadn't. It gave him a way of controlling me, because he knew I needed him. After that, he started asking for more, for different things – to meet me in real life, to buy me things other than just lingerie and flowers and… things. He started offering to send money directly to Mum, making all these promises. I didn't know what to do – he was getting too close to the real me. He started to creep me out. And now he's found our house – it just feels so close. Way too close. He could find out where I work, if he found me here. He could find Renzo and tell him.'

I didn't ask her what the 'weird shit' was; I didn't want to know.

'He won't tell Renzo,' I said, wishing I truly believed it.

'If only I knew how he'd managed to find me, I'd feel better. I just can't understand it. How did he find me here?'

'I don't know, babe, I really don't. I can ask Pavel or someone at work. But if you told Renzo yourself, then Travis wouldn't have that power over you any more. You wouldn't have to worry.'

'I can't. I could never tell him. You know, when we were in Paris, when we slept together the first time, I couldn't stop thinking about Travis and the others. Even though sex with Renzo was – is – so amazing, I felt so ashamed, so dirty, so guilty. I knew I could never, ever go online again. And I didn't. As soon as I got home I deleted my account. I didn't tell Travis or any of my regulars, I just disappeared. Being with Renzo made me realise how grubby and pathetic it all was. There was no way I could be both things at once – Renzo's girlfriend and bloody Saskia. I'd already started to hate being her. And you know what the really horrible thing about it was? Because I was doing it for Mum, I kind of found myself resenting her for needing the money, like she was making me do it. And that was just the worst feeling ever. I couldn't even feel proud that I was helping my mum.'

The memory of Tansy's tears made me start to cry too.

'Charlotte,' Xander said now. 'Your friend will be okay. She has you. Don't cry.'

And he reached out and patted me on the shoulder, giving me a little squeeze.

It was the squeeze that did it. I buried my face in his coat, not caring how scratchy the tweed felt against my skin, and sobbed and sobbed.

Xander patted me a bit more, ineffectual and embarrassed the way blokes usually are when women cry, then I heard him mutter, 'Oh God,' and he wrapped his arms around me and held me close until I'd finished.

Then he passed me a handful of paper napkins left over from our lunch, and held my hand mirror for me while I repaired my face, which was hard because I couldn't meet his eyes, knowing they were so kind and concerned I'd start to cry again if I did.

'I don't know how he found your friend,' he said. 'I'll ask around, outside of work. But we may never get the answer.'

Chapter Nineteen

I spent the rest of that afternoon at the mercy of Piers's latest stack of business cards. He'd been to a conference in China and come back with an absolute mountain of the things – I didn't count them because it would have been too depressing, but there must have been at least three hundred – and each one had to be entered into our database. Of course, to make matters worse, the names on the cards weren't easy to remember, like John Smith and David Jones, but were things like Zheng Xiaoteng, so I had to check the spelling of each one multiple times, and I kept putting the first name and family name in the wrong fields and losing track of how many digits there needed to be in the mobile phone numbers.

Plugged into my headphones to help me concentrate, I was shut off from Tansy and her problems, Myles and his irresistible body and horrible flat, the memory of how my imagination had summoned Xander into my bed – anything at all going on in the office or in the world beyond it. So it was only when I was on the Tube home that I went onto Twitter and found out the massive news I had missed.

I'm not exaggerating: I literally squealed, and got odd looks from the commuters surrounding me. Without pausing to think, I tapped out a text to Maddy.

Woe! Woe for you and me and every other woman on the planet! Prince Harry's getting married! I can't believe it, can you?

I added an assortment of emojis – a crying face, a diamond ring, a bottle of champagne and a hat – and pressed send.

And then I remembered. Maddy and I weren't speaking; we hadn't spoken since her hen weekend almost a month before. I wasn't even sure if I was still going to be a bridesmaid, after I'd spent half of it with Myles instead of with the hens, and been excluded from the business-class upgrade on the way home. Even though none of them had unfriended me on Facebook, I suspected that I'd been put on a limited profile, because the flood of wedding-related posts on my feed had entirely dried up.

Unfortunately for me, the train was in a station when I pressed send, so instead of getting stuck in a signal-free dead zone and allowing me to delete it, the text had been delivered.

'Shit,' I muttered, and the woman next to me glanced at me again, then edged slightly away. Rule one of London Underground: you don't talk on London Underground. Not at seven on a Monday evening, anyway. Unless you were the group of German teenagers standing further down the carriage, who evidently hadn't got the memo.

Well, it was done. The text was sent. Maddy would either reply, or ignore it. I thought wistfully how, if things were how they used to be, she'd have replied straight away, sharing my excitement, adding a bunch of emojis of her own, and pretending to be much more gutted than she actually, realistically, could be.

You see, I know that millions of women up and down the country have nurtured crushes on the handsome prince, but with Maddy it was serious. Ever since she was little, she'd said that she, one day, was going to marry Harry. It was our first year of secondary school, and other girls were announcing their ambitions to win *The X Factor* or be supermodels or, in the case of the more high-minded among us, become heart surgeons (there weren't many of those), and Maddy had calmly announced that she was going to be a princess.

She had it all worked out. She was going to study veterinary medicine and specialise in horses, and then she'd move down south and work in Berkshire, and when Harry's favourite polo pony developed a mystery illness that no other vet could diagnose, she would be on hand to find a miracle cure. The prince, hollow-eyed from a sleepless night, would look at her over the stable door and say he couldn't thank her enough, and the friendship that grew from that would soon blossom into love.

I'm sure it was only that fantasy that got Maddy through vet school, which as far as I could tell was bloody hard work and involved spending a lot of time with your hand up cows' fannies.

At some point in the process real life intervened and Maddy got a job as a junior vet in a practice in London where the patients were mostly obese cats and dogs with behavioural problems, with the odd stressed-out house bunny thrown in for variety, and she must have realised that her dream was slipping away. Still, though, when Prince William got engaged, she went all giddy and said, 'See? See? It can happen to anyone!' and spent a few weeks wearing lots of black eyeliner and nude L.K.Bennett heels and trekking across London on her days off to go shopping on the King's Road.

And now, even though Maddy was about to get married herself, I knew she'd be following the news avidly, buying every single tabloid newspaper for the commemorative colour supplements, watching the official interviews on telly and planning a party even more over the top than the one she'd hosted for William and Kate's wedding.

Fuck, Maddy, I really miss you, I thought, but I managed not to say it out loud. I checked my phone at every stop, but there was no reply from her even though I could see she'd read my message. If she didn't respond, I decided, I'd officially resign from being her bridesmaid, accept that our friendship was over and move on. There was no point, as Prince Harry doubtless knew all too well, in flogging a dead horse.

But just as I was walking past The Daily Grind, my phone buzzed. I rummaged in my bag and extracted it, and saw a slew of text messages.

> *Hey – how was your day? Did you manage to find anything out? I'm at home – do you want dinner? Thanks again for offering to help, I really appreciate it x*

From Tansy.

> *Hi gorgeous. I've been thinking of you all day. Last night was amazing. Fancy a rematch? I'm at the flat alone and it seems very empty without you xxxx*

From Myles.

> *Hi – I've just heard from Maddy. Have you? We need to talk.*

From Molly.

And from Maddy: *Hello lovely. Thanks for your text. I owe you a massive apology. Any chance you're free tonight? We could meet in town somewhere? PS Harry though, OMG!* and a succession of emojis even longer and more random than my own.

I thought about it for a while, but not very long. Then I sent four texts back.

Nothing to report yet, sorry, but my colleague Xander is going to think about it. I'm out tonight – home by 11. Don't answer the door and don't worry, it will all be fine. Think you should talk to R about it though! X

It was amazing for me too. You're amazing! But I'm busy tonight, sorry. Tomorrow? Xxxx

Yeah, I think we do. I'm seeing Maddy this evening.

And *Where shall we meet? London Bridge somewhere? That tapas place? Can be there in half an hour.*

And, not waiting for Maddy to reply because I knew she got her train home from London Bridge and loved tapas, I turned round and got back on the Tube.

Sure enough, when I arrived at the restaurant, she was waiting in a booth for two, a bottle of our usual kind of sherry and two glasses in front of her. She jumped up when she saw me and we had a massive hug, and by the time we'd finished we both had tears in our eyes.

'Come on, sit down, let's have a drink. I need one and I need to talk to you,' she said to me.

I sat down and poured sherry into our glasses. Then, at exactly the same time, we both said, 'I'm so sorry.'

'No, I'm sorry,' I said. 'I abandoned you on your hen weekend.'

'Only because I was being a total, copper-bottomed, ocean-going bitch,' Maddy said.

'You weren't!' I protested.

'I was,' Maddy said.

'Okay, you were,' I admitted, and we both laughed.

'So I owe you an apology, and an explanation. I've been a dick, and now it's coming back to bite me in the arse and I don't know what to do.'

'Bianca?' I asked, grateful for the intel I'd received from Molly.

Maddy nodded. 'It's my fault, really. When we moved house, she was just so helpful, waiting in for deliveries for us and shouting at the builders and just being so competent about it all. I know you thought I was coping fine with the move and the wedding and everything, because that's what I wanted you to think. But I wasn't. I was missing you and missing Hackney and wondering if I'd made a terrible mistake. Not with Henry, obviously, but *life*. Moving on to a version of me that felt all strange and wrong. Being a fiancée and having a house in the suburbs with rising damp and... I don't know. I just wanted to go back to my old life. I wanted to hang out with you and watch trash TV and pop by The Daily Grind whenever I felt like it. But you can't, can you?'

'No, you can't.'

'And so when Bianca offered to help with things, I was really grateful. And I kind of realised, with the wedding, how much there was to do. I mean, because we're having it at Henry's parents' place there was no venue to book or anything, but suddenly there was only a few months to go and all these things that I hadn't even thought about, like going to France to buy the wine and organising favours for the tables and having a rehearsal dinner and buying the bridesmaids' dresses and – just everything. Everything Bianca said I had to have, otherwise their family would think I was doing it all wrong.'

'You could have asked me,' I said softly. 'I would have helped.'

'No you wouldn't. You'd have told me to stop being a bridezilla and what the fuck did I want a rehearsal dinner for, anyway?'

'Maybe,' I admitted. 'But if you wanted all that stuff, I'd have tried to make it happen. Although with work and everything…'

'I know. Trust me, I get it. I don't have time for any of it myself. But Bianca does. And she just kind of took over, and then it all took on a life of its own and of course I had to ask her to be my chief bridesmaid, because she'd put so much effort into it, even though it was you I really wanted to do it.'

Maddy took a tissue out of her bag and blew her nose. The waitress came over and asked if we were ready to order, and I chose olives, smoked almonds, manchego cheese, serrano ham, padrón peppers, vegetable tortilla – all the things we always had, without having to ask Maddy. Which was just as well, because she was having a discreet little weep into her sherry.

'Bianca said you'd said you weren't interested in the wedding stuff,' Maddy went on, dabbing at her eyes. 'She said you told her you thought I'd changed, that I was all into becoming a suburban housewife and you didn't feel like you knew me any more. And I believed her. It hurt, Charlotte, partly because I knew that if you had said those things, they would have been true.'

'I didn't say them, though,' I said, mystified. 'I've literally never even seen Bianca without other people there. Why would I bitch about you to her?'

'I don't know. Of course you wouldn't. But the way she said it – like she was really hurt and confused too – and feeling the way I felt about it all, it kind of made sense. Fuck, what a mess. I can't believe I ever thought that stuff about you could be true.'

'How do you know it's not? You believed Bianca then, so why don't you now?' I asked.

'Because she's doing the same thing to me,' Maddy said miserably. 'Pamela – Henry's mum – started acting all weird. We've always got on really well, you know we have. But when we were there for Sunday lunch a couple of weeks ago, she was being all off with me. You know, polite and everything, but just kind of cold. And then when we were loading the dishwasher – they're so fucking unreconstructed, that family, the men never lift a finger; thank God between us we managed to house-train Henry – she was like, "Madeleine, if you were unhappy with my mother-of-the-bride outfit, I would have been quite happy to have chosen something else. You had only to say." And I was like, what? Because her outfit is pretty awful, but only in a standard kind of way, like something the Queen would wear, and I hadn't said anything about it to anyone.'

I wrapped a piece of ham around a breadstick, ate it, and carried on listening.

'And now some other friend of Bianca's – she seems to go through friends really quickly, I can't think why – is having problems with her marriage and at the same time Bianca's helping her do up a flat for a client of hers, and she's all over that like she was all over my wedding, and she's not answering my texts and the wedding's in three weeks and it doesn't even feel like fun any more, it just feels like this massive load of fucking stress, and if it wasn't for loving Henry, I wouldn't even want to do any of it.'

She looked like she might be about to start crying again. I put some ham and cheese croquettes on her plate to distract her, and topped up our glasses.

'Look,' I told her. 'You've got three other bridesmaids who love you. I'm not counting Charis. What chance does she have, with a mother like that? But we can sort it all out together. Seriously, last week I had to magic a drinks reception for sixty at the Chiltern Firehouse, which as you know is booked up months in advance, out of thin air. We can do this. Sack her off.'

'I can't,' Maddy said, but she was looking a bit more cheerful. 'She's Henry's sister.'

'Okay, so don't sack her off. I don't care about being chief bridesmaid. Honestly, I don't. I care about you having a lovely wedding and not panicking about it. We'll sort it, me and Molly and Chloë. We'll even do it all on Bianca's Slack group so she doesn't feel left out. And you know what? In five years' time, you'll have a lovely set of photos and a sister-in-law you manage to rub along okay with, and all of this will be ancient history. You won't care about any of it. I promise.'

Maddy ate a croquette, then a piece of ham, then a piece of cheese. Then she said, 'Oh my God, I am so hungry,' and started eating all the other things as well, like she hadn't had a square meal in weeks, which I suppose she hadn't.

In between bites, she said, 'I'm such a crap friend. Tell me what's been going on with you? How's mad Adam? How's Tansy the Barbie doll? How's adorable Freezer from next door? And most importantly of all, how's the man you've been shagging?'

I told her that Adam was still Adam. I said that Tansy was actually really nice and becoming a bit of a mate and was dating Renzo, but I didn't over-egg it because our recovered friendship was still too fragile for me to want to make her think she had been supplanted with me as well as with Bianca, and I didn't want to go into any detail about Tansy's past and the sinister Travis. I told her about work. I told her that Myles was utterly delectable and fantastic in bed, but that it was early days, and I didn't go into any details about his past, either.

And then I told her about Freezer and how he'd gone missing and come back and then disappeared again, and I wasn't sure whether he was currently at home with Luke and Hannah or not. Maddy said you could just never tell with cats, and reminded me that he was microchipped, she'd done it herself at her vet's, so if the worst had happened, at least they'd know.

She told me that she and Henry were going to get a cat as soon as they were back from honeymoon, a rescue obviously, probably a black one as they were always the hardest to find homes for because they're the least Instagrammable, and I said how excited I was for them about that.

And so we spent the rest of our dinner chatting aimlessly about things that didn't matter as much as the things we'd started out talking about. Afterwards, when I was on my way home, I realised that I'd been holding back from telling her the important stuff, and I wondered whether that was how it would always be from now on, between me and my best friend.

Chapter Twenty

Hello again girlfriends, and welcome back to Sorry Not Sorry. *I kind of feel like the name I gave these podcasts has never been more appropriate than it is now.*

You see, I've had the week from hell. Everything that could go wrong, has. I pulled a muscle in my yoga class and my back is killing me. I had an argument with my mom when she asked me one time too many if I'm still single. Yes, Mother, I am. What do you want me to do about that? Oh, hold on, I am *doing it. Except the guy I went on a date with last week and thought I really connected with just ghosted me, so I'm back to square one there. And I screwed up at work by accidentally copying in a client on an email to my boss telling her that she – the client, that is – was being totally unreasonable.*

So, am I sorry about any of those things? Actually, no, I'm not. I don't regret looking after my body. I'm allowed to tell Mom to butt out of my love life. I had a great date that didn't work out. And the client – well, she's hopefully a better person for reading what I said about her, although I did have to say *I was sorry, like a million times, even though I'm not.*

But you guys aren't here to listen to me vent – you're in this for the challenges, right? So here's one for you. When shit things happen, take them on the chin and learn from them. If you're in the wrong, own it. If you're not, stand up for yourself. And if life gives you lemons – well, you know what to do with those babies.

Over the next three weeks, it felt like I hardly had time to eat or sleep. My clothes all felt too baggy. There were dark hollows under my eyes. My skin, normally the bit of me with which I was happiest, went on strike and broke out in a mixture of spots and flaky patches. My nails went all flaky too, and started to split and break, and I hadn't time to go and get gel overlays put on. My hair got so lank and flat I didn't even have to use my straighteners, which was probably just as well, because I didn't have time for that, either.

Work, in the build-up to our year-end, was manic. Xander was compiling a report on the firm's impact investment strategy, which he'd told me was 'a blatant exercise in green-washing', and was too busy to stop and perch on the corner of my desk for a chat as he usually did. Piers was in full back-slapping mode, out every day at client lunches and every night at Christmas parties, and his permanently hungover state made him more demanding than ever. When, two days before Maddy's wedding, he dumped a scribbled-on printout many pages thick on my desk and said, 'Here's my Christmas card list, darling. Choose cards from a worthy charity, won't you, and please make sure they're all handwritten. You can print out the address labels,' I actually had to escape to the loo and have a little cry.

There, I thought bitterly, went my chances of sneaking off to have my hair and nails done in time for the wedding. There went my chances of getting a decent night's sleep after having left the office before ten o'clock at night precisely zero times in the past two weeks. There went my chances of going to Hoxton that evening to meet Myles.

I'd only seen him once more at the empty flat and, that time, it hadn't been empty any more. In fact, it had been transformed. The walls had been painted a clean, even pale grey. The suede sofa was still there, but it was scattered with orange and gold cushions and had been joined by two squashy grey armchairs. The dangling wires had been connected to a new widescreen telly. There were fluffy white towels in the bathroom and dove-grey sheets on the bed and even glasses and plates in the kitchen cupboards.

'This is a bit more civilised, isn't it?' Myles had said, undressing me and kissing me until my knees gave way and I collapsed onto the bed. It was definitely more civilised and the sex was as blissful as ever, but somehow I couldn't feel at ease there with him, cutlery or no cutlery. And when I'd invited him to come for pizza at The Daily Grind with me and Tansy and spend the night at ours the next Friday, he'd said he was sorry but he had a work function, and perhaps we could see each other one night during the week. But then I was too busy, so it didn't happen.

Maybe, I thought mournfully, assessing Piers's Christmas card list, being single was how it was going to be for me, for ever. He'd made notes next to most of the names in his indecipherable, spidery handwriting, saying things like, 'Jewish. Non-religious card', 'Orthodox. Traditional' and 'Call office to check whether in London or LA'. If I followed all his instructions, the job would take days – days I didn't have, because every spare second had been spent on the phone to Molly and Chloë, making last-minute plans for the wedding now that Bianca was off the scene.

The seating plan for the reception had to be finalised. Black and white balloons and feather table centrepieces had to be ordered. A table for thirty had to be found and booked for the rehearsal dinner, a challenge that would have made me cry again if Xander hadn't overheard me making my fifteenth phone call to a fully booked restaurant, and said, 'I just heard that Fredericks Brothers has gone bust. Want me to ask my contact where their Christmas do was booked?' And, miraculously, it had been on the right night, at a restaurant so famous even Bianca would be impressed.

Somehow, that Thursday afternoon, I had begun to feel that it was all coming together, even if it was at the expense of my sanity. I checked my calendar. If I could finish typing Colin's report and send it to Greg for Colin to sign off, reply to the caterers' email about whether to substitute the quail's eggs (evidently there'd been a surge in demand pre-Christmas and the nation's quail were on a go-slow, for which I didn't blame them one bit) with devilled mushrooms or sun-dried tomato crostini, and forward the progress report on the office refurb to Margot, remembering to delete the filthy covering note from Myles, I could go to the hairdresser, take a bunch of Piers's cards with me, and write them while my roots were being done.

But, when I clicked on my email icon, I was met with a spinning hourglass, and then a message saying that my computer couldn't connect to the proxy server.

'What the fuck's going on with the internet connection?' asked Greg.

'Where the hell is Pavel?' said Renzo.

'Someone call that cyber woman,' ordered Piers, emerging from the gents', flushed from his lunch. 'Even if she can't fix the problem, at least we can all look at her tits.'

I opened my mouth to call him out on his sexism, then closed it again. There was no point, not with him in this mood. Besides, by 'someone', he presumably meant me. Only problem was, I couldn't for the life of me remember her name. I could picture her as clearly as if she was standing right in front of me, petite, olive-skinned and pretty. Her name was pretty, too, something Greek: Elleni or Antigoni or something. But what?

And then, as if summoned by the urgency of my thoughts, she emerged from the boardroom, closely followed by Pavel, Colin, Margot, the Head of HR and the Head of Legal.

'We seem to have a problem with our server, Chryssanthi,' Xander said. 'Just as well you're here.'

She and Pavel hurried to Pavel's desk, Chryssanthi pulling a laptop out of her bag.

'Everyone switch off,' Margot said. 'Log out, if you can, otherwise just power off. Do it now.'

She paused in front of my desk. 'Charlotte,' she began, and then stopped.

'Yes? Is there anything I can do?'

Margot said, 'You're wanted in the meeting room.'

My mouth immediately turned as dry as paper and my stomach churned so violently I was glad I hadn't had time for lunch. Vomming all over my line manager's covetable green suede wedges would have got me into even more shit than I was evidently in.

But for what? Had I made a disastrous error in the annual forecast? Maybe I had, but as it hadn't yet been signed off, disaster would have been averted as soon as it was spotted. Had Piers got wind of my plan to decamp to Studio Vincenzo for the afternoon? Impossible – and again, if he had, it wouldn't matter, since I was planning to carry on with the task he'd given me while I was there.

Then I felt even sicker. What if it was something to do with Tansy? What if Renzo had somehow found out, and I was going to be asked what I knew? What if Travis had… I couldn't even begin to imagine what he might have done. But that fear was instantly allayed when I saw Renzo talking into his phone with the uncharacteristically soppy look on his face, in the uncharacteristically low voice I'd come to recognise as the one he used when talking to her.

'Might be really late, or I might be able to get away early,' he was saying. 'I'll call you, okay? *Ciao.*'

Suddenly, it dawned on me. What if they'd found out about me and Myles, and sleeping with a supplier was a disciplinary offence?

'Charlotte?' Margot repeated. 'Now, please.'

Fuck. 'Sorry, sorry,' I said, gathering a notebook and a pen and hurrying in the direction of the fishbowl.

'Not there,' Margot said, gesturing discreetly towards the other meeting room. The one no one could see into. The one where executions took place. 'You might want your handbag.'

The churning nausea in my stomach was replaced by an icy stillness. I knew what this meant.

I saw Xander watching, appalled, as I gathered up my things and followed Margot.

'Have a seat,' she said, when I'd completed the walk across the office that, although short, seemed to last as long as one of Piers's PowerPoint presentations. 'Normally Colin would have joined us, but as he's a little tied up right now—' in spite of my terror, I had to bite back a hysterical giggle '—Robert and Melanie are standing in.'

Legal and HR nodded gravely. At least no one was going to shout at me, I thought.

Margot said, 'Charlotte, we've asked you here to let you know that you are, with immediate effect, suspended on full pay, pending an investigation into allegations of gross misconduct and possibly criminal charges.'

'What?' I tried to say, but something wasn't working: my lips were stiff and immobile, as if I'd been hitting the Restylane big time, and my throat and tongue were completely dry. All that came out was a sort of rasp. 'I didn't... What are you saying I've done?'

'We'd like you to return your company phone and laptop,' Margot went on, as if I hadn't spoken. 'A letter inviting you to attend an investigatory meeting will be couriered to your home address early next week.'

'My laptop's on my desk,' I muttered, so indistinctly I might as well have been speaking Russian. I pulled my handbag onto my lap and fumbled in it for my phone. A stack of blank Christmas cards and Piers's printed spreadsheet slithered out onto the table.

'And those,' Margot said. 'And any other company property you have in your possession.'

The Christmas cards weren't even company property, I thought: I'd paid for them with my own money, planning to claim them back on expenses. But right now, the seventy pounds I'd spent on assorted tasteful and gaudy, spiritual and agnostic designs in aid of Save the Children was the least of my worries.

I tipped my bag upside down on the table and the three of them watched as I rifled through the contents.

In their direction, I pushed my work mobile, a Dictaphone, a spiral-bound notepad half-full with two months' worth of scribbles, a Sexy Fish business card, several leaking Colton Capital pens and two unopened protein bars.

On my side were my purse, my house keys, my personal phone (an iPhone 5 that had seen better days), an Oyster card I hadn't used in ages because my travel all went through my work mobile, a plastic box of Smints, a jumble of make-up and tampons, some disintegrating tissues and, mortifyingly, an empty condom wrapper.

I put the bag back on my lap and used my forearm to swoosh everything back across the table and into it, the way Maddy slides chopped onions into a pan with the blade of a knife.

I looked at them. Melanie and Robert's faces were carefully composed, stern and still. Margot looked like she wanted to say something else, but she didn't.

This is it, I thought. *Three years here, and it ends like this.* I knew what happened when people were suspended on full pay: they never came back. Not ever. I'd never again push the boardroom door open with my hip because my hands were busy carrying a tray of coffee. I'd never get changed into my gym kit, then check my phone and find an email from Piers and have to go back to my desk. I'd never have to sort out yet another new pass for Xander.

Work pass. I unlooped the lanyard from my neck and pushed that across the table as well.

Then I stood up. Margot stood too. She gave Robert and Melanie a glance that said, 'BRB,' and she walked me to the lift, escorted me to the ground floor, and out into the street, then gave me a little pat on the back to send me on my way. She didn't say anything more. I expect Robert had told her not to.

I spent the journey home trying my hardest not to cry. If talking to yourself on the Tube makes your fellow passengers feel uncomfortable, crying is pretty much torture. It helped that I was almost too shocked and confused to give in to tears. Until the whole enormity of what had happened to me sunk in and the injustice of it all properly began to bite, I was dry-eyed and dry-mouthed, my hands shaking violently as I clutched my bag against my chest.

What the fuck had happened? I hadn't done anything wrong. Literally the only thing I could think of that was even the tiniest bit improper was sleeping with Myles, with whom – or with whose firm – Colton Capital had a project worth six figures on the go. It had hardly occurred to me to ask anyone if what we were doing was okay, partly because I'd been too busy worrying that it wasn't okay for totally unrelated reasons. Maybe it was wrong; maybe it was horribly unethical, compromising me or the firm in some way. But one thing I knew for sure was that if, under some code of conduct I'd never seen or heard of, relationships between client and supplier were forbidden, Myles would have known. He'd have known and, however much he wanted and fancied me, I'd have been off limits until the last inch of carpet had been laid, the last television screen installed.

I might not know how to look after my interests, but I was pretty sure he did, and the risk – if there was any – was more on his side than mine.

I tapped out a text asking him if he was free that night or the next day, and sent it when the train stopped at Holborn, but by the time I got off at Liverpool Street there'd been no reply. I considered going straight to the flat – to The Factory, as he called it – but arriving there unannounced would look too desperate, and the prospect of being turned away with an impassive shake of the concierge's head was too mortifying to contemplate.

I fought my way to the Overground through the crowds of early commuters and out-of-town Christmas shoppers, remembering that I hadn't bought a single Christmas gift for anyone yet. It was going to have to be a last-minute splurge on Amazon for me, yet again. The usual overpriced and under-thought-about gifts for my nan in Newcastle and Mum, Jim and their – his – family in Spain, something extravagant and pampering for Tansy, something for the house for Maddy… But what was I even thinking, compiling a mental Christmas list when in just a few days I would have no job and no income?

The thought brought me back with a jerk to the cold reality of my situation. *What do they think I've done?*

After last year's Christmas party, one of the traders had been summarily dismissed because he'd had an argument with one of the quants and punched him on the nose. Earlier in the year, a portfolio manager had been caught selling information about our investment strategy to a rival fund. One of the women on the sales team had been fired for coming to work totally looped on cocaine.

I hadn't done any of those things. I hadn't done anything wrong at all that I could think of.

Maybe I'd displeased Piers in some way. Displeasing Piers was easy: no matter how hard I worked, he always had fresh demands for more lists to be compiled, more PowerPoint presentations to be edited, more dinners to be booked. But I'd done everything he'd asked me to do, if not always as quickly as he'd like. He'd even said he was impressed with my work, just two weeks before. I'd been excited about getting a decent bonus on the back of it, to go into my flat-deposit fund.

Well, I could kiss that goodbye now. If Colton Capital fired me, no other firm would take me on. I wasn't a genius analyst or a shit-hot systems engineer: I was just a junior admin girl. I'd be untouchable and unemployable. I'd have to move back up north and claim Jobseeker's Allowance until I found some horrible, poorly paid work with no prospects. I'd never see Myles again.

Mired in self-pity, I walked home and went straight upstairs and got into bed. I wondered what the Bad Girl would have done in my position. Own her mistakes? I couldn't have – I didn't even know I'd made any. Stand up for herself? I'd totally failed on that score too. Life had given me lemons, and even if they'd been limes it wouldn't have helped, because I'd run out of tequila.

I was woken not by the insistent beep of my phone's alarm as usual, but by sun streaming through the window. My first thought was what a beautiful day it was – icy cold but sunny and crisp, my favourite kind of winter's day. My second was that I hoped it would be the same tomorrow, for Maddy's wedding. Then, with a horrible thud, I remembered what had happened. I was going to be sacked.

I needed to talk to a lawyer first and, once it was all over, find some way to pay the rent. I needed a plan, and fast.

But, with Maddy and Henry's rehearsal dinner that night, there was no time for planning. There was no time for anything, certainly not for having the good long cry I badly wanted.

I got out of bed and looked out at the morning. There was frost on the grass and a robin perched on the bare branch of the ash tree. Whether it was the weather or the effect of a decent night's sleep for the first time in ages, I suddenly felt a bit more optimistic. I had things to do, but a whole day to do them in. I could make a plan.

After a shower, I made tea and toast and called Chloë. Employment law wasn't her area, as I knew, she said, but her colleague Rashid would contact me on Monday. In the meantime, she said, I mustn't panic: nothing was going to happen today.

'Apart from you taking yourself off and getting your hair and nails done,' she said. 'We're meeting at seven for the dinner tonight, so take the rest of the day off. Everything's under control, thanks mostly to you. I'm going with Bianca to pick up the dresses and drop them off at Henry's parents' place ready for tomorrow. The florist will be there first thing in the morning, and Molly's collecting the cake with Maddy's mum. Take care of yourself. Switch your phone off; I'll text Maddy and tell her to call me if she needs anything.'

I did as I was told. By eleven o'clock, I had newly blonded roots and a rather fabulous bouncy blow-dry.

'Oh my God,' the stylist said. 'You look just like Blake Lively.'

'Really? Not like Ivanka Trump?'

'Who?' she said, and I gave her a fat tip and skipped happily out into the sunshine. Then, as the cold air hit my face, the reality of my situation came crashing down again. Work. Margot, Melanie and Robert's stern expressions. The letter that would arrive in just a few days, telling me what they believed I had done.

It was terrifying – a void I couldn't bring myself to stare down into. But there was also absolutely nothing I could do about it now, and I couldn't let Maddy down all over again by being in bits over the loss of my career at her wedding. So, more soberly, I hurried down the street to the nail salon, where I had my nails transformed from a chipped, ragged-cuticled mess to shell-pink perfection and my eyebrows tinted and threaded, but I drew the line at the beautician's suggestion that she thread my face as well. There's looking like a yeti, and then there's going through excruciating pain in order to not look like one, and I knew which I was going to pick.

My life might be spiralling into chaos, but at least I could look my best while it was happening, I thought. It was amazing how the little things helped.

On Monday, I'd deal with the nightmare of my career. At some unspecified point in the future, I'd get in touch with Xander and find out whether he'd learned anything that could solve the mystery of Travis and keep Tansy safe. Maybe I could even persuade her to do the right thing and come clean with Renzo about her past, so that their relationship could move forward without secrets. But for now, I needed to focus on my friend's wedding.

I went home and packed an overnight bag with the essentials Google had told me a bridesmaid should have to cover any emergency: sewing kit, tissues, cereal bars, hair spray, straighteners in case Maddy's ones blew a fuse, nail file, spare tights and every item my make-up collection contained, as well as my own clothes, including the industrial-strength control pants I'd bought to wear under my bridesmaid's dress and a sparkly black dress that would do for the rehearsal dinner.

I'd bought it to wear to the Colton Capital Christmas party, but I guessed I'd been uninvited from that around about when they told me to pack my bag and leave the building.

Chapter Twenty-One

Hey girlfriend! How's it going? My last podcast caught me on a bit of a downer, but I'm over it now – in fact, I'm totally psyched to be sharing with you the next of the Sorry Not Sorry *dating challenges! How are you getting on with them? Maybe Mr Right hasn't shown up yet, but I hope they're helping you to have more fun dating, and maybe even learn a bit more about yourself. Today's challenge is kind of all about that.*

You won't believe how often I hear women say, 'Oh, no, he's just not my type.' But when you ask them more about that, it turns out that's not quite what they mean. Let me explain. Like, say your mom's always told you how happy it would make her to see you settled down with a nice Jewish doctor. And so you get into the mindset of thinking that nice Jewish doctors are your type, and it's not worth dating anyone else – not even the hot Puerto Rican musician who lives in the next-door apartment, who you could have loads of fun and hot sex with, even if he doesn't turn out to be The One!

So that's your challenge for today. Think about guys who you wouldn't necessarily think of as your type, and why not. And get broadening those horizons!

I'll say one thing for Bianca: her sense of dramatic timing was epic.

She was on best behaviour all through the rehearsal dinner. She sat next to Adam (who had scrubbed up amazingly well for his role as one of Henry's ushers, and actually looked quite handsome with his hair decently cut and his clothes clean and even ironed) and chatted pleasantly away to him. I kept my distance, eyeing her warily from the other end of the table, but there didn't seem to be anything to worry about.

Maddy and Henry were radiantly happy. Their parents were in getting-to-know-each-other mode. Charis was rushing around, completely overexcited, getting under the waitresses' feet and fiddling with the decorations on the Christmas tree while being completely ignored by her mother. The vicar beamed benevolently at us all and said grace before the meal, which was an unqualified success thanks to Xander's tip-off of a spare table for thirty at the River Café.

We all got taxis back to Henry's childhood home, an enormous house overlooking the Thames, and Bianca showed me to my bedroom and said, 'So, tomorrow's the big day! Thanks so much for all your hard work. I hope you get a good night's rest.'

As soon as the door closed, I thought in amazement that she was behaving almost like a normal human being, and maybe it was all going to be okay after all.

But I was wrong.

The next morning, we all got ready together in what was Bianca's old bedroom, which, like the rest of the house, startled me with its size and luxuriousness. Henry's mum had brought in a couple of bottles of champagne, 'Just to take the edge off, darlings,' and we

all had a few glasses. Maddy didn't seem nervous, just giddy with
excitement, and we all kept breaking into fits of laughter over silly
things, even Bianca (although her smile never quite reached her
eyes, possibly because whoever did her Botox for the occasion had
done it with a bit of a heavy hand).

She waited until we were all dressed, our hair and make-up done.
I am pretty sure that Bianca had slipped Monty a few quid to take
my humbug dress in slightly too much, so that I'd look like a total
heifer in the photographs and possibly burst a seam, but thanks
to my recent weight loss and the awesome power of elastane, it
actually looked good on me.

Molly and Chloë looked lovely too, and – annoyingly – Bianca
herself, who with her red hair and porcelain skin suited the harsh
colour scheme perfectly. Which, of course, was why she'd chosen it.

Maddy, in her ice-white column dress and elbow-length gloves,
a feather head-dress on her glossy dark hair and a matching boa
wrapped around her shoulders, was so beautiful I couldn't look at
her for too long because otherwise I'd cry.

The hair and make-up woman had packed up her kit and
left. Outside in the frosty sunshine, we could see the caterers
staggering to the marquee with their crates of glasses and the
first of many trays of food. The mums, who'd been bustling in
and out all morning (Henry's mum, as Maddy had said, looking
like the Queen in powder blue; Maddy's mum in a fitted fuchsia
number that made her look about twenty years younger than the
mother of the groom) asking Maddy if she was sure she didn't
want another piece of toast to keep her strength up and telling
us how pretty we all looked, had gone to check that the heaters

in the marquee were working and to supervise Charis having a run around the garden.

Molly looked at her watch and said, 'If it takes five minutes to get to the church, we should leave in ten. That way, you'll be just a tiny bit late, but not so late Henry starts worrying he's been jilted.'

We all broke into a last-minute frenzy of selfie-taking and make-up checking, and into the happy babble of chat, Bianca said, 'This must feel really strange to you, Charlotte.'

'What, Maddy getting married?' I asked. 'Of course it does, a bit. But she and Henry are made for each other, anyone can tell they are. And we'll still be best mates.'

'No.' Bianca raised her voice a bit to make sure no one would miss a word, 'Not that. I mean, going into church and hearing them say their vows, promising to be together forever, when you're fucking a married man.'

Her words hung in the air like a toxic cloud. I felt my face go very cold, then very hot. 'I don't know what you're talking about.'

'Oh, I think you do. "I've got a boyfriend. His name's Myles, he's an architect,"' she said, mimicking my accent. 'It's a small industry, you know. As it happens I've been working with him on a number of projects, and over time I've got to know him quite well. Him and Sloane, *his wife.*'

'They're separated. He moved out a few weeks ago. They're getting divorced…' My words spilled out, and when I heard them I realised no one would believe them, and I didn't, either.

'Bullshit,' Bianca spat. 'Next thing you'll be saying she doesn't understand him, and they never sleep together. They're trying to have a baby, you know. They're going through fertility treatment.

I've been supporting Sloane through her journey, and it's been a long and painful one for her. One that's involved having lots and lots of sex. Sloane's told me all about it. I guess she knows she can trust me.'

If that's what this Sloane thinks, then she's a pretty poor judge of character, I thought. And then I realised that if she didn't know her husband was cheating on her, then she almost certainly was. And that I, believing what Myles had told me, was even worse.

I remembered the sense of power I'd felt when he had looked at me, the feeling of heady elation his desire had given me, and I realised that it had all been an illusion. All along, he'd had all of the power, because he'd known what he wanted from me and coldly, calculatedly set about getting it.

He'd thought that telling me his marriage was, for all intents and purposes, over would be enough to persuade me, and then when it hadn't been, he'd upped the ante and told me that it *was* over, and like an idiot I'd believed him. Or at least, I hadn't examined what he said closely enough to imagine that it might not be true.

Still, faced with Bianca's attack, I found myself wanting to defend myself – and that meant defending him.

'He has left her,' I said, my voice coming out in a thin squeak. 'I've been to the flat where he's living.'

Bianca laughed. 'The flat – I presume you mean The Factory? The flat that belongs to two of Sloane's clients, that Myles offered to handle the sale for, because he's got a contact who's an estate agent? The flat I spent a weekend dressing for sale as a favour to my friend? I did wonder why there was an empty champagne bottle and condom wrappers in the trash. You little slut.'

I looked around at my friends. They were all frozen, bewildered and shocked. Soon, I thought, they'd stop being shocked and start judging me, just like Bianca was.

'I didn't know. You have to believe me, I didn't know. I thought he was telling the truth.'

The tears I'd managed to hold back since Margot had delivered her news on Thursday couldn't be restrained any more. I flopped down on one of the twin beds, put my face in my hands and started to cry.

'I totally understand if you don't want me to be your bridesmaid any more, Maddy,' I said between sobs.

I felt warm arms around my shoulders. Chloë and Molly had sat down on either side of me and were squeezing me tight.

'Don't be ridiculous,' Maddy said. 'That bastard, stringing you along like that, lying to you and lying to his wife! You don't owe her anything. You're not married to her – he is. He's the one who's betrayed her, not you. And besides, you had no idea! You weren't to blame. You're my friend and you always will be and of course I want you to be my bloody bridesmaid. On the other hand…'

I raised my face and saw the look Maddy was giving Bianca. So, fortunately, did Molly.

'That's enough drama for now,' she interrupted. 'Bianca, surely you must realise that this is a totally shitty way to behave? Are you trying to ruin your brother's wedding? Because quite frankly, from where I'm standing, that's what it looks like.'

'I—' Bianca began.

But Molly was in full flood. 'Ever since you got involved in planning this wedding, you've made every effort to shut Charlotte out, to alienate Maddy and us from her, to make things awkward and miserable for everybody. What are you thinking? If Charlotte made a mistake – if she believed what this creep told her – that's none of your fucking business, is it?'

'Sloane's my friend,' Bianca said, sticking her bottom lip out like a child. Whoever did her fillers had a bit of a heavy hand, too.

'And I'm going to be your sister-in-law,' Maddy said. 'Blood's thicker than water, right? So stop trying to fuck up my wedding day, and stop being foul to my friends. If I'm going to sack a bridesmaid at the last minute – and I have to admit I'm really tempted – it isn't going to be Charlotte.'

'I might be imagining things, but is that Charis out there, halfway up that tree?' Chloë asked.

Bianca turned white under her make-up. 'Oh my God,' she shrieked. 'My baby! I'll fucking kill that woman.'

Then she remembered that 'that woman' was Maddy's mum, shut up, flung open the French doors to the garden and went pelting across the lawn faster than I thought anyone could run in heels.

'I hope she doesn't fall,' Molly commented.

'Bianca?' I asked. 'I don't.'

'No! Poor wee Charis,' Molly said, then she realised I was joking and all at once, impossibly, we all started to laugh.

We watched as Maddy's mum came hurrying out of the marquee. She and Bianca reached the tree at the same time, and both stood looking up in horror at Charis, who was about five feet up and had started to cry. Then Maddy's mum kicked off her high heels and shimmied up onto one of the lower branches. Balancing like a tightrope walker, she reached up, grabbed Charis firmly under the arms, and passed her down to her mother before jumping gracefully down herself.

'They don't teach you that shit in Surrey,' Chloë said admiringly.

'Right,' Molly announced, now disaster had been averted. 'We should have left five minutes ago. Someone text Henry and say we're running late. We need to fix Charlotte's face.'

'And Mum will need new tights,' Maddy said.

'I've got stuff in my bag,' I offered, sending up a silent prayer of thanks to my Google search. 'Make-up and everything. And spare tights, and a sewing kit.'

'I'll get it from your room,' Molly said. 'You stay here.'

Like a bridesmaid SWAT team, we sprang into action. Chloë cleaned the mascara smudges from under my eyes and slathered on concealer. Maddy texted Henry, after fussing for a few seconds about whether it was as bad luck as him seeing her on their wedding morning. Molly handed Maddy's mum a fresh pair of ten-denier nudes and filed the nail she'd chipped in her climb.

But there wasn't much anyone could do about Charis's dress, much to Bianca's disgust. The front of it was all smeared with green slime from the moss on the tree, there were little snags in the hem from the branches, and her white tights and shoes were white no longer. But Charis didn't seem to care – in fact, she was incredibly pleased with herself, asking if we'd seen how high she'd got and insisting that she hadn't needed rescuing at all. I couldn't help wondering what Bianca had been like as a child, and how Charis would turn out when she was grown up. I felt a bit sorry for Henry's mum and a bit less sorry for Bianca herself.

'What are we going to do?' Bianca demanded. 'What about the photos?'

Maddy said, 'Let her go as she is. Badge of honour. And it'll be a great story to tell on her own wedding day. I'm not bothered if people think she's got a neglectful mother.'

Bianca's mouth opened and closed a few times, like an enraged goldfish, but there was nothing she could say, really, and no time to make other arrangements.

'Are we all ready then?' Maddy asked. 'Sure? No more drama? Right. Then let's get going, because it's almost quarter past two and I'd quite like to get married at some point this afternoon.'

After that, the day went without a hitch – apart from the one that was meant to happen, of course. We followed Maddy as she walked down the aisle on her mum's arm and I felt a big rush of melty happiness when I saw Henry waiting there next to his brother, all proud and nervous in their morning coats and black and white striped cravats, and watched his face change to amazed delight when he saw how beautiful the bride looked.

We relinquished Maddy to her soon-to-be husband and the vicar and took our seats, and although the ceremony was as moving and lovely as weddings always are, I couldn't help my attention wandering a bit. I watched as the winter afternoon slowly darkened the stained glass windows, and I listened to the voices of the choir seeming to light up the church from within.

Maddy wasn't religious and nor was Henry, but they'd decided to go all traditional because it would please Henry's parents and also, as Maddy had frankly admitted, because the church was such a stunning venue, especially with the advent flowers packing every corner and the vicar in his white and gold vestments. Also Henry, being a bit of a traditionalist in some ways, thought the words of the Anglican marriage service were among the most beautiful ever written, and he wanted to say them to Maddy and hear her say them to him. (Although, I noticed with satisfaction, she made no promise to obey him. As if Maddy had ever obeyed anyone in her life.)

But I wondered, as the joyful and serious occasion went on, how they'd feel in a few years' time about the things they were promising now. 'For better, for worse, for richer, for poorer, in sickness and in health' – Myles must have said those words, however long ago it was, to Sloane, his wife. Infertility wasn't a sickness exactly, but it must have been as horrifically painful for them as any disease.

And, as Henry was doing, Myles must have promised to forsake all others, and be faithful to his bride as long as they lived. He'd broken his vow – broken it because of me.

It's funny, given how deceptive I knew Bianca was in all sorts of ways, but I didn't doubt her version of events for one second. Myles had, after all, told me just enough of the truth. And the feeling of unease and impermanence I'd felt in that empty, cavernous flat, even once Bianca had worked her magic on its decor, had been strong enough for me never to have had any sense of us having a future together there. It had been just as artificial as Oleg's mansion, in its way.

Suddenly, in the harsh light of day, as I watched my best mate marry her best mate, I realised that I hadn't been in love with Myles. I hadn't even felt the profound sense of connection he'd said he felt for me. The feelings I'd had for him – apart from a serious case of lust – had been more about the way he made me feel about myself. It was validation: a new, wonderful knowledge that someone wanted me; that I was worthy of desire.

And, after the depressing doldrums my life had fallen into, I'd loved the giddy excitement of being with him, the thrill of having something to look forward to, something that was just for me, after so long, when I'd almost given up hope of ever finding anyone.

Which was pretty hollow, knowing what I knew now.

And now, I'd have to decide what to do. I wouldn't see him again: I knew that for sure. Not in the sense of shagging him, anyway. I'd have to decide what to do about telling him, and whether I should tell Sloane before Bianca did. The idea made me feel like I was going to be sick. I knew who she was. I'd known since the first time Myles had mentioned her, when I'd spent hours stalking her on social media.

But, I realised, as the opening chord of the final hymn burst from the organ and Molly dug me in the ribs to bring me back to the present, that was a decision for another day, one to add to the growing mountain of intractable problems I faced.

For now, I was going to discharge my bridesmaid duties as best I could, secure in the knowledge that my friends had my back, and then I was going to get shitfaced.

So I did. Well and truly shitfaced. And as a result, I made another, even bigger mistake. I blame the bad girl that the podcast had unleashed inside me.

Chapter Twenty-Two

I woke up the next morning with the worst hangover I'd ever had in my life. No word of a lie. I hadn't felt this bad during freshers' week at uni, or when Maddy and I went to Zante on holiday, or even after the last Colton Capital Christmas party. I felt like my brain had been replaced with boiling cheese and if I opened my eyes it would ooze out onto the pillow and I'd be dead. I knew that if I opened my mouth I'd be sick, so I didn't.

I pulled the duvet further up over my head and hoped I would be able to fall asleep again and miss the worst of it. But then, memories of the day and night before started to invade my battered head, and each one felt like Aunt Lydia from *The Handmaid's Tale* was coming at me with her cattle prod.

I remembered standing in the marquee after the reception, chatting to a couple of university mates of Henry's, and waitresses circulating with bottles of champagne and platters of canapés, only somehow I got all the champagne and missed out on all the food.

I remembered sitting down to the meal, only I'd passed the stage of being hungry and just kept drinking. It seemed as if every time I made the decision to be sensible and switch to water, someone would top up my glass and I'd decide to just finish this, and *then* switch to water, but it never happened.

I remembered hearing the opening chords of 'Amazed' by Lonestar and rushing over to see Maddy and Henry having their first dance, looking as happy and in love as any couple possibly could. I remembered having to drag Molly off to the loo so I could have a little cry about how I'd never fall in love with anyone who loved me back, and I'd be single for ever, and her patting my back and telling me it would happen when the time was right, there was someone out there for me, I just had to be patient and keep trying to meet new people or, who knew, the love of my life could even have been there all along, right under my nose.

I remembered the warmth of the marquee suddenly feeling oppressively hot, and going outside to get some fresh air, and standing under the stars breathing in great gulps of cold, and starting to feel slightly better.

I remembered a familiar voice saying, 'I came out to find you. I just wanted to tell you how beautiful you look,' and the Bad Girl's words coming back to me and my judgment being so impaired that I actually thought, 'Yes! Maybe this is it!'

I remembered feeling a surge of happiness and clarity, and going back inside and dancing and dancing, and then Maddy and Henry cutting the cake, and the slab of rich, fruit-laden sweetness being the most delicious thing I'd ever tasted, and being overwhelmed with hunger and eating two bacon sandwiches as well, when those were served at ten o'clock for the evening guests, but realising even at the time that it was too little, too late.

I remembered Maddy standing on a chair and Henry removing the garter from around her thigh to whoops of encouragement from all the men, and seeing who caught it, and then joining the throng of women around her and thinking that it was very, very important that I should be the one to catch her bouquet, and just beating Molly to it and then feeling guilty and giving it to her.

I remembered looking at my phone and seeing that it was eleven o'clock and it suddenly seeming even more important that I get the last train back to London, instead of sleeping in the spare room I'd used the night before, and Chloë trying to dissuade me, saying I'd had far too much to drink and I wouldn't be safe on my own, and the tall, suited figure by my side saying, 'Don't worry, I'll take Charlotte home.'

I remembered the almost empty train to Waterloo and us being all alone in the carriage, and shivering with cold because I hadn't gone back into the house to pick up my coat, and him taking off his jacket and wrapping it around my shoulders, even though he must have been cold too. And shortly after that, realising that he was going to kiss me, and thinking that was a good idea.

And I remembered the kiss. Every detail of it. Seeing his eyes when I opened mine, looking down at me with such intensity that I dropped my eyelids again and lost myself in the moment. His mouth on mine, so different from how Myles's mouth had felt. His hair, thick and soft when I buried my hand in it. I remembered the kiss ending, and us looking at each other with amazed smiles.

And that was it. The rest of the night was a blur. We must have got an Uber home after that – or maybe we didn't, maybe we got the night Tube and the Overground, or a bus or something. I had no idea: it was all a blank. We must have got home, let ourselves in and gone up to bed. I hadn't cleaned my teeth or taken my make-up off, I knew that for sure thanks to the vile taste in my mouth and my gummed-together eyes.

But at least I was home, safe in my bed.

My bed. Wait. Something wasn't right. The room smelled all wrong – familiar, but wrong. When I opened my eyes a tiny bit, head throbbing, I could see that the duvet covering my face had a dark blue cover on it, not my white one. I stretched my legs experimentally over to the other side of the bed, but there was no one there. That was something, at least.

Reluctantly, I opened my eyes and sat up.

'Good morning, Charlotte,' Adam said. He was sitting at his desk, the computer screen in front of him alive with flickering code. He'd showered – I could smell the deodorant he used – and was wearing jeans and a jumper. There was a mug of tea and a plate scattered with toast crumbs next to him. And curled up on his lap, as if this was the most normal place in the world for him to be, was Freezer.

Adam smiled and caressed the cat's white fur, looking just like the villain in that Bond movie.

I said, 'I'm going to be sick,' and sprinted for the bathroom.

Adam. Adam and me. Kissing! Kissing loads. Kissing like I'd kissed the leopard man in Lisbon. The memory whirled in my head as I lay sprawled on the bathroom floor.

A few hideous minutes later, I got gingerly up. The room felt like it was tilting sideways like a fun house in an amusement park, but then it steadied and I started to feel reasonably confident that

I wasn't going to throw up again. I cleaned my teeth and looked gloomily at my face in the mirror.

I was not a pretty sight. The make-up Molly had applied yesterday after I'd cried off the professionally applied stuff was still there in patches, where my skin hadn't flaked it off. There were deep black smudges under my eyes. My hair was partly still pinned up on top of my head and partly falling down in messy hanks, still stuck through with pins and rigid with spray.

But all that was just detail. The most important thing, which made me mutter, 'Thank you, whoever the god is that protects pissed people,' was that I was still wearing my bra, pants and tights. I supposed that if I had shagged Adam, I might conceivably have done so with my bra still on, and possibly I might have replaced my pants afterwards. But not the tights. Tights were definitive proof. I'd kissed him, and either he or I had taken my bridesmaid's dress off – I remembered seeing it lying in a crumpled heap on his bedroom floor – but the shenanigans between us had gone no further.

'Oh, thank God,' I said. The realisation that I hadn't had sex with Adam and then blacked out like a teenager, as well as having been copiously sick, made me feel a lot further from death than I had before. I spent ten minutes painstakingly – and painfully – removing the forest of pins and grips from my hair, and then I soaked a couple of cotton pads in eye-make-up remover and dissolved the rest of my mascara.

Then I had a long, boiling hot shower, from which I emerged feeling almost human. I pulled on a pair of leggings and a baggy sweatshirt and went back to Adam's room to have the talk I knew we were going to have to have.

He was still at the computer, Freezer still in a furry white puddle on his lap. I addressed that issue first; fraught as it was, it was easier to talk about than the other one.

'Adam,' I said, trying hard to steady the wobble in my voice. 'What are you doing with Luke and Hannah's cat?'

'Whose cat?' Adam said. 'He's mine. He adopted me. He just strolled in one day and I gave him some tuna and he stayed. I've called him Ethereum.'

'Adam… He's not yours. His name's Freezer and he belongs to the couple that live next door. They've been crazy with worry about him. They've put up posters and everything.'

Adam looked mulish. 'He's mine. He lives with me. If he wanted to live next door, why doesn't he go?'

'I can't claim an in-depth knowledge of cat psychology,' I said. 'But I imagine the tuna might have something to do with that. And anyway, he does go. Luke said he came home for a bit, and then vanished again.'

'They can't look after him very well. Otherwise he wouldn't have left. He likes it here. We're mates.'

I wondered, with a stab of sadness, how many friends Adam actually had.

'You can't just steal people's cats,' I said, as reasonably as I could. 'It's not on. And besides, we're not allowed pets here. It's in our lease.'

Adam looked furtive. Clearly he'd known that all too well. 'No one knows he's here. You didn't even know.'

I thought about the times I'd seen empty bowls on Adam's floor, the scurrying sounds I'd heard at night that I'd thought were mice, the tins of tuna stacked in the kitchen cupboard. If I'd only used my brain for five seconds, I would have worked it out. But I hadn't.

'We'll have to take him back,' I told him. 'If the estate agents did an inspection and found him here, they'd evict us. Never mind that he's not your cat.'

'He wants to be, though,' Adam insisted. He scratched Freezer behind the ear and the cat opened his bicoloured eyes, yawned hugely and started to purr, pressing his head against Adam's hand and digging his claws into his knees. I felt terrible, like I was tearing away a child from its parents. Except, I reminded myself, this child already had two loving parents and was probably just exhibiting the feline equivalent of Stockholm syndrome.

I said, 'Adam, for God's sake. Don't be a dick. I've got a foul hangover, I've found out that the guy I thought was my boyfriend is someone else's husband and I don't have a job any more. Don't make my life worse by giving me a load of grief about a cat.'

Adam looked aghast. He stood up and Freezer jumped off his lap and stood looking reproachfully up at him. 'You've lost your job? Why?'

'I don't know. But I've been suspended, the lawyers are sending me a letter on Monday, and eventually they'll sack me. So I've really got quite a lot on my plate right now.'

Plate. The word made me realise I was bloody starving. As soon as I'd sorted this mess out I was going to go to The Daily Grind and order the biggest fry-up they'd sell me.

'I'm so sorry, Charlotte,' Adam said. 'That's awful. I—'

'Yes, well,' I interrupted. 'Come on. Let me take Freezer back to his owners, and then we can go and get some breakfast.'

'Okay. I guess.'

He picked Freezer up and cuddled him, and the cat started to purr again. Adam buried his face in the white fur and I was pretty sure he was either crying or about to start.

'There's no reason why he can't come and sit with you during the day, while Luke and Hannah are at work,' I said. 'I expect he'd enjoy the company.' *And so would you.*

'Really? You don't think they'd mind?'

'I doubt it. So long as I don't tell them you've been basically falsely imprisoning him. I could just say we found him in the shed, or something.'

'Really? Thanks, Charlotte.'

'You're welcome.' Then I added, 'But no more tuna. And you kick him out at six o'clock every evening. Right?'

Adam said, 'Fine. If you say so.'

'Adam! He's not your cat. Seriously. Stop with the tuna and don't keep him in your room overnight, or I'll tell Hannah you're trying to kidnap him and they'll probably ground him. Or move house, to somewhere where there isn't a cat abductor next door.'

'Do you think they'd do that?'

I didn't, of course, but I carried on with my lie, even though I felt guilty about it.

'They might. And then you'd never see him again.'

'Fine,' Adam said. 'Take him.'

He passed Freezer over to me. I don't know much about cats, but this one did seem to be an unusually biddable animal. He snuggled into my arms, turned himself upside down and started purring again, and I said, 'Awww!' He really was very cute.

'Come on then, Freezer,' I said. 'Let's take you home to your mum and dad.'

Hannah, her red hair tangled, answered the door wearing a dressing gown, fluffy slippers and the slightly annoyed expression on her face that people have when they're dragged out from a Sunday lie-in. It changed as soon as she saw her cat, to one of amazed delight.

'Oh my God,' she gasped. 'You found him! Where was he?'

I opened my mouth to come up with the story I'd prepared, and then realised I couldn't do it – not just because it was wrong to lie, but because Freezer looked far too well-fed and glossy for a cat that had been sleeping rough for several weeks.

'Come in,' Hannah said. 'I can't believe he's home! We've missed him so much. Luke's been saying we should get another cat, but I couldn't, not until we knew what had happened to him. And now here he is.'

I handed Freezer over and followed Hannah inside. She took him through to the kitchen, put him down on the floor and poured some cat biscuits into a bowl. Freezer snuffled them and then gave Hannah a look that quite clearly said, 'What the fuck is this?'

Cringing, I explained. 'I'm afraid he's got used to eating tuna.' And then I told her the whole story.

To my great relief, she laughed. 'The naughty boy! Freezer, I mean, not your housemate. I do see his point, though, we often worried that he got lonely during the day. I mean the cat, not…'

'Actually, I think Adam does too, you know. He works from home and they kind of kept each other company. I thought, if you didn't mind, he could maybe still come round to ours sometimes and they could hang out with each other.'

Hannah's eyes crinkled up at the corners. 'Play Xbox games together?'

'Yeah, while scratching their balls. That sort of thing.'

'Not talk about their love lives, just kind of go, "Women!" and shake their heads and roll their eyes.'

'And then say, "So, how do you rate QPR's chances against Forest on Saturday?"'

Hannah burst out laughing. 'Sounds reasonable to me.'

'But I told him he can't feed Freezer any more, and he's got to impose a curfew.'

'Deal,' Hannah said. Then the smile melted off her face. 'When you said Freezer had been with your housemate, I thought at first you meant the other one. The tall blonde girl.'

'Tansy,' I replied. 'No, definitely not guilty. She's not even home that often these days. She's seeing a guy I work with, and she spends three or four nights a week at his. It's gone from nought to a hundred in just a couple of months.'

'Right, okay. Only there was a weird thing… Would you like a coffee?'

I said I'd love one, if it wasn't too much trouble, and watched as she fired up a serious-looking bean-to-cup machine, filled two thick china cups with espresso, frothed milk, put some mince pies on a plate, and carried it all through to the front room.

'Oh, wow,' I said. 'Christmas has definitely landed here.'

There was a huge, real tree, glimmering with gold and silver lights and laden with ornaments, filling the air with its scent. The room wasn't tidy – there were books and magazines scattered over the coffee table along with rolls of wrapping paper and ribbon. The sofa was piled with knitted throws and an assortment of cushions, and a random battalion of Christmas cards threatened to jostle one another off the mantelpiece. But, at the same time, it looked both homely and elegant, like it had been styled by Kirstie Allsopp when she was in a bit of a hurry.

'It's our first Christmas together,' Hannah said. 'We wanted to do it properly.'

She passed me a cup of coffee and offered me a mince pie, which I accepted, remembering again how starving I was.

Freezer sat down in front of the fireplace, looked balefully at the cold logs and started washing his face.

Then Hannah said, 'So, your housemate. Tansy. Is she okay?'

I blinked. 'What? Yeah, she's fine, as far as I know. I haven't seen her for a few days because I've been away at a wedding and work's been… kind of frantic. But Renzo's going to Italy for Christmas, and she's been texting me about our plans, which are basically eating chipolata sausages and selection boxes and drinking prosecco in front of the telly with some mates.'

'Okay. That's good. It's just something that happened a few weeks ago. Luke said I should call the police but I didn't want to. I tend to overreact a bit about stuff and I thought I was being silly. But I've thought about it some more and every time I do I'm like, "No, still weird."'

Travis, I thought. This was about Travis. My mouth felt suddenly much drier than the mince pie I was scoffing should have made it.

I swallowed and drank some coffee. 'Go on.'

'So a guy came into The Daily Grind,' Hannah said. 'He brought this.'

She rummaged behind the sofa and produced a crumpled Selfridges bag, and took out a navy blue cashmere scarf. It wasn't new, but it wasn't old either. It looked like something you might be delighted to find in a charity shop, if you had the time to rummage through all the other stuff you'd never want, or something you'd be made up to get for twenty quid on eBay, if you could be arsed to sort through all the Buy It Now fakes from China.

'I wasn't there,' Hannah carried on. 'I'm a teacher at the Queenswood primary school. You know, on the other side of the station? I just help Luke out in the evenings sometimes, if I'm not busy marking or in late meetings or whatever. I don't love being at home on my own. But that night I was, so I went to bed early, and the next day Luke showed me this.'

'What, he thought it belonged to Tansy?'

'That's right. Apparently the guy said he'd been at our first pizza evening, when you three were there, and that she'd left the scarf on her chair and he picked it up. Only Luke thought it was weird because, first of all, if that happens you hand whatever it is in at the bar, don't you? You don't take it home and then bring it back weeks later. And second, Luke said he could have sworn he'd never seen the bloke before, and he's got the most incredible memory for faces. But he described your housemate and he knew the date and everything. So Luke said that she lives next door to us, and he'd drop it off, and the guy said thanks and put a note in with the scarf in case she wanted to ring and say she'd got it back. And we thought that would be the end of it.'

I said, 'That seems like a hell of a lot of trouble to go to for a scarf, even if it is cashmere.'

'I know, right? But to be honest, we forgot all about it. Hence not dropping it round. We're so busy, you see. And then the other day Luke told me he saw the guy hanging around outside your house. Luke thinks he must've followed him home from work.'

'Oh my God,' I said. 'That's seriously creepy.'

'It really is. And like I say, I'm a bit paranoid about that kind of stuff. My ex… Anyway, I told Luke I was being daft and there was nothing anyone could do, because all the guy had done was return a piece of clothing someone had left behind.'

I said, 'That scarf isn't Tansy's. I've never seen it before. And even if it was, she wasn't wearing one that night. It was really warm still, remember?'

'So this man – he's an ex of hers, right? – must have worked out that she comes to The Daily Grind and bought it especially to try and track her down.'

We looked at each other. Hannah put her feet up on the sofa and wrapped her arms around her knees, hugging them against herself as if for comfort. I wondered what had happened in her past to make her so anxious, but I wasn't going to correct her assumption that Travis was an ex-boyfriend.

I said, 'But how could he…'

'Have known about the coffee shop and the pizza night, if he wasn't there?' Hannah finished. 'I think I can guess.'

She took her phone out of her dressing gown pocket and a few moments later passed it to me. On the screen was a YouTube video, paused on a frame that showed the beautiful girl with the violet hair who'd been at the table next to ours that night, talking into

the camera. Behind her, quite clearly, I could see Tansy, laughing
with a glass of wine in her hand.

'Your friend has a YouTube channel?'

'That's right. Her name's Gemma Grey but she's called Sparkly-
Gems on YouTube. She's got more than five million subscribers. If
the guy has a teenage daughter, chances are she watches Gemma's
channel.'

I didn't say anything for a bit. I imagined a young girl, engrossed
in her tablet, and her father looking over her shoulder to check what
she was watching. A little girl who only saw her dad on weekends,
maybe, so he had lots of nights alone to look for entertainment of
his own online. I imagined the shock of recognition he must have
felt – 'That's *her*!' – how he must have gone back and found the video
and watched it again later, once his daughter was in bed or back
home with her mother. 'That's *definitely* her!' And how Gemma's
unwitting promotion of her friends' business had led him to Tansy.

I said, 'I'll tell Tansy what happened. Take the scarf to a charity
shop, if you want. If I see him again, I'll call the police.'

'Okay. If you're sure it's not hers, I'll put it in the school jumble
sale. But there was a note with it. You should take that.'

She passed me a small envelope, slightly bendy at the corners
from being squashed down the back of their sofa. There was nothing
written on it.

I said goodbye to Hannah and wished her a merry Christmas,
then walked back next door, let myself in and climbed the stairs
to Adam's room. He was still sitting at his desk, hunched over his
keyboard – the pose in which, I realised, he must spend almost all

of every day and a lot of the night too. No wonder Freezer liked him: a warm human who sat in the same place for hours – only moving to dispense tuna and play nocturnal pouncing games – had to be pretty much cat nirvana.

Adam must have been too engrossed in what he was doing to hear my feet on the stairs, because he took no notice of me for a few moments, just carried on tapping away. He wasn't coding, I noticed, he was posting on Slack, the same messaging system Bianca had used for our wedding planning group.

Well, we were going to have to have a conversation about what had – and what hadn't – happened between us the previous night, and it might as well be now. What would the Bad Girl do if she were me, I wondered. *Duh, she'd go right in there and say what she felt.* So, dry mouth and all, I did.

'Hey,' I said.

Adam jumped as if he'd been stung and spun around on his chair, closing the tab on which he'd been typing.

'Hey Charlotte.' He was actually blushing, looking as alarmed and guilty as if I'd caught him on Pornhub.

'What's wrong?'

'Nothing. I was just…'

Then, to my surprise, he stood up and wrapped his arms around me.

'Charlotte,' he said into my hair. I could feel his warm breath tickling my skin and I wanted very badly to move. 'Last night. You were…'

'Very, very drunk.'

He laughed. 'Yes, you were. You were really sweet. You fell asleep sideways across my bed, with your feet on the floor. I took your shoes off and I managed to turn you around and get the duvet over you, and then I slept in your bed. I hope you don't mind. I'll wash your sheets.'

The god who protects pissed people had been putting in some serious overtime, I thought.

'I don't mind a bit,' I said, easing myself out of his embrace and looking up at him. 'I thought…'

Adam blushed again. 'I'd never do that. I mean, you weren't even awake. And even if you had been, I wouldn't have known you were sure that you wanted me to… you know.'

'I know. And thanks, I guess. For being decent. And for getting me home safely.'

I moved away from him and sat down on the bed. He sat next to me and took my hand.

I said, 'Still, it shouldn't have happened. I'm sorry.'

'Sorry for what? You didn't do anything wrong.'

Shit, I thought.

'Look, Adam. You don't even like me. You fancy Tansy. It was just a stupid, drunken—'

'I what?' Finally, he let go of my hand – in fact, he dropped it as if it was red hot. I resisted the urge to wipe my palm on my leggings. 'No I don't! She's really pretty, obviously, but you're different. You're special.'

Oh no.

'But you hate me. You never even talk to me. When the three of us went out that night, you could hardly bear to look at me.

The only time we actually had a conversation, you told me you think I'm evil.'

Adam pushed his hand through his hair, raking his dark fringe back over his head. Immediately, it flopped down again. He reached for my hand again, but then changed his mind and twisted his fingers together in his lap.

'I'm not great with women. When I like someone, I can't show it. I get all tongue-tied. And I thought you didn't like me, until last night.'

Oh no. Oh no, no, no, make it stop.

'Adam, like I said, I'm really sorry about last night. It was a mistake. I was pissed and overemotional. Weddings do that to people, even when you haven't just had all the shit happen in your life that I have. Not that that's any excuse. I shouldn't have kissed you.'

'Okay.' Adam frowned, then looked directly at me and smiled a sweet, gentle smile that showed his white, even teeth and made dimples appear on either side of his mouth and the corners of his eyes crinkle up. I'd never noticed his eyes before: they were a very dark blue. I saw again what I'd seen at the rehearsal dinner (and at the wedding reception, obviously): that Adam was, in his way, quite the hottie. Unfortunately for us both, it might as well have been C-3PO sitting there next to me for all the chemistry I felt.

'Can't we just pretend it never happened?'

'You mean, like, start over?'

'Yes,' I said, then hastily added, 'As housemates. Maybe even as friends.'

'I see. You don't feel the same way about me as I do about you.'

Feeling almost as guilty as I'd felt an hour before, when I'd told him he couldn't keep Freezer, I said, 'No, Adam. I just don't. I'm sorry.'

I stood up and so did he. For a second I thought about giving him a hug, and then I thought it would almost certainly make things worse.

'I'm going to get some food, if you want to come?' I suggested.

'Nah. I've got stuff to do.'

'Okay. See you later.'

I left the room and, after a second's hesitation, closed the door behind me. Almost immediately, I heard the rumble of Adam's chair wheeling across the wooden floor, and then the rapid tap of his keyboard.

Chapter Twenty-Three

Hi and welcome back to Sorry Not Sorry. *Today I'm going to talk about one of the less pleasant bits of dating. In the beginning, if you decide someone's not for you – or vice versa – ending it is pretty simple. Some people believe ghosting is okay – although I'm not one of them, as I've said before – and in the very early stages, after maybe one date, or a few messages on Tinder or whatever, you can just delete, block and ignore. Or you can do what I favour, which is sending a polite, kind message to say that this isn't working for you and you think it's best to call it quits. Of course, some people – some guys, mainly – don't take that so well and try to argue the toss. If that happens – why, then you block, delete and ignore.*

But, a little further down the track, if you've had a few dates with someone, maybe even spent the night with them, and you decide it's not working for you, then calling the whole thing off becomes a little harder. So brace yourselves, because today we're going to talk about ending it.

I spent the rest of that Sunday and most of the next Monday in bed, emerging only to go up the road to the M&S Simply Food and stock up on random snackage. My plan had been to go and sit in The Daily Grind and cure my hangover with lardy food and possibly a Bloody Mary while reading the papers in a grown-up and civilised fashion, but somehow I couldn't face being around people. I tried to listen to a podcast, but the upbeat tone only annoyed me.

I replied to texts from Chloë and Molly saying that yes, I was fine, no, Adam and I hadn't shagged, yes, I'd pick my bag up from Chloë's place later in the week, yes, the wedding had been amazing in the end, and no, I'd never met a bigger bitch than Bianca.

I replied to a text from Tansy saying that she and Renzo were on their way home from Zürich, where they'd been exploring the Christmas markets in the snow and it was so amazing and so romantic, and would I be home tonight? I said I would, but that I was knackered and planned to be asleep by nine, and she must tell me all about it when we saw each other. I didn't tell her about work, or Adam, or Freezer, or what I'd learned about Travis – I figured she was probably not in the right frame of mind and I barely knew where to begin.

Then I binge-watched almost all of *The Crown* on Netflix, stopping only when I found myself drifting into sleep and missing chunks of it.

But before I fell asleep, I texted Myles.

The next day felt really weird. My alarm didn't go off at seven as usual; it didn't go off at all. I lay in bed, drifting in and out of sleep, wondering what the hell I was going to do with my life. I felt no sense of optimism or purpose, and even though it was only a week until Christmas, I didn't feel even a tiny bit festive. I finally got up when I heard the crash of the door knocker and went downstairs in my pyjamas to answer it, and even the sight of Freezer trotting purposefully in the other direction on his way to spend the day with Adam didn't cheer me up, because I knew what the knock on the door meant.

'This needs a signature,' the postie said and, reluctantly, feeling like I was signing my own death warrant, I provided one.

I opened the letter, which began, 'I am writing to inform you that Colton Capital has deemed it necessary to conduct an investigation into your actions…' I read it and called Chloë's colleague Rashid, who said that he was sorry but he was booked solid all week and then off until the New Year, and could I come and see him on the second of January. I mustn't worry, he said, it would all be sorted out. Then he added ominously, 'One way or another.'

I spent the rest of the day sitting on the sofa with my laptop, googling and worrying, until it was time to go to The Factory and finally wake myself up from the dream I'd been in for the past four months.

When I got home afterwards, I found Tansy in the living room, shrugging off a long, white wool coat that was utterly beautiful, clearly expensive, and probably the most impractical garment I'd ever seen. She was surrounded by shopping bags and her suitcase was open on the floor. She'd obviously just got in.

'Hey!' she said. 'How was the wedding? I stayed over at Renzo's last night because it was really late when we got back. I brought you perfume and gin and a Toblerone – look, a proper one, not one of those pissy Brexit ones – and I got us some decorations from the Christmas market and loads of ginger biscuits and cheese. Zürich's so beautiful but my God, it was cold. Are you okay?'

'I just dumped Myles.'

'But you…'

'Yeah,' I said. 'I dumped him months ago. But then I kind of undumped him again, in Lisbon. Because he told me he'd left his wife, only he hadn't, they were still together the whole time and trying to have a baby. I didn't tell you, because…'

'Because I was so busy with my own dramas.' All the happiness had melted off Tansy's face, and she looked concerned and miserable. 'Fuck, Charlotte, you've been through all this and I didn't even know. You listened to me going on about Renzo and… and the other thing, and I never even asked about what was going on with you. I'm a shit friend.'

'You aren't a shit friend. You brought gin.'

She brightened. 'Not just gin. Give me two seconds.'

She rummaged in her duty free carrier bags a bit more, then disappeared into the kitchen, clanking bottles. I heard the rattle of ice in the cocktail shaker, and a few moments later she returned carrying two frosted glasses filled with clear liquid.

'Kirsch martinis,' she announced. 'They made them in the bar at the hotel where we stayed, and I liked them so much Renzo made the barman give us the recipe. He reckons they served them on the *Hindenburg* before it blew up, which is nice.'

'Appropriate,' I said, sipping. 'Jesus. I'm not surprised it blew up if they had this stuff on board.'

'Right. Now, tell me everything.'

So I did. I filled her in on Myles's surprise appearance in Lisbon, how he'd rescued me from Maddy's disastrous hen weekend and I hadn't been able to resist sleeping with him. I explained to her about the flat in Shoreditch and the times we'd met there, and Bianca's revelations before the wedding.

'I guess I could have just ghosted him,' I raised my voice, because Tansy was back in the kitchen shaking another round of cocktails. 'But I felt like I needed to confront him, to see what he was going to say.'

'To see if he was going to keep lying to you?' Tansy strained what was basically pure gin with added cherry flavour into our glasses. 'Or to see if he could convince you that he wasn't?'

'Both, I guess. Or neither. And you're right, he did try to lie. He said Bianca was a malicious bitch, which she is, of course. But I actually believe her about this, and I told him I did.'

'You called his bluff,' Tansy said. 'Renzo taught me to play poker over the weekend, and… But carry on.'

'It was weird,' I said. 'I could almost literally see him thinking. Like there was a computer in his head calculating probabilities – quite a bit like poker, actually, or chess. Like, "If I say this, that or the other might happen. But if I say that…" And so on.'

I took a huge gulp of my cocktail and almost choked, it was so strong. In hindsight, it was easy to see what had been going through Myles's mind, but it hadn't been at the time. Looking at him next to me on the suede sofa, his legs long and lean in his jeans, his familiar face half-turned towards me, all I could think was, *Who is he? Who is this man who I thought I knew, thought was someone special?*

'You lied to me,' I'd said coldly. 'I told you how I felt about you being married. I told you I wouldn't see you again. And so you lied. Are you proud of yourself?'

'Charlotte, you have to understand how hard it's been,' he said. 'She – Sloane – is just so fragile at the moment. I wanted to leave her – I meant to, I've been spending nights here, honest. But it just wasn't the right time to make it official. You don't know what it would do to her.'

'About the same as what her husband fucking someone else would do.'

'She wouldn't have found out. I was just waiting until she was in a better place emotionally, and then I could move on, and be with you. I didn't ask to fall in love with you, you know.'

There they were – the words I would have given anything to hear just a few weeks before. Now, they filled me with hot rage.

'Maybe you can't help what you bloody feel, but you can help what you do.' I stood up, too angry to stay still, and paced over to the balcony and looked out. But I could see nothing in the black winter night, only my own reflection looking back at me, white-faced.

'You don't know what it was like,' he said softly. 'The pressure, the rows. Sloane in tears all the time. She's been taking these hormones, and they sent her—'

I spun around again. 'Hormones to help her have your baby! You think she put herself through that for fun? And instead of supporting her, you betrayed her. And you betrayed me.'

'Oh Charlotte,' he said. 'If I could just have more time. Just a few more months, to get things on an even keel. It's been so hard, being so torn between my loyalty to her and what I feel for you. I need to work it through. I don't want to hurt either of you.'

'You don't give a single shit about either of us.' I was surprised how calm I managed to sound. 'You only care about yourself and having your cake and eating it and making fucking trifle.'

He crossed his arms over his chest, his face petulant, like a little schoolboy caught cheating in a test.

'I just wanted some pleasure in my life,' he muttered. 'Aren't I entitled to that?'

'Entitled? You think you're entitled to a wife and a bit on the side? Tell you what, why don't we call Sloane right now and ask her what she thinks of that little plan?'

I'd stood over him, my phone in my hand, so pissed off I must have actually been quite scary. Even remembering it now made my heart beat faster and my hands clench into fists.

I'd managed to finish my drink and drunk another one that Tansy had made without me really noticing, while I remembered the scene and described it to her. She took my empty glass from me.

'Oh my God, you never called his wife?' she breathed, filling up our glasses again.

'Well, no. I don't have her number, for one thing. But he didn't know that. He literally begged me not to call her. It was horrible. I looked at him and I just couldn't see why I'd ever fancied him. He was pathetic. I actually felt sorry for him, but not as sorry as I feel for Sloane.'

'So what did you do?'

I sighed. 'What could I do? I told him I was going to go home, and so should he. And I told him that if he doesn't tell Sloane so that she can make a proper, informed decision about what to do, I would. And I will, too.'

'Maybe you should tell her anyway,' Tansy suggested. 'It would be easy to find her, send her an email or whatever.'

'Maybe you should tell Renzo about Travis, and the others.'

'It's not the same thing at all,' Tansy said. 'For fuck's sake, Charlotte, it's just not.'

She had that wide-eyed, panicky look again, and I immediately regretted what I'd said.

'You're right. It's not. Your past isn't the same as their relationship now, it's definitely not. But I still think you should tell him, because it'll be worse if he finds out another way.'

'He won't find out.' But Tansy didn't sound at all confident about that.

We sat in silence for a moment. 'I'm sorry I mentioned it,' I said.

'That's okay.'

'So yeah,' I carried on. 'After that I told him I was going, and I went. And here I am. And I'll never see him again.'

I wouldn't, I realised. Not even at work, because I didn't work there any more.

'You must feel amazing,' Tansy said. 'Telling him off like that. Like Superwoman, or Professor McGonagall or someone.'

I got up off the sofa. I felt like I'd been sitting there for a long time. My head spun a bit when I stood, and I realised I needed a wee desperately, and then I needed to be alone and sleep for a long time.

'I feel... okay. Thanks so much for the gin and stuff. I should go to bed.'

Tansy leaned over to me and gave me a tentative half-hug. I hugged her back, grateful for the comfort, and went upstairs. It was only when I cannoned off the landing wall that I realised how pissed I was from her lethal cocktails. I waggled my toothbrush around in my mouth for a bit, drank a load of water out of the tap, then went to bed.

I didn't feel like Superwoman, not at all. And certainly not like Professor McGonagall, unless you focused on her dowdy dress sense and unluckiness in love (and, at the rate I was going, I'd find myself as single at seventy-two as I was now). I just felt lonely, sad and afraid.

I was woken the next morning by the persistent trilling of my phone, which seemed to have synchronised itself with my pounding head. I turned over and peered blearily at the screen. Half past nine, and an unfamiliar mobile number. For a second I considered rejecting the call and going back to sleep, but then I realised that it could be someone from Colton Capital. All their numbers were stored on the work phone I'd returned to Margot. It could be her, telling me a terrible mistake had been made and offering me my job back. It could be Piers, asking why his Christmas cards hadn't been posted, in which case I'd take great pleasure in telling him where he could shove them.

'Hello,' I croaked. Then I sat up and said it again, hoping I sounded a bit less like someone who'd just woken up with a vile hangover for the second time in four days.

'Charlotte? Are you okay? It's Xander.'

I'd never spoken to him on the phone before. He had a nice voice, I realised, to go with his nice eyes and nice smile and nice... well, everything. Colton Capital might have ruined my life, but I was reminded with a sick thud how much I was going to miss it, and everyone there, not least my hapless, kind former colleague. But maybe not Piers.

I said, 'I'm not supposed to be talking to you. You could jeopardise the disciplinary process. I read it on Google.'

'Don't worry, I'm not in the office. I chucked a sickie. I need to see you – or rather, you need to see me. I've got some serious intel.'

'Some what?'

'Charlotte! You're still in bed, aren't you? I don't blame you. But I can't tell you all this stuff when you're half asleep. I need to see you. Where do you live?'

'Hackney.'

'Great. It'll take me as long to get there as it'll take you to get up. I'll be there in forty-five minutes. Where do you want to meet?'

I said, 'There's a place round the corner from where I live, just by the station.' And I told him how to find The Daily Grind. Then I showered, washed and straightened my hair, did my face and put on skinny jeans, a scarlet cashmere jumper I'd bought in last year's sales and never worn, and trainers. I looked at myself in the mirror and changed the trainers for taupe suede over-the-knee boots because... Well, because Xander was quite a bit taller than me. And it was cold. And... But I had no time to analyse my wardrobe decisions, or I'd be late.

The morning rush had died down at The Daily Grind. A group of Lycra-clad women with babies in buggies were refuelling after their British Military Fitness class with lattes, almond croissants and eggs and bacon at a table in the corner, next to a Christmas tree sparkling with rainbow lights. There were several people engrossed in whatever was on their tablets and a woman with a huge wheelie case of legal paperwork, clearly settled in for a morning's work. And, alone at a table in the corner with a laptop and a teapot, was Xander.

He looked entirely at home amongst the industrial beams – which were twined with more fairy lights and sparkling with tinsel – vintage movie posters and racks of vinyl records, just the same way he fitted into the aggressive, moneyed gloss of Colton Capital. Or perhaps he didn't really fit in anywhere, but just became part of his environment, because no one saw him as an intruder. Maybe working in places like Colombia and Bangladesh did that to a person. I didn't know, and I felt somehow inadequate because I'd never learned that skill myself.

But I needed to stop hovering in the doorway and letting cold air into the fragrant warmth of the café, so I hurried over to Xander and said hello. The pretty Spanish barista hurried over, too, and asked me what I'd like to order, whether Xander needed more tea, and whether we'd like anything to eat.

'Charlotte, you'll have a coffee, won't you?' Xander asked.

I looked at the earthenware pot and the tobacco-coloured dregs in Xander's mug, and remembered drinking strong tea just like that in my nan's kitchen in Gateshead.

'Actually, I'll have what he's having.'

Xander said, 'I was going to order scrambled eggs and beans.'

'Our beans are guaranteed GM free,' explained the waitress.

'Sounds great,' I said, although quite frankly I couldn't have cared less if they were made from extruded cow udder or something. I just wanted a vat of builder's tea and all the toast, eggs and beans I could fit in.

We troughed in silence for a bit, and drank lots of perfect tea, and Xander didn't say anything until every last crumb was gone. Finally he said, 'So I took Chryssanthi for a drink last night.'

For a moment I wasn't sure who he was talking about. Then I remembered – the petite, shiny-haired IT consultant. For some reason, I found myself hating her very much.

'Oh, yes?'

Xander said, 'She told me a bit of background about the security breach, and what's come out of their investigation. I'm not sure she was supposed to, but she did.'

I bet she did, I thought. Like everyone else, she'd have fallen for Xander's ability to listen to people in a way that made them tell him things.

I said, 'You know they think it was me, obviously.' You wouldn't have to have Xander's ninja skills to know that; confidentiality inevitably fell by the wayside when there was truly juicy gossip going round at Colton Capital, as I knew only too well.

'Yes. And I'm pretty sure they're wrong, which is why I'm here.'

'Why?'

'Why do they think it was you, or why do I think they're wrong?'

'Both, I guess.'

'It's complicated. I don't know anything about cyber security and I ended up getting a bit of a crash course last night.'

I wondered if cyber security was the only thing he'd got a crash course in from Chryssanthi.

'You must know more about it than I do, then,' I said. 'Oh no, wait – I'm this hacking mastermind. I'm basically the girl with the dragon tattoo.'

'I think that's what they're thinking, a bit. You see, they're all terrified of you.'

'What?' If I'd still been drinking tea, I'd have spat it all over the table.

'They are,' Xander carried on. 'Piers, Colin, all of them. They think you're this super-intelligent ice-maiden. Piers says you could do his job better than he does, so he keeps you busy with mundane shit. Renzo reckons he'd have asked you out in his first week there, but he was too scared. Pavel says he's cut right down on Red Bull because when he asks you to order it you look at him like you can see the weakness in his very soul.'

The Red Bull orders *had* dropped off a bit, now that I thought about it.

'But I'm not! I just have resting bitch face.'

Xander said, 'Actually, I like your face.'

I met his eyes across the table. They were a sort of greeny-brown, fading towards grey in the centre. We looked at each other for a long moment, then he smiled and I blushed absolutely scarlet and felt something weird happening around my ribs, like wearing a too-tight sports bra, so my breath came faster and more shallowly.

For God's sake, Charlotte, I told myself, *stop acting like a teenager! Your entire career is at risk here – you need to focus. And you can't fancy him – you work with him.*

Then I remembered that I didn't, any more.

I cleared my throat. 'Yes, so, anyway. Chryssanthi.'

'Right,' Xander said. He took out his phone and tapped the screen a couple of times. 'I made some notes, afterwards, because some of what she said was quite technical and I didn't want to forget.'

Afterwards. Did that mean their drink had been just a drink? A picture popped into my mind of Chryssanthi asleep, her dark hair spilling over a pillow, while Xander sat next to her, bare-chested, recording their conversation into his Notes app. It was so vivid that I missed the first bit of what Xander was saying and had to ask him to say it again, while I frantically tried to erase the picture from my mind. *It was just a drink.*

'She said the initial attack was caused by something called Black-Nurse. Apparently it's in a category of malware called BWAINs.'

'What the hell is a BWAIN?' I asked.

Xander laughed. 'That's what I wanted to know too. Get this – it's an acronym for Bug With An Impressive Name. You know – like Orpheus Lyre and TORMoil and WannaCry and so on.'

'They all sound like eighties heavy metal bands,' I said.

'Exactly. Which probably tells you all you need to know about the people that write this stuff. Anyway, the original attack didn't actually do very much. It sent a bunch of fake control message packets to the router, so the server was temporarily prevented from working properly. And then once they'd tweaked the firewall somehow, the problem went away.'

'So what was the point of it?'

'That's what Chryssanthi and Pavel couldn't figure out. The servers have apparently been running a lot more slowly for the past couple of weeks, like they're taking massive strain, which as you know is a huge issue for us.'

I did know – I'd done enough PowerPoint slides for Piers explaining how the speed of our fibre-optic cables, the processing power of our servers and our high-frequency trading algorithms allowed for maximum execution speed, with a consequent impact on profitability. I could practically recite the words in my sleep, but I'd never given much thought to what they actually meant.

'Right,' I said. 'But they couldn't find what was causing it, so what did they do?'

'They focused on tracking down the source of the original malware attack.'

'And they found it?'

'They did. Normally it would have been a lot more complex, because they would have had to involve the police to persuade the internet service provider to release the data. But in this case, apparently, the IP address matched one that was already recognised by the system.'

I said, 'And it was mine.'

Xander nodded.

A lot of the questions that had been whirring around my mind had been answered, and now the solution to the biggest one of all clicked into place like I'd always known it. I knew I hadn't hacked into the server, and I knew only one other person who could have.

'Okay. I think I know what's happened – kind of. But there's something I need to ask you.'

'Ask away.'

'Why are you so sure it wasn't me?'

'Well, for a start I guess I don't share the popular view that you're the girl with the dragon tattoo. I mean, I know you're brainy and stuff, but you don't strike me as the criminal mastermind type. And I know you love your job – I couldn't imagine you doing anything that would jeopardise it. And…'

'And?'

'I think you're a good person, Charlotte. It's a simple thing. And I like to think I'm an okay judge of character.'

I sighed. 'I think the person who's done this is a good person, too. Just maybe he sees the world a bit differently.'

The waitress came over and asked if we wanted more tea, but we both shook our heads, and Xander asked for the bill.

'What are they going to do? If they find who did it, I mean?' I asked.

'They haven't involved the police yet, and I don't reckon they will. Think about it for a second – if it gets out that our systems are vulnerable enough to be compromised like that, the fund will haemorrhage clients. Far better to shut down the attack, beef up security and say no more about it.'

I said, 'Okay, then. Let's go and ask him.'

Xander followed me out into the biting cold. He held the door open for me and then met my eyes for a second when I turned to thank him, and I wondered with a thrill of excitement whether he might be about to put his arm around me, or take my hand. But he just brushed the back of my coat with his hand – almost a caress, but not quite – and we walked together around the corner and down the familiar road to my house. The blind in Adam's window was down, but I could see cracks of light around it. Reluctantly, I fitted my key in the lock and opened it. Xander followed me upstairs and we both stopped outside Adam's door.

I knew I was doing what I had to do. I knew there was nothing else at all I *could* do, short of taking the blame myself. And even if I wanted to do that, which part of me did, my technical knowledge fell so far short of what was needed to hack into a hedge fund's secure server – even if it wasn't nearly as secure as it should have been – that no one questioning me about it would believe me for more than about five seconds.

Still, it felt like yet another betrayal of Adam.

Before I could knock, he opened the door. He didn't look like he'd shaved or brushed his hair since the wedding. He was wearing the same jeans he'd had on when I'd woken up in his room, and a T-shirt that looked like it had made its way from Adam to the washing machine, to the tumble dryer, to the floor of his room and then back onto Adam.

I couldn't see Freezer – presumably, with Hannah home for the holidays, he was staying in his own home.

Adam stared at us for a moment, then he asked, 'Are you Charlotte's ex-boyfriend? The married one?'

'Nope, not her boyfriend and not married. I work with Charlotte. I'm Xander.'

Adam said, 'Adam,' and, absurdly, the two of them shook hands. 'You'd better come in.'

We did. Adam sat in his familiar place on the wheeled chair by the computer. I sat on Adam's bed and Xander glanced at the computer screen, then stood in the corner by the window.

'Adam,' I started. 'You remember I told you I've been sacked? Well, suspended, which is the same thing.'

'Yes. I'm sorry.'

Xander said, 'You know why, don't you?'

'Yeah. It's my fault. I installed the cryptomining malware.'

Xander and I both said, 'The *what*?'

'What, they haven't worked that out yet? Sheesh, some people shouldn't be left in charge of a Space Invaders console, never mind a server. They need to take a serious look at themselves.'

I didn't want to say so, but I was beginning to think he had a point.

'Look, why don't you just tell us what you've actually done,' I said.

'Explain like we're five,' Xander suggested.

Adam sighed. 'Right, okay, so you know what bitcoin is.'

We both nodded.

Adam said, 'And you know it's increased in value a bit recently. Like, almost a thousand per cent this year.'

We did, of course.

'Buying bitcoin's a mug's game right now,' Adam went on. 'The price is peaking, and the bubble's likely to burst. But you can still mine it. You know how that works?'

I said, 'It's like solving a puzzle, isn't it? Like a maths problem?'

'Kind of. But it's not like doing Sudoku on the Tube. It's massively complex. It takes powerful computers weeks and weeks.'

'And you don't have that kind of equipment,' Xander said.

'No,' Adam smiled. 'But I know a place that does.'

'So you basically stole the Colton Capital server to make money mining bitcoin,' I said.

'No! Of course I didn't. I don't give a shit about that – money, and stuff. I didn't even think about bitcoin at first. I just kind of had a look, and I saw how vulnerable their systems were, how easily they could be accessed. And I thought, why the hell are you so proud of working for these people? They're managing billions of pounds, they could chuck loads of pensioners into poverty, and they can't even get their own servers secure.'

Xander and I looked at him, not knowing what to say. But we didn't need to say anything, because he was in full flood.

'So I installed some malware, just because I could. I wanted to show Charlotte that they're not as clever as they think they are. It was interesting – a challenge. That's all. But then I was telling some guys about it online, and they were like, "You know what you can do with that kind of processing power?" I didn't, actually. But now I do.'

Xander said, 'So then you did the bitcoin… thing.'

Adam nodded, looking down at his hands again. 'It's not theft, you know,' he said. 'Anyone can mine it, if they've got the gear.'

'But you didn't,' I said. 'Colton Capital does.'

'Yeah, so I borrowed it. I wasn't going to carry on for ever. I just wanted to make enough of a point.'

'Enough for what?' Xander asked.

Adam looked down at his hands, then up at Xander. I knew what he was going to say, I was pretty sure. I really didn't want to hear him say it, but I knew I had to let him.

'Enough for Charlotte to see I was better than them.'

I said, 'Adam, I'm so sorry. I didn't realise. Not until the other day. I really had no idea that you were even…'

'It's okay, I get it. You don't feel the same. You told me. You don't have to tell me again. I'll uninstall the code and we can all pretend this never happened.'

Xander said, 'Unfortunately it's not that simple. They're blaming Charlotte, remember? They've suspended her from her job. Unless she can prove she wasn't responsible, she won't get it back and she'll never be able to work in the industry again. Even if they don't bring criminal charges.'

'Oh. Right. That.' Adam glanced longingly at his computer screen like it offered some kind of escape route, then looked back at Xander.

Really, I thought, *how can such a brilliant man still be as thick as mince?*

Xander said, 'You'll have to tell them. I can't see any other way to resolve this.'

'Tell Charlotte's boss?' Adam's eyes widened.

'Well, yes, I suppose so,' Xander said. 'Colin. Or Pavel.'

There wasn't much to choose between them, I thought. Colin would shout, undoubtedly, but Pavel's silent rage might be even more terrifying to confront. Then I remembered that Pavel thought I was intimidating, and suppressed a smile.

'It'll be okay,' I said. 'What are they going to do? You'll be saving them from a massive headache, actually. They might even be grateful.'

'We can go there now. I'll come with you,' Xander suggested.

Adam blinked. 'Maybe tomorrow.'

'Come on, mate. No time like the present.'

Not so much no time like the present, I realised – the present was the only time. Tomorrow Colin would be playing host to sixty of Svetlana's mother's closest friends for her birthday lunch at Claridge's, and then hosting his own staff and their other halves for the Colton Capital Christmas party in the evening. The party Tansy would be attending as Renzo's plus-one, and I wouldn't be going to at all. And the following day the office would be more or less shutting down for Christmas, with Colin flying to Dubai, Renzo to Italy, Pavel to Vegas, and only a skeleton staff remaining to keep things ticking over.

I'd been going to be one of them. Now, I wasn't.

'Come on,' Xander said again, encouragingly. 'Let's do this thing.'

Adam stood up very slowly, tucked his phone, wallet and keys into the pocket of his jeans and replied, 'Okay then.'

'Won't you need a coat?' I asked.

Adam looked out of the window. I could see drizzle glossing the pavement and hear the branches of the tree outside whipping against the window. It was almost three o'clock and already the day was darkening towards evening.

'Nah.'

Xander said, 'I'll call you, Charlotte, once I know what's happening.'

Adam said, 'See you later. And, Charlotte?'

'Yes?'

He hesitated. 'I'm sorry I got you in trouble. I didn't mean to. If I'd thought…'

I didn't say anything. I just reached over and gave his hand a little squeeze.

And they both started down the stairs.

Through the crack at the edge of the blinds, I watched the tops of their heads emerge from the front door, Adam's dark and Xander's chestnut. I saw them walk away up the road, Xander's coat collar turned up against the wind and Adam seemingly impervious to the cold, his hands hanging by his sides as he walked.

It felt weird to be in his room on my own, as if I was trespassing, so I went and sat on my own bed, staring out into the gloomy not-quite-dusk.

Chapter Twenty-Four

Hello again, bad girls! How are you doing? Before I started recording this podcast, I got thinking about the journey I've been on, and how far I've come. I don't want to big myself up, but I'm feeling like setting myself these challenges – and I promise you, if you've found some of them tough, so have I! – has really helped me to connect with a side of myself I didn't know was even there. I'm feeling braver and more confident, and of course I've been having a whole lot of fun.

And tonight I've got a date! It's a second date, actually, and it's with a guy I really like. We're going for cocktails and dinner at this really cool new Mexican restaurant, and every time I think about it I get the most mad butterflies in my stomach. Why? Because I think tonight will be the night we sleep together. And my challenge to myself is to make the first move. Eeeeek! I don't know where you're at in your dating adventures, but if you're like me, and you've met someone you like, why not join me? Come on. Go in for that kiss and let your inner bad girl do the rest!

'What do you think?'

Tansy hovered in the doorway to my bedroom. She was wearing a black midi dress with long sleeves and a polo neck, and patent black kitten heels. Her hair was twisted into a knot on the back of her head. Her make-up was perfect, subtle and glowy. She looked beautiful.

'Babe,' I said. 'No. Fucking. Way are you going with Renzo to his Christmas party dressed like that.'

'Like what? But it's the first time I'm going to meet his colleagues and your – his – boss. I want to look serious. Like I'm marriage material.'

'Tansy, take that Gilead wife shit off right now. Honestly, trust me, I've met Colin's wife – the power behind the throne, right – and she wears leather skirts up to her minge and heels Kim Kardashian wouldn't be able to walk in. Renzo will want you to wow. You look stunning – of course you do, you'd look stunning in a spud sack – but it's a party! Give it some.'

'Okay.' Meekly, Tansy pulled the dress off over her head, pulling her hair down too, so it cascaded down her back in all its tousled blonde glory. I opened her wardrobe and looked inside.

'Try this.' The dress was red and glimmering with tiny sequins. Draped over my arm, it looked like a snake that had got its festive skin on.

'Are you sure that's not too…' She stretched out a hand and touched the dress as if it might burn her.

'Too what? Too sexy? Too Christmassy? Don't be daft. Get it on.'

She kicked off her modest heels and stepped into the dress, and I zipped her up. It flowed and clung in all the right places. She must have gone for a spray tan or something, because her skin was golden and glowing, and for a blow-dry, because her hair was all shiny and swishy and bouncy like Kate Middleton's. Putting that up was literally a crime against hair, I thought.

But no salon could have given her the sheen of happiness and excitement that lit up her face. She wasn't anxious about how she looked this time; she was blazing with confidence.

I said, 'You look absolutely fucking amazing.'

'Are you sure?' She reached out and squeezed my hand. 'What if they hate me?'

'They won't hate you. They might hate him, because he gets to shag you and they don't. But they'll love you, I promise. Especially if you wear these.'

I produced a pair of strappy gold stilettos from her wardrobe – it was like Aladdin's cave in there, honest – and she slipped her feet into them.

'I wish you were going to be there, Charlotte,' she said. 'Are you sure you can't…?'

'Just turn up? No way. It would be too weird. And seriously awkward if they kicked me out. I'm still suspended, after all. I haven't seen Adam or Xander since yesterday, and neither of them have replied to my texts. I haven't heard anything and it's killing me. And anyway, I've got nothing to wear.'

'Will you be okay?' Tansy asked. 'I feel really bad leaving you here. It should be you going to the party.'

'It's just a party. I'll be fine. I'll have an early night, and you can tell me all about it when I see you again.'

'Which will be tomorrow,' Tansy said. 'Renzo's flying to Rome at lunchtime. God, I'm going to miss him. He says he'll call every day, but… Anyway. I'd better go. We're meeting for drinks first. Are you sure I look okay?'

I said I was absolutely sure, and gave her a hug and watched her shrugging on her new white coat, putting her phone, lipstick and keys into a little gold evening bag, and practically levitating downstairs.

I waited a few minutes, then went down too and looked around. The house had a kind of sad, unlived-in look that it had never had when Maddy and Henry were there. Henry sometimes used to buy flowers for Maddy, and she'd put them in a jug on the kitchen table. Maddy often left sourdough bread proving in a special basket or chicken stock simmering on the cooker, making the house smell like a home. When we were all in of an evening, we'd eat together and have a bottle or two of wine. If they still lived here, we'd have had a Christmas tree.

But Maddy and Henry were in Bali on honeymoon, and anyway this hadn't been their home for months. I thought of the cushions and throws and little bits of art I'd planned to buy to replace what they'd taken when they moved out, and never got around to. There didn't seem much point: Tansy and Adam and I were mostly out, or in our separate rooms upstairs.

I lived there still, but I didn't feel like I belonged there any more.

I thought of the Bad Girl, getting ready for her date with the man she fancied, going in for that kiss, maybe going the whole way. I wondered how it had worked out for her and thought about listening to the next episode to find out, but I knew it would only depress me – she'd already left me far behind.

I thought of Xander, chatting and laughing with his colleagues at the party, fitting in even though mentally he'd already checked out. I wondered if Chryssanthi would be there, petite and polished in a little black dress, swishing her smooth curtain of hair and smiling at him.

I wandered downstairs and opened the fridge, finding only a pint of sour milk, an almost-empty bottle of wine, three ready meals that were past their use-by date and a bag of salad leaves that had wilted to a slimy mess. I chucked everything in the bin, went back upstairs and ran a bath, and while it was filling I opened all the doors of the Liberty advent calendar I'd bought myself as a treat and forgotten all about, scattering the lovely, expensive beauty products over my dressing table.

Perhaps if I used enough of them, I'd feel better.

An hour later, I'd straightened my hair, painted my nails, rubbed scented body lotion all over myself and used four different creams on my face. I was still miserable, but at least I smelled great – not that there was much point in that, since no one was going to be smelling me.

And then I looked again at the small, not-quite-square envelope that had been sitting on the table next to my bed for almost – but not quite – long enough for me to be able to stop seeing it. It wasn't mine, it was for Tansy. I should give it to her, even though she didn't want it. But there was an alternative: I could protect her from it, defuse it like a bomb.

I picked it up and looked at it for a moment, then used my thumbnail to lever up one corner of the flap and rip the paper across. There was no going back now. I took out the card inside. It wasn't a Christmas card; it was plain white, but there were tiny flecks of glitter on it and one edge was slightly askew, as if it had been cut with scissors.

I pictured Travis again, a man who hadn't sent a card to anyone since he was a child, because his PA had done the business ones and his wife the personal ones. I imagined him alone at night, tucking the scarf into a bag and knowing he needed to include something else too, and finding something his daughter had left lying around, the daughter who loved SparklyGems and sparkly things, and cutting off the bit with the princess or the unicorn, and writing. It was beautiful handwriting, done with a fountain pen like Piers used, only much neater.

Saskia. I don't know if that's your name, but I promise mine is really Travis. It's Travis Doyle. I don't know what has happened to you. You went offline and I haven't seen you for weeks, except once, by accident. I had to find you because I can't stop thinking about you. What we had was so special. I know you loved the things I gave you: I saw you wearing them. I thought you cared for me like I cared for you. I still think you do. So why not call me? We could have something amazing together. We could support your parents together. I know we could, and you know it too.

There was a mobile number, but I didn't call it straight away. I googled the name first. Travis Doyle. And there he was, right there on LinkedIn: an insurance broker working for a company in Oxford. There was no mistaking the photo on his profile.

And then I did call the number, after switching off my own caller ID. It went to voicemail, but I wasn't fazed by that. I left a message: a long one. I told him that Tansy – although I used the name he knew her by – never, ever wanted to see him again, and that after he'd turned up at our house late at night and scared the living crap out of me, nor did I. I told him that if he ever came near her or me again, I'd be straight on the blower to his employer and the police, because stalking was a criminal offence now, in case he wasn't aware of that. And then I added, for good measure, that I'd find his wife and tell her all about his pervy ways, and that then his daughter would be the one who lost out because he might never see her again outside of a contact centre. I didn't know for sure about the daughter, of course – it was pure conjecture – but it seemed like the magic bullet.

I finished by saying, 'Goodbye, Travis,' as menacingly as I could, and ended the call.

Then I flopped back on my bed feeling a bit sorry for him because I'd taken out my rage against the entire world on the poor fucker. But not *that* sorry, mostly just exhausted.

I was drifting into sleep when I heard the crash of the door knocker and raced downstairs, my heart pounding. A delivery from Travis, somehow? Adam, having lost his key? Hannah, looking for Freezer, who wasn't here because Adam wasn't?

But it was Xander. He was wearing a dinner jacket and carrying three zipped garment bags on hangers, and I couldn't help noticing that he scrubbed up quite amazingly well.

'I've come to take Cinderella to the ball,' he announced. 'If she wants to come, of course.'

'What are you talking about?'

'The Colton Capital Christmas party, obviously. It's tonight, you may remember.'

'Of course I remember. Tansy left ages ago.'

'Well. You and I will just have to be fashionably late.'

'But I can't go. I'm totally uninvited.'

'You need to read these.'

He handed me two white envelopes with the Colton Capital logo on them.

'What the… You'd better come in.'

We sat at the kitchen table, and I opened first one letter, and then the other. The first informed me that the investigation into my misconduct had been withdrawn and suggested I contact HR to arrange a meeting to discuss my return to work. The second was the standard letter all staff received at Christmas, revealing the amount of our annual bonus.

I read it and said, 'Wow.'

'I guess Colton Capital's had a good year.' Xander grinned. 'Apparently it's been the best for hedge funds since 2010.'

'Did you also…?'

'Yep. Although unfortunately if this was meant to inspire loyalty, it's not working in my case. I'm handing in my notice in January.'

'But you've only been there a few months.'

'Seven. Enough for me to decide that the world of high finance isn't for me. It's been fun, but I've been having doubts, and then the way they behaved to you made my mind up. I guess I lack the killer instinct. And anyway, I want to take some time off, travel, maybe work abroad for a bit. Or not work, just explore. And thanks to Colin, I can afford to do that now.'

Thanks to Colin, my savings pot would at last contain enough for a deposit on a flat. The only problem was, I wasn't sure that was what I wanted any more.

'But enough about that.' Xander stood up. 'Come on, you need to get ready, unless you want to turn up at the party in your bathrobe.'

I glanced down. My shabby towelling gown was sagging open, showing an awful lot of my chest. I tugged the belt closed, but not before I'd noticed Xander noticing too.

'I've got nothing to wear,' I said.

'Yes you do. I asked Margot to help me order some stuff online. I didn't realise you could get same-day delivery of designer frocks. What a time to be alive. Come on.'

He picked up the garment bags, followed me upstairs and laid them carefully on my bed.

'Margot said to go for two classic black options, one long and one short, and then something a bit more out there,' Xander said. 'She had to guess your size but she says she's got a good eye and they should all fit.'

'Jesus, Xander. This is crazy. I mean, nice-crazy, but… Thank you.' There was a strange feeling in the pit of my stomach: not nervousness but a kind of giddy excitement. I felt like I was about to start giggling and not be able to stop.

Xander smiled. 'Thank Colin. If it weren't for the bonus, I'd have had to go shopping at New Look. I'll wait outside while you try them on.'

Long black, short black and something more out there. As soon as I opened the bags, I knew which one I wanted to wear.

It was gold velvet, the sheen of the fabric making it look almost liquid. It had a slit up one thigh, and an asymmetric neckline that left one of my shoulders bare. If the black dresses, lovely as they were, were the choice of a woman who was happy to blend into the background, this was a dress that said, 'Fuck you, here I am.'

I stepped carefully into it and did up the zip. It was a perfect fit – I could tell without even having to stand on the bed and inspect myself from all angles in the mirror over my dressing table. I had a perfect pair of simple, ridiculously high-heeled black shoes in my wardrobe to go with it – it didn't need anything else.

I opened the door, giddy with excitement to see his reaction.

'I just need to put some make-up on. We'll only be a bit late.'

Xander looked at me and smiled. 'I hoped you'd pick that one.'

'It was the obvious choice,' I said. 'It's the most amazing thing I've ever worn. Thank you.'

He shook his head, muttering that it was nothing, it was his pleasure. It wasn't like him to be tongue-tied, and there was something in his face I'd never seen before – a kind of tension. Suddenly, I could feel it too – it was like the air in my bedroom had become electrically charged, or filled with some kind of invisible, odourless gas that made it hard to breathe, or like microscopic particles of glitter were floating under the pendant light, making it impossible to see anything except sparkles.

I thought of the podcast's challenge: make the first move. I didn't even know if Xander fancied me. Until that moment in The Daily Grind the day before, when I'd found myself suddenly, irrationally jealous of Chryssanthi and blushing when he'd said he liked my face, I hadn't even realised I fancied him. But I did. I fancied the arse off him. And there was only one way to find out whether he felt the same.

Make the first move.

I walked over to him and put my arms around him. He hugged me back, very gently, as if I was made of tissue paper, then bent and kissed my bare shoulder, and smiled at me again.

That kiss did a weird thing, like flicking a switch inside me, even though it was only the lightest brush of his lips against my skin. Or maybe it was the way he looked at me, or the way his shoulders felt under my hands, the warmth of his body coming through the smooth black fabric. Whatever it was, it made me want him so much I could hardly breathe.

I said, 'Xander, come here.'

'I am here.' Then he kissed me properly. For a man who couldn't walk across a room without tripping over the pattern on the carpet, he was amazingly good at it.

'I've fancied you ever since I met you,' he said.

'In spite of my resting bitch face?'

'Maybe because of it. I love that you take no prisoners.'

I don't quite know what came over me then. It wasn't just realising how much I liked him and wanted him – it was knowing that I could take charge, that I could be the confident, powerful sexy self I'd spent the past few months discovering, without fear of rejection or regret.

'Only the ones who want to be taken,' I said wickedly.

Without taking my eyes off his, I reached up and carefully untied his black bowtie and unbuttoned his shirt. I ran my fingers down his chest then back up again, and pushed the sleeves down over his arms. He kissed me again, harder this time, and I kissed him back, then moved away.

I felt like I was melting from the inside, I wanted him so much. I wanted to yield my whole body to him and give in to the pleasure I knew he'd give me. But I was going to take charge here – I wasn't just going to make the first move, but all the other moves, too.

I guided him gently back into my bedroom and onto the bed next to the two bags holding the black dresses. I knelt in front of him and unsnapped the braces holding up his trousers.

In the end, we were quite a lot late for the party, but it didn't matter.

Partly, it was because this was the Colton Capital Christmas do and there was no question of the food or the drink running out, and in fact when we arrived the second of six courses was just being served.

But mostly, it was because I was floating along on a cloud of happiness, and if they'd turned us away at the door I wouldn't have cared one bit; I would have taken Xander straight back home to see whether the second time would be as good as the first, which I was pretty sure it would be.

They didn't turn us away at the door, though. When we arrived, Colin and Piers were standing outside smoking cigars, and they both welcomed us like we were long-lost children. Piers said, 'Beautiful dress, darling, like the angel on a Christmas tree.'

Colin said, 'I believe I owe you an apology,' and although he didn't actually make any apology, he did put his arm around my shoulders (having to reach up to do so, thanks to my high heels) and only stopped when Svetlana came stalking out in a black leather dress and gave him a look that made him drop both me and the cigar and scurry back inside.

We followed more slowly, collected glasses of champagne from a passing waitress, and stood together under one of the luminous fish tanks, looking at the room. It might have just been me, but everything seemed to sparkle: the fizz people were drinking, the women's dresses, the Christmas lights that were festooned everywhere.

I could see Margot, faultlessly stylish in chartreuse satin, chatting to a few of the traders. Briony, Alice and Greg, all with their husbands, had commandeered a table, an ice bucket full of bottles and a platter of food and looked like they were settling in for a good old session. Renzo and two of the other portfolio managers were standing in a little group that seemed entirely focused on Tansy, radiant in her red dress. She caught my eye across the room and looked amazed, then delighted, and mouthed, 'Talk later?'

And, in a corner, I could see Pavel, deep in conversation with a familiar figure – at least, he would have been familiar if he hadn't been wearing an entirely unfamiliar tuxedo.

I said to Xander, 'Look over there. Is that who I think it is?'

Xander smiled. 'Yes, it is.'

'What the hell happened? I was going to ask you, but then…'

'We got distracted,' Xander said, and distracted me again for a while with a kiss that I didn't want to end.

When it eventually did, leaving my lips tingling, I said, 'Go on, spill.'

'I think you should let him tell you himself,' Xander said, 'Just as soon as I've got you a margarita.'

We walked over and said hello, and there was a huge amount of back-slapping between the men. Pavel gave me his usual shark-like stare, only it didn't frighten me any more, especially when he suddenly smiled in a way that wasn't shark-like at all, kissed me on both cheeks, told me I looked beautiful, and summoned over a waitress to fill up my glass.

'What are you doing here?' I asked Adam.

'I was invited.' It wasn't just the dinner jacket that made Adam look different; he was standing straighter, he'd tidied up his beard into a sharp-as Van Dyke, and although he wasn't smiling, he was looking around the room with happy assurance.

'But you…'

'I was shitting myself,' he said. 'Your bloke there basically frog-marched me to Mayfair and stuck me in this glass room like a torture chamber and then fucked off to find your boss. And then he came in like a guided missile in a suit and started shouting at me.'

Oh God. Poor Adam. Even people who'd endured Colin's rages for years were sometimes reduced to tears by them.

'I'm so sorry,' I said.

'It was only words. I let him finish, and then I explained.'

Fuck, I thought, imagining Adam quailing and stammering while Colin got more and more ranty and spitty. I felt a bit sick imagining what it must have been like for him.

'And then what happened?'

'Then,' Adam said, taking a big glug of champagne, 'he offered me a job. Head of Cyber Security, working alongside Pavel here. I started today, but I knocked off at lunchtime to go shopping.'

Pavel grinned ingratiatingly, clearly well aware that he was extremely lucky to have kept his own job.

Before I could properly process this new information – or cheekily ask Adam how he felt about going over to the dark side – Briony came over and hugged me, sweeping me off to join her little group, where I stayed for a while, eating and gossiping. Then I mingled for a bit, marvelling at how much nicer my colleagues were when they weren't all working round the clock and operating at maximum stress levels, and wondering whether they'd be my colleagues at all for much longer. Already, I felt a certain detachment from it all, a feeling of having been untethered and of drifting away, like I was looking at them from a distance.

But that might have just been the booze.

When the food was finished, Xander came and found me and we danced together. He danced like he kissed and like he fucked: like a man in his natural element. I felt as if I was in my element, too – or at any rate flying or floating towards a destination where I belonged, except I belonged right here, in the moment, too. I didn't have to take the lead now – we felt perfectly in synch, our bodies fitting together like we'd been made to dance together – to be together. I felt giddy with excitement, but at the same time serenely content, as happy to be me as I was to be with him.

It was almost as if I'd taken some of the same stuff as the little group of traders I'd noticed slinking ever so subtly off to the toilets together, and emerging a few minutes later sniffing ever so discreetly.

But I didn't care – if people behaved badly at the Christmas party, it was business as usual, and if they behaved *really* badly, it would be Legal and HR's problem to sort out in the new year. And I wasn't even going to think about the new year and what it might bring for me.

Then, quite suddenly, the night turned sour.

I was dancing with Xander, our arms wrapped tightly around each other and my head pressed against his shoulder, so I didn't hear anything at first. But I felt Xander's shoulders stiffen under my hands, and he stopped looking down at me but instead looked away, towards the little nest of sofas and tables that had been set aside as a chill-out zone. I raised my head and listened too.

And then we all heard it, even above the buzz of chat and laughter. Even above the music.

'Get away from me, you whore!'

Xander and I sprang apart and we both looked and listened, then he went one way, as quickly as he could through the press of people who'd been dancing a moment ago but weren't now, towards where the shout had come from. I went the other way, towards the exit, following the sparkling red lightning-flash that was Tansy's dress.

I found her outside in the street. She was crouched against the wall, the neon lights giving a sick greenish-yellow cast to her skin, clutching her knees to her chest and sobbing. I squatted down next to her and put my arm around her shoulders. She was shivering with cold and so was I.

'Tansy. Babe, what happened? Did he hurt you?'

She shook her head violently.

'Did you have a row?'

Her hair whipped against my face as she shook her head again. I rummaged in my bag for a tissue and handed it to her. I'd used it to blot my lipstick, but I didn't think she'd care about that. Not that one ragged tissue was going to go far to wipe away the tide of tears that had made black rivers of mascara down her face.

I squeezed her close and patted and shushed as if she was a small child, and waited.

After a bit she took a huge, trembly breath, looked up at me and said, 'He told me he loved me.'

And then she sobbed even harder, and I patted and shushed and waited some more, because these weren't tears of joy, that was for sure.

It took a while, but Tansy's sobs eventually abated. By the time they did, we were both shuddering with cold, clinging onto each other for warmth as much as comfort.

'Do you want to go inside?' I asked. 'We can go into the ladies' and talk. It'll be warm and no one will see you.'

She shook her head again. 'I can't go back in there.'

'Okay. We'll stay here. It's fine.'

It wasn't, but a moment later Xander came out with a big wodge of paper napkins and both our coats. I helped Tansy to her feet and we put them on.

'Want anything? Fag, drink, Uber?' he asked.

Tansy said, 'I want to go home.'

'Uber, then,' Xander said, tapping rapidly at his phone. 'It'll be ten minutes, they say demand is peaking.'

'And surge pricing, I expect. Sorry,' I said.

Xander nodded, then hesitated for a second, kissed me and said he'd call me later, and disappeared inside.

At last our cab arrived and we clambered gratefully into its warm, pine-scented interior.

I took Tansy's hand and said, 'Do you want to tell me what happened?'

She shook her head again, grimaced and blew her nose. Then she said, 'Yes.'

I waited.

'He told me he loved me. And I...'

Now I knew what she was going to say.

'Oh, Tansy. Oh, no.'

'I told him I loved him too. And I told him I didn't want there to be any secrets between us. And so I told him about the…' She glanced at the driver, who was expressionlessly watching the road ahead and listening to Magic FM. 'You know.'

'Oh shit,' I said. 'And he was horrible about it?'

Tansy started to cry again. 'It was awful. He said… he said the most vile things to me. He was like a completely different person. It was like he thought *I* was a completely different person. He called me the most awful names, things the men… the punters used to call me. I minded it when they said it, even though I expected it. But when he did…'

I squeezed her hand, a cold knot of remorse twisting inside me. I'd told her to tell Renzo. It was my fault. But then, she couldn't have hidden it from him forever. Could she?

'I told him I'd stopped. I said, as soon as we got back from Paris, I never went online again. And he said he wasn't surprised, because I'd found someone else to bankroll me. He called me a money-grabbing slag.'

'Oh fuck, Tansy. How could he?'

I tried desperately to think of words to say that would comfort her. I could tell her that now she'd seen who Renzo really was, she'd had a lucky escape. But I didn't believe that, not really. I believed that the person he'd been when they were together had been the real him – at least, an aspect of him. A man who was kind, sincere, smitten, even a bit insecure. I believed he'd been in love with her – or at least in love with the image he had of her, the parts of her she'd let him see.

'The worst thing, Charlotte,' she said, gulping and starting to cry again. 'The worst thing is, he's right. I did go after him for his money. He's right to say that about me.'

'No, of course he isn't,' I said. 'That's a terrible thing to say.'

'But it's true. You know it is. But then, I fell in love with him. And I still am in love with him.'

We spent the rest of the journey in silence. When we got home, Tansy went upstairs and took off her make-up and her dress, and I made tea and took her a cup in bed.

I said, 'Try and get some rest. See how you feel about it all in the morning.'

'I will get him back, you know. I'll find a way to make him realise he was wrong.'

'Whatever happens,' I said. 'You'll be okay. I know it hurts like fuck now, but you'll be okay. I promise.'

I knew that, in the grand scheme of things, I was right. I also knew that my words must have sounded as hollow to her as they did to me.

Then I went and sat in the kitchen in the dark, drinking my own tea and texting Xander. He said he missed me and he wished he was there with me, and I said I felt the same, and we spent a few minutes sending rows of kisses and silly emojis to each other, until I was giggling with happiness in spite of myself. But before we sent our final goodnight text, he told me he'd tried to talk to Renzo but got nowhere, and that Renzo, after drinking most of a bottle of Grey Goose, had left with Pavel and Piers... and gone on to Gaslight.

Chapter Twenty-Five

Hello and welcome back to Sorry Not Sorry, *and the last of my dating challenge podcasts. Why the last, I hear you ask? Well, on one level, I'm really sad to be ending this little project, because it's been so much fun and I've so loved having you along for the ride.*

But on another level, I'm over the moon. You see, that second date went really well, and the third and fourth did, too. I'm thinking that I've met The One. It's early days, but you know when you just feel that connection? I'm feeling it, and he says he is too. So much so that we're both deleting the Tinder app on our phones – and I guess these days that's a pretty serious sign of commitment, right?

If things work out with him, it's going to mean some pretty big changes in my life – maybe even leaving my whole life here in New York behind. And that's kind of daunting, but really exciting too – and then I tell myself I'm getting ahead of myself!

We'll just have to see what the future holds – but, for now, it means the end of these podcasts.

It felt weird and wrong to record this last one without one last challenge for you, though. So here it is: be your best self, and follow your heart.

The podcast ended abruptly, right there. How random, I thought, that she should have met someone at almost exactly the same time I had. And then I remembered that she hadn't, of course – the recordings were a few years old now. I wondered what had happened to her – whether the man she talked about really was The One, whether they'd got married and had babies, whether they were happy.

But then the Tube train pulled into my stop, and I stopped thinking about her and focused on the task in hand.

It was the second working Monday in January – the day the media calls Blue Monday – and a week since Xander and I had both handed in our notice at Colton Capital. I had loads of holiday that I hadn't had time to take, so I was working bits and pieces of my notice period and using my free time to plan the trip we were taking to Asia, which might last three months or six or maybe even longer. My mind was full of images of sparkling beaches, neon-lit streets waiting to be explored, narrow pathways leading through lush vegetation – a whole host of things that were almost as enticing as Xander himself.

When he'd suggested I join him on his travels, I'd hesitated.

'Isn't it too soon? I mean, we've only just started… you know. This.'

'It's soon,' he said. 'But I don't think it's too soon. I can't think of a better way to get to know each other. And anyway, it worked for Prince Harry and Meghan.'

I burst out laughing, absurdly delighted that he knew that detail about the royal romance.

I'd thought about the money I'd carefully saved to put down a deposit on a flat, about how that was the sensible thing to do, and about my dream of buying somewhere of my own to live. But that could wait. I had a different dream to follow now. Just as the Bad Girl had said she planned to do, I was making big changes, stepping bravely into the unknown, ready to take on this new challenge.

Tansy and I had spent Christmas together, like we planned, staying in our pyjamas all day and watching telly. Adam wasn't there – he was in Richmond with his aunt and uncle, along with Bianca, Henry, Maddy and the rest of the Wilmot clan, who were no doubt as delighted as they were amazed that the black sheep of the family had come good and got a job at a hedge fund.

I was worried about Tansy, and kept asking her in an infuriating mother-hen sort of way if she was okay. Calmly, she insisted that she was. She was going to get Renzo back, she repeated over and over again, sounding a bit like Scarlett O'Hara at the end of *Gone With the Wind*. She just had to figure out how to. I didn't say so to her, but I privately hoped she would figure out why not to, instead.

We – Tansy, Xander and I – spent New Year's Eve with all my friends, including Maddy and Henry. Maddy and I spent about half an hour apologising to each other all over again for our bad behaviour, and saying how much we regretted almost ruining our friendship. It wasn't ruined, but I knew it had changed.

I asked Maddy and Henry that night what I ought to do about Myles. Well, obviously I was going to do nothing about him – if I ever saw the bastard again I'd take great pleasure in kneeing him in the balls or chucking my pint over his head. Okay, I wouldn't – that would be undignified. But I'd take pleasure in looking straight through him and carrying on being happy, like the better person I knew I was.

It was his wife I was worried about, and her I asked them about.

'Should I tell her? I mean, I know her email address and where she works and everything; I could, easily. But is it the right thing to do?'

Maddy said, 'For sure it is. If it was Henry who'd cheated on me, I'd want to know. Not that you would, obviously.'

Henry squeezed her hand. 'Would you, though? I mean, maybe it was just a one-off transgression and he'll never do it again. Maybe – sorry, Charlotte – maybe she's found out she's having a baby, and you'd be telling her at the worst possible time.'

'He's done it once, he'll do it again,' Chloë said. 'Leopards don't change their spots. Chances are she knows already, or at least suspects, and she's just in denial.'

'Maybe he'll tell her himself,' Molly said. 'You should give him a chance to. After all, you said you'd only tell her if he didn't.'

'Would you really be doing it for her?' Tansy asked perceptively. 'Or just to make yourself feel less guilty about the whole thing?'

I remembered the horrible secret she'd carried for so long, and how I'd encouraged her to come clean to Renzo, and what had happened when she had. I genuinely didn't know the answer.

'What do you think?' I asked Xander.

'I think you must do what you believe is right,' he said, correctly but unhelpfully.

Molly dropped a bombshell that night. She told us that she'd finally got sick of waiting for William to ask her to marry him, and asked him instead. William, she reported, had hummed and hawed and said he wasn't sure the time was right, and Molly had promptly dumped him.

'It felt great!' she said. 'I was like, "Right, if you're not serious about me, I'm off to find someone who is." And he looked like he'd sat down on the toilet and found someone had left the seat up, and I know exactly how that looks because I've seen my face in the bathroom mirror often enough when he's done it. Fucker.'

'Fucker!' we all chorused.

I said, 'You know, when you're ready to start dating again, there's this great podcast you should listen to…'

But now, all the glitter of the holidays had worn off. I'd thought about it a lot, and I'd decided what I needed to do: not to assuage my conscience, not for revenge, but because it felt necessary.

I'd spent a long time online, finding out about Myles's wife. You know how it is: you do one quick Google search and the next thing you know it's two in the morning and you're still down the rabbit hole, clicking on thing after another and never reaching a point where it seems logical to stop, turn your phone off and go to sleep. And that's when you're just looking for the perfect slouchy black jumper or trying to understand what the hell is actually going to happen with Brexit, or whatever – never mind when you're trying to get inside the head of a woman you've wronged in the most horrible way.

I'd found her employer pretty much straight away: a talent agency called Ripple Effect, which apparently specialised in representing social influencers. Which, I discovered, meant people with massive numbers of followers on YouTube and Instagram. Some of them I'd even heard of: Lisa Summers, whose make-up tutorials I'd watched a few times; Glen Renton, whose name I'd seen on lists of top earners under the age of twenty-five; and SparklyGems, whose name, face and violet hair I knew only too well. But there were far more unfamiliar names, and I'd clicked on a few of them and watched some of their videos, baffled by the world of unboxing, live gaming and pranks they revealed.

Then one link took me to a video by a guy called Charlie Berry, and as soon as the first frame flashed onto my screen, I practically hurled the tablet away in horror, then closed the window and stopped watching, because Charlie Berry lived in the flat that I'd thought was Myles's, and filmed his videos on the sofa where we'd had sex, and if I needed any more confirmation that Bianca had been right, there it was right in front of my eyes.

So I avoided YouTube after that, and focused on how to contact Sloane Cassidy. I'd wondered why she had kept her surname when she married Myles, thinking with a brief pang that if he'd asked me to marry him when I thought I was in love with him, I'd have given up my name without a backward glance. But then, he'd loved Sloane, I presumed, enough to marry her – but not enough to be faithful to her.

I'd thought about other ways to do this, of course. She was easy to find online – she had a social media presence all over the place. I could have emailed her, sent her a message on LinkedIn, requested she respond to me on Facebook Messenger, followed her on Twitter and hoped she followed me back, or even ventured for the first time in my life onto Snapchat and tried to contact her there.

I had gone the old-fashioned route and called the Ripple Effect office and asked to be put through to her, but when the receptionist had asked who was calling I'd hung up, unable to go through with it. So I was going to wait for her to leave work and accost her in the street. The idea was frightening and humiliating in equal measure, but it seemed like the only way.

First, though, I had a morning's work to do at Colton Capital. For once, it was easy enough – the firm's year-end figures had been so staggeringly good that all I really needed to do was work with the PR agency to make sure our press release was circulated far and wide, and help Piers juggle the many meetings with prospective clients that had his diary bursting at the seams.

Margot, though, wasn't having such a leisurely start to the year. I'd witnessed several tense meetings between my line manager and Colin in the fishbowl, from which she'd emerged looking anxious and flustered, not her usual serene self at all.

'Is there anything I can do to help?' I'd asked her a few days before.

'Not unless you can get Myles Taylor's head out of his arse and the office renovation back on schedule,' she replied grimly. 'He's headed for a second yellow card right now.' I felt my face burning with embarrassment just at the mention of his name, and said nothing more.

But that Monday morning, my mind was on Myles's wife, not on the man himself. So when I saw the familiar silver-haired, suited figure following Margot past my desk, I thought I must be hallucinating. He stayed looking straight ahead, not even glancing at me, and I kept my eyes firmly on my screen.

What the fuck is he doing here? Why didn't they go into the boardroom?

Almost immediately, it became clear. Margot escorted Myles into the fishbowl and sat him down with a glass of water. No biscuits today,

I noted. No coffee, even. Margot left him there alone and returned to her desk. I watched her turn to her screen, move her mouse, tap her keyboard a couple of times, then roll her shoulders and close her eyes for a moment as if she was trying to find her happy place.

Then Colin emerged from his office. His face was already flushed brick red over his cheekbones, and I could see beads of perspiration on his temples. He loosened his tie slightly and walked slowly towards the fishbowl.

All around me, my soon-to-be-ex colleagues followed his progress with their eyes while their heads stayed facing firmly forwards. Greg got up from his desk, picked up his shorthand notebook and Dictaphone and followed Colin, white with apprehension. Margot closed her eyes again, took another deep breath, then shook her head and stood up and legged it to the ladies', where she remained for the next half-hour.

Only the traders, safely tucked away in their bank of desks at the back of the room, let their true feelings show. Messages began to pop up on my phone from the WhatsApp group they'd added me to a while before, which included Xander, Renzo and Colin's PAs, but not the man himself, or Piers or Margot.

Five to one on he gets the boot. He's two months behind schedule and half a mill over budget.
I'm offering evens on the boss dropping the c-bomb.
Greg's gonna have to share the audio to verify that. Otherwise all bets are off.
So who gets the gig when Taylor's sacked? I'm offering 15/1 on Purcell, 10/1 Capita, 5/1 Atkins, evens Fosters, 33/1 the field.

There was a brief shout of laughter from the trading desks, then Colin looked in their direction and they all buttoned it and pretended to be working. With a final glare over his domain, my boss entered the fishbowl and shut the door.

It was awful to watch. Colin shouted and shouted. Myles cringed. At one point he turned and opened the door to leave, but Colin grabbed him, literally by the collar, and the whole office heard him bellow, 'Haven't finished with you yet, you—' before the door swished shut again.

Eventually it was over. Colin flung open the door and headed straight for the lift. Greg followed seconds later, pale and trembling, and went back to his desk for a bit of trauma counselling from Briony.

Myles remained in the fishbowl, alone. He had his elbows on his knees and his face in his hands. He stayed there until I went and found Margot in the loo and told her it was all over, and asked her to see him out.

'Right,' she said, squaring her shoulders. 'Girl's gotta do what a girl's gotta do.'

The whole of Colton Capital was watching as she went into the glass-walled office and touched Myles gently on the shoulder. He literally flinched, but he stood up obediently. The two of them paused for a second before she opened the door, gripping his elbow firmly, and guided him out.

There was a burst of ironic cheers from the traders. Myles didn't look up. He let Margot lead him to the lift as if he was incapable of finding it on his own. He looked like someone you see on telly being escorted to court by police officers when they've committed a shameful crime, only he didn't have a hoodie to cover his face.

And then it was over. I didn't feel sorry for him – not one bit. There was another person I felt I owed something to, and now I was going to find her, tell her what I'd done, and take on the chin whatever she had to say to me.

I bought a coffee and stationed myself on a high stool at the counter by the window of the coffee shop in Soho, just a short walk from Colton Capital's office, taking out my laptop for camouflage. Surrounded by other people whose afternoon work base this appeared to be, I was as inconspicuous as I could hope to be, even though I kept my coat and scarf on, knowing I'd have to make a dash for it as soon as I saw her leave the office through the glass door.

It sounds stupid, and it felt stupid, but I made sure I had an image of her on my screen so that I could be sure I had the right person. I sat there like the world's worst private investigator for literally an hour, looking at my screen, then at the door, then at my screen again, getting tenser and tenser and boreder and boreder.

And also, needing to wee more and more. I blame the coffee.

If I'd been a private investigator on a stake-out, I'd have used my coffee cup. But that's if I'd been in a car, and had a penis. I wasn't and I didn't. I looked at the closed glass door across the street, and then at my phone. It was quarter to five.

Surely, surely no one left the office at quarter to five? If they were going to a meeting, even a five o'clock one, they'd have left already. It was too early to leave to go home. I could take two minutes – surely? And if I missed her, I'd just come back another day.

Or, of course, not.

I closed my laptop and put it in my bag, gathered my things and dashed in the direction indicated by the arrow underneath a wrought-iron plaque of a woman in an old-fashioned flouncy dress holding a parasol, praying that no one would steal my vantage point. I went through a set of wooden doors, down a flight of stairs, along a passage – fuck, was this some kind of joke? – and eventually found the door I was looking for.

I used the loo at warp speed, washed my hands and hurried out again, along the corridor, back up the stairs, into the coffee shop.

And there she was.

She was standing at the bar, holding a reusable bamboo coffee mug, which the barista had evidently just filled for her, chatting away to him like they were old friends, which, given that her office was five seconds away, they probably were.

I paused, wanting to be completely sure. She was smaller than she looked in photographs, a couple of inches shorter than me, although she was wearing red patent leather boots with a kitten heel. Her piled-up dark hair made her look taller too. I wondered for a second if I'd got it wrong, but her style was unmistakeable: her waisted black coat, the flicks of eyeliner, the red lipstick – all the things I'd seen in all the pictures I'd looked at of Myles's wife.

Then I heard the barista say, 'See you tomorrow, Sloane,' and I knew I had to do it.

I rushed over, catching up with her just as she put her hand on the door.

'Excuse me,' I said. 'Are you Sloane Cassidy? Can we talk for a second?'

In the time it took for her to respond, I realised I'd made two stupid mistakes.

The first was not realising the way her job would make her respond to people. This was a woman, after all, who could make or break the careers of aspiring celebrities. She probably got accosted all the time by young women who'd emailed and called and tweeted in vain, thinking that if she saw them – really *saw* them – she'd recognise their potential and sign them up as clients.

She knew just how to deal with them, and she dealt with me like that.

'Honey,' she said, 'I'm due somewhere in like minus one minute. But it would be so amazing to talk with you! Please let me give you my card.'

She held out a glossy scarlet rectangle, but I didn't take it. She looked at me for a moment longer, then pushed the door open with her hip and hurried out.

If only I'd let the receptionist put me through to her. That was my second mistake. Even if I'd got her voicemail, I'd have known. After all, I'd listened to her for hours and hours over the past six months.

She was the Bad Girl, the woman who was *Sorry Not Sorry*.

Epilogue

I leaned back, settling more comfortably into the white canvas-covered cushions, and took a gulp of sour cucumber-and-gooseberry beer from the frosty bottle in my hand. My feet were half-buried in sand, still warm although the sun was sinking and the fierce heat of the day was giving way to a balmy evening. The sea looked like crinkled aluminium foil in the fading light. Above my head, palm fronds made jagged black scribbles against the indigo sky.

I could see Xander waiting at the counter, his legs long and brown in his baggy cut-off denim shorts. His hair was bleached almost gold by the sun, and freckles had appeared on his cheeks and shoulders. I thought how strange it was that just three months before, I'd only ever seen him in work clothes; now, it felt like I knew every inch of his body as well as I knew my own. I knew how he smelled when I pulled him towards me in the morning, the saltiness of his skin when I kissed him, the way he laughed after we had sex like we were some kind of mad geniuses who'd invented this incredible, generous, never-ending pleasure.

I knew that – curiously, for a man so well-travelled – he still got nervous when a plane went through turbulence, and that gripping my hand comforted him. I knew he was game for trying anything new, so long as it didn't involve eating dead animals. I knew he started conversations with taxi drivers and random people on buses and in the lobbies of hotels. I knew that when I nibbled the base of his spine, he squirmed with ticklish delight.

And I knew that he was finding stuff out about me too. How I couldn't stand the smell of bananas, but loved papaya. How I got anxious about going anywhere without my factor 50 sunblock. How I'd never learned to swim properly but loved wading into the water up to my waist, then floating on my back, knowing that he was there to scoop me back to my feet if a big wave came. How I loved prawns but hated peeling the shells off them, so he did it for me even though he wouldn't eat them himself. How I loved having my feet massaged and loved it even more when the massage was finished and he kissed his way from my ankles to my calves and then up and up some more.

Now, he was waiting in a bit of a queue for what was apparently the best green mango salad in Cambodia. Judging by the number of people crowding around the little wooden shack that served it, he was going to be a while, but I didn't mind. I was almost liquid with relaxation, content to wait idly and watch the people and the sunset, my beer still two-thirds full.

I fished my phone out of the wicker beach bag Xander had bought me so that I wouldn't keep losing my sunglasses and lip balm, and swiped over to WhatsApp, glancing briefly at the icon for the Slack app Bianca had made us install when she was planning Maddy's wedding. I should probably delete it, but I couldn't be bothered right now. She couldn't hurt me any more now, and nor could her cloud-based team collaboration software.

I had a message from Maddy. Actually, it was a photo. A pic of her long, denim-clad legs, and Henry's next to them. Except I couldn't see much leg at all, because draped across both their laps was the biggest, fluffiest black cat I'd ever seen. Seriously, until I read the text below, I wondered for a second whether they were being devoured by a bear.

But Maddy had written, *Meet Wayne. He moved in this afternoon and already he is the boss of us.*

I responded with a load of hearts and feline faces, and told her that Wayne was clearly the best cat ever and was going to be the most spoiled, and then I flicked through to my email and tapped the drafts folder, as I'd done again and again without pressing send.

Dear Sloane

I'm not sure about sending you this email. I tried talking to you in person, in the coffee shop in Soho back in January. You probably don't remember – it didn't go well. I suppose it was a bad idea, but it felt like the right thing to do.

You see, I did something really bad. I didn't know I was doing it, not exactly, although of course I should have done. There's no nice way to write this, so I'm just going to have to come out with it. I had an affair with your husband. With Myles. It lasted about four months, until I found out in December that you and he were still married, and then I ended it.

I won't go into any details unless you want me to. I completely understand that you'll hate me for this, and I'm more sorry than I can ever say. I hope you're okay, and that whatever you decide to do, things work out for you.

That was as far as I'd got. The problem was, I couldn't decide how to sign off. 'Love' felt far too intimate, although I did want to send her love – the supportive, sisterly kind – not that she'd want love from me. 'Kind regards' was even worse. And just signing my name felt far too abrupt and cold.

I'd considered telling her about the podcast, the months I'd spent listening to her voice on *Sorry Not Sorry*, and how it had changed me. But that didn't feel right either – I remembered the joy in her voice when she'd recorded the words, 'I'm thinking that I've met The One.' She had – but it had been an illusion. The man she'd thought would love and cherish her forever had betrayed her trust, and I was sure she wouldn't want to be reminded of the happy confidence she'd felt back then.

So the email had sat there unsent, and every now and then I opened it and tinkered with it, adding a few words and taking out a few others, but never solving the dilemma of what the final words would be, and never pressing send.

I didn't press it now, either. Sighing, I switched back to WhatsApp to look at Maddy's cat again.

And, right there as I watched, a new message appeared. It was from Myles. I felt a little jolt of surprise and waited to see if the reaction I'd got used to feeling when I saw his name – back in London, a whole half the world away – would come: the rush of excitement, the visceral twang as my eyes registered his name and my body responded. But there was nothing. Like Bianca, he no longer had any power over me. I dug my toes deeper into the sand and my finger touched the screen to find out what he had to say.

It was fewer than ten words.

I told her. She's left. Hope you're happy now.

It was a spiteful message, I realised. He was trying to put the blame for the break-up of his marriage onto me, instead of taking responsibility for it himself. And I wasn't happy – of course I wasn't. Not about that, at any rate. But at least it was over. Sloane's decision – however agonising it must have been for her – was made. When I got back to London, I promised myself, I'd arrange to meet her, apologise in person and let her say whatever she wanted to say to me, taking it on the chin like I deserved to.

I put my phone away. Xander was walking towards me across the beach, holding two banana-leaf plates piled high with food, two cold bottles of beer wedged under his arm. I stood up to kiss him.

'Everything all right?' he asked when he saw my face.

'Yes,' I said. 'Everything's all right.'

A Letter from Sophie

I want to say a huge thank you for choosing to read *Sorry Not Sorry*. If you enjoyed it, and want to keep up-to-date with all my latest releases – and (whisper) find out what happens next to Tansy, Adam and Freezer – just sign up at the following link. Your email address will never be shared and you can unsubscribe at any time.

www.bookouture.com/sophie-ranald

I wrote *Sorry Not Sorry* in a building site. Well, obviously not any random building site – I'm talking about my house. While I was working on the novel, walls were knocked down, ceiling joists were hammered into place, holes were drilled everywhere for wires and pipes to fit through. There was even something called a builder's crack stitching kit involved.

And it struck me that the process of gutting a house and that of writing a novel aren't very different. In the beginning, you have an idea on paper of what it will be like when it's done – all perfect and squared away, just how you want it. And then the work begins and it's a total nightmare: dust and shavings and piles of rubble everywhere (or words that just look wrong, characters who misbehave and plot holes you can't get to close), and you wish you'd never started.

But, as I write this, my house is somewhere close to being finished – and Charlotte's story is complete. Did you enjoy it? I'd love to know what you thought of *Sorry Not Sorry*, and the best way to let me know is to leave a review online. I read every single one of them, good and bad, and I'm sincerely grateful to each reader who takes a few minutes to write one.

Of course, there are other ways to get in touch too. If you'd like to be kept up-to-date with news about my writing, you can sign up to my mailing list above. (I promise I will never spam you or share your details with anyone else.) Or use the links below to connect with me on Facebook, Twitter and Instagram.

Most of all, though, thank you for choosing to read this story.

@SophieRanald

SophieRanald

@SophieRanald

Acknowledgements

It's funny how the idea for a novel sometimes jumps into a writer's head based on something entirely random – at least, it does for me! In this case, it was a conversation with my high-flying friend Katie, who mentioned that at the hedge fund where she works, the fridge is kept permanently stocked with high-quality protein. I don't know what it was about that idea, but something made me think, 'I want to write about the person whose job it is to do that.'

So, over many cocktails and many delicious plates of food at the fabulous Kitty Fisher's in Mayfair (if you go there, try the whipped cod's roe – it's off the scale), I picked Katie's brains about the inner workings of the hedge fund world, and what else the protein-orderer's job might involve, growing more fascinated all the time as the career of the character who would become Charlotte came to life. Thank you for your help, lovely Katie – any errors or inaccuracies are of course my own.

In the meantime, at the content marketing agency where I freelance as an editor, I was learning more about the world of high finance through one of my clients. I'm happy to say that the people I work with there are nothing like Colin, Piers or Pavel, but I did borrow their cappuccino-coloured leather meeting room chairs for the novel. I also picked the brains of my lovely colleague Ellie for insights into the world of dating as a twenty-something.

For advice on computer hacking and bitcoin mining, I turned to Anne Miles, who generously put me in contact with an acquaintance of hers. Thank you, Anne and VN – your insights were invaluable and, once again, any mistakes are mine alone.

Although he is not their cat, I'm enormously grateful to my dear friends Sarah and Lea for introducing me to Freezer, who became such a central character in this novel.

Huge thanks as always go to the team at LAW, who have represented me for the past six years. Alice Saunders, Niamh O'Grady and Araminta Whitley have provided unstinting support, excellent advice and constructive criticism that have made this book far better than anything I could have achieved without them. You're all amazing and I am so grateful.

After self-publishing my previous five novels, it has been a joy and a privilege to have been signed by Bookouture for this one. Huge thanks to my editor, Christina Demosthenous, who has worked tirelessly and meticulously on this novel and improved it beyond measure, while also being encouraging, inspiring and an all-round delight. Also at Bookouture, the utterly wonderful Peta Nightingale, who's been involved in my writing career right from the beginning, provided support, encouragement and advice. Thank you, Peta.

Finally, always at my side have been my darling Hopi and my precious little Purrs. I love you both and I couldn't have done it without you.

Made in the USA
Columbia, SC
29 April 2020

R00219